PENGUIN BOOKS
Birthday Girls

Annabel Giles is a TV and radio presenter, and an actress. She also wrote and performed a sell-out one-woman comedy at the Edinburgh Festival, *Looking for Mr Giles*. She has two children and lives in London. This is her first novel.

Birthday Girls

ANNABEL GILES

PENGUIN BOOKS

PENGUIN BOOKS

Published by the Penguin Group
Penguin Books Ltd, 80 Strand, London WC2R 0RL, England
Penguin Putnam Inc., 375 Hudson Street, New York, New York 10014, USA
Penguin Books Australia Ltd, Ringwood, Victoria, Australia
Penguin Books Canada Ltd, 10 Alcorn Avenue, Toronto, Ontario, Canada M4V 3B2
Penguin Books India (P) Ltd, 11 Community Centre, Panchsheel Park,
New Delhi – 110 017, India
Penguin Books (NZ) Ltd, Cnr Rosedale and Airborne Roads,
Albany, Auckland, New Zealand
Penguin Books (South Africa) (Pty) Ltd, 24 Sturdee Avenue,
Rosebank 2196, South Africa

Penguin Books Ltd, Registered Offices: 80 Strand, London WC2R 0RL, England

www.penguin.com

First published 2001
1

The extract on p. 85 is from *The Language of Letting Go* by Melody Beattie,
copyright © Hazelden Foundation, 1990. It is reproduced by permission
of the Hazelden Foundation, Center City, MN.

Printed in England by Clays Ltd, St Ives plc

For Molly and Ted,
with love from the lady in the shed

SCARLETT MATTHEWS
10 today

My Birthday list:

Anything with cats onit of course for my collection
   Body Shop bubble bath and animal soaps
Vouchers (but not book tokens) please please please
   Getto blaster like Jade
A pony
      Fluffy pens
Girls World
(a big head thing that you put make-up on)
   Grease video
My own tv in my room
   Nail polishes
~~Jowlry~~ ~~Jewlly~~ ~~Jyewl~~ a neckless and some bracelets
   Mosaic Kit
      Hair thingies (sparkling ones)
   Picture frames that blow up

25 February

'Mu-um – I think I'm going to be sick again . . .'

'Oh golly, Scarlett, can't you hang on a little bit longer? We're nearly there now . . .' Sophie was driving like they do in films, only without the squealy screechy tyres going round the corners bit. So it was very lurchy.

'I don't think I can, no . . .' Scarlett's eyes began to fill with tears, she could feel a funny taste like tin foil coming into her mouth.

'Oh look just get out of the way will you!' her mother yelled to a very dirty car which had stopped right in front of them without using its indicators or anything, typical. A Datsun Cherry it was – Scarlett and her dad played the Wotcaristhat Game all the time, he said she was quite good at it now.

'Mu-um . . .' She wasn't going to be able to keep it in, she felt really hot as well, and freezing. She didn't want to, but she started to cry.

As she beep-beeped the horn, Sophie turned to look at her baby girl. 'Oh darling, please please don't be sick in the car if you can help it – Dad'll be furious and I'll never get the smell out. Move your bloody arse!' she yelled and beeped to the other car.

Scarlett was a bit scared – she'd never heard her mum

swear before. Maybe she was iller than she thought. Oh no, it was all coming up now, she could tell . . .

'Oh sweetheart – look, use this,' said her mother, reaching down onto the passenger floor as she tried to keep the other hand on the wheel and two eyes on the road. 'Oh thank god, I can get past him now, it's just down here I think –'

Too late. Scarlett was sick into her mother's handbag.

When she woke up, all she could see was a curtain with some really bad drawings of teddies on it who were sposed to be playing with some abc bricks. 'Mum?'

'She's gone to telephone your father,' said somebody who was fiddling around at the bottom of the bed. 'But don't you worry,' the kind-sounding lady said, 'you're most likely a bit sleepy still, aren't you?'

Scarlett tried to sit up a bit in the bed, but couldn't. It hurt. She burst into tears. 'I don't feel very well,' she sobbed.

The nurse came and sat on the side of the bed and took Scarlett's little pink hand in her big squashy black one. 'Of course you don't,' she said, 'you're in hospital and we only have people who don't feel very well here. As soon as they start to feel good we send them home.' She laughed even though it wasn't very funny, and her whole face split into a really enormous smile. 'Can you remember what happened to you?'

'Well I woke up this morning with a bad tummy ache and then it just got worse and worse and then I was sick so Mummy took my tenjebra and it was really high and so she phoned Dr Eager and he said I had to go to hospital and so Mummy drove me and it took ages and it really hurt and then she carried me in cos I couldn't stand up proply and then I was sick again all down her back and in her hair.'

'Oh dear me,' said the nice nurse, 'was she cross?'

'No, my mum doesn't get cross about stuff like that.' Scarlett thought about it. 'She doesn't really get cross about anything actually. Except sometimes.' But she wasn't sposed to know about that.

'Well you're a lucky girl, aren't you? I used to scream at my kids all the time when they were little – still do in actual fact.' Her face went into a what-are-they-like face. 'My youngest, Michael, now he's really bad –'

'What's wrong with me?' asked Scarlett, not sure if she wanted to hear the answer before her mum came back.

'You had something called appendicitis,' replied the nurse, who was so fat she looked as if she was going to burst out of her uniform any minute now.

'I'm not going to die, am I?' Scarlett had seen lots of sad films with people in hospital in them on the sofa with her mum, like *Beaches*.

'No,' the nurse's eyes got really big, 'you are not.' And she laughed her head off and that big smile was all over her face again, and it was quite scary if you weren't expecting it.

'Scarlett?' Her mum's voice came from behind the curtain. She was punching it, trying to find a way in. Scarlett tried to laugh but she couldn't, it hurt her tummy.

The nice big nurse stood up and pulled the curtain open right around the bed. 'She's awake now and very chirpy, all things considered. Proper little chatterbox, isn't she? I'll leave you to it – just come and find me if you need anything, my name's Ellen.' And she walked off, making a swishing sound as she went.

'How're you feeling, darling?' Sophie smoothed back her little girl's fringe. 'Gosh, you gave me a fright. I've just been trying to get hold of Dad – his mobile's off, I've left lots of messages on it though. Where on earth can he be?'

Scarlett patted her fringe back down again and tried to think. She was used to keeping track of her parents for each other. 'I think he said he was going out to buy more stuff for the party bags, and then he was going to pick up the cake – oh no! Mum! What about the party? I can't go now, can I?'

'Well not really, no. I've just tried to ring the bowling alley, but I couldn't get through and I haven't got any school mums' phone numbers with me to tell them not to go there – I just hope your father got the note I left him on the kitchen table. Where on earth can he be? He shouldn't be out shopping anyway, he's supposed to be at home pumping balloons! Oh I wish he was here . . .' Oh no, thought Scarlett, looks like she's going to cry, she's fiddling with her sleeve, looking for her hankie. Better say something, or she'll go into one of her spins, as Dad called it. And Scarlett really hated seeing her mum cry – which she did, a lot. It made her feel scared, like everything was going to go wrong, but then Dad always made it better. Scarlett wished he was here too. Oh help. Change the subject?

'Will I have another party, later?' (Jade was going to be furious with her, she'd never hear the end of this thing.)

'Yes, yes of course.' It worked! Sophie put on a bright

smile and took a deep breath. 'Now let's see if we can get you some ice cream – or is that tonsils?'

The other children on the ward looked much more worst than Scarlett, but the woman in the next-door bed seemed absolutely fine. She had been sitting up, silently playing with her Game Boy (which is probably why she's in with us kids, thought Scarlett) but as soon as Sophie left to make some more phone calls, she started talking. Without taking her eyes off the game once, which Scarlett had been told was rude but anyway.

'What's the matter with you then?'

'I had to have an emergency operation on my tummy,' Scarlett said dramatically, her mum having explained everything earlier. 'I was in Great Pain. What about you?'

'Tried to kill myself.'

'Oh.' Scarlett couldn't think of anything to say. 'Did you?'

'No of course I didn't or I wouldn't be here now, would I? Anyway my mum found me just in time, which was really boring of her.' She made a 'duh' face into her Game Boy and carried on twiddling her thumbs into it.

As Scarlett watched her, she noticed that the other girl's hair was two different colours. It came out of her head black, but then it went bright yellow. If it came out yellow again she'd look like a bumble bee, thought Scarlett. Her own hair was the same colour all the way down, 'glorious mouse' Constance called it. Anyway. 'What's your name?'

'Becca. You?'

'Scarlett.'

'What kind of a wanker name is that?'

Scarlett knew this was a swear word of course, Jade had told them all to everyone at Lunch when they were about six, but she couldn't remember most of them now and anyway she was proud of her name and this girl, even though she was older than her but not a lady like she first thought, just shouldn't be so rude. 'Well actually, I was called after Scarlett O'Hara who was in my mum's favourite film which is called *Gone With The Wind* which you probly haven't seen because it's very old, you can only get it on video. Unless you get TNT or TMC. Which we do. It's on there sometimes. Actually.'

Becca wasn't saying anything.

Scarlett carried on regardless, being a Proper Little Chatterbox. 'And my middle name is Viola, because she was the only woman in Shakespeare with any spunk.'

'Bet you don't even know what spunk is.' Becca actually managed to look up for a split second.

'I do, actually,' said Scarlett, who didn't – she had just heard her father saying this lots of times before.

Becca pressed pause. 'What is it then?'

But really luckily, before Scarlett had to say anything, she spotted her father at the door of the ward, looking round for her, all worried. 'Daddy!'

Becca imitated Scarlett silently in a horrible babyish way into her Game Boy and went back to what she'd been doing.

'Scarlett!' Simon rushed over to her bed and tried to do his usual bear-hug with her but it was a bit difficult as she couldn't sit up proply. 'Hello, you poor old thing, how're

8

you feeling?' He gave her such a smile as he plonked himself down on the bed, it made her want to cry but she didn't want to look a kind of a wanker in front of Becca so she gave him a bit of a wobbly one back, a bit blinky. Thank goodness he'd come, it was all going to be all right now.

'My tummy really *really* hurts,' said Scarlett, relieved to be able to tell the truth now that her mum wasn't there.

'I bet it does,' he said. 'And it probably will for some time. Still, let's think about the good side – you won't have to go to school on Monday, you'll be spoilt rotten and – um – you've given Mummy something proper to worry about at last, she must be really pleased!' He grinned.

'Don't be funny, I can't laugh,' said Scarlett a bit grumpily, she didn't like it when he said things against Mum. 'Does she know you're here?'

'No, where is she?'

'She's on the phone, trying to get hold of You actually.'

'Well I came as soon as I got the four hundred messages she left on my mobile.' He got up and moved over to the armchair by Scarlett's bed.

'Did you see the note?' she asked.

'What note?'

'At home.'

'Oh, no, I came straight here.' He smiled over at Becca as he sat down. She pretended not to notice.

'So you haven't cancelled the party?'

'Oh – well no, I thought she would – oh god, Scarlett, I – well never mind, I –' He did look like he felt bad about it.

'Simon! Where've you been?' Sophie arrived, a bit red in the face, a bit cryey. 'I've been trying to get hold of you for ages, I've rung everybody I could think of, even Mother and Jessica.'

'I'm really sorry Soph, the phone must have been out of range or something – honestly, they're more trouble than they're worth sometimes … what's that terrible smell?'

'Oh dear, it's me,' said Sophie, trying to run her fingers through her long blonde hair. 'Poor old Scarlett was sick all over me when I was carrying her in. I must really pong, sorry.'

'He hasn't cancelled the party!' said Scarlett, who didn't normally like to land her dad in it but this was very important – what would people say when they turned up and she wasn't there?

Eventually they agreed that Sophie would go home to change and try to phone everyone before they left, and Simon would be at the bowling alley in case some people didn't get the message in time. Of course there was a lot of 'will you be all right here on your own darling' from Mum in her best trying-not-to-worry voice, and Dad kept saying things like 'of course she will she's in good hands' in his best make-it-all-better voice. But then Dad's mobile rang which made Ellen bustle over and tell him off because it could make all the machines go wrong and people could die and so eventually they left together, promising to be back first thing in the morning even though Mum wanted to stay the night. So Dad just took her by the arm and led her out of the ward, looking back at Scarlett and grinning that way they did when Mum was being a bit too mad. To tell the truth, she felt better when they'd gone anyway because now she could get on with the business of Being In Hospital, sure that she was going to have to write a composition on it for Miss McFarland when she went back to school.

Even though she was absolutely starving, Ellen had said she couldn't eat anything proper yet until things had settled down, whatever that meant, and so Scarlett had had to make do with a plastic beaker of Ribena Toothkind while everyone else got nuggets and beans from some ladies with a trolley.

Then Becca had pretended to be asleep when her parents had come to visit her, but Ellen had made her wake up and now they were sitting one either side of her bed holding a hand each. She can't play her Game Boy now, can she? They were talking to her very quietly so that Scarlett couldn't quite hear what they were saying which was annoying, not that she wanted to be nosy or anything. But it looked like Becca was pretending she couldn't hear them either as she wasn't talking back, just staring up at the ceiling and doing really loud sighs every now and then. Why is she so mean to her parents, wondered Scarlett, who was a bit wishing hers were still here as everyone else seemed to have visitors now and she only had a very old copy of *Princess* to read. Grown-ups were sometimes so silly about children, they thought that just because you were smaller than them you wouldn't be interested in anything except Disney stuff. She'd asked for a magazine – like her grandmother did at the hairdressers – and they'd given her a comic.

Ellen was going round all the beds now, telling the

parents to go home because it was half-past six and the children had to get ready for bed. Half-past six?! Bed?! That's far too early, she was ten now, double figures and Becca was probably about twenty-five or something. And anyway, if she was at home now and it wasn't her birthday, she and her mum would be doing their usual Girls Night In thing, which meant pizza and a video and loads of chocolate in the sitting room with all the lights turned off just like a cinema, snuggled up just them and Brando together on the sofa under the Cosyblanket. And if it wasn't a school night she didn't have to go to bed until sometimes eleven o'clock, or until Dad came home, whichever happened first. They'd listen out for his car, which they knew the sound of, and if it was him Scarlett would run upstairs and pretend to be asleep and Sophie would gather up all the sweet wrappers and ice-cream cartons and all the other rubbish and rush into the kitchen and bung them in the bin before he got in. She loved their Saturday nights in. And even if Dad was home, it was just as cosy only they didn't pig out so much and she wasn't allowed to stay up so late. She'd sit on the sofa between them and they'd all watch an old black-and-white movie, from Dad's collection. He'd always pick exactly the right one to watch, her and Mum just didn't know how he did it. They hadn't done that for ages now though, she must remind them. Scarlett began to feel a tiny bit on her own even though she wasn't and sad and just wanted to go home actually.

She looked over at Becca's parents who were trying to kiss their daughter goodbye, but Becca kept turning her head away. Her dad looked like he was going to get cross, but her mum hissed at him 'Stop it, Ivan! Just leave it.' So they just said goodbye instead and walked off separately, and Scarlett thought it was a bit mean actually when they didn't even wave at Becca before they went through the double swing-doors.

Which swung back open again with a huge long squeak and an enormous bunch of flowers came in. It was a very smart lady with a big black hairdo and bright red lips holding a really big handbag as well, and her high heels made a loud clacking noise on the shiny floor. Constance! Everybody went quiet and looked. Ellen, who was turning out to be a bit of a bossy boots, rushed over. This should be good, thought Scarlett, most grown-ups were a bit scared of Constance for some reason. Dad always said she could kill at fifty paces with that tongue. Maybe she was going to lick Ellen to death right now.

'I'm sorry, madam, but visiting hours on the children's ward are over.'

'Oh don't be so ridiculous,' said the other woman in a very loud posh voice, 'the traffic was appalling, even the cab driver said so. I've come to see my granddaughter,' she announced whilst scouring the pale faces in the beds, 'and I haven't come all this way in the godawful rush hour to be prevented from doing so. Ah, Scarlett, there you are!' She pushed past Ellen (who muttered something about just two minutes and no more) and made her way to the little girl's bed as everyone else started their goodbyes all over again. 'Have you got a vase for these?' She held out the flowers for Ellen to take without even checking behind her to see if she was there. Which she was, face like thunder.

'Hi Constance!' Scarlett was thrilled, she loved her granny even though she wasn't allowed to call her that as Constance said it made her feel old. Everyone called her by her first name – except Mum and Jess who called her Mother.

'Darling, what a dreadful birthday you must be having!' She bent down to kiss her granddaughter with her powdery cheeks and Scarlett was nearly suffocated as usual by the really strong perfume she always wore. 'I couldn't believe it when your mother eventually managed to tell me what had happened, how ghastly for you. Now you mustn't worry about tonight, I've given the tickets to Mrs Mac who's going to go with her little Filipino friend, they're thrilled.' She perched herself on the arm of the chair beside the bed.

Scarlett had been so worried about her party in the afternoon that she'd completely forgotten she was going out to the theatre that night with her grandmother. They were going to see *Cats* and then going to meet Luigi (Constance's Italian boyfriend who was dirty rich) for dinner in a really smart restrong afterwards and it was going to be a really late night and now she was stuck here in this horrible hospital with a really fat nurse not letting her do anything and now she was supposed to go to sleep really early like a baby. It's just not fair. She couldn't help it but her eyes began to fill up with tears and so she bit her bottom lip to try and stop it.

But Constance had seen, and even though Scarlett knew her grandmother didn't like crying she didn't actually say anything, just raised an eyebrow and fumbled in her great big handbag instead. She eventually came back up with a small but beautifully wrapped present, all silver and glittery with those funny hologram thingies and a great big bow on top which had got a little bit squashed but it didn't matter. 'Happy birthday, darling!' she said very loudly, probly hoping Ellen would hear and feel bad for being such a meanie.

It had been so beautifully wrapped that Scarlett's bitten fingernails (her and Mum had tried everything but she just couldn't stop) weren't able to get into it, and so Constance's perfectly manicured dainty red ones did it instead.

'Oh my gosh,' exclaimed Scarlett very loudly, hoping Becca would hear as she wasn't actually looking being too busy with her own, 'a Game Boy!' (She hoped she sounded excited enough, praps Mum hadn't told Constance that she'd already got one.) 'Oh thank you sooooooo much!' She tried to sit up and give Constance a hug, but she'd forgotten that her tummy wouldn't let her. 'Ow!'

'I wouldn't get too excited darling, it's only bubble bath. As you know, I disapprove of big presents, you children are given far too much these days. It's very realistic though, don't you think?! I was quite fooled into thinking it was the real thing!' Scarlett heard the most terrible snort come from Becca's direction. 'You don't have to open the card right now, you can save it till later when you can take a moment to inwardly digest what I've written inside.' Scarlett wished yet again that she had a grandmother who just bought her stuff, like everyone else's – and not one who thought long letters about Life (Wise Words, Mum called it) were worth more than money can buy and so on. Constance loved words, she was a writer now and sometimes read Scarlett her stories to make her go to sleep. Which they did.

'And I also brought you this,' said her grandmother, producing an enormous, really huge, giant size bar of Galaxy which she knew was Scarlett's favourite. Ah.

'I'm afraid she's not allowed that,' said a stern Ellen, standing at the foot of the bed behind the flowers which had been dumped into a vase made out of the bottom of a big plastic bottle of lemonade. 'You'll have to go, it's lights out.' Big smile; no teeth this time.

'Oh really, this is quite preposterous, is the NHS cutting back on visiting hours as well?' asked Constance, as she stood up anyway and smoothed down hers and Scarlett's favourite black suit with the white edges and the shiny gold buttons with two Cs that crossed over on them. Picking up her handbag, she said to Ellen, 'Look, can't you move her to a private room? I'd be happy to pay. I really don't think a dormitory full of bald children is a suitable environment for a nine-year-old girl, do you?' (Scarlett wanted to say ten now, but decided not to.)

'The others seem to manage OK,' snapped Ellen, 'and anyway, she's probably going home tomorrow.'

'Oh well all right, I suppose it is only for one night, darling,' said Constance as she bent down to kiss the little girl goodbye, fluffing up her pillow as she did so. 'You'll just have to grin and bear it.'

It wasn't till her grandmother had gone and the lights

were turned to almost off completely that Scarlett realized Constance had secretly slipped the big bar of chocolate under her pillow, right under Ellen's nose. She wriggled her toes with delight – that was what she really loved about her granny, she was just so naughty!

It was no good, she just couldn't go to sleep. One of the littler children had started to cry which had set another one off and the lights above their beds kept going on and off and then a new arrival was wheeled in very loudly by a man with a big limp and put into the empty bed opposite and the nurses were chatting and laughing really loudly in their room and the bed was really uncomfy and Scarlett was used to a fluffier pillow and the hospital nightie thing wouldn't do up proply and so she kept getting a draught down her back and even though she kept trying to think nice thoughts bad ones kept coming in anyway like was Brando missing her because he would notice that she wasn't in her bed and he always curled up in a furry purry ball at her feet every night and what did everyone say when they found out about the party and would she still get their presents anyway which she knew was bad because it's the thought that counts but still.

And Becca's always sniffing was getting on her nerves too. Did trying to kill yourself give you a runny nose? 'Becca!' she whispered loudly in the direction of the other girl's bed.

'What?'

Scarlett was surprised, she'd expected Becca to tell her to wanker off or something.

'D'you want a hankie?' She didn't have one of course, but it was what her mother always said when she wanted Scarlett to stop sniffing.

'No.' An even bigger sniff, the biggest one yet. And then, 'Thanks anyway.'

She was crying! Blimey. 'I've got some chocolate if you want.'

'Where?'

'Here, under my pillow.'

'Well bring it over, then.' She was sounding better already.

'I can't, I'm not sposed to get up until tomorrow, case I burst my stitches.'

The double swing-doors of the ward squeaked open for the ninety-ninth time that night, and the squinty hall light showed up a very skinny nurse with bright orange hair coming in with what Scarlett now recognized as medicine for the new arrival who had been making a bit of a fuss.

The two girls kept quiet until she'd gone out again and then Scarlett was a bit surprised to hear Becca at her bedside hissing at her to budge up, which she did as best she could. She opened the chocolate under the bedclothes, to stop the gold paper rustling too loudly. She gave quite a big chunk to Becca (bigger than she meant to actually but it was hard to break) but didn't have any herself because she wasn't allowed.

'Bet you're glad you didn't kill yourself now!' she giggled quietly to Becca.

'Not really,' she said with her mouth full. 'You saw my parents.'

'Aren't they very nice then?'

'No, they're bastards.'

'Oh, I see.' Scarlett had a vague memory of her mother explaining to her the proper meaning of this word when they'd heard someone say it in a shop once. But she couldn't quite remember what it was. She'd have a go anyway. 'Aren't they married then?'

'Yeah, but only just. My dad keeps shagging other women, just like all men. Your dad probably does it too.'

'Oh no, I don't think so.' Scarlett wondered if Becca could tell she wasn't exactly sure what that meant, but she could guess. 'No, my dad really loves my mum. He kisses her all the time.' Then she thought that might make Becca feel worse again, and she didn't want her to try and kill herself right now. 'Your mum looks nice though?'

'Well she's bloody not. She's a prick.'

'Oh no,' said Scarlett, completely lost now, 'that must be awful.'

'Yeah, it is. She spends her whole life either shopping or having lunch or flicking through bloody wallpaper books or drooling over my stupid baby brother.'

'Still, at least you've got a brother,' said Scarlett, determined to get Becca to look on the bright side. She sighed. 'I'm an Only Child. I nearly had a baby brother once, which would have been nice but then my dad said that –'

'It wouldn't have been nice. Everything changes when babies come along; they don't love you any more, they're too busy with the baby, trying to keep you away from it. My therapist said they handled it really badly.' She helped herself to more chocolate without even asking. 'Wish I was an only bloody child. You lucky shit,' said Becca, literally stuffing it into her mouth, 'bet you get loads of money spent on you.'

'Are you poor, then?' Scarlett wasn't quite sure how to put this. Jade's mum Mirabelle (or Mirrorball as Dad called her) always said they were filthy poor but as far as Scarlett could see Jade's dad (who didn't live with them any more) bought loads of stuff for them and so they weren't that poor because Jade got loads at Christmas and wasn't out on the street selling matchsticks in bare feet or anything. But actually their house wasn't very nice. 'Do you – well do you live in a council house?'

'Fuck no!' Becca laughed, quite loudly actually, they might get caught if she wasn't careful. 'We've got a massive house in Chiswick. But I don't go to a private school, thank god.'

'You lucky thing,' said Scarlett, 'I do.'

'You poor cow – nah, my dad's a socialist. He's got a Labour Party credit card and everything.'

'Oh no, that's really terrible.'

'No it's not, it's really good! You bloody Tory. For fuck's sake, it's people like you who are bringing this country to its knees.'

'Oh. Sorry.' Scarlett thought about that and felt really, really bad about it.

'So,' Becca continued, 'who d'you prefer – your mum or your dad?'

'Um – gosh,' replied Scarlett, 'I don't know – I've never really thought about it.'

'OK, let me put it another way – if they were both drowning who would you save first?'

'Um, well, um . . .'

'Oh come *on*,' said Becca, 'it's not *that* hard.'

It is, thought Scarlett. 'Well I love my mum because she helps me with my homework and doesn't tell my dad and so he thinks I'm really clever; and I love my dad because he lets me have a McDonalds just before lunch and things like that.'

'Yeah, and . . .'

'What?'

'What don't you like about them?'

'Well my dad can be a bit strict sometimes, and I keep thinking Mum's going to leave the brake off the car when she's left me in it and we're parked at the top of the hill and it's going to roll back down again and I'll be killed and it'll be because she can't remember things.'

'Right.' Becca sighed loudly. 'That's the worst answer I've ever heard to that question. Really pathetic.'

'Oh, sorry.' Oh dear. 'So who would you save first out of your parents?'

'Neither. I'd leave them both to drown.'

'Oh. Right.' Scarlett really wished she'd thought of that. Maybe it'd be good to change the subject now. 'How old are you?'

'Thirteen.'

'Really?!' Scarlett was shocked.

'Why, how old d'you think I was?'

'Well, you know, about twenty or something.'

'Yeah, it's my tits that make me look older. They just started sprouting when I was ten, I developed really quickly.'

'Really?' said Scarlett, who was wondering if you just

woke up one morning and they were ginormous or if you got some kind of warning first or what. Jade'd know.

'Yeah, my boyfriend Steve really loves them, he's always squeezing and sucking them.' She laughed, Scarlett couldn't think why, that was a disgusting thing to do to someone. 'Yeah, everyone thinks I'm like really old, it's great – I go clubbing most weekends y'know.'

'Gosh, do you?' Scarlett was really impressed, she'd seen a little bit of *Ibiza Uncovered* on Sky once before her mum came in.

'Yeah, with my mates from the fifth year, we get really pissed, it's great.'

'Yeah,' said Scarlett. 'Don't your mum and dad mind?'

'They don't bloody know, do they? Most Saturdays they're either having one of their stupid dinner parties or having a row. I just say I'm going to bed and jump down from the bathroom window.'

'Don't they check on you before they go to bed?' Hers did, every night.

'I dunno.' Becca paused. 'Obviously not.' She shifted in the bed. 'Have you ever given someone a blow job?'

'Um no, I don't think so. Or maybe I have, I can't really remember.'

That really made Becca laugh. Oh good, thought Scarlett, I've managed to make her happy again.

'And what exactly is going on here?' It was Ellen, shining a really bright torch in their faces.

'She was crying and so I was just trying to cheer her up,' said Becca, not Scarlett, who just about managed to slip the chocolate back under her pillow. What was left of it, mind you.

'You get back into your own bed right now, madam, or you'll find yourself with both legs in traction by the morning!' She held the bedclothes back for Becca who sloped off into the darkness, as Scarlett wondered where Traction was exactly. Then Ellen plonked herself down on the bed. If they had been in a cartoon, Scarlett would have ended up on the ceiling. 'Now then, Miss Scarlett, you lie down on your pillow like a good girl and tell me what's the matter with you.' She was almost whispering now, she seemed much nicer again.

Scarlett said that she was homesick, which was true, she had been a bit earlier.

'But you're going home tomorrow,' soothed Ellen, 'you're lucky. Some of these children have been here for months and they're going to be staying here for a very long time. Some of them,' she stroked Scarlett's cheek, 'will never go home again.' Her face was coming nearer and nearer, Scarlett had a horrible feeling that Ellen was coming down to kiss her. Help!

'But you'll be all right, little one . . .' Ellen continued, Scarlett shut her eyes really tight and braced herself '. . . you'll be out of here tomorrow – if you don't die of chocolate poisoning!'

She opened them again. Ellen had her hand stretched out. 'Give!'

As she bustled off with the chocolate towards the swing-doors, Scarlett heard her laughing to herself, something about being born yesterday. Scarlett was beginning to wish she'd never been born at all.

Next morning, while she was eating breakfast of one of those little boxes of Coco Pops and toast with not enough butter and too much apricot jam, the weedy nurse with the orange hair came up to Scarlett and said that Mum had rung and that Auntie Jessica was going to come and get her because she couldn't because she had to take Dad somewhere. Now normally Scarlett would think this was brilliant because she adored Jess but today that's not what she wanted to happen because Jessica wasn't very good about not being late and so she might be here for ages just waiting and it was horrible and she just wanted to Go Home.

Then an old doctor who had done the Emergency Operation came round, checking up on everybody. There were lots of other people with him too, all in white coats like the men in the butcher's shop but with less blood down their fronts thank goodness, all staring at her tummy, which was quite embarrassing as she'd had to roll down her pants and they could nearly see her front bottom. He said Scarlett was fine to go home now, and that she was going to be off games until he saw her next month at the check-up. He talked to her like she was about six, but he was quite cross when he got to Becca and said she had to stay another day so's they could keep an eye on her. If she didn't watch it she was going to end up in a cycle hat-trick ward, which sounded quite fun to Scarlett but anyway. Becca was about to get cross back with him, but then her boyfriend Steve came to visit her and so she was happy again. (He was quite good-looking actually, quite like Stephen Gately out of Boyzone but with much greasier hair.) But she did make him go back outside and wait until she'd put her make-up on. Then when he came back in she was all giggly and hopeless, which was a bit odd but anyway.

While she was waiting for her aunt to come, Scarlett went round telling the whole ward all about her. (She thought it might cheer up the ones who were going to die here, and as she didn't know which ones they were she'd better tell them all.) How Jessica used to be on *Krazy Kids* every Saturday morning and how Scarlett had had to shout at Terry the Dactyl one time because the little girl who was sposed to do it hadn't turned up and she and Dad were there anyway and so they used her instead. They'd phoned Mum to tell her to tape it but she hadn't been able to work the video.

Most of the other children were too young to remember *Krazy Kids*, but Becca and Steve did and he said that he used to really fancy Jessica, which made Becca cross and she said she thought Jessica was really uncool. But Scarlett said that in real life she was really nice, you wait till she gets here, she wears really fashionable clothes – she'd be really good on *Top of the Pops* or something but they only wanted Babes now you see. And she's got loads of famous friends and she's really rich too.

'Big fucking deal,' said Becca.

Scarlett pulled up her sleeve which was hiding her Barbie's Diving Watch to check what time it was yet again and began to get worried that she was never going to go home. Why hadn't Mum and Dad come to pick her up, anyway? She was getting quite annoyed with Auntie Jessica for being so late. As per usual. But she knew she wouldn't be able to be in too much of a huff once Jess had got here, as she was one of those people you just couldn't be cross with, she made you feel a bit silly for getting so worked up about nothing.

Jessica Rose Big Star arrived at last, wearing huge black sunglasses even though it was raining outside. But she wasn't looking very smart – her dark hair was all tangled at the back and she only had on a pair of black jeans and a baggy jumper and trainers, not even her pink snakeskin boots. She was quite grumpy too – Scarlett had told everyone she'd give them her autograph but she said she didn't have time.

Ellen was quite nice when she went to say thank you to the nurses for having her, even though she said she didn't want to see Scarlett back here again.

Becca and Steve were snogging like mad, but Scarlett tapped her on the shoulder and gave her the piece of paper she'd written her address and phone number on, just in case – well, you know – she felt a bit fed up again. Becca said she only really bothered with email and told Scarlett her email address, which Jessica said she could memorize; it was easy as it had the word 'slag' in it. Steve grinned and winked at Jessica who said it was now really time to go and so they did.

Scarlett had tried to tell Jessica all about the hospital and everything on the way home but she'd got a massive hungover and said she didn't feel that chatty and so Scarlett spent the rest of the journey not looking at the lights cos that makes them go green quicker.

'Hello, darling, good to have you back home!' said Sophie as she squeezed Scarlett tight on the doorstep. She waved at Jess who was in her car outside making sure Scarlett got in OK, and called out 'Thanks!' as Jess sped off. 'Didn't she want to come in for a cup of tea?'

'No,' replied Scarlett who hadn't even bothered to ask – they didn't really get on, you see, though nobody ever said that. 'I think she's got to do some things.'

'Oh, right,' said Sophie, shutting the door behind them. 'Now let me see you – are you hungry, darling? Did they give you breakfast? It's nearly lunchtime actually – fancy a baked potato? Banana milkshake? With cheese? On the potato, I mean. And beans? Or perhaps you want a lie-down? No? OK then, let's go and see what's in the fridge . . .'

'Um . . .' said Scarlett as she followed her mother through the hall and down the steps to the kitchen, 'I'd like a –' she knew she'd have to come up with something or her mum would keep on listing random food '– peanut butter and marmite sandwich with no crusts.' Sophie looked at her. 'Please.'

While Mum was pottering about in the kitchen, Scarlett went into the playroom and the sitting room and then upstairs into all the bedrooms even the baby's room and the bathroom and then went round again, looking in all the cupboards. She got a bit waylaid in her bedroom, because she suddenly remembered that before she got ill, the day before, she had been just finishing making her Posterity Tape and just hoped that Mum hadn't listened to it when she came in to tidy up; but no, it was still there in her old Fisher-Price tape recorder. Phew. But where was he?

Scarlett would have run back down the stairs if she could, but instead she held her tummy and hobbled back down as quickly as possible.

'Where's Brando?' she asked her mother, who was drying her hands on an old bib of Scarlett's hanging from the Aga.

'There you are, darling, all ready!' said Sophie, pointing to the sandwich sitting on Scarlett's Beatrix Potter plate in the middle of the kitchen table. 'D'you want to eat it in the sitting room with a video?' Sophie moved to the dishwasher.

'Mum. Where's Brando?'

'Um, well, he's not here.' Mum did one of her brave smiles.

'Yes, I know, I just had a look for him. Where is he?'

'Well, it's been a bit of a day round here, I'm afraid.' Sophie sat down at the table and motioned for Scarlett to do the same but she didn't.

'What d'you mean? Mum?'

Sophie got out her hankie from up her sleeve. She started to cry. 'Oh Scarlett, it's just so dreadful. I'm so sorry . . .'

'What's happened, Mum?' The little girl knew all her mother's different types of crying and this one was a bad one. 'Come on, Mummy, please don't cry.' She went round the table to Sophie and put her arm round her mother's shoulders. Sophie was sobbing into her hands, it was awful. Scarlett cupped her arm round her mother's head and kissed her on the side of her forehead. She had to straighten up, though, because her tummy was killing her and so she eased herself onto the kitchen table instead and looked down at her mother, waiting for it to all stop.

At last Sophie blew her nose. 'Well, you see – oh dear, I don't know where to start.'

Scarlett knew how to deal with this, she'd watched her dad do it a million times before. 'Just take a deep breath, Mum.' She wanted to say 'and get on with it' but didn't.

Sophie's big wet blue eyes looked up at Scarlett. 'Well,' she took a deep breath. 'Well, we got a phone call really early this morning, about half-past seven I think it was – I can't really remember – and it was your Gran's old friend, Isa – you remember her, Mrs Wood, we met her one night with Gran when Daddy was at the Edinburgh Festival the first time?'

Scarlett nodded but she didn't remember at all. Anyway.

'Well, she was worried about Gran because she hadn't seen her for a couple of days and she hadn't turned up at Bingo last night, and that was most unlike her as she never missed it; and so Dad said to knock on the door and she said she had, and Dad said to call the police and ring him back.'

Scarlett was having trouble working out what this had to do with the missing cat, but never mind. She knew not to interrupt and then it was over quicker.

'Well, after what seemed like an age, the police called us and said they'd broken into the flat and she was – well –'

'Out?' said Scarlett, interrupting anyway.

'No – dead!' She started crying again and Scarlett had time to take all this in.

She didn't really know Gran very well as she lived so far away, not like Constance who she saw all the time because she lived in London too, really near them. So did Jess, too. But Gran had come down from Scotland to stay every Christmas for as long as she could remember and she was really very nice even though Scarlett sometimes found it difficult to understand what she was saying because of her accent. And only yesterday morning she'd opened her birthday card and there had been a ten-pound note in it which Dad said was a lot of money for an APE and that had probly been the last thing she did before she died and it was probly her fault and maybe the walk to the postbox had worn her out. She wanted to cry, but couldn't somehow. And anyway, Dad never got sad too when Mum was like this, he said you had to keep strong for her.

'Gosh, Dad must be really really upset.' How awful if your mum died. 'Where is he?'

'Well,' said Sophie, holding her hankie in a little ball on the end of her nose, 'of course he wanted to go up to Glasgow as soon as possible and so we quickly got dressed and I rang Jess and begged her to come and get you because I didn't know who else to ask,' she took a deep breath, 'and then we jumped into the car so that I could take him to the airport to catch the next shuttle. But – oh god . . .'

Scarlett always thought you caught a plane from the airport but anyway. 'Did he take Brando with him?'

Sophie was holding her head in her hands again. 'Oh Scarlett, I'm so sorry . . .'

'He wasn't in a plane crash, was he?' She was really worried now.

'Oh god no, nothing like that! No no, it's just that – well, when I came home again after dropping him off, I was just turning in to put the car back in the garage when I saw – oh god . . .'

'What?!' Scarlett couldn't help it, she was getting cross now.

Her tone of voice shocked Sophie into spitting it out. 'Brando lying in the driveway . . .'

'What?'

'Oh Scarlett, I must have run him over when I left – we were in such a hurry and everything, Daddy was crying and I was so upset . . .' Her voice trailed off as she studied her little girl's face which had frozen into shock.

Silence.

'You – killed – Brando?'

'Oh Scarlett, I'm so sorry, it was an accident, I –'

But Scarlett had jumped up off the table, forgetting her sore tummy, and sweeping the sandwich off the table so hard and so far that it broke her baby plate, she screamed at her mother, 'I hate you! You are a fucking, shitting, bloody SOCIALIST!' And with that she stomped off and slammed the kitchen door really, really hard. For fuck's sake, it was people like her that were making this country be kneeling.

DELLA O'HARA
21 today

```
##___      I    ( ##
##__    )0=I     )##
## I I   I      (##

##___   /   /   ##
##__   )I      )   ##
## I I t    t    ##

##___      I    ( ##
##__    )0=I     )##
## I I   I      (##
```

5 April

'Bloody hell, Nance, don't ever have anal sex, it really fuckin' hurts, my arse is killing me!'

Della wriggled and giggled in her bed, juggling the phone in one hand while the other scrabbled about chasing a Marlboro Lights packet round the bedside table.

'Yeah, Darren's idea of course – bastard! Just as well I was paralettick at the time. Oh bloody hell he's taken my last fag an all, and my fucking lighter – I'll kill him . . . No, course he's not here, I've got my mum staying on the sofa, haven't I – it's quite funny really, I have to keep sneaking him in when she's asleep – mind you, she snores so bloody loudly he was saying he's going to go in there one of these days and tell her to keep the bloody noise down, he can't hear himself fuck! He was bloody furious last night, he hates it that he can't stay the whole night, gives him the right hump; but as he won't let me stay at his mum's place because she wants him to get back with bloody Mirabelle and so she doesn't like me, he's got no choice has he?'

Della sat up a bit in the bed and propped her pillows up against the pine headboard. Leaning back she said, 'What, let them meet each other? Don't be stupid, Nance, she'd have a fit! They've probably never even heard of sex before marriage where Millicent comes from. If she knew what we done last night, she'd have to go to church even more, maybe have to turn into a nun! Mind you, that'd be one way to get rid of her. God, I hope she finds somewhere to bloody go soon, she's been here what, nearly a week now and she's driving me fucking mad. And I don't know how long Darren's going to put up with it, he's not happy about this at all, Nance. He didn't stay here Monday or Wednesday if you remember – yeah, used her as his excuse. Well fuckim, that's what I say.' Della stuck her long pinkie fingernail up her nose, had a little scoop and examined the results closely.

'Nah, she won't stay at Auntie Ellen's no more, says she's got a full house – well so've I, Nance, I've only got the one bedroom, haven't I? Oh I dunno, maybe she'll find some Montserrat support group or something, maybe they'll take her in, maybe she'll fall in love with the vicar, who bloody knows – all I know is I can't take this much longer, she's really crampin' my style, Nance, know what I mean? Anyway, let's not think about that now, let's think about fun and tonight and exactly how hard we're going to party . . .'

She wiped the bogey onto the back of the headboard. 'Yeah, well I can always meet you after, can't I? I'm not going to bloody be there all night, am I? I'm hardly likely to want to not see my best friend on my twenty-first birthday night – yeah, come on girl, you and me are going out – hey, maybe we could try that new place that bloke Adam was telling us about the other night. You know, Adam, the one from last weekend, the one who actually let me pour that champagne into his shoe and then he actually drank it, yeah – aaaagh! Rank! Yeah, all right then, see ya later – what? Well I don't know, probably not till about ten thirty, eleven, something like that – does it matter? No right, OK then darlin', I'll give you a call, whatever – see ya later then, love you lots, bye.'

Della replaced the receiver and sat up in her bed (wincing a bit) and surveyed the scene. The bed was out a bit from the wall – well it would be, wouldn't it – and Darren had left his mark, so the new plan was working. His Calvins were on the floor, beside his socks which he'd left for her to wash. Bloody cheek really, considering he doesn't live here – yet. But hey, this time he'd left his jacket too, not on the chair but near the chair – good, there might be something in the pockets, she'd have a look later. Everything else seemed in order though. Quick scout round just in case he had actually managed to do something romantic for once like leave her a bloody birthday present to find in the morning . . . no. Chance'd be a fine bloody thing.

No fucking fags either. Well she would just have to have the rest of that joint. It was her birthday, after all. Della eased her long legs out from the lemon duvet and was grateful once more for having naturally brown ones and not having to bother with fake tan like poor Nancy, who spent all summer looking like she'd tried to colour her own legs in with orange felt pen and missed a bit around the ankles. Well actually it looked like she'd let a three-year-old do that bit. That's quite funny in fact, thought Della to herself, I must tell Nance that one.

Della padded over to the door and took the imitation silk kimono off its hook, walking as she put it on over to the mantelpiece. Picture – same old black-and-white photograph she'd always had, in the same old cardboard frame which was still falling apart – of her mother when she was much much younger and still quite nice-looking; it had been a bit of a shock when they'd met her at the airport, she'd looked like an old lady. If Auntie Ellen hadn't been there Della would have let her walk past. My mum? Are you sure? Couple of candlesticks from an arty stall down Portobello, chosen to match the room, hadn't got round to candles yet. Jewellery box she got for her eighteenth from Auntie Ellen and Uncle Desmond, really naff but useful even though she didn't have any proper valuable jewellery to put in it, just cheap silver stuff that looked good. (Darren hated gold, which was odd for someone like him, but that was partly what was so good about him, he was classy, he had taste and style.) Fishbowl given to her by one of her clients with book matches in it. And her confirmation bible, sent over from Montserrat. Usual sort of stuff that gathers dust. Not now though, not now Millicent had taken it upon herself to dust and scrub and scour and polish the flat till it fucking shone and Della couldn't find anything any more. Oh my god, she's probably dusted here too. Oh no.

She grabbed the bible and opened its black leather cover. Thank god for that, still there. She obviously hadn't thought to look in here. Well she wouldn't, would she? How could she guess that her daughter had hollowed it out and now used it as a drugs box? And anyway, if she came across a packet of Rizlas and a little brown lump in clingfilm and what looked like herbs in a plastic bag from the bank then she wouldn't know what they were for anyway, would she? She was only just off the fucking boat, for christ's sake.

Della gingerly removed the tiny yellowing roll-up from the inner sanctum, put it to her lips and lit it with a fiddly match from The Pharmacy. When had she eaten there? Must have been with Darren on one of their wild nights. Boy, he knew how to have fun, he was the only man she'd ever known who was able to keep up with her. They just egged each other on, it was brilliant. And nobody had any idea what they were laughing at most of the time, especially Nancy who used to laugh along anyway which only made them more hilarious, ah dear . . .

Della smiled inside as she inhaled deeply, savouring the burning throaty woodsmoky taste, and suddenly remembered her mother in the next room. Bollocks! Shutting her mouth really tight to hold her breath in, she rushed over to the window, pulled the stupid string that held up the Ikea blind and wrapped it round the stupid hook thing, then tried to open the window but couldn't – damn, bloody Millicent always locked everything, burglars through a third-floor window, I don't fucking think so – then had to fiddle with the ancient lock for far too long because it was so bloody rusty, must have another go at the Polish landlord if he understands English yet, and eventually Della managed to fling the sticking sash window up and finally, finally blew out onto a chilly Ladbroke Grove.

It was already heaving of course. It always was; no matter what time of the day or night there was always something going on. It was buzzy out there, that's why she liked it, made her feel at the centre of things, just where she liked to be. Admittedly, it wasn't a pretty place to live what with the Westway thundering on twenty-four hours a day and the shops being mostly takeaways and newsagents and offies, and that bloody pedestrian crossing beeping all the time, but at least it had a life to it; not like Notting Hill which had gone even more poncy than ever since that film. Mind you, you still got your fair share of trendies round here, the ones who couldn't afford to buy in W11 but were happy to rent in W10, showing off their trendy clothes bought with their trendy low wages. But it was everyone else who made Ladbroke Grove a busy place: all the ethnic mixtures, the white trash, the old people with attitude – it's carnival every day round here mate, all you have to do is look out your window.

She smiled to herself as she looked down over the road and spotted a couple of girls just like her and Nancy used to be, hanging out outside Hippos, chatting up the Greek boy as he unpadlocked the pizza box on top of his moped. They were supposed to be at school of course, you could tell because they were wearing a kind of uniform based on the one they were supposed to wear at school, but with a few bits of their own so's it looked cool out here too. Her and Nance used to do the same thing, in fact they invented the mini-tie look. Of course the kids wore sweatshirts now so it wasn't exactly the same, but the shoes were still a bit too high, the skirts a lot too short and the make-up was far too heavy to be mistaken for natural beauty. One of them, the coffee-coloured one, was quite pretty – that's me, thought Della – but shy, a little bit nervous – that's definitely not me, thought Della. Nancy used to be more like that, quiet, but she was a bit better now, she was really coming out of her shell these days. The white girl was making all the running, chatting and laughing as she twisted the gum in her mouth. She wasn't as fat as Nancy was – still is, thought Della – and probably quite plain under that elaborate hairdo; and obviously they weren't so fussed about the no-jewellery and plain-hairslides-only rule any more, there can't have been anything left in Claire's Accessories the day that one'd been in. And as for the colour, well – roots, girl, roots, thought Della. Not even Madonna was doing that any more.

'Hey, Spiros!' The boy looked up, found Della hanging out the window and smiled. 'You all right mate, need any help?' He smiled back, shrugged his shoulders and the white girl shot her a very practised if-looks-could-kill. 'You need to watch him, girls, he's a right one!' Della laughed, bless him. At that moment a middle-aged black woman with one of those red-and-blue checked launderette bags bustled up out of nowhere and started screaming at the group, shoving Spiros nearly off-balance as she grabbed the two girls and bundled them along to the bus stop, still ranting and raving at the top of her voice. Reminded Della of the time Nancy's mum caught them smoking round the back of the German sausage stall near the tube and went mental at them. Auntie Ellen had gone bloody apeshit too, started to check Della's blazer pockets after that, but she soon forgot to keep doing it. Didn't matter anyway, they only nicked Nancy's gran's fags instead.

Della stubbed out the remaining sliver of joint underneath the windowsill and flicked it into the air. It landed on the roof of Mickey's Datsun Cherry with the shot suspension that he was having trouble starting again –

some bloody cab service, it was like paying to hitch-hike. Still, they wouldn't use anyone else, her and Nance. He had loads of kids and a worn-out wife to support.

She pulled herself back in and closed the window, without locking it as a little act of so-there to Old Mother Neighbourhoodbloody Watch, and quickly stuffed Darren's give-away socks and pants into a big Warehouse bag that was hanging off the door handle being a laundry basket. Feeling nicely protected now from whatever the morning was going to bring her, Della took a deep breath and opened her bedroom door.

She could see at the other end of the corridor that wonders will never cease, today's mail was still lying there on the doormat. Tiptoeing along the passageway, avoiding the squeaky places (Darren and her had worked out where they were one really funny night), she grabbed the letters, commando-style, and hurried back down the corridor, ducking into the bathroom for a look and a pee. (Well she wasn't even going to try anything else yet.)

'Good morning, Della!' she heard her mother call out. Bollocks. Well tough shit. It wasn't right that she was having to be like this in her own flat, locking herself in the bathroom for a bit of privacy, smuggling her boyfriend in and out. It wasn't fair, man. If there really was a god he'd get rid of her.

Flipping the loo seat down (and that was another thing, hadn't she noticed there wasn't a man in the house?) Della sorted through the letters. Phone bill, mobile bill, one for P Hartley Esq who used to live here straight in the bin with that, postcard from a gym offering her reduced membership

– sorry mate, wrong kind of club – and a birthday card from Nancy of course. Nothing from Darren. Not like last year, when he'd given her one of those really big giant padded ones with a teddy on.

At least Nance still loved her. Usual big fat writing on the envelope, and Della noticed with glee that she'd marked it 'Privit' on both the front and the back, just in case Millicent opened it by mistake – yeah right. Ooh – looked like a fake Purple Ronnie. Bloody hell, she'd made it herself! Mind you, she'd always been good at art at school – 'bout the only thing she was good at in fact, god love her.

Della

You are my best mate you are
I really do love you
Even when your off your face
Or crapping in the loo!!!!
We've had some right good times we have
And it has all been fun
So have a good birth day today
Now that your twenty one.

Brilliant! Must have taken her ages. Aaah. She was a good girl, Nancy. They'd known each other since they were babies, went to the same childminder and then the same schools, but they didn't really start being proper friends until senior school.

She'd always hung out with her cousin Barbara before that, what with them being brought up together and everything, but Barbara had gone all serious when they'd got older and started to work really hard and do tons of homework and go to bed early and shit like that. But Della had just discovered boys, and Barbara wasn't interested (lezbo) and Nance had a gorgeous brother and so Della had to get more friendly with her.

But then they discovered some magazines under Declan's bed which showed that he was gay. They didn't tell any of the other girls who all fancied him like mad too, they just kept taking their messages to him anyway and making ones up from him back, trying not to laugh. Shelley Chong's probably still not using tampons now.

Anyway, they'd sort of just become best mates, it wasn't on purpose or anything. Nance used to do little things for Della, like always bring two Lion Bars into school or always remembered when Della said remind me, came to the doctors with her for the pill that first time, that kind of thing. Della hung out round Nance's house a lot, they didn't shout at each other so much there and her mum was nice, brought them cups of tea in bed in the morning. Really looked after you, not like Auntie Ellen who was always too busy and too tired. And Nance didn't seem to want much back, just having Della as her friend was enough, she said. She said she felt sorry for Della because she didn't have a proper family and didn't even know who her dad was. So they promised to be best mates for ever.

Which was just as well because nobody else really liked them, they all thought they were weird. Her and Nance used to spend hours in Nancy's room (now that her sister had moved out to live with her boyfriend) plotting and scheming, Della thinking up the plan and Nancy carrying it out – nobody ever suspected her, she didn't look clever enough, it was brilliant. They were a good team, you didn't want to get on the wrong side of them two. There had been one time they still laughed about now, when Kevin Khan had aksed Nancy out on a date (probably for a bet) one Saturday night and he bloody stood her up and she'd ended up looking a right twat outside the cinema, all squeezed into Della's second-best top and nowhere to go. So they gave it a couple of weeks and then one afternoon at the bus stop there was the usual pushing and shoving to get on the bus when it came and Nance managed to stick a compass in Kevin's bum, and then she dropped it on the floor. He didn't half scream, but they never found out who did it.

Both of them left school as soon as they could, and didn't really do much after that. Nancy's family were Irish Catholics and there were so many kids in her house her mum didn't hardly notice if she was there or not. And Auntie Ellen was always either working at the hospital or sleeping off the night shift or paying more attention to her own kids so Della and Nance just carried on doing what they did when they were at school; just roaming the streets or looking round the shops or just hanging out in caffs seeing how long they could make one Diet Coke last before they were chucked out.

Even though Nancy wasn't as beautiful or thin or funny or even as smart as Della (in fact Darren once said she looked a bit like that girl in Harry Enfield, y'know Wayne and Waynetta, which was awful but she knew what he meant – in fact that was the same night he'd said Della looked like Scary Spice only much more prettier), anyway they were still bezzies now, better than ever even. Nancy was always there for Della, listening to her going on about Darren, happy for her when it was going well, really understanding when it wasn't. And you could trust her too, Della knew that – if she was ever in trouble, Nance would drop whatever she was doing and come running. She would, she was a last Rolo kind of girl.

The only thing about Nancy that pissed Della off was her copying. Della had moved out of Auntie Ellen's as soon as she could into her flat, so then Nancy got a bedsit. Della became a hairdresser, now Nancy was training to be one too. The worst had been when Nancy started copying her clothes, she'd looked like a pig up on its trotters all tied up in lycra bandages. (Della went shopping with her now, showed her what looked good on her and what didn't.) Della hadn't really minded the copying thing at first, she liked them being the same. But now it looked a bit sad, like they didn't have a life.

And there was a little naggy thing going on at the minute, which was that if Della was being honest she knew she wasn't giving Nance as much time or attention as she used to because of Darren. Last week she'd not called Nancy back until the next day, she'd forgot, it was terrible. She didn't like to think about it really, but she did feel a bit bad about it. Even though Nance hadn't said anything, she knew it must be pissing her off. But Della'd understand if it was round the other way, if Nance was the one with the boyfriend, even though that wasn't very likely. But they had agreed long ago that no man was ever going to split them up and of course Darren wouldn't, but –

'Della?' Millicent was knocking on the bathroom door. God, what had she done now? 'Are you all right in there?'

'I'll be out in a minute!' Della called back. She flushed the toilet and just remembered in time to brush her teeth – didn't want the Gestapo to smell weed on her breath, did she.

'I've made your breakfast . . .' she heard Millicent say as she slowly shuffled back down the corridor, treading on all the squeaky bits. Probably wearing those bloody awful slippers again, looking like the black mammy in *Tom and Jerry*. Della quickly spat out the toothpaste, rinsed her mouth by cupping her hand under the tap (where the fuck was the old Wella mug that was always there?) and stormed into the other room, where Millicent was standing behind the breakfast bar in what Della could tell she now saw as Her Kitchen.

'Look, you know I don't eat breakfast!' Della protested, and then stopped her mouth from moving back to the shut position. It looked like her mother had gone grey overnight.

'What's happened to your hair?' she managed to say.

'Well, I don't know,' Millicent replied, slowly. Too bloody slowly; speed up, woman, get the pace. 'I just woke up with it like this. It must be stress. I have read of it happening to people who've had a rough time.'

Della began to laugh. 'You look like Don King.'

'Who's Don King?'

'You know, that boxing bloke – oh well look, it doesn't

matter, d'you want me to do something about it for you?'

'No thank you, I'm sure you've got a very busy day ahead of you. I thought I might have it done professionally anyway, for tonight – perhaps I'll try the hairdressers downstairs.'

'What, Have It Off?'

'No, I'll just get them to dye it back.'

Della couldn't be bothered to go into that one, she'd work it out eventually. 'Well anyway, I've got to get on. You're right, I have got a busy day.' Getting paid to be a professional hairdresser actually, but never mind.

'But what about your breakfast?'

'I've told you, I don't eat breakfast.' Della looked at her mother's disappointed face. 'I'm sorry, but I haven't got time; I've got to have a bath and do my hair and make-up and get dressed and then I've got to do two clients this afternoon and then –'

'But you're so thin.'

Does she know nothing? 'I'm supposed to be thin, it's my job, I'm a hairdresser, my clients are supposed to want to look like me, I tell them what's in and what's out. And fat is really, like, Out.'

'But everybody knows you're meant to start the day with a nice breakfast.'

'Yes, I know,' Della was losing her patience, 'but I'm not hungry, OK?'

'It's only bacon and eggs. Done just how you like them . . .'

That was it. 'And how would you know how I like them?

You've never cooked bacon and eggs for me before. I don't even like eggs, I could be allergict for all you know!'

Pause. Well, for god's sake. She can't just come over here after all these years and pretend to know me. Play the loving mother. Oh bloody hell, now she looked all crushed again. This was all going wrong.

'Look, I'm sorry, it's just that – well, breakfast is something I just don't kind of do.' Della scrabbled about in her mind. 'And anyway, we're going to have a big dinner tonight, aren't we? Tell you what –' yes, that's it '– why don't you give Auntie Ellen a ring and see if she needs a hand? I could give you a lift over there if you like.'

'Now that's a good idea,' said the greying Millicent, as if she was speaking to a small child, 'how thoughtful of you, Della.' She pushed a mug which had been sitting on the breakfast bar towards her daughter and smiled. 'Do hairdressers drink coffee in the mornings?'

Saved by the mobile, which was ringing somewhere. Not in this room, not on the table where it normally was, not in the fruitbowl which was full of fruit now for god's sake. Bloody hell, where was it?

'I put it on that chair in the hallway, with your keys so you won't forget them as you leave. You're always in such a hurr–' but Della had worked it out for herself.

'Hello? Oh, hi, yeah. Listen, can I call you back? I'm a bit busy at the – yeah, yeah, OK, well you call me when you can then; yeah, OK, bye.' Just go away. She walked back into the room, phone in hand and tried to explain to her mother that the reason she kept it in here was because you had to charge it up every night, and there was no plug point in the hall and so – what was the point, she wasn't bloody listening anyway.

Millicent was over by the telly, on her hands and knees, big bum in the air, rummaging in her suitcase (she'd been given that corner for her stuff, or Pile of Shit as Della secretly called it), pulling out bag after rustly bag of godknowswhat, muttering to herself. Della picked up the mug of coffee from the counter, went round into the kitchenette and put it in the microwave to heat it back up to drinkable.

'Here it is!' Millicent leaned on the tv to ease herself up and turned round with a triumphant smile. She looked just like Auntie Ellen when she did that. She walked towards her daughter holding something out. 'Your birthday present. I brought it all the way from home. One of the men made it for me. I hope you like it.'

Oh god. Here we go. What the fuck was going to be in that bag?

'Oh, thanks.' Della leaned across the bar and took it from Millicent's hand which was stretching across the back of the sofa. They just met. 'You shouldn't have.' Well that was a mad thing to say, of course she should, she was her mother for christ's sake.

Inside the bag was something quite bulky wrapped in lots of thin blue paper. Della slowly undid the package, trying to buy time to think of a good thing to say.

It was a . . . well, a Thing, made out of old bits of what must have once been coconut shells. Bing! went the microwave. OK if you liked that sort of Thing, but who did?

'Wow, that's great, really. It'll look really good on, er, the telly, won't it?' Let her look at it all bloody day. 'That's really clever, isn't it, how they've sort of stuck the bits of stuff together, isn't it . . .' Oh god. 'Really looks like a fish.'

The two women smiled at each other. 'There's something else in there,' said Millicent.

Bloody hell. Now what?

Della peered into the bag. 'Oh yes, so there is.' Saying the bleeding obvious again, then.

She pulled out a little brown box, with gold writing on the lid saying 'Jewels of Plymouth', made of plastic but made to look like tortoiseshell. Inside was a top layer of manky old yellow cotton wool, the kind you only ever see in these little boxes, and then underneath was a thin gold chain with a sort of wonky teardrop-shaped pendant thing with curly edges attached to it.

'Oh, that's lovely,' said Della as she picked it out with her longest nail and held it up. 'What is it – I mean, what's it of?'

Millicent was beaming. 'That's a map of Montserrat. My mother gave it to me when I passed my final examinations, and it was one of the few things I managed to take from the house before we had to leave. I thought that you would like it for yourself. Give you a bit of roots.'

'Yes, well, that's really nice, thanks ever so much. I'll put it on now, if you like.' Della fiddled with the clasp but couldn't do it, nails too bloody long, so Millicent came round into the kitchen to help. As she stood there holding her hair up off her neck, Della had to admit to herself that she was touched, yes, but her roots were here in West London, she'd never even been abroad, let alone to the

Caribbean. No need, it was like Jamaica-in-the-cold round here anyway. She'd have been better off giving her a necklace with a little can of Red Stripe hanging off it.

'There you are. Turn around now. Yes, that looks very nice on you.' Millicent beamed proudly at her daughter who couldn't look back any longer.

'Thanks.' Della reached for the microwave door, took out her coffee and squeezed past her mother into the safety of the rest of the room. She knew they were supposed to have hugged each other, maybe even kissed, but she just couldn't do it.

Fucked off yet again (it had been a lukewarm bath thanks to the Dawn Patrol using most of the hot water earlier on), Della got dressed. She carefully did her hair and make-up (sponsored by her clients who passed on their expensive mistakes) at the mirror above the mantelpiece. She went to make the bed but decided against it (these stains were in a class of their own – ugh) and stripped it off instead. She shoved the sheets into the Warehouse bag and picked it up, grabbed his designer leather baseball jacket off the floor and pulled it on as she left the bedroom. Mmm, it smelt of him. It smelt of her man. She felt protected, like he had his arms round her.

Millicent said she didn't need a lift over to Ellen's this morning after all, which was just as well as Della hadn't left enough time for that anyway. Besides, her mother said, she had a lot of other things to do today.

'Oh OK, bye then.' And then, as an afterthought, 'Have

a nice day.' Funny, didn't matter how you said that, it never sounded like you meant it. I am so outta here.

She left the washing for Maggie to do next door in the launderette, carefully avoiding having to pay for Darren's suit that she'd left there last week. He could bloody well come and get it himself. Only he'd be angry that she'd taken it there and not to Sketchleyses down the road. Well too bad, who was she – his mum? Della expertly performed the Traffic Dance across the road to the newsagent's, bought forty fags and yet another lighter and a scratch card – nothing – left the shop and hung a left into Cambridge Gardens.

'Oi! Raj! What the fuck d'you think you're playing at?'

Too late. He was already punching it all into his stupid little machine. 'Sorry, Della, but you know, I have to, it's well over time.'

'But you know this is my car, I only live round the corner.'

'Yes, but it's not parked in a residents' space, is it? This is a meter.' The little shit was going to try and stick up for himself. 'What would happen if everybody did that?'

'The world would be a much better place and you would be out of a fucking job, that's what.'

He smiled. 'Well then the world wouldn't be a better place, would it? How would I support my fam–'

'Look, Raj, don't try out your customer relations shit on me. I was at school with your brother and I'm telling you, once he gets to hear about this, you're – oh fucking hell, hang on.' Della rummaged in her handbag, pulled out the phone, paused to look at it, didn't recognize the number, took a deep breath and answered it in her nice-person voice in case it was a client or Darren being mysterious about his whereabouts.

'Hello? Oh hi, how are you? Yeah no, sorry, it was a bit difficult earlier, my mum and everything.' Raj carried on punching his buttons. 'Oh thank you, you remembered. Let's just hope the rest of the day goes a bit better than it is right now.' She glared at Raj. 'Well, I'd like to, but I'm quite busy actually – oh have you? That's very nice of you, well maybe we can meet later or something. Yeah, that'd be nice . . . very nice . . .' She looked up, smiling a naughty smile that vanished as she saw Raj wrapping up the ticket in its plastic bag. 'Well look, tell you what, can you get away at dinnertime? No, not tonight, dinnertime, about twelve thirty – my mum's usually out by then and we can have the flat to ourselves . . .' He stuck it on the windscreen, and walked off down the road. She could tell from his back that he was smiling, the fucker. 'OK then, see you then, bye.' Red button, phone back in bag, car keys.

One last go at the disappearing Raj. 'It's my birthday today, you CUNT!'

The trouble with Jill was that she was bored. Or lonely. Probably both. Della couldn't understand why she complained about it all the time. Massive house in the poshest part of Chiswick, rich husband, both kids at school all day and an overworked underpaid au pair for when they weren't, dirty great Range Rover to swan about in – the lot. What was wrong with these women?

Della had lots of clients like Jill. She'd met this woman, Kerry, who was one of her first ever clients when she worked in the salon in Soho. They really got on, even though they weren't anything alike – Kerry was much older but quite sparky still, what with being a career woman and no kids. She was in the film business, well, tv adverts more like, but she wasn't snotty or anything. Anyway, she loved the way Della did her hair because she said it made her look younger and more hip so she told all her friends – even got her a bit of film work – and then Della became top stylist at the salon because Toby the owner said she'd brought in so many new clients (though she knew damn well it was because he fancied the pants off her) and then she found herself thinking fuck this, why's he making all this money out of me, and so she went freelance. She thought it would be a lot easier, less stressful, but in fact what happened was that she now spent most of her time driving around London in the little car Darren had bought her from one posh house to the next, listening to women like Jill waffling on about nothing.

'And so I thought, why not do an interior design course?' she was saying. 'I mean I did do up this whole house myself. And that was no mean feat, I can tell you. Of course Ivan just thinks it's a case of popping down to Interiors in the High Road to look through a few wallpaper books, but it's not, Della, there's much more to it than that. But then, do I really want to be an interior designer? My life would be just a sea of swatches and tassels. Oh I don't know . . .'

Della moved to the fringe, blocking Jill's view of herself reflected in the gilt mirror propped up on the kitchen table by Delia's book for people who weren't confident enough to boil an egg on their own.

'Ooh actually,' said Jill, 'be careful with my bits at the front. I don't mean to be rude or hurtful in any way, but last time you cut them a bit thinner than usual and so my wrinkles really showed when I moved my eyebrows. And maybe I'd better keep the fringe a bit longer this time, might cover up those ghastly frown lines in the middle, what do you think?' I think you're due a facelift, thought Della.

'D'you think I should have a facelift, Della? Actually, a friend of mine had some of those Botox injections recently, I must say it has taken at least two years off her. Terrible con, of course, because you've got to keep having more areas done to match up with the ones you've had done already, if you see what I mean.' Della didn't. 'But it doesn't seem right to me, getting yourself injected with poison. And she had a black eye from where he'd missed. Do those non-surgical facelift thingies really work?'

How the fuck do I know, thought Della. 'Oh yes, definitely,' she replied. 'What you should do is get that done, and then if that doesn't work then do the injections, and then if that doesn't work have the full operation.' She loved spending other people's money. 'Anyway, what are you talking about? You don't need a facelift yet, you still look great.' And this is why they like me.

'D'you think so? I mean, I am going to be forty-four this year. And I have to say, my confidence isn't exactly at an all-time high right now. I don't know if it's just me, but I just feel so old at the moment and so I thought if I looked better on the outside it might help. I mean I go to the gym every day and watch what I eat and all that but I just feel so awful all the time, I just don't – well I can't sort of, oh god, sorry, Della, it's just that, er – oh god, the thing is, that I think Ivan's, well you know, I don't know but I'm pretty sure that he's, he's–'

Here it comes, thought Della.

' – having an affair! Oh dear, I'm so sorry, I didn't mean to do this . . .' Della tore off a sheet of kitchen roll from its built-in Shaker-style holder and handed it to Jill who was looking up at her like a baby seal with a wet shoulder-length bob.

'Bastard!' said Della and meant it. She was sick and tired of hearing this same old story. Why did these women always let their lives fall apart when they reached this age? Now she was going to have to go through all the usual questions, yet again. She put her scissors down and flicked on the kettle. 'How do you know?'

'Oh you know, all the usual signs,' sniffed Jill into her makeshift hankie. 'Working late, credit card statements, secretive phone calls, lipstick on his pants.'

That's a new one, thought Della. 'And I spose you have no way of knowing who she is?'

'Oh, it could be anybody. You know what it's like, commercial directors are surrounded by beautiful models and hairdressers – no offence – and make-up artists and over-attentive PAs all day. That's how I met him, I was his producer and he just couldn't keep his hands off me, even though he already had a girlfriend – oh god, this is such a cliché, isn't it?'

'Has he done it before?' Skip to 'What happened that time?'

'Well,' said Jill, peering in the mirror to check the state of her mascara, 'he said he finished it because he loved me and the kids too much to leave us.' She brightened up a little at the memory of that victory, which Della thought sounded suspiciously easy.

'There you go then, doesn't sound like he's got the nerve to leave you anyway.' Grateful for the chance of bringing this to an end, Della started to make the tea.

But Jill hadn't finished. 'I mean, what sort of woman is it who has an affair with a married man?' she wailed like someone off *Jerry Springer*. 'Doesn't she realize that she's ruining my life, and the kids' too? Poor Becca's already completely messed up, she's been even worse since she came out of hospital – I blame Ivan's behaviour entirely for that – and even baby Anton's started to bite the other children at nursery. This woman is tearing our family apart! Just what does she think she's playing at?'

Della began to feel, for the first time in ages, just a little bit guilty.

Trying to eat a packet of Walkers cheese and onion crisps, drink a strawberry and banana smoothie, have a well-earned fag and drive a car at the same time was proving a little tricky, but she was going to be late for her little bit of afternoon delight back home if she didn't step on it. Bloody Jill, bloody men, bloody hell there goes the bloody phone abloodygain. Never a red light when you want one.

As she stretched down to scrabble about in her handbag

on the passenger-side floor (didn't want those thieving bastards to attempt a roadside smash-and-grab on her car, thank you very much) whilst trying to keep one eye on the road, the bottle of red juice which had been wedged between her thighs spilt itself all over her white Capri pants. Fuck!

Yes! Darren's number was illuminated on the phone. Right, well he can just bloody wait, thought Della, and she enjoyed hearing the phone play its twiddly-diddly-dee until it switched over to voicemail. A sense of power surged through her at the thought of him hanging on, wasting a few of his precious moments. She knew he wouldn't leave a message, he never did. He'd just keep trying until she answered, and then he'd make out he was too busy to talk anyway. Probably ringing about tonight, he couldn't really have forgotten it was her birthday, could he?

She really didn't know any more. This time last year, he'd taken her to a really posh hotel in Holland Park and they had a big room with a sitting room in it as well and not one but two tellys, and he'd got them to put a huge bunch of flowers in there before, and a bottle of champagne in a bucket full of ice which was right beside the biggest bed she'd ever seen in her life. It was like something out of a film.

That was the first time she'd let him have proper sex with her. She'd seen him around of course, he'd tried to chat her up in a club but she wasn't interested, she told him she didn't really fancy old black men. (He was twenty-eight.) But they kept bumping into him after that and, as Nance had quickly pointed out, he was obviously loaded, so they thought she might as well give it a go. They worked out that he was the type you'd got to play it really cool with, not like the stupid boys they knew, and anyway she'd worked her way through most of them – not because she was a slapper, but because they all turned out to have something wrong with them. And so she'd played really hard to get, made him beg for it. They made him wait about six months in the end – she'd do things like arrange to meet him and not turn up, let him see her flirting with other men, that sort of thing. He was going crazy with it. In the end he'd given her a car for her twentieth birthday; so she gave him her body.

Even now, after a year, they still shagged each other's brains out which was odd because, if what Della's clients said was true, you usually did it less and less the longer you'd known each other. But Darren just wanted it all the time, and she loved the power of deciding whether he could have it or not. But he always got to her in the end. He was like that, Darren – you couldn't really say no to him, he had that cheeky smile and such deep brown sexy eyes. And the more time she'd spent with him the more she liked him. He was really sorted, you know, knew how things worked – she always felt safe and looked-after when she was with him, he was always in charge. And he treated her like a princess, spent loads of money on her, took her everywhere in his big black car, they went to every bar and club there was and he'd be welcomed like royalty. Everyone loved Darren and soon she did too.

But he wouldn't let her. Every time she tried to tell him about how she felt, he'd just laugh at her and change the subject and then not call her for a while, go missing for a few days. One time, when he could tell she was trying to get him to say something lovey-dovey to her, he'd got angry, which he never did, and told her she wasn't to fall for him, she couldn't rely on him. She knew why of course, but it didn't bother her, she'd deal with that when it happened. And anyway, she knew he loved her deep down from the way he looked at her when they were out and she was being naughty and extroverted, the way he touched her after sex when they were lying there knackered, the way he'd kissed her last night when he was leaving, thinking she was asleep.

So Della had learnt to keep quiet, pretend she was just putting up with him. Look like she didn't care either way. Made him think he could come and go as he pleased, got on with her own life when he wasn't around, but it bugged her. She was always on the look-out for his car, his friends, anything, and of course Nancy always phoned in any sightings so they had a rough idea of where he was most of the time. He was getting a bit harder to track down these days, though; he was a slippery customer, our Darren – wouldn't even have his own toothbrush at her place, just left it in the bin.

Him doing that had really annoyed Della, it showed that he really didn't want to make it official. But why not? Everyone knew they were a couple, her and Nance didn't have to pay for anything when they were out, they all knew she was Darren's Girlfriend. Hours and hours of plotting and scheming had gone into that toothbrush, and he'd just thrown it away.

What they really wanted was to get him to move in with

her. Right at the beginning he'd said he'd never live with another woman again after that bitch Mirabelle, but surely he didn't mean that now? Surely he didn't think that Della would get herself pregnant too? (And even if she did, their kid wouldn't be like that spoilt brat Jade, she'd make bloody sure of that. Della hadn't actually met Darren's daughter yet, but you could just tell from the way he went on about her.)

So her and Nance had come up with the buy-him-stuff-of-his-own-to-leave-in-the-flat plan, but it hadn't worked at all. They'd realized he was cleverer than that. Or had it fallen into the bin by mistake? Anyway, Nance in fact had come up with a cracker which they'd put into action a while ago. Della had got her already dropping hints to Darren and it seemed to be working – after all, he'd started to leave his pants and socks and now his jacket round at hers, hadn't he?

Smiling to herself as she scoured Ladbroke Grove and the rest of West London for a parking space, she noticed The Other Man's car sitting right outside her flat. Her and Nancy called him T.o.m. as a secret code. Look at him, preening himself in the mirror all ready for me, it's pathetic. Like I bloody care.

Miraculously, that stupid twat from the video shop moved his Beetle from its permanent spot in Oxford Gardens and so Della got in there, flicking a quick V to the passing Raj as she did so. As she approached the flat, handbag carefully positioned in front of the spreading red wet patch on her pants which was looking like an early period, she noticed her lover quickly picking up a copy of the *Evening Standard* from his passenger seat and acting as if he was really interested in it. With a look skywards, Della turned into the front door and rummaged in her bag for the keys.

'Hello, sexy!' He was right behind her, and as she reached up to the lock he grabbed her crotch and pulled her buttocks towards him. 'God, you're so wet – you just can't wait for me, can you?'

Following her tight arse and his growing dick up the two flights of stairs, he went on:

'It's the same for me, you know. I had such a huge stiffie when I woke up this morning, I didn't know what to do with myself. I mean I can't face doing it with her any more, so I had to dash to the bathroom to have a wank into the basin. It was a good one, actually, all the spunk went everywhere, all over the soapdish and even the tooth-brushes!'

And on. 'I was thinking of you, of course, I always do. I was remembering that first night when I gave you a lift home and you put your hand on my cock before I'd even done up my seat belt! And then when we did it up against the door to your flat, with your keys still in the lock, and when I'd come you just calmly turned round and let yourself in and I was just left there with my trousers round my ankles and a great big – oh my god, Della, get the bloody door open, I've just got to fuck you really hard, right now, you dirty little whore . . .'

And on. 'That's it, ohmigod, let's do it right here, no, no, over there on the kitchen table! Come on –'

'Della, is that you?' To the sound of the toilet flushing

Millicent, resplendent in coat and hat, appeared in the doorway.

God almighty. 'Er, hi, Mum – I thought you were out today, you know, doing things.'

'I'm just about to go out now in fact. What's happened to your trousers? And aren't you going to introduce us? In actual fact,' Millicent studied the red face in front of her, 'I think we've met before, haven't we? You look very familiar . . .'

'Er, I don't think so,' was all he could manage.

'He's just here for a haircut,' said Della.

'Yes, we were just going to do it on the kitchen table actually.' All cocky again, he took his jacket off and hung his rucksack on the back of a chair. 'Can we get on with it, Della, I haven't got much time.' Sounding really pleased with himself now.

'Well it won't take much time, will it!' snapped Della.

'I'd better be getting on my way anyway.' Millicent adjusted her hat and smoothed down the bosom of her coat. 'I'll see you this evening, Della. We'll go together, shall we? Nice to meet you. Don't work too hard now.' And after what seemed like the slowest exit from a flat ever known to a man with a hard-on, she left.

Della was bending over the kitchen table on her elbows being (somewhat painfully but it had to be done) fucked from behind when Darren called again. She'd hoped this might happen, and had taken the precaution of placing her mobile phone within easy reach.

'You're – not going to – answer it – are you?' he puffed as he pumped.

'Course. I have to, it might be a client,' said Della, not quite as carried away as she might have been. 'Hello?'

'Where are you?'

'I'm bending over my kitchen table being fucked by a man with a big cock.'

'Yeah right.' Darren cackled. 'You will be soon!' Good, he may be on his way round, he'll catch them at it. Make him realize how much he cares about her, like Nancy said.

'What are you doing now, anyway?'

'I'm shaggin' your mate Nancy.'

'Yeah, of course you are.' Della laughed.

'Well, I will be later! Wanna come and join in?'

'Not really. I'm going to come anyway thanks.'

The man who now thought he had a big cock pushed harder and gathered speed – this conversation was too much of a turn-on and he wanted them to climax together.

'Anyway, I was just seein' if you could still walk after last night, it was great that, wannit? Gotta do that again soon – wanna do it now?'

'Er, yeah, great –'

'I knew it, you fuckin' loved it, you bad, bad girl. Oh, hang on a minute, babe, I've got another call comin' in . . .'

While she was waiting, Della slipped her hand in between her legs to make sure she'd come as she could tell he was about to finish. She didn't bother to cover up the mouthpiece of the phone when he let out his over-dramatic groans at the grand finale, and barely noticed him pulling out of her as she was making a mental note to repair her nail polish before tonight.

'You still there?'

'No.'

'Yeah well, I've gotta go. Jade's school's just been on – she's hurt herself in the playground and I'm gonna pick her up.'

'Can't her mum do it?' Della snapped, not meaning to.

'They can't get hold of her.' He cackled again. 'And neither can I now, according to you!' She'd always been jealous of Mirabelle and Darren knew it. In Della's darker moments she sometimes thought they were still having sex – that bitch still seemed to have some sort of hold over him. 'Anyway, gotta go get my baby, see ya later.' End of call.

If only he really meant that he would actually see her later. No mention of her birthday tonight. Bastard. Probably teasing her, knowing him. He was so hard to work out – Nancy said that's why she liked him.

Della eased herself up to a standing position, and turned round to discover her lover lying on his back on the spotless kitchen floor, naked from the waist down, giblets akimbo, fast asleep. Honestly, this plan of Nancy's had better work soon, she couldn't keep this up much longer. She'd said to Nance that she didn't really want to have sex with someone else that much, but her friend had said it was the only way, it was all Darren understood, and she was probably right there. But look at him, silly sod.

'Wake up, I've got to go.' She prodded him in the balls with her foot. 'Come on, you can't stay here.'

He put on his best little boy face as he propped himself up on his elbows. 'Can't we just snuggle up together on the sofa and watch *Through the Keyhole* or something?'

'No, we can't. I've got to have a shower, dash out to do another client, dash back cos I've got a family party and then I'm going to celebrate my birthday with my boyfriend all night long.' She knew that would get him going, he liked to think she belonged only to him.

'Ooh, that reminds me.' He sprang to his feet and opened up his rucksack. 'I've got you a present.' He proudly produced a little pale turquoise box that said 'Tiffany & Co.' on it, wrapped in white ribbon.

Inside was a silver chain, with the outline of a slightly crooked silver heart dangling from it, not held in place neatly with a little loop like a normal pendant, just sort of hanging there really. 'That's a bit romantic, isn't it?' said Della. She'd noticed several of her clients wearing these necklaces, gifts from their husbands. Must be very popular with that lot – personally she thought they looked like they hadn't been finished off properly.

'Yes, well,' he was blushing, 'it's sort of meant to show you how I feel. You see, the thing is, Della – well, I've known many women in my time, but I've never felt like this about any of them. This is just not like me, I think I must be going mad – normally I can handle myself a bit better. The thing is, Della, I don't know how, or indeed why, but you've got under my skin and into my heart somehow, and I just can't stop thinking about you.' He smiled, apologizingly.

Oh for god's sake, this was like something out of

EastEnders. 'Yeah well, that's all very nice and everything but can we do this another time? I've just got to get on or I'm going to be late.' Bit rude, maybe, got to keep this going for a bit longer. Smile. 'Thanks for the present, it's really nice.'

'Look, why don't I drive you to wherever you're going? Then you don't have to worry about parking your car. I could wait for you outside and bring you back home again if you like. Anything to spend more time with you.' That soppy little boy face again.

'I don't think that's a very good idea.'

'Why not?'

'Because I'm going to be cutting your wife's hair.'

'He's not been the same since his mother died . . .' Sophie was saying. 'I suppose it came as such a shock. Just dropped dead, well, not dropped exactly, she was sitting on the loo at the time. Imagine the poor policeman who found her.' Della examined some split ends in a section of Sophie's long blonde hair very closely. 'I mean it's not a very dignified exit, is it? To be found slumped against the cistern, with your knickers around your ankles. Only she probably wore big old ladies' pants, didn't she, great big salmon-pink bloomers . . . Della, are you laughing? Gosh, you are such a bad girl, it's not funny, honestly –'

The two women giggled like naughty schoolgirls in assembly. Della picked up her mug of coffee from the dressing table and took the opportunity to have a quick look round Sophie's bedroom. Big high-up brass bed, white lacy pillows, patchwork quilt probably made by Sophie herself, big pink roses on the walls. Everything tidied away into the pine cupboards either side of the fireplace, which was overloaded with family photos in those old-fashioned silver frames. Floor-length pink rosy curtains to match the wallpaper, with more matching things to hold them back. Laura Ashley would have been so proud, thought Della.

As she bent down to put the coffee mug back, she caught sight of her and Sophie reflected in the dressing-table mirror. We really couldn't be more different, could we? Della said to herself. She's all blonde and creamy white and pink and round and squashy, and I'm tall and slim and toned and firm and well, exotic, really. What they call a dusky maiden. No wonder he comes to me for sex, she thought, fucking her would be like shagging a blancmange.

'The strange thing is, he seems to have gone sex-mad!' Sophie continued. 'I thought he'd do the classic Cancer thing, retreat into his shell and have to be gently coaxed out. That's what he did when his father passed away. But that was a long time ago now, and he was away filming *Postman's Knock* quite a bit, so I didn't really see that much of him. But when Daddy died, the last thing I wanted to do was to be ravaged, I just wanted Simon to hold me and cuddle me and tell me everything was going to be all right again. I suppose I did take to my bed, but not with him.'

No, he prefers kitchen tables, thought Della.

'But Simon – well, he just can't seem to get enough of me at the moment!' Sophie blossomed with the boast of a woman having regular sex. 'Maybe it's because he's taking some acting classes at the moment – did I tell you about that?'

'No, really?' said Della, as she snipped off a bit more than was necessary. Sophie was off on her favourite subject again. Him.

'Yes, he decided that even though he has all the natural talent necessary to be one of the country's best actors – and no one would deny that he is – it might be a good idea to do a few refresher lessons, sort of get back into the swing of things, make new contacts, hear of any jobs coming up. I mean his agent is really not very supportive – every time poor Simon rings he tries to palm him off with bit parts on *The Bill*, if you please. Hardly a good place for an actor of his stature to be seen, is it? I mean, he still gets people shouting out "Got any letters for me, postie?" when they spot him in the street.'

'Does he really?' said Della, chopping rather than cutting. She'd only heard someone say 'Didn't you used to be Simon Matthews?' when she'd persuaded him to come out with her once.

'Oh yes – even on holiday, people are always coming up to say hello. It sold to thirty-seven different countries, you know. Trouble is, most of them don't realize he's an actor and think he really is Robbie the sexy postman! It was quite funny once actually, he –'

'So he's gone sex-mad, has he?' Della moved round to do the fringe.

'Well – yes! I think these classes are doing him the world of good, raising his self-esteem, making him feel more manly or something.' Sophie giggled. 'It's the Improvisation With Movement session that really gets him going . . . in fact he's gone to that one today so I'll have to change the sheets yet again tomorrow morning . . .' She sighed happily. 'I don't think the washing machine's ever seen so much action – and frankly neither have I!' She laughed loudly at her own not-funny joke.

'Well at least you know he's not getting it anywhere else,' said Della as she cut Sophie's fringe unflatteringly short, something she always did if they were pissing her off. Poor cow, she hasn't got a clue what he's really like.

'Oh no, Simon would never have an affair, that's one thing I am sure of. Scarlett's always going yuk when he kisses me in front of her, which he does all the time.' She looked at herself in the mirror, putting her chin down the way women do when they've seen one good photo of themselves like that. 'What about you and Darren? Would he ever have an affair?'

'Nah, he wouldn't bloody dare!' retorted Della, though the thought had crossed her mind most days and every night he wasn't with her. 'But my best mate did once say she should offer herself up to him, so's he'd appreciate me more!'

'Gosh, she wouldn't actually do that, would she?' Sophie was so shockable.

'God no, never,' replied Della. 'And I don't think he would go for it either!' What a disgusting thought, but quite a funny picture. 'There you go, all done!'

Sophie ruffled her hair so that it looked exactly the same as it always did again. Della hated it when they did that before she'd even left the house. 'That's lovely, thank you.' She stood up. 'Right then, I think that cake should be just about defrosted by now. You are a naughty girl not to have told me it was your birthday before, honestly Della. Now if you can just hang on a couple more minutes I'll quickly ice it and pop on a couple of candles, and you and Darren can eat it tonight, in bed!'

'Thanks,' said Della. 'He'll be really pleased.'

'I hope Ellen's giving us some good nourishing Caribbean soul food this evening,' Millicent said as she was trying to get the seat belt to meet its holder, 'we need to fatten you up, get you a little bit healthy-looking.'

Della didn't know how much longer she could be nice about this. 'Look, I've already told you, I don't want to be fat.' And I don't want to be going to this bloody family dinner either, but Barbara had had one for her twenty-first and so it was only fair that she did too. The little car pulled out and slotted into the rest of the traffic.

Millicent continued. 'But where we come from, it's a compliment to be called fat, it's a sign of wealth you know.'

'Correction.' Bollocks to that. 'Where you come from, you mean. I've never even been to the Caribbean, I'm a West London girl, born and bred.'

'Correction.' Millicent took a deep breath. 'You know you weren't born here, Della.'

How could she forget, thought Della, who didn't enjoy remembering those old feelings of not belonging here or there or anywhere.

'Wouldn't you like to know a little bit about home?' Millicent ventured.

Here we go. 'Like what?' Della stared up at the traffic lights, willing them to go green.

'Well, what do you want to know?'

'I don't know, you tell me.' Della began to feel like she couldn't escape, which actually she couldn't as she was driving. Even though Ellen's was only five minutes away, she always took the car there – they didn't know how she got it, she preferred to let them think she was doing really well.

Millicent tried again. 'Well, don't you want to know about your family, your background?'

'Well, I already know most of it from Auntie Ellen, don't I?' Della adopted her usual sing-song tone when repeating her family history. 'You sent me over here with her and Desmond because you thought she'd be able to give me a better life, didn't you? And I think you were right, I had a great childhood.' When they weren't shouting at me or each other, when they were too busy working to notice what I was doing, when they let me get away with murder. When I could get away from them.

'Did she ever tell you about Montserrat, what went on there?' Millicent shifted in her seat.

'Well, you know, bits and pieces.' No, she'd never aksed. What did she need to know? Everyone lying under palm trees to the tune of 'Yellow Bird' on the steel drum, waiting for the next coconut to fall on their heads – wow. She swung the car into Westbourne Park Road and had to swerve in order to avoid an Irish Wolfhound that was running wild-eyed across the road. Bloody irresponsible, having a dog that size in London, poor animal.

Millicent gripped the seat belt with both hands but

clearly wasn't going to be put off. 'Perhaps I should explain exactly how things work back home, make it a bit clearer for you.' Oh whoopee.

'You see, in the Caribbean we have a slightly different family system to the one they – you – have over here. Some girls are unfortunate enough to fall pregnant when they are very young, around sixteen sometimes, and so the grandmothers help bring up the children while the mothers are still young enough and strong enough to work. It's sad if these are your circumstances of course, but it's a good system in many ways, because much of the child-rearing is done by the time the grandmothers are about forty and then they are free to do what they like.' Millicent adjusted her hat, satisfied with her explanation.

'And what about the men?' aksed Della, who'd had to stop while a black cab poured its drunken contents out onto the pavement.

'Well they work hard to support all their children financially when they are young, and then they marry when they're older.'

'What d'you mean – don't they marry the mother of their children?' Come to think of it, Darren hadn't been married to his babymother as he called Mirabelle. And of course he always made sure darling Jade had everything she always needed as well as lots of things she didn't.

'Oh no, these girls have children by different fathers, I'm afraid. Then when they have finished raising *their* grandchildren, they choose someone from the island who they've known all their lives and marry for love. So it all works out very well in the end, you see.'

'So what happened with me? Why wasn't I brought up by my grandmother?' Della regretted asking the question as soon as she had said it, she didn't like all this talk of family.

Millicent spoke slowly. 'Well, our situation was a bit different. I mean a lot of people in the Caribbean send their children overseas of course, but –' She looked across at Della. 'Has Ellen told you none of this?'

'No, but we're nearly there now.' She decided to overtake the cab anyway, never mind if anything was coming in the other direction. Those old horrible feelings that she'd pushed away years ago were creeping back into Della's stomach and she could feel herself going all on the defensive as Darren called it.

'Well then, child, I think it's time you knew a bit more.' Millicent cleared her throat, just like someone who was about to embark upon something very important.

Della had been dreading this. She didn't want to know after all these years. 'Stop it! Just – don't.' Why can't the bloody woman just leave things alone? Everything was fine until she came along. If she really cared about me that much then why didn't I ever hear from her? Why didn't she come and see me? Where was my mum when I needed her? 'I'm sorry, but can we do this later? When we've got more time?' All those old hurts and angers and losses and longings were going round in Della's head and she didn't want to feel like this right now, or ever again for that matter.

'All right, if that's what you wish,' said Millicent quietly. 'I can wait.'

So Della turned on the radio and let her little heart thump along with Capital's beat for the rest of the journey.

'Ladies and gennlemen . . .' Uncle Desmond was pissed of course. As he stood up, raising his can of Guinness to them, all squashed round the kitchen table, his chair clattered backwards onto the lino floor.

'Ha-ha-ha-ha-ha!' shoutlaughed Michael in his most annoying eleven-year-old way.

'Oh shut up, Michael!' said Della and Barbara at the same time, for the hundredth time that evening. Barbara smiled across the table at Della who didn't smile back, just sighed.

The meal had been exactly as she expected, even though secretly she had hoped it would be different. When she first left home, Della used to look forward to coming back; then once she'd been here a while she'd remember why she left; now she could only do about half an hour until she was desperate to get out of this madhouse and away from this bloody family once and for all.

'Dad.' Felix. Della used to really look up to him when she was a little girl but after he got the room in the attic nobody saw him again, except at mealtimes. This was the first time he'd spoken all evening. 'Dad!'

'What?'

'Say "bacon"!'

'What?'

'Say "bacon", as in bacon sandwich.'

'Why?'

'Just say it!'

'Bacon.'

Felix actually smiled. 'No, not "beer can", say "bacon".'

Desmond looked confused. 'That's what I said, "bacon".'

'No you didn't, you said "beer can"!' Felix sniggered into his Red Stripe, and everyone laughed at poor old Desmond swaying at the top of the table in his ill-fitting suit. Except Millicent, who started to clear the plates. 'Does Italian food keep?' she aksed her sister.

'Oh just cover it with clingfilm and shove it in the fridge,' replied Ellen, yawning.

'Clingfilm? What's that?'

'Mu-um,' whined Michael, 'can I go and watch telly now?'

'I'm off.' Felix got up.

'You know, that plastic stuff you put over the bowl –'

'You can't go now,' said Barbara, 'Dad's not done his toast and we haven't given Della her presents yet.'

'Come on, Mum, please, it's my favourite programme –'

'I'm just borrowing a tenner till Friday, Mum, OK?'

'Oh, Gladwrap!'

'Dad, come on, get on with it –'

'Where do you keep it, Ellen?'

'Mum, tell him to sit down again!'

'Where's your purse, Mum?'

'Ladies and Gentlemen . . .'

'Please, Mum, let me, Mum, come on, or it's going to be finished –'

'SHUT UP, MICHAEL!' shouted everyone.

A split second of silence, then Felix's mobile went off. Or was it Barbara's? Or Michael's? No, it was Della's.

Darren. She went out of the kitchen and shut the door behind her. 'Hello?'

Nobody there. One missed call. She waited a bit to see if he was going to call back. He didn't. She wanted to call him, but she could hear Nancy in her head telling her not to.

The kitchen door opened. 'Della?' Millicent. 'I think your presence is required in here.' She held the door open for her daughter, who couldn't resist smiling again at the coiled spiral hairdo sitting on top of her mother's head. Have It Off had done her proud; she looked like someone off *Rikki Lake*.

They'd turned the lights off and Ellen was carrying the cake towards the table, her face was lit up by the candles from underneath, making her look like something out of the *Blair Witch Project*. 'Happy Birthday to you,' they sang, blah blah blah. 'Make a wish!'

'I wish,' wished Della to herself as she plunged the knife into Sophie's soft sponge, 'I wish that I'm going to be really rich and that Darren will love me for ever and that my mother would just fuck off and stop making me feel bad.'

'I would like to say a few words now,' announced Millicent.

'Right, I'm off!' Felix grabbed his keys and phone from the table.

'Mu-um –' said Barbara and Michael as he left just like that.

'Oh, just leave him,' said Ellen, who looked knackered.

'I'm going to watch tv then.' Michael knew exactly when to cash in on somebody else's good thing.

'I would like to propose a toast,' Millicent continued as Ellen pretended she couldn't see her youngest sneak out the door, 'to absent friends.'

'To absent friends,' said Desmond, probably thinking of his mates waiting for him down the club.

'To Mother,' toasted Millicent, who was looking slightly pink in the eye.

So was Ellen. 'To Edric,' she said, quietly.

Bloody hell, thought Della, they're all going to start crying – on my birthday. Miserable fuckers.

Barbara broke the silence. 'What about Della's presents?'

Ellen didn't say anything. Barbara tried again. 'Shall I go and get them?' She read her mother's face. 'It?'

'I've been so busy, I just haven't had the time.' Ellen rubbed her face in her hands and looked at Della. She sighed that old sigh. 'I'm sorry, Della, I really am.'

'Oh Mu-um . . .' Barbara whined it in the same way Michael did. 'That's really crap.'

Desmond got up. 'Don't speak to your mother like that,' he said, but he didn't mean it. Della could see he wasn't that bothered either way. Never had been.

'Well I think it's enough that your aunt has given you this lovely party in honour of your coming of age, Della,' said Millicent, smiling. Party? What, some pasta and a jar of ragu with a packet of salad; she'd even got Michael to cut up the cucumber which had ended up covered in blood. Couple of cans of beer and some Asti Spewmanti – I'll show you a bloody party! What's the time anyway?

'I've got you something, it's upstairs in my room – wait here!' Barbara nearly knocked her father over as she pushed past him out of the door.

Bloody hell, it was only just past nine. Good, her and Nance could start early. 'Where you going, Uncle Desmond? I can give you a lift if you like.'

'Thank you, Della, that's very kind of you. I just thought I'd go out for some fresh air . . .' Ellen clearly didn't believe a word of it, but she'd long ago given up trying to control Desmond's movements.

'Well, Ellen,' said Millicent with a big smile, 'that leaves just the two of us. I think we should put the kettle on. We can have a nice long stroll down memory lane at last.' The older woman rubbed her hands in anticipation.

'I'm sorry but I'm going to bed.'

'Oh.' That bloody crumbly face again. Damn her.

'I'll take you home.' Go on, try it. 'Mum.' It was no use, she still choked on that word, just couldn't say it.

It wasn't until she'd dumped the old people and her car and was on her way round to Nance's in the back of Mickey's Datsun Cherry that Della got the chance to open Barbara's present.

Her cousin had muttered something about being a student and not having any money and all that, but this was ridiculous. For a start, she'd bought a Forever Friends card which was just rank, but what could you expect from a girl who bought her trainers at Marks and Spencers? But worst than that, it wasn't a present at all. Inside the free tissue paper was a little tin, which Della recognized straightaway.

When her and Barbara were really little, they'd made up this sort of club thing called the Happy Huxtables. They'd dreamt that their dad and mum were Bill Cosby and that beautiful woman who was his wife called Clare in the tv programme. And somehow that got turned into making wishes, and somehow those wishes got written down on little tiny strips of paper that were folded up really really small and put into an old throat-sweet tin which they filled up with talcum powder, and once the wishes were in there they weren't allowed to come out until they'd come true. And Barbara, the soppy sod, must have hung onto the Happy Huxtable tin all these years. Probably to get out of having to buy a present.

They were still about five minutes' away from Nancy's road, and so Della thought fuck it, I'll have a look. Why not, it'd be a laugh and she couldn't really do it in front of Nancy, she might get upset, she'd always been a bit jealous of Barbara and her – even though Della had told her over and over again that they didn't get on now, that she couldn't be friends with someone whose idea of a good night out was a game of squash and half a lager in the student union bar. So she prised the little tin open really carefully, and took out one of the little slivers of paper.

It was all silky smooth from the powder and really fiddly, they'd folded this one up really tight. In Barbara's writing, ever so neat and tidy even then, it said: 'I wish my brother Felix was dead and then I would be the favourite.' Della laughed to herself, it was so true – Barbara had always thought they preferred him. But Della had always been bottom of their pile, even after Michael arrived. Anyway, don't want to think about that now.

Got to try and find one of hers, though. Maybe this one – fiddly thing it was too. Here we go: 'I wish my proper mummy would come and get me now.' Oh god, how pathetic.

The car stopped suddenly, really suddenly – so suddenly that the little tin flipped over and spilled its contents out onto Della's favourite black pants. 'Oh for fuck's sake, Mickey!'

'That'll be six quid, then,' said Mickey.

'How much?!' Della tried to brush off as much of it as possible, and shoved the little tin under the seat in front with her foot, fucked if she was going to clear it up. 'Are you having a fucking laugh or what?'

'Look, Della, I've had to put me prices up and that's what it is now from Ladbroke Grove to Hammersmith.' Mickey was doing his best to be firm.

'What, are the dog hairs all over this back seat extra, then? And it smells like one of your bleeding kids has been sick in here. You can have a fucking fiver as usual, take it or leave it.' And she stuffed it down the back of his neck. 'Bloody cheek.' She slammed the car door, thinking maybe he didn't fancy her after all. Well he could just fuck off. Everyone could fuck off.

As she was rummaging through her handbag to find the mini hairbrush keyring with Nancy's keys on (they both had the same) she took yet another look at the mobile. No, no more missed calls. Not even one of his stupid saucy text messages. Well fuck him. You wait till he finds out about T.o.m., that'd teach him to forget her birthday.

She'd never thought she'd be this pleased to be going up the smelly damp stairs to Nancy's bedsit, but now she was looking forward to feeling safe again. She couldn't wait to tell Nancy all about how bloody awful the so-called party had been, how they hadn't bothered at all, how they still didn't care or even try to treat her like one of the family. And Nance'd be really shocked about the no-presents bit, she knew how much Barbara had got on her twenty-first, she couldn't wait to see her face. Wonder what Nance had got her?

The birthday girl felt a surge of excitement at what lay ahead, they were going to have a really good night tonight. They'd probably do a tour of all their usual bars and clubs plus a few extra places where Darren may or may not be, who cares anyway.

As Della went up to Nancy's door, she could hear music – Marvin Gaye – coming from inside. Brilliant, thought Della as she put the key in the lock and opened the door – the fun starts right here.

But Nancy, it seemed, had already started without her. There she was, right in front of her, on the bed, on all fours, big white tits slapping about while Darren, yes Darren, was fucking her up the arse.

SOPHIE MATTHEWS
30 tomorrow

Sadness   **May 20**

Ultimately, to grieve our losses means to surrender to our feelings.

So many of us have lost so much, have said so many good-byes, have been through so many changes. We may want to hold back the tides of change, not because the change isn't good, but because we have had so much change, so much loss.

Sometimes, when we are in the midst of pain and grief, we become shortsighted, like members of a tribe described in the movie *Out of Africa*.

'If you put them in prison,' one character said, describing this tribe, 'they die.'

'Why?' asked another character.

'Because they can't grasp the idea that they'll be let out one day. They think it's permanent, so they die.'

Many of us have so much grief to get through. Sometimes we begin to believe grief, or pain, is a permanent condition.

The pain will stop. Once felt and released, our feelings will bring us to a better place than where we started. Feeling our feelings, instead of denying or minimising them, is how we heal from our past and move forward into a better future. Feeling our feelings is how we let go.

It may hurt for a moment, but peace and acceptance are on the other side. So is a new beginning.

(from *The Language of Letting Go*
by Melody Beattie)

19 May

Home, 8.30 p.m.

My darling Sebastian,

I'm so sorry I haven't written for so long, only things have been a bit hectic lately round here. This is the first time I've had to myself for a while – but now Scarlett's in bed and Simon's in Glasgow, so here I am, my darling – I'm all yours for the rest of the evening! Speaking of which, it's my big 3-0 tomorrow and Simon's taking Scarlett and me out for an early supper tomorrow night – gone are the days of romantic candlelit dinners for two! Still, at least I don't have to arrange a babysitter. We were going to have a big party, but of course I didn't get round to organizing it. Maybe we'll wait till Simon's 40th and have a joint one or something. Even I should be able to get that together, with 3 years' notice!

So – what news to tell you? Well, our everyday lives are bumbling along quite nicely. Simon actually went for an audition last week (after quite a lot of fuss, he didn't see why he should have to read for it as everyone knows his work) but he got the job! It's a tour of a Sherlock Holmes play, and he's got the part of the great detective himself which is marvellous. They haven't started it yet, but he says the rehearsal period is going to be pretty intensive. I know this isn't a very nice thing to say, but to be honest, Sebastian, I'm secretly looking forward to him going away – he keeps picking holes in everything I do, I just can't seem to get anything right these days. I'm sure it's coz he's bored and hasn't got enough to do. Those acting workshops I told you about don't seem to be doing the trick – he comes back from them more grumpy than ever. But at least he's got something to focus on now, at last; he can feel more like The Man again. You know, he can be the caveman and go out and hunt and gather while I sweep the cave clean. (And even though this job isn't particularly well paid, it'll help.) No, to be quite honest, I can't wait for it to start. Apart from anything else, once I've got him out of the house it gives me more time to do my own things like talk to you, doesn't it?

And what about Scarlett, I hear you ask – well, she's fine in that she's not got a terminal illness or anything like that, thank goodness, but if you ask me she's growing up a bit too quickly. Apparently they do these days. I saw a terrible *Sally Jesse Raphael* the other afternoon when they had a girl of 12 on who was drinking and taking drugs and having sex, sometimes with more than one man at a time, can you imagine? That's only two years away for us! And there was a dreadful *Maury* on last week, where the teens were so bad they had to be sent away to a boot camp! At least Scarlett's not showing any signs of bosoms or anything yet – her father will just want to lock her up and throw away the key when that happens! And thankfully the swearing seems to have stopped since Simon blew his top that time she called him a bollock.

No, she's sort of gone all lethargic and doesn't want to do anything any more. And all her sentences are going up at the end, which is like really annoying. (Can't believe I've typed that, you can't hear me, can you?!) She's just sort of changed, almost overnight, it's awful. OK, for example, remember the Posterity Tape I told you about, that we decided she should make to mark her 10th birthday and then put it in a box and bury it in the garden for the people of the future to find? (And I secretly listened to a tiny bit of it, remember, and it was all full of how she loved her mummy and daddy, and admittedly the cat, and lots of stuff about her little life, just so adorable and sweet.) Well, she just wouldn't finish it, kept saying it was a really babyish idea. So I began to get a bit of a thing about it, I just thought it was a terrible shame, so Simon made a deal with her (when I wasn't with them, of course) that if she completed it she could have her ears pierced. (I'm not even going to go into that now, honestly she has him so round her little finger.) So we buried it in the garden, under your rhododendron bush (which is out right now and absolutely beautiful, like you!), but I have to confess that the next day I dug it up again and had a listen. Well. I wish I hadn't. It was awful, Sebastian. A torrent of filth, abuse and spite and venom, all from that pretty little mouth. I can't imagine where she's getting all this bad language from – Miss McFarland says it's unusually young to be using those words. I have a horrible feeling it might be Jade, actually, though I'm not sure I'm brave enough to have a word with Mirabelle about it, she'll only shout at me and I don't think I can take it at the moment.

We were talking about Scarlett the other night, in fact –
my personal theory is that you can pinpoint the change in
her to when I ran over the cat, I suspect I traumatized her
for ever, I still feel so bad about that. Killing Barbie the
goldfish with furniture polish was bad enough, but poor
old Brando . . . anyway, Simon reckons she's hormonal.
Hormonal?! My baby? She's only 10, Sebastian. Mind you,
I got my period when I was 11 (as Mother keeps insisting
on telling her) but that was different, I was a big girl, I took
after Dad. Scarlett's only a tiddler! Still, I suppose she has
to grow up one day – I just wish it wasn't today, that's all.

We get on fine, most of the time. But sometimes she
tells me she hates me, and though I know the best thing is
to tell them that you still love them anyway, it still hurts a
little bit – even though Scarlett isn't particularly good at
big dramatic scenes, she hasn't got the authority yet. But
apparently you mustn't let them see that they've got to you,
or they'll start to think they're in charge, and then you're
in trouble. So I'm really trying hard to keep calm and stand
up to her when I have to. But it seems so silly to be thinking
like this now – I look at her little red crying face and I just
want to hug her, she's still a little girl to me. Did you know
that when you hug children, you should always let them be
the first to break away, because then you know they've got
enough love for now. Isn't that a lovely thing?

But anyway, it seems to me that Scarlett's hitting teenage-
hood a little earlier than her mind or body want her
to, which means that she's learning it from someone or
something else. Too much tv, d'you think? Should I limit
her hours? There was a documentary on the other night,

about tweenies (in-between ten and teenage) and it looks like life's going to be hell now, for several years.

I wish Dad was here, he'd know what to do. I still miss him like mad, Sebastian. I'm sorry, but I do. I know it's silly, but every time the doorbell goes I hope it's him, popping by for an illegal cup of tea and a chat, like the old days. Oh well, Simon says I'll get over it soon. (Though I don't think I'll ever get over it, but perhaps I'll get used to it instead.)

And Mother isn't exactly helping either. Did I tell you about her renting out *Notting Hill* the last time Scarlett went to stay with her? She said it was a good movie for Scarlett to see because it was all filmed locally – it's a 15, for goodness' sake! And Jess isn't any better, of course. Last time she saw Scarlett she told me they were going to Planet Hollywood, but apparently 'the plan changed' and Jessica put an old bra of hers on Scarlett and stuffed two condoms filled with water down it, to make her look older, and they went to the *Rocky Horror Show* instead. Can you imagine?! She came home with masses of make-up on, covered in bright red lipstick and about to break her neck on an old pair of Jessica's stilettos. She looked like a transvestite dwarf, it was awful. And all Jessica could do was laugh.

As for her – well, it's sad, but we're not getting on any better than last time I wrote. We haven't fallen out or anything like that. I don't know what it is, one minute I feel sorry for her because she's on her own and doesn't have much home life, as far as I can see; then I think good for her, she's succeeded in what is, after all, a very competitive world, you've got to admire her – you wouldn't catch me interviewing someone upside down in a Red Arrow, I can tell you; and then at other times I'm just a bit scared of her. Always have been, ever since I was a child. I used to look up to her and long for her to come home from school, but then when she did she'd be a bit horrid and so I'd end up a bit hurt, and disappointed. Then she'd go away for just long enough for me to forget how mean she was, and I'd look forward to seeing her again and then it wouldn't be long before I'd be crying on my bed in my bedroom because she'd been awful again. Those people are so hard to be with, because you don't get any warning of when they're going to do it, so it's a bit like treading on eggshells when they're around. You don't think I'm jealous of the fact that Scarlett thinks she's the most exciting woman who ever walked this earth, do you? I mean, I do try to be exciting for Scarlett and keep up with the new trends and everything, but she just collapses in giggles and calls me 'sweet'. Or if someone else is there, she tuts really loudly at the ceiling. Maybe it's Jess who's teaching her how to be moody, what d'you think?

The terrible thing is that neither she nor Mother will listen to me, they just think it's funny that Scarlett's in such a hurry to be a grown-up. Well that's as may be, but I don't want her turning into a grown-up like either of them, do I? Constance is getting worse in her old age, you know, she doesn't even pretend to be concerned about me any more. (It's a bit like that bit in the *Simpsons* – you know, when Marge's mother turns up and says, 'I can't talk very much, I've got a sore throat so I'll just say this: you never got anything right.' Actually, you've never seen the *Simpsons*, have you? So you don't know what I'm talking about! Well, Marge is this yellow woman with tall blue hair – actually, maybe I'll tell you another time.)

Where was I? Oh yes, Constance. I suppose I still can't quite forgive her for phoning Jess when she found Dad dead in the bed beside her, and then getting Jess to phone me instead of doing it herself. I'll never forgive her for that. Cow. Bitch. (Gosh, that's so naughty! Feels good, though. Lucky it's you, anyone else would be shocked.)

But the silly thing is, and I really hate myself for this, it seems that the meaner Mother is to me the harder I try to please her. Now what's all that about? I must be mad. Last weekend, for example, I dropped Scarlett off and, just as I was leaving, she gave me a picture she'd torn out of a magazine and said that as I was probably going shopping perhaps I would buy that skirt for her. Well actually I wasn't going shopping, I was going to pick up Simon and then we were going to a matinée of *A Woman of No Importance* because a friend of his was in it, but what did I do? Yes, that's right – Simon went to the theatre on his own and I spent the rest of the day running round the West End trying to track down this blooming skirt which it turns out you can only get in Italy. You know I am so pathetic, Sebastian – I really hate myself for not being able to say no to her. One day, one day. Sometimes I wonder what Dad saw in her, I really do. But he was the only one who could control her at all – he'd let her go so far and then he'd put his foot down and, strangely, she'd stop it. Like when she launched a campaign for them to have single beds. He let her bang on about it for a while, but then when Harrods delivered them he sent them straight back and she shut up about it. The double bed stayed.

But it's not as if they were that close, not like me and Simon. In fact, if you think about it, our family was kind of split down the middle, with Mother and Jess on one side and me and Dad on the other. The Chalk Team versus The Cheese Team! It was a bit like that, actually – things like on holiday, they liked to lounge round the pool while (or is it whilst, I never know) we went exploring the surrounding area, visiting other places near by, etc. They liked to read their magazines and have beauty treatments, Dad and I liked to play games and go swimming. Funny, isn't it? Jess and I have always been very different, but I suppose that's to be expected. Ten years is a big age gap, isn't it? And of course she went to boarding school and I didn't, because Dad told Mother he didn't want to miss out on my childhood as well, he'd learnt his lesson. And he reckoned she was becoming a bit of a tearaway. Maybe that's what bothers Jess about me, that I got all his attention. What do you think? One for Oprah's Dr Phil there!

You wouldn't even know we're sisters, if you were just looking at us – she's dark, I'm blonde; she's thin, I'm fat (yes I am, bless you though); she's really clever, I'm really not. Well you know, not in that way – only 4 O levels, I couldn't even be a nurse. Simon says I'm much nicer than her. But I'd die for a figure like hers. Perhaps it is because of Dad – but I didn't turn into a mean person because she was Mother's favourite, did I? Oh I don't know, families are all a bit complicated, aren't they? She'd probably be much happier if she could find a nice husband and have a baby to think about – ooh, which reminds me, did you see that article in the *Mail* the other day? No, of course you wouldn't have. Well, it said that because they're pumping loads of female hormones into chickens to plump them up, it was all getting into our drinking water. And that also explains why men's fertility levels have reached an all-time low now. Interesting, isn't it? Could explain our problem. Anyway.

I've just gone off and made a cup of tea and read back what I've written to you so far whilst/while I had my Penguin, and I see that I've been a bit mean about Mother and Jess and I don't want you to get the impression that I don't love my family because I do, you know, of course I do. I can't imagine why I should be so bitchy about them, perhaps it's because Scarlett's being a bit tricky at the moment, I do worry so about her. D'you think she'll be a drug addict?

And me – well, I'm fine. Still putting on weight unfortunately, but at least I don't have to be spooked by that one-eyed trolley man at Sainsbury's any more – I order it all on the internet now! I got Scarlett to show me how it all works, it's much easier than I thought, you know. But of course it does mean that we're often arguing over whose turn it is to be on it, she's always sending her little chums emails and MSN-ing, whatever that is. And I can't really say no when she wants to send a message to the little friend she met in hospital, can I? Scarlett could be her only lifeline with the outside world, she might only have days to live for all I know.

And I buy all my books from the internet too. Ooh, I

had my first Book Club meeting the other day which was a bit nerve-wracking – all the other mothers seemed to have such forceful opinions and I just couldn't think of anything impressive to say, so I just kept quiet and pretended I hadn't read the whole book because I hadn't had time. But of course I had, and I'd read all her other stuff too, you know what I'm like! Honestly, if Simon knew how much time I spent lying on the sofa during the day reading I think he'd have a seizure, don't you?! But the thing is, what else do I have to do all day once I've done the housework and popped a wash on and tidied up? Do you think God'll give me a medal when I get to heaven for being the perfect wife and mother? Except I'm not really, but only we know that.

Oh Sebastian, what are we going to do? This is getting more and more unbearable, I'm not sure how much longer I can go on like this. I sound like someone in *EastEnders* or something, don't I? The thing is, my life is indeed turning into a bit of a soap opera actually – I'll tell you all about it, see what you think. You're the only person I can really confide in, as you know. It's funny, with everyone else I get all in a muddle about things and they must think I'm a complete simpleton; but with you I feel quite calm and clear. We do have a nice time, don't we?

Hang on a minute, just got to go to the loo . . . .
Right, back now! Anyway, where was I? Oh yes.

You know I thought Simon might be having another affair? Well, I'm sorry to say that I've found out that he definitely is. As you know, I had my suspicions, and so I planned this whole thing like a military operation, you would have been proud of me. I just had to know once and for all. So about a month ago I put my car in to be repaired again on purpose, on a day when I knew he was going in to Ladbroke Grove for a class, and asked him to give me a lift to Notting Hill because I was meeting Jess for lunch. (He's so wrapped up in himself at the moment – actors get like that when they're out of work – he didn't even think that was odd.)

So, once he'd dropped me off, I jumped into the minicab I'd pre-arranged to pick me up outside The Pharmacy (that's a very fashionable restaurant, a typical Jess place) – it was the perfect decoy car, absolutely filthy. And then I actually said the words 'Follow that car!' But it wasn't like the movies at all, he didn't hear me so I had to say it again. But he did do a huge squealy u-turn and held up all the traffic, he just didn't care – they obviously drive like maniacs in Ireland.

Anyway, eventually Simon parked up – on a yellow line, mind you, obviously wasn't planning to stay long and thought it was worth risking a ticket for – outside a hair-dresser's shop in Ladbroke Grove called Have It Off. (Where do they get these names from?) So we parked too, a little bit further up the Grove. He stayed in the car for ages, and as I sat there I suddenly felt awful – what if I was wrong, and he was using these workshop thingies as an excuse to get away from me? I mean, I have to confess, I have been a bit miserable lately – largely about you, my darling, as ever – and probably not very good company.

So anyway. I didn't think I should go through with this, so I told the grumpy driver to take me back to the tube station, but just as I did I saw Della, yes Della – hair Della, walking past us in a bit of a hurry. I thought she maybe worked at the hairdresser's, I knew she lived somewhere round there, but lo and behold Simon jumped out of his car, grabbed her round the hips in a very suggestive manner and they both disappeared into a doorway. Can you believe it?

I was so shocked, Sebastian. I'd imagined that it might be one of the other actresses on the course – God knows Mother has enough stories of that lot behaving badly. But Della?! I felt so betrayed – I mean I've told her everything, all about the babies, Simon's other affairs – the lot. Well you do to your hairdresser, don't you? I couldn't believe she could do this to me! I was just open-mouthed, stunned really, couldn't believe what I'd just seen. I was so angry, I was half-tempted to jump out of the car and drag him out of her love nest by the roots of his floppy hair. But of course I didn't.

My head was spinning on the tube back, I just didn't know what to feel. I began to piece it all together once I'd got home and had a cup of tea and a packet of biscuits, calmed down a bit. I reckon it all started about three months ago, around the time his mum died. He gave Della a lift home one night, for some reason she didn't have her car. She'd done all of us that evening and I'd even given her some supper, wish I'd put weedkiller in it now. Anyway, when he came back he was all sort of fired up and whisked me upstairs to bed and we did it like we haven't done it for ages. I was thrilled, thought we were back on course again. (Can you believe it, I was actually silly enough to think that my new hairdo had made all the difference! But no, it wasn't the hairstyle – it was the blinking hairdresser.) But now, well I just can't believe it. How could he do that? And as for her, well I'd always counted her as a family friend! So she does it to him, and then she sends him home to me – what a nerve! He probably didn't even have a bath in between us that night. I've just thought – he would have used a condom, wouldn't he? Ugh – makes me shudder.

But the awful thing was that Della was due to come round to give me a trim that very afternoon, can you imagine? Here was I in bits at the kitchen table, and The Enemy was about to walk in through the door. So I decided to do a little bit of weeding, which as you know is what I always do when I'm feeling bad. And as I was ripping out that wretched bindweed I tried to think how I was going to be with her. Do I confront her? (I decided not to, because she'd only tell him.) Do I ring her and say that I'm ill? Do I answer the door with a shotgun?

I have to say I'm rather pleased with the plan I came up with, and I think you will be too. I pretended that we were at it like rabbits (I even managed a little joke about the washing machine), just to see what her reaction would be. Well I have to hand it to her, she completely kept her cool but I know it got to her because she gave me the worst haircut I've ever had. (I got Nancy, that junior at A Cut Above on the corner, to even it up for a fiver, she's really very good actually. And a very sweet person, maybe she'd make a good babysitter.) Anyway. So now we know. What d'you think? I w

Sorry, I just had to get the phone – Mirabelle saying she

can't do tomorrow morning's run as usual, that woman is so flaky I don't know why I bother – and I've just realized that I don't exactly sound heartbroken by all this Simon and Della business, do I? Well I am, of course. I've cried and I've cried about it, as you would expect. But it's not the first time this has happened, is it? And he always comes back to me in the end, never really leaves in fact. I never thought I'd say this, but his playing around just doesn't hurt as much any more, I suppose I'm almost immune to it now. No, that's not true. I think I've just learnt to deal with the pain a bit better. What is it they say? You've got to accept the things you can't change, and change the things you can – something like that anyway. But it doesn't hurt nearly as much as the first time, when I found out about that stupid make-up girl. And I've managed to change my reaction to his behaviour now, you see, that's the trick.

Actually, what nonsense. Who am I kidding? The truth is, I'm really blooming furious with him. But if I say something, if I let him know that I know, then I'll have to do something about it – issue an ultimatum, make him leave, maybe I'd have to leave him. And the fact is that I don't want us to split up. I know it's unfashionable to say this, but I love being Simon's wife and Scarlett's mother. Who wants to be a single parent? To be really really honest, Sebastian, I don't think I could manage on my own and I don't think I really want to try for that matter. He'd never cope with it either, and Scarlett would be absolutely devastated of course. And anyway, it's only sex, isn't it? What we have together goes much deeper than that. You can't just wipe away 10 years with a few infidelities here and there.

No, I think the clever thing to do is to just hang on in there and wait for it to blow over.

D'you know, even though I'm really cross I'm more disappointed in him than anything else. What a silly thing to be doing. He's just going to make such a fool of himself, she can't be really interested in him, a beautiful young girl like that. She'll probably dump him soon, they usually do, don't they; and silly old muggins here will be left to pick up the pieces.

So I have to just sit tight, which will be agony, but I've done it before and so I can do it again. And as long as Mother and Jess don't find out, it'll be all right. They did once – did I tell you about that? – and they've never let me forget it. Constance blamed it all on me, if you please – said it was my fault for not being a good enough wife! Secretly a small part of me did agree with her, I have to admit. Perhaps it is a bit my fault he's turned into a womanizer, what with all my worrying and not being much fun a lot of the time. Jess always says I should never have married him. (Not that anyone asked her for her opinion, but anyway.)

But how was I to know he would be like this? When I think how we were when we first met, it seems incredible that he would even look at another woman. I've never told you about all that, have I? Well I think I should, it seems only fair that you know. Settle down now, this could be a bit of a long one! I'm just going to get a drink, hang on.

OK. I was 19, and working in Richmond Theatre (that's quite near here, but it's not one of the big West End theatres even though it still has good plays on) as a dresser, helping various actors and actresses to get in and out of their costumes, doing quick changes with them behind the scenes, that sort of thing. I'd always loved going to see Mother in her various productions, and so I was thrilled when she got me the job. (She was on the committee or the board or whatever it is of the theatre, so she swung it for me.)

I was still living at home, not because I couldn't afford a flat of my own – Daddy had offered me one of his, there are some advantages to having a father in property! No, I wanted to stay at home because I knew Dad liked me being there. Jess had moved out years ago, and Mother could be a bit rough on him sometimes and so he'd stay up waiting for me to come in from work and we'd have a good old natter while he had a nightcap. He was just so great, Sebastian, everyone should have a father like that. I could tell him about anything, anything that was troubling me and he'd always know what to do about it. You'd have loved him – and he'd have loved you. Anyway.

So one evening I was standing in the wings, waiting for a very grumpy actor to come off and age 30 years in about 30 seconds, and I noticed this rather gorgeous stagehand who I hadn't seen before. I didn't say 'hi' or anything, I was too shy – and anyway the audience might have heard me – but I think he winked at me. (He always says he didn't, but even though it was dark, I know he did!) Anyway, I just thought he was gorgeous, the most handsome man I'd ever seen. Well in real life, that is. (I'm still waiting for a reply from John Cusack, by the way, d'you think they actually go to their own websites to pick up their fan mail?) And I just

knew that I wanted Simon to be my boyfriend, as soon as
I saw him. And one thing about me, which I keep jolly
quiet, is that if I want something – and I mean really really
want it – then I get it. I can be quite ruthless, you know.
(Otherwise, I'm very very lazy, I'm afraid.)

Anyway, over the weeks we sort of kept bumping into
each other – or so he thought; I just kept turning up for
the quick change earlier and earlier! It turned out we both
lived in West London, and so we'd race to get the last tube
or night bus home together sometimes. At first he sort of
pretended he hadn't noticed me running down the station
steps behind him, or standing a little way off at the bus
stop; but gradually we began to make eye contact, and
eventually we started chatting. I can still remember his first
words to me: 'If they could see us now, they'd think we
were having an affair!' Which of course, we weren't. But
we did start spending more and more time together – if
there was a matinée, we'd pop out of the theatre between
shows and grab a coffee or just go for a walk round the
Green or something. We used to play this game where you
had to look in a shop window and say which one thing
you would get if someone was holding a gun to your head
– Buy or Die, he called it.

Oh Sebastian, I just thought he was the bee's knees. Still
do. I'd never met anyone like him. Still haven't. He's all big
and brave on the outside, all confident and self-assured
(not actually certain what that means but I think it's right!)
and if you didn't know him very well you'd think he was a
perfectly normal man, leading a nice calm life with everything sorted out in his head. You'd think he was the sort

of person you wouldn't mind going on holiday with because you know he'd get on with everybody without offending anyone, he'd not get drunk and go on the rampage through the resort with an axe, and you'd definitely feel OK handing over your tickets and passport to him because you know he wouldn't lose them.

And you'd be right to think all that. But what people can't see is that under that cocky, tough, manly shell of his (he's a Cancer – that's a crab) is a kind little boy who's very sensitive but very scared. He's troubled by his emotions, Sebastian, and it's a real struggle for him to keep them under control. He's really insecure, you see, he's not sure people like him and no matter how much I try to reassure him that they do, he still worries about it all the time. Of course this makes him a bit touchy, because if I even slightly raise my voice to him he thinks I'm going to abandon him and he goes back into his shell and won't come out for some time. So I have to be careful with him, and look after him like you would a difficult child. I just keep on loving him and loving him and loving him, and he trusts me to do that.

But you mustn't think he's wet. Oh no, a lot of people make that mistake but that's because he saves his real personality for his family. You see, being a moody person himself, he's sensitive to others' feelings; and so if he sees someone's hurting one of his loved ones, then god help them. He would defend Scarlett and me right to the end, lay down his life for us if necessary. I know that. He protects us. And that's the deal, you see, we look after each other.

But of course I didn't see all this back then. In fact I

thought he was quite cold, and unfeeling – except when it came to the theatre; he was as passionate about it as I was. (I just loved it, all my school holidays I spent working at our local fringe theatre for free, helping them paint scenery and make costumes and sometimes I even did the box office too, all at the same time. I was mad keen!) He was a drama student then, you see – he'd just moved down from Glasgow where he'd been working as a van driver for a bakery. He'd always wanted to be an actor, and when he got the place at LAMDA he leapt at it. He was working at the theatre in the evenings when he could, to get some spare cash; his parents weren't very well off. And he'd never admit it, but I think he was quite lonely, didn't know many people down here.

Anyway, so we'd chat away about everything and nothing – he told me all about his ex-girlfriend – apparently she was very bossy, a wee herrie as he says. (Or used to say – at drama school they taught him to iron out his accent and lose all the mannerisms and funny speech patterns, so you wouldn't even know he was Scottish any more. Shame really.) And I used to prattle on about stuff – he loved all the stories about Mother and her theatrical exploits – and quite soon I knew this was what they call It.

It was quite gentle really. I mean I fancied him lots, but there was no flash of lightning or anything, it just felt as if my heart was now complete, sort of rounded off, more a comfy feeling than anything else. But I didn't know if he fancied me back – I was a lot thinner then of course, but he didn't make a move for absolutely ages. Gosh, we took a lot of stick from the rest of the crew, though; they'd do that thing men do with their fist and their elbow to him and tease me relentlessly about my blushing thing, which was really bad in those days.

Of course, I told Dad all about Simon and even though he wasn't sure about the 7 yr age gap, he relaxed once he found out Simon was Scottish too. (Did I tell you I've decided to learn how to play the bagpipes? I thought it was a good thing to do to get back to my roots. Haven't told Simon, going to keep it as a surprise.) And he said he knew how I'd felt because he'd had a similar experience when he first saw Constance on the stage. We were the backstage version if you like! And how weird is this – it was Richmond Theatre where my parents met too! Coincidence – or Fate? Dum dum dum!

Anyway, I ended up thinking we were going to be Just Good Friends. I wanted more, of course, and didn't intend to give up on my campaign; I thought he'd probably go out with a few of the actresses first, they were far more glamorous and interesting, and then he'd realize that I was the best one for him because I was solid and reliable and not so flighty as them, and he'd realize that he'd loved me all the time, and we would kiss one night and live happily ever after. But he didn't even go for a drink with any of them – he later told me he didn't have the courage to ask any of them out. Lucky for me!

So one night on the way home, I was saying goodnight to him as he was getting off at his usual stop and he just grabbed hold of my arms and looked straight into my eyes and said, 'Don't go, Soph, not tonight. Come with me.' Ooh, I'm getting little tingles just thinking about it again!

And how could I resist that little boy face? So I got off with him, and rang Daddy from a phonebox (he wasn't very pleased but he understood) and we went back to Simon's little bedsit in Shepherd's Bush.

It turned out it was his birthday that night and he just didn't want to be by himself. It was also a sort of birthday for me – I was still a virgin, and somehow I managed to tell him that, even though I think he'd guessed. Oh Sebastian, he was so loving and gentle with me, so understanding, so kind and yet in control. He talked to me all the way through, checking I was still comfortable with everything, so sweet. It was the happiest I had ever been, the next day I just wanted to shout to all the birds in the trees and the people on the streets, write on all the big buildings that I Love Simon Matthews!

So that was how it started really. I was so in love with him it actually hurt. Still hurts now sometimes. I've never stopped loving him, never. Does that sound mad? I suppose a more sensible woman would have given up on him by now after everything he's done, but I'm afraid I just couldn't bear the thought of never seeing him again, never smelling him, touching him, feeling him – I still get that huge surge of excitement when he walks in the door. Do you think I'm being a bit silly? Sometimes I think I might even be addicted to him, it's like he's my drug and I can't rest until I get the next fix. I even used to get withdrawal symptoms if he was away for too long – real panic attacks. I'm so pathetically soppy on him still, it doesn't even bother me that much when he's bad-tempered with me – it's not as if he's like that all the time, he can be absolutely lovely if he wants to. If he's happy, I'm happy. And if he's unhappy, then I just do my best to make him happy again! And he would do the same for me. It's all quite equal really, even if it doesn't look that way.

I mean it's not as if he's a bad person. He's never really too horrible to me, I know he truly loves me – otherwise he'd have left me by now, don't you think? You see only I know the real man, the person he actually is, and though lots of things have happened over the years he's still my Simon underneath, the man I fell in love with. He can pretend to be the Big I Am all he likes; to me he's the little boy from Glasgow who was lost and lonely and frightened of life, and deep down he knows perfectly well that without me he couldn't survive. No one else would understand him like I do. I am his strength, his safety and his comfort and as far as I'm concerned that will always be true. In sickness and in health and all that. You see, we make a very good team – he just forgets that sometimes, or tries to. But if he was ever in trouble, wherever he was in the world, I just know he'd come to me and we'd sort it out and everything would be all right again. We have a bond, you see, we're like brother and sister in a funny way, and nothing but nothing (including pretty little chocolate hairdressers with pert bottoms) will ever break that bond. We will be together for ever, we both know that. We understand that we are better together than we would ever be apart. Right from the start I knew that he would be my world, and that I would be his – whether we liked it or not. We sort of had no choice.

It's a terrible feeling when you first fall in love. Your

mind just gets completely taken over, you can't function properly any more. The world turns into a dream place, nothing seems real. You forget your keys, no one seems to be talking English and even if they are you don't care as you can't hear what they're saying anyway, and it doesn't matter since you're not really there. Things you cared about don't seem to matter any more, and things you didn't think you cared about suddenly do. I must become a brilliant cook, I don't want to waste time seeing my friends when I could be with him, I feel no sympathy for all those people in India killed by an earthquake last night; what is the matter with me? It's a kind of hell, but you feel like you're in heaven.

Even your body goes out of control, you can't eat, you don't sleep properly, your legs turn to jelly as you're not sure where the floor is any more. You have butterflies permanently, not only in your tummy but all over your body – your hands, your shoulders, your chest, your eyes, everything's just a jangling mess of nerve endings tingling with fire. It makes you feel so alive. And yet it's like being suffocated, you don't seem to be able to see or hear anything real any more, it's like people are speaking to you through treacle, and so you stay in your cosy place with him, the place that only you two understand. Occasionally you're forced to come up for air by your biggest enemy, Real Life, so you do the minimum required and then head back down under your love blanket for more, knowing it's uncomfortable but compulsory.

And then, once you think you've got him, the panic sets in. What if he goes off me? What if I blow it, say the wrong thing? What if he meets someone better than me? Prettier, thinner, funnier, more like him? Who doesn't bite their nails? Perhaps he doesn't feel the same, maybe this is all in my head and this is just a quick fling for him. Why did I tell him that stupid story about not owning up that I knew who spilt ink on the teacher's bag and so everyone was punished for it? Does he think I'm a liar? What if I'm not very good at the blow job thing and he's just being patient with me? He says he loves me; yes, well, we can all say words, can't we? Perhaps he's just being polite.

Of course you do your best to keep all this to yourself, you don't want him to think you're a neurotic nutcase, but now when he's away doing Real Life it's agony, your mind won't leave you alone, it tortures you and examines your every moment spent together, pointing out how stupid you've been to allow yourself to get this carried away, how insane you are to imagine someone would feel like that about you. Dad did his best to reassure me, but nothing he said made any difference – it was like I wanted to see Simon, but didn't want him to see me.

Eventually, of course, it all came out, after we'd made love in the middle of the night. Extraordinary to think of it now, but we'd go to bed and do it, and then he'd wake up at about two or three in the morning and start kissing me down there and I'd slowly come to and we'd make slow long love all over again. It was just blissful.

Anyway, one night during this I just started to cry. I couldn't help myself, I was so happy and yet so unhappy at the same time, I knew I'd die if this was ever taken away from me. The poor man, all he said was 'What's the matter?'

and that was it, it was like an emotional pressure cooker going off in his face.

He was so good with me, Sebastian. He stayed awake all night, just listening. I went through absolutely everything, all my insecurities and niggles and worries and he took them one by one and made them go away. And that was when he began to show me the person he really was. That night was the turning point, that night we decided we'd be together for ever. At last I could relax.

So we just settled into each other after that. I took Daddy up on his offer and we moved into a little flat in Ravenscourt Park, only about 15 minutes from here actually, a little attic flat which we used to call The Snugbug because it was so cosy. We carried on working at the theatre because we needed the money (even though he was a student, Simon wanted us to be as independent as possible) but every spare moment I had was spent looking after him. If, for example, he was in a production at college I would spend all day planning a delicious supper for him and then I'd scour the shops for the best-looking vegetables and cuts of meat, and time it just right so that when he came home absolutely exhausted I'd have a nice hot bubble bath waiting for him, and I'd sit on the loo to hear all about his day. And then after we'd eaten we'd go through his lines and he would make me be all the other parts (of course I was terrible at it but he didn't mind) and so it went on, each day was idyllic. We were together all the time, didn't really have much of a social life as his friends were the other students at college and I only needed him to be happy.

Anyway. When he left college to do *Postman's Knock* I

was so thrilled for him, and I have to admit I did a little bit of told-you-so to Daddy. (Mother quite liked him then; as she's always said, 'It takes a lovey to love a lovey', which was probably more of a dig at Dad than anything else.) But as he was on location in Scotland most of the time, I found the loneliness unbearable, I missed him so much, Sebastian, it actually hurt – I had real physical pain. My stomach hurt, my arms and legs ached, my heart was freezing a hole in my chest. It was as if my life were pointless, I had nothing to concentrate on, nobody to look after. I didn't know what I was for any more. And I couldn't go and visit him because I had my job at the theatre. I remember I'd dash home straight after the show, I couldn't wait to lie on our bed and imagine him there beside me. I've never admitted this to anyone before, but I used to leave his washing in the laundry basket until the day before he came back so that I could smell his smell any time I felt the need! And I'd play our answer-machine message over and over again, just to hear his voice. Don't tell anyone, but I even made a tape of all the messages he left on it telling me he loved me, and I used to listen to it on my Walkman on the way to work, or as I did the ironing – it made me feel like he was with me, like I was being protected, I could sense his arms around me.

But it was an awful time, Sebastian, I felt like only half a person, my soulmate had abandoned me. In fact I was so miserable that Daddy insisted I do a secretarial course to keep me busy, but I absolutely hated it, it just wasn't me. (Now, of course, I'm very grateful for that as it means I can type my letters to you, saves you having to decipher my appalling handwriting!)

Actually, sweetheart, I've just got to go to bed now. I'm terribly tired, and I've got to get up early in the morning. I'll try and find time to finish this tomorrow – in the meantime, don't forget that I love you. Never forget that. Night night, sleep tight, don't let the bugs bite! Sweet dreams . . .

xxxxxxxxxxxxxxxxxxxxxxxxxxxxxxxxxxxxxxxxxxxxxxxxxxxxxxx

*

Archie was sitting in his usual armchair, smiling at her. He looked as handsome as ever; thick silver hair combed perfectly into place, lightly tanned face setting off his twinkly blue eyes, immaculately dressed as usual. The others used to laugh at him because no matter what he did, he always looked perfect. Even when he'd come home after a long stressful day at the office, even when he'd just finished mowing the huge lawn in the country on a hot summer's day, even when he'd cooked Sunday lunch for everyone (the only meal he could do, but still) – nothing ruffled him. He was a big man with big hands and a big heart.

He was the kindest man in the world. He'd do anything for anybody who asked him, and even if they didn't he'd sort it out without making a big thing about it. Sophie had been amazed by the number of people who turned up at the funeral, most of them had had to stand at the back of the church. And lots of them, complete strangers mostly, had come up to her afterwards and told her about the nice things he'd done for them and she hadn't even known. Made it worse really.

She just wanted him back. And here he was, smiling at her.

'Say something, Dad, please?' But Archie stayed the same.

Sophie moved closer to him. Knelt at his feet, put her hands on his strong knees, looked up at her father.

He didn't seem to know she was there. Took a sip from his scotch on the rocks and replaced it on the little table beside him, ice clinking in the glass. Kept looking straight ahead, still smiling.

Sophie began to cry. 'Dad, oh Dad . . .' She buried her face in him, sobbing. 'Please, please – just talk to me, please – help me, I need you, please?'

Nothing. She looked up at him one more time, at his warm kindly face and loved him completely. 'Don't go, please, please don't go, Daddy, please, I'm still here, I can't cope without you, don't leave me, please . . .' She must have been holding really tight, because he looked down at her and smiled the old way, their smile, but before he could say anything Sophie had woken up.

'You all right, Mum?' Scarlett's worried face was there instead of her father's. 'You were making a funny noise.'

'Yes, yes, I'm fine. Just having a dream, that's all.'

'A bad one?'

'Um, sort of, but sort of nice as well. Go back to sleep, darling, it's only –' she blinked the tears away to look at the alarm clock beside the bed '– six thirty. You've got another half an hour.' So that meant Sophie had only had – she did the mental arithmetic on her fingers – seven hours sleep, one hour short, oh god. And she hadn't slept that well either, never did when Simon wasn't there, always thought she could hear burglars and kept having to get up to check the front door was locked properly. Four times last night, it was ridiculous. She'd be tired today, she'd better have an early night tonight. But they were going out. Well then, she must have a nap in the afternoon. But was it her doing the school run? She knew she was doing Mirabelle's morning one, that was arranged last night – but who was doing this afternoon? Sophie couldn't remember, she'd have to ring Fleur's mother. Only she'd no doubt be roped into doing something she didn't want to do; last time, Sophie had found herself agreeing to pick up Charlotte's dry cleaning on the way home, which was a bit much but she was the sort of woman it was difficult to say no to. Never mind, she'd drive to the school anyway, pretend she was just passing if it wasn't her turn and pick up Scarlett, save whoever was supposed to be doing it the trouble of dropping her home. But when would she have her nap?

Scarlett had thankfully dropped straight off again. She always slept better in their bed. Sophie shut her eyes, but no matter how hard she tried she couldn't get her father back and so she lay there worrying instead, staring up at the peeling ceiling. (Simon was going to have to fix that soon, before it all came down on their heads in the middle of the night when they were asleep and somebody died.)

Maybe she should go to a psychic. Was Daddy disappearing because it had been just over four years now? Why wasn't he talking to her any more? Had she done something wrong? Something to upset him? No, couldn't be that, he'd never got cross with her – she couldn't remember him even raising his voice to her when she was a child, he hadn't even been angry when she'd failed most of her exams despite the expensive education, and she'd felt worse than him when he'd had to pay off her credit cards because she was hopeless with money.

Still am, thought Sophie. I just don't know where it goes. They'd been quite rich once, what with Simon's *Knock* money and her father's generous allowance; but Simon hadn't had a job as well paid as that for a while now and her inheritance was dwindling fast, mostly on school fees and household bills and well, if she was honest, food.

I've really got to lose weight. I've really got to. The more I eat, the fatter I get, the more clothes I have to buy in bigger sizes, the more money I spend. And gyms are so expensive to join nowadays, and they're full of thin people. Perhaps I should bicycle everywhere instead of using the Merc which had always been greedy with petrol but was now really expensive to run as it was so old, kept breaking down, little things going wrong all the time because she couldn't afford to have it regularly serviced. Not to mention the odd little stupid prang here and there which she'd always somehow managed to get fixed before Simon could notice. He said she should buy herself a new car, but she didn't want to as a) little did he know they didn't have that kind of money any more, and b) it was Daddy's old car, she couldn't possibly get rid of it. She still got some comfort from knowing that he'd also sat in that seat, his feet had pushed those pedals too.

But how much were bicycles these days? And then Scarlett would want one as well, hers was far too small now – actually, maybe if Simon got one too they could go out on family bike rides on Sundays, that'd be good. But three bikes? Not to mention all the helmets and reflective clothing, it'd cost as much as a new second-hand car in the end. And anyway, he'd only make fun of her, she could hear it now – 'Sorry, I just steered my bike into the back of yours, Soph, only I couldn't see where I was going, your big bum was filling my view.' And she would just laugh, like she always did, and then plan to drive her bike into the back of his and make him fall off accidentally on purpose, but they'd be home before she'd had the chance, knowing her luck.

He'd be right, though. It would be his way of saying you're too fat. (Does my bum look big *on* this?) Wouldn't just come out with it, that'd be too mean, wasn't his style. Maybe she'd go to the bookshop today, buy a few diet books. Ooh no, more money. That powder stuff, instead of food? No, disgusting and again probably very expensive. Weight Watchers? Wasn't that for old ladies? And anyway, she'd have to get a babysitter, you couldn't rely on Simon to be in every Tuesday night or whatever. No, she would just have to eat less and take more exercise, it was as simple as that. Bit of self-discipline, that's all it needs.

Sophie moved quietly in the bed, she didn't want to wake Scarlett up, and gingerly opened the cupboard door in the bedside table. She'd taken to hiding her bibles in here, to stop Simon going on about pop psychology any more. If he'd only bother to have a look for himself, he'd realize they weren't about music anyway, they were to do with feeling good about yourself. He may not worry about setting a perfect example to their daughter, but she did. She didn't want Scarlett growing up with low self-esteem and a bad self-image. She'd been wrestling with those issues herself for years.

Sophie was still trying to find the one that had that bit on Self-discipline Within The Body when the alarm went off. Scarlett didn't move. Not even when Sophie kissed her softly to wake her up. Stroked her earlobe, like she used to do when she was a little baby and it was time for the midnight feed. Nothing. She began to panic. 'Scarlett! Wake up!'

'No,' said her fuzzy voice, still thick with sleep. 'I'm not going to school today.'

'Come on, darling, you've got to. We don't want to be late for Jade and Fleur now, do we?'

Scarlett opened her eyes and looked directly at her mother. 'I thought we'd made birthdays Bank Holidays.'

'Yes well, we did, but –' Sophie looked away. 'Well, I said I'd do the run for Mirabelle this morning and so I'm afraid we've got to get up anyway, but –' she interjected before Scarlett could tell her how hopeless she was '– you can have tomorrow off instead. Which is better anyway, because Daddy's taking us out to supper tonight and so it's going to be a late night for you and you can have a lie-in tomorrow morning.'

'Oh god –' Scarlett knew without even looking at her mother that she'd made a mistake '– sorry, gosh.' She smiled. 'Happy Birthday, Mum! Stay there . . .' And she scrambled out of the big brass bed and ran into her room. Not too old to enjoy birthdays, then, thought Sophie to herself and she smiled.

'Do we have to have this on?' Jade complained. 'I prefer Virgin.' I'm sure you do, thought Sophie, but that Chris Evans is very smutty sometimes and you understand too much for someone your age.

'Yes we do,' said Scarlett, 'it's my mum's birthday today and she can play whatever tape she wants.' And, as an afterthought, 'And anyway, I like Inkzis.'

'In Excess!' laughed Sophie.

'Never heard of them,' said the disgruntled Jade.

'They were big ooh, ages ago now,' Sophie said. 'They were my favourite band, it was the first gig I ever went to with Scarlett's father. But it's very sad now because the lead singer died and then so did his girlfriend, which meant that their baby was left an orphan, all on her own –' Sophie could feel a lump growing in her throat at the thought of this terrible tragedy.

'– and Dad's got so sick of Mum playing the cd at home that he won't let her play it any more, which is why I bought her it on cassette for her birthday,' finished off Scarlett, quickly.

'Anyway, it's better than my mum and Parleyarmo Italiarno,' piped up little Fleur. Charlotte had decided it was a good idea for them all to learn a foreign language as they sat in traffic.

'Yeah, and it's better than the blooming Spice Girls!' said Scarlett and the others all joined in, laughing at the band they would have died for when they were little girls.

'But not as good as M&Ms!' said Jade, determined to be older and wiser than the others.

Silence. Scarlett kept quiet. 'Who are they?' asked Fleur, who wasn't going to fall down the kind of chocolate trap, but had to know anyway.

'*He*. Who is *he*. He's really wicked, he hates everyone. He's got a mask and a chainsaw. I really fancy him –'

'Nearly there now,' said Sophie.

'Much better than stupid Boyzone. Or Westlife, for that matter.'

'Yeah,' said Scarlett. 'Tell Mum about that Boyzone thing, Jade, go on, it's really funny.'

'Well,' said Jade, glad to have centre stage at last, 'my dad got us tickets to go and see them, ages ago now, when they were still cool. He really pulled his leg backwards to get them.' Sophie smiled to herself instead of interrupting with the correction, which tended to spoil the flow. 'Anyway, he said I could take a friend and so I took Mimi because she'd been nice to me.'

Sophie remembered now; Scarlett had been very upset not to have been asked but Jade was a difficult little girl who had learnt too early in life how to manipulate others into being slightly scared of her.

'Anyway. So it was great and everything, blah blah blah but when we were in the car coming home we unrolled the posters we had made to wave at them, just for one last look and Mimi discovered she had spelt Boyzone wrong, hers said "Bozone" instead!' The other two girls laughed loudly, even though they'd heard this story a hundred times.

'Poor Mimi,' said Sophie all too sympathetically, 'how awful for her.'

'No, it wasn't awful,' retorted Jade, 'it was really funny. My dad laughed and laughed, I thought we were going to crash he laughed so much. And Mimi was just sitting there, crying!'

Sophie had made the mistake of criticizing Jade's father before so she kept quiet. He didn't sound like a very nice person at all, but Jade was devoted to him. And Mirabelle wasn't exactly a candidate for Mother of the Year so one had to be a bit understanding.

During the rest of the journey Sophie learnt that Miss McFarland had been seen in Sainsbury's with a man, Max G was going to be expelled soon if he didn't stop hitting people and Sofia was probably going to be tired again today because her new hamster kept her awake at night going round and round on its wheel which was squeaky. Oh and six eights were now thirty-eight, according to Jade.

But instead of going straight home from the school as usual, she drove towards the airport, grateful for the chance of listening to her favourite album in peace.

He hadn't been there. She'd waited and waited, but he hadn't turned up. Maybe she'd got it wrong, but she was sure he'd said he'd be on the nine-thirty flight. Admittedly, he hadn't asked her to meet him but she knew he knew she would. Never mind, Sophie thought as she opened the front door, he'll turn up eventually. He always did.

As she stepped into the hallway, she tripped up and went flying face first onto the stripped wooden floorboards. Ow, that really hurt! Oh no, the door was still open – quick, agh – phew, she just managed to kick it shut with her foot before the startled kitten managed to escape.

Sophie stood up quickly (even though there was nobody to see that she'd fallen over) and rubbed her chin, which she'd grazed quite badly but it wasn't bleeding yet. She hung her handbag on the stairpost and her jacket on the hatstand by the door; then she took the post out of the wire basket behind the letter box as she scooped up the bewildered little cat and carried it through to the kitchen.

'You are a silly thing,' she said, 'I could have killed you, and then – well, it doesn't even bear thinking about.' She put it back in its bed and carried on chatting to it as she launched into her daily morning ritual. 'I wish we knew whether you were a boy or a girl, I suppose the vet will tell us when we take you for your you-know-what.' She shuddered at the thought, Simon would have to do that, he knew how she hated needles. 'Now what we've decided is this – if you're a boy, Daddy wants to call you Baldrick and if you're a girl, then I'd like to call you Jill, after poor Jill Dando, so that every time we say your name we remember her. We did think just Dando might do, until we realized that it rhymed with Brando. Anyway, Scarlett hasn't come up with a name for you yet, but she will. She'll love you in the end, you wait and see.'

Sophie flicked on the portable tv in the corner and opened the fridge to embark on the second part of breakfast. She'd missed *Trisha*, which was annoying as it was all about incest today, so Richard and Judy were banging on about what they've got coming up instead. Sophie was doing her best to go for the healthy option but that pancake mix was going to go off soon and the maple syrup was positively winking at her. And she'd better finish off the proper milk before she changed it over to semi-skimmed. (They'd only had full fat because of Scarlett still growing; she was almost there now though, and it wouldn't hurt her to slow down a bit actually.) Though she didn't want to put Alan the milkman out at all, maybe it would be inconvenient for him to change their order?

The *Daily Mail* had a double-page story about an heiress who'd turned to drugs and prostitution, and one of Simon's old mates was the special guest on *This Morning*. Both of these things were totally absorbing and so Sophie didn't hear him come in.

'Where the hell were you? I waited for ages, had to get a cab in the end, cost me thirty quid!'

'I was there, honest, Simon. I even got them to page you.'

'And the cab driver was pissed off that I was only going to Acton.' He looked at her. 'Ah – which terminal did you go to?'

'The same one as usual, the one we went to Portugal from last year.'

'Oh for fuck's sake, Soph, this was an internal flight, they always land at Terminal One.'

'Oh yes, sorry, I forgot. I'm really sorry.' Why couldn't she just remember stuff like this?

'Never mind, doesn't matter now, nice to see you. Happy birthday.' She knew he wouldn't forget. He came over and kissed her on the top of her head. You needn't bother, thought Sophie, she's not here. But it was nice anyway.

'How was it? Not too harrowing, I hope?' Sophie looked up at her husband, concerned. He looked a bit pale around the edges.

'Awful. Really awful. I'll tell you about it later.' He glanced at the telly instead of meeting her big blue-eyed gaze. 'Isn't that Steve Venables? What's he doing on this?'

'He's written a book about secret love affairs in the theatre or something, I don't know, I wasn't really listening.' She had been, of course, but she was bound to get it all wrong.

'He's what?!' Simon slung his coat on the back of a chair and went over to the fridge. 'Honestly, some people will do anything to keep their flagging careers going.' At least he's done something with his unemployment, thought Sophie. 'Still, I'll give him a ring anyway, tease him about his receding hairline . . .' said Simon, running his fingers through his own as if checking to see it was still there. It was. All floppy still. He'd hardly changed since they met, she still fancied him like mad. 'What's for breakfast?'

'Well,' said Sophie, getting up from the table and removing her sticky plate at the same time, 'what d'you want? There's lots of cereal of course, I've managed to track down those Apricot Wheats you like, Safeways is doing them now; and there's toast – brown or white – muffins, crumpets in the freezer. Or . . .' she was behind him now as he was still peering into the fridge '. . . we could go upstairs . . .' she placed her hands over his crotch '. . . work up a bit of an appetite . . .' he moved away from her '. . . or I can do you bacon and eggs!' She smiled, pretending she hadn't noticed.

'This today's post?' he said, picking up the letters from the table.

'Yup,' said Sophie, standing by the open fridge door with her arms by her sides, not exactly sure what to do with herself next.

'One for you,' he said, handing it to her without looking up. Sophie knew without opening it that it was a birthday card from Mrs Mac. Bless her, she never forgot. 'Bills, bills and more bills,' he said, sorting through them but not opening any. 'One from the hospital – what on earth's that about?'

'Oh you can just leave that one,' Sophie said quickly. 'It's bound to be for me – you know, something to do with my, er, troubles.'

'Oh, right,' Simon said, putting it to the bottom and dropping the whole pile onto the table. 'Oh hang on,' he said, picking up the top letter again, 'this one looks like a cheque.' He opened it while Sophie picked up his jacket from the chair and went to hang it up on the hatstand in the hall where coats lived how many times do I have to tell you. 'Bloody hell!' she heard him exclaim, and she hurried back into the kitchen.

'What?'

'You know, I give up. You spend hours of your life, no – days, slaving away at an inferior script for those bastards at Radio 4 and what d'you get? One thousand measly pounds, that's what.' Here we go. 'Six episodes I did for them, six whole bloody episodes in front of a live studio audience consisting mostly of social rejects in from the cold clutching their BBC Experience carrier bags, and this is all the thanks I get. Well, I'm going to get on to Sandy about this, this is just not good enough, how dare he accept this sort of fee for an actor like myself – and I bet Steve bloody Venables turned it down first, well he can just fuck off!' Simon tried to throw the cheque at the tv but it didn't go very far, just fluttered down onto the floor instead.

'It seems like quite a lot of money to me,' Sophie ventured. He stared at her. 'And it's not as if you had to learn any words or anything . . .' Anything to make him feel better, calm him down. Though she could sense she was probably too late.

'Typical. Fucking typical!' Oh dear, he was fuming. 'And since when were you the world authority on acting?' He moved towards her. 'What the fuck –' coming closer now '– what – the – fuck –' his spit landed on her face '– do you know about it?' His angry, reddening face was shaking in front of hers which was also red, but for a different reason.

'I was just – trying to help . . .' she stammered, annoyed with herself that she'd chosen the wrong thing to say. But even though her chin was quivering she still managed to look him straight in the eye. You're not going to break me, she was thinking.

'Don't you dare bloody cry!' He turned away, looking for his coat. 'I'm sick of this, I'm sick of you, I'm sick of bloody everything!' Sophie kept quiet, she knew not to interrupt the Big Exit. He stormed out of the room and up to the hatstand in the hallway, pulling his jacket off it so hard that she heard it clatter to the ground.

'Ow!' he yelled. Sophie suppressed a giggle. Stepping

over it, he shouted, 'I'm going out!' and slammed the front door behind him. He'd come back, he always did.

And this is what it's like now, she thought. We only communicate properly these days when we're talking about Scarlett. He's trying to push me away to make him feel less guilty about the affair. Just now was a perfect example – he'd come in and created a one-man fight. He'd done this a few times now; it was a good excuse to storm off and see Della. It was still going on, then; she hadn't tired of him yet. Normally his affairs finished when the production did; this one was a bit different, and she lived near by, very convenient. Sophie heard an alarm bell of insecurity go off in her head, she hadn't known any of the other women. She could sort of see what he might see in this one. And of course Della was beautiful, he must be very pleased with himself.

Hmm. The fridge door was still open. Sophie closed it, of course, but not before removing the leftovers of yesterday's bread-and-butter pudding first. No cream though. Or custard. She'd have to make do with ice cream instead.

Having performed that day's chores like a well-choreographed domestic dance, Sophie was sitting on her bed surrounded by all the necessary diaries and charts and two different kinds of thermometers as well as the latest thing from the chemist which told her all the information she needed – tonight was The Night.

But how was she going to get him to do it? Obviously he was going to drink this evening, but if recent nights out were anything to go by he'd get too drunk to perform. She got off the bed and opened the bible cupboard, squatting down to have a look. Aha! Oh yes, *How To Keep Your Man Tuned In And Turned On*, that had come in very useful last time. She looked at the chapter headings in the index and despaired, she'd done all this already. Flicking through anyway, she came across a tempting suggestion involving tinned peaches and chocolate sauce, but Sophie wasn't sure if in that situation she could trust herself to get on with the job at hand. And it would make a terrible mess of the sheets.

There was an alarming diagram further on in the book, in the Toys For Your Boys chapter, of something called The Rabbit, which looked like a very painful contraption indeed. No, she drew the line at electronic gadgets; according to those naughty girls in *Sex and The City* the batteries always ran out at the wrong time, and she'd seen enough *ER*s to know that all the doctors and nurses would be sniggering behind her back if she had to go in with one stuck up her. And what if Scarlett found it?

She was going to have to use the old tried and tested method after all. Sophie got up and walked over to her chest of drawers and opened the one at the bottom. There it was, her sexual history lovingly folded and wrapped in tissue paper, with lavender she'd gathered from the garden scattered throughout. Gosh, she hadn't been in here for a while.

Too long – she'd chucked in some pot pourri that Jessica had given her last year for her birthday (thoughtful as ever) to give it some extra flavour and it seemed to have somehow worked its way through the tissue paper and left nasty little stains all over most of her favourite white and cream silk underwear. Looked like a mouse with diarrhoea had gone berserk in there.

So she was left with very little choice really. There was one of the first ever Wonderbras, which was purple (the only colour they'd had) and which Sophie remembered as being incredibly uncomfortable, leaving huge red welts and blisters on her skin when it finally came off; and a red nylon peephole bra with a black fluffy trim which Simon had bought her from Ann Summers when they first met. It was absolutely hideous, but held happy memories – she'd only worn it once and they'd been almost too giggly to do it, especially as he'd bought a knitted willy warmer for himself with a smiley face on it. She'd chucked that out years ago (in fact she'd given it to the scouts for their jumble sale by mistake, god only knows what they thought) but had kept the bra for emergencies. Perfect. Sophie whipped off her fleece and t-shirt, released her pendulous breasts from their struggle in her old favourite greying M&S bra and put the sexy little number on.

She saw in the dressing-table mirror (the full-length one had been banished to the cellar ages ago) that although to her it looked ridiculous, Simon would probably love it. Her bosoms had got a bit bigger over the years and were pouring out of the black fluff like a couple of long pale-pink balloons that hadn't been fully blown up, with dark pink nipples on the ends. She'd always wanted a chest more than a bust, but Simon was a boob man. This should do the trick.

And as for her bottom half – well. Her old trusty black

satin French knickers looked far too tasteful to match the sex shop monstrosity and she knew that she was just going to have to do the full suspenders thing anyway, so she might as well try it all on and be done with it.

After far too much fiddling about with stockings and suspender belt, and trying to work out whether the pants go on top or underneath and then taking them off anyway – they were like a cheesewire and if she wasn't careful she'd get thrush or cystitis or herpes or shingles or something – Sophie rummaged through Scarlett's old dressing-up box and eventually found the old pair of slightly battered red stilettos that Jessica had passed on. They were far too tight, at least two sizes too small for her but they looked just the job. She'd better practise in them before tonight, she didn't want to twist her ankle like an amateur as she walked in the street.

Doorbell. What?! Doorbell. Oh no, who was this? She hadn't been expecting anyone. Or had she? I really must remember to write things down in the diary, thought Sophie as she teetered as fast as the high heels would let her back into her bedroom and grabbed her old pale-blue dressing gown from the back of the door.

As she negotiated the stairs she realized that today would be a bad day to break her neck as it was her birthday after all and there was no need to make everyone sad, and so she kicked off the wretched shoes and ran down the rest of the staircase to the front door, wrapping her dressing gown around herself as she opened it.

'Read the meter?' said the middle-aged man with a tiny moustache as he thrust his card too close under her nose for her to study properly but she never liked to anyway, it looked like you didn't trust them.

'Well, um, it's not very convenient at the moment, I was about to – er – take a bath!' she spluttered, quite proud of herself for coming up with something so quickly.

'Won't take long,' he said, 'just a question of looking in your cupboard. Under the stairs,' he explained.

'Oh, I see. Of course. Don't want the bath to get cold or anything!' she elaborated as she let him in. 'I don't normally have a bath during the day actually. Just today. Not that I'm dirty or anything. It's my birthday!' Oh dear, too much information, as Jess would say.

'Right. Well, don't let me get in the way of the festivities.' He dived into the cupboard. Normally Sophie would offer him a cup of tea and have a bit of a chat, but what if he could see what she was wearing under her dressing gown, which wasn't that thick actually. He might get completely the wrong idea. Maybe just a glass of water, or some elderflower cordial perhaps. Toast?

'All done!' He backed out of the cupboard and tucked his torch into his breast pocket.

'Bye, then,' said Sophie as she followed him towards the door. 'Thanks for coming!' What a silly thing to say.

'Bye!' he said as he opened it. 'Oh, and happy birthday!' he called out as he walked down the garden path, narrowly missing Constance who was just coming up it.

'Mother!' exclaimed Sophie, staggered. The last person she'd expected to see. 'What are you doing here?'

'I just thought I'd pop by,' she announced, looking over her shoulder at the disappearing man. 'I haven't come at a bad time, have I?' she said, taking in the dressing gown as she marched straight past Sophie and into the hallway.

'No, no – he'd done what he had to do.' Sophie shut the door.

'So I see,' said Constance, clocking the abandoned stilettos on the stairs. 'I'd get him to shave more often if I were you – your chin's a mess.'

What? Ow! Oh yes, she'd forgotten about that. 'Oh no no no, you d-don't understand –' stuttered Sophie as she followed her mother through to the kitchen. 'It's not what it looks like, he –'

'Do spare me the clichés, Sophie,' said Constance as she sat down and looked around the room. 'What you do in your own house is none of my business. Something's different in here, what is it?'

'Well, I did redecorate a while ago,' said Sophie, putting the kettle on. 'You can tell I did it because I bished up in that corner. And the colour wasn't quite what it said on the tin.' Always best to point out her mistakes before her mother did. 'Tea?'

'Herbal. You haven't got pink grapefruit with mandarin and lime, have you? No. I'll just have a cup of hot water with a slice of lemon, then. No lemon? Oh dear, Sophie, you really must be more prepared for all eventualities – sign of a good wife.' She threw Sophie a Look.

'But I didn't know you were coming!'

'No, well neither did I! But Luigi had to zoom over to Italy suddenly this morning, some wealthy relative struck down by a mystery illness, and so he made me take him to the airport. But it was quite convenient in the end, meant

I could pop by and see you on the way back.' Big fake smile.

Sophie knew it, she always combined her royal visits with something more important. Never came just to see her. Bloody Luigi.

'You still don't like him, do you?' Constance's perceptive powers were as witchy as ever. 'I don't know why not, he's a darling really, you should give him a chance. He's been part of this family for nearly four years now, Sophie, and no matter how much you want him to, he's not going to go away. And anyway, a woman of my age still has strong physical urges, you know, we're still sexual beings, creatures of desire –'

'Will a bit of orange do instead?' Sophie had to stop her now.

'Well yes, I suppose so. But the whole point of coming here was to deliver your birthday present, can't trust the post office these days with something so valuable.'

Even though she knew there was probably disappointment ahead, Sophie allowed herself to get a little bit excited as Constance produced a package from what they used to call her Mary Poppins bag.

'Sorry about the Christmas paper, darling, it was all I could find.' Constance watched with glee as Sophie opened her present. 'I can't believe you're thirty now, I don't look old enough!'

Inside was something made of navy-blue velvet. Sophie picked it up out of the paper, and it revealed itself to be a lovely long dress which she held up against her. It was just the right length, and it looked just the right size. 'Oh Mum, it's beautiful!'

'It's Betty Jackson,' Constance declared, 'though you wouldn't know that, the label seems to have fallen off – which is an absolute disgrace at that price – you really must take good care of it, Sophie.' Meaningful Look. 'Well, what are you waiting for, you silly goose, try it on!'

'OK!' said Sophie, carried away with excitement. Oh no, the underwear. 'Actually, maybe I'll leave it till later. When I've had my bath. That I was just about to have.' Phew.

'No, come on, put it on now. Nobody can see you, it's only me. Go on, darling, I'd love to see it on. In fact, I'll take a photo! I've got my camera here somewhere . . .' She was scrabbling about in her bag again.

Maybe if I quickly do it now, while she's not looking. But be quick, for goodness' sake. Sophie let her dressing gown drop to the floor and reached for the dress. FLASH!

'Golly! Sorry, darling, it's one of these new digital ones. It just went off in my hand!'

Once Constance had managed to stop laughing and had made all the horrible deliberately-misunderstanding-the-situation remarks she could think of, she finally left the house. Sophie changed into her cosiest fleece and favourite leggings, and with her feet snuggled in their soft sheepskin slippers she sought solace in the study. She'd really become quite a whizz at the computer now that Simon had given her the dummies book after she deleted the final draft of his lengthy CV by mistake. And Scarlett had shown her a few little email tricks too, like how to do a smiley face sideways – not that she had much cause to send many emails, but anyway. Constance insisted on communicating family arrangements via Scarlett's hotmail address, apparently to 'make her feel involved' – Sophie just saw it as another way of her mother avoiding having to deal with her. But the whole computer thing was growing on her now – it was something the whole family could enjoy after all, even though they couldn't all do it at the same time.

The internet was her new favourite thing, and she was getting really quite good at it. She'd made herself a BLT with some chicken and grated cheese with a great big dollop of mayonnaise (it was her birthday and anyway it was only Thursday and all diets start on Mondays, everybody knew that) and she'd treated herself to a packet of crisps as well, to go with it. So with one hand on her sandwich and the other on her mouse she surfed away to her heart's content. This was a great way to lose yourself in the big wide world, the best way to find information, it was just great. Having found out quite a lot in quite a short space of time, Sophie tore herself away from the superannuation highway and inserted the floppy disk. She started typing.

*

Thursday, 20 May

Sorry, sweetheart, it's the next day now – my birthday, hooray! Gosh, I don't feel thirty years old, you know. Not that I mind being that old – this old, rather! – as I never really was one for the twenty-something lifestyle. I've never really wanted to go on 18–30 holidays (in fact I can't now, can I?!) and get really drunk until I'm sick, and sleep with every boy I meet and all that. I know it's not a very fashionable thing to say in this day and age, but I like being just a homemaker, as the Americans call it. And anyway, I'm quite good at cooking and cleaning and ironing and sewing and all those traditional mummy things – what job could I have where I would get to do all of those?

Anyway, where were we? I've got to finish this, or I won't get back to it for ages and I don't want to leave you in suspenders, do I? Which reminds me, I've got a brilliant plan to tell you about later. Now then . . .

Oh yes, right, I was just telling you about me and Simon – we were madly in love, he was away filming, and I was really miserable, wasn't I?

So you can imagine how delighted I was when I discovered I was pregnant. I should have known then, really. Simon was absolutely furious about it. I was so shocked – I thought he'd be thrilled, we'd often talked about babies, how ours would look, etc. Of course I was on the Pill, but I have to admit (and I would only ever tell you this) that I had been a little careless about taking it every day. I didn't deliberately set out to get pregnant, but I think subconsciously I must have wanted to. And actually, why not? His career had really taken off, and I thought it would bring us even closer together, make us a real family. Looking back on it now, I think I had a fantasy going on in my head of us all living together happily in a big house in the country, with the children running barefoot through the wild poppy fields, straw from playing in the hayloft threaded through their wild blonde hair, or something equally ridiculous.

Anyway. Simon did his best to convince me to get rid of the baby, but somehow I just couldn't. I had this little life growing in my tummy, our life, and it felt like he wanted to murder it. I just couldn't even contemplate not having it, and was really quite fierce about it all. He came up with every reason in the book for terminating (no one dared mention the 'a' word) – we'd not known each other long enough, potential financial insecurity in the future, what if it was handicapped – the lot. It was a terrible time, I've never cried so much. In the end, Daddy said he'd buy us a house as a wedding present. And so we got married. I was so blinkered at the time that I thought I'd managed to talk him round, that it had just taken him time to get used to the idea but, looking back – well, who knows. It makes sense anyway, doesn't it, to get married to the other half of your orange. (I think that's an old Chinese thing but I'm not sure.)

He was away filming for most of my pregnancy, but I didn't mind so much because I had a part of him inside me now; I could carry him around with me wherever I went. He managed to get back from location just in time for the birth (I hung on for as long as I could but in the end I had to have an emergency Caesarean), and when Scarlett eventually arrived – well, everything changed. He just fell in love with her from the minute he set eyes on her (so did I, that squashy little button face!) and I can remember lying in my hospital room, watching Simon snoozing in the armchair beside me with baby Scarlett sleeping on his chest, just thanking God for letting this happen. It was so peaceful, there was so much love in that room, I can honestly say that was the Happiest Moment Of My Life. Just us, just the family – mummy, daddy and baby.

And give him his due, he has been the most marvellous father. He would lay down and die for her if he had to. He was so good with her when she was tiny, he'd spend hours playing with her on the sofa while I pottered in the kitchen, and took great pride in changing nappies, taking her for walks to feed the ducks, driving her round and round the block to get her off to sleep, etc. Of course it was always me who got up in the night to give her a bottle (I couldn't breastfeed, sadly, because I got abscesses) but actually I enjoyed that because it was almost the only time I was on my own with her, I just loved it. And he really needed his sleep or he'd turn into Mr Grumpy overnight. They became a great team, he took her everywhere with him in her babysling, and people would stop him on the street and coo away – he loved it. Loves her. Call him what you like, no one could ever deny he's been an excellent dad. They're still thick as thieves now – always ganging up on me! (Did I ever tell you, that stupid counsellor I went to see a couple of years ago tried to convince me that I was secretly jealous of their relationship! I mean, as if. Apart from anything else, I was very close to my father so I'm glad Scarlett has that too. I stopped going when I discovered she wasn't married and didn't even have any children – what would she know about it?!)

But after Scarlett was born he changed towards me, he was different. An outsider wouldn't notice, but I could feel that he was a little distant, less giving, less loving. Of course I was very tired a lot of the time when she was a baby, and she was absolutely hopeless at sleeping when she was a toddler – I always ended up in her bed – but I absolutely promise you I did everything in my power to make sure he was as well looked-after as she was. I always managed to have supper on the table and the house clean and tidy, I sent him little cards and photos of me and Scarlett when he was on location, I never refused sex, even instigated it occasionally when it was the last thing I felt like doing – I did everything I could. But it never seemed to be enough. It felt as if I had done something very bad to make him cross, and no matter how hard I tried I just couldn't get us back to normal. Maybe he couldn't forgive me for standing up to him about the baby, 'getting my own way' as he said; maybe he felt emasculated because Daddy had bought the house; maybe he felt trapped into marrying me – I don't know. But he had Scarlett now, wasn't she worth all that? And whenever I tried to talk to him about it, he would just dodge the issue – change the subject, change the channel, even just leave the room. I suppose I could have tried harder to make him communicate with me, but I didn't really want to push it as I didn't want to push him away from me either.

So we pottered on, both of us focusing on Scarlett instead of each other, but we were still having a nice enough life. *Postman's Knock* went to another series, and another and eventually we had enough money to buy a bigger house, this one, admittedly in Acton, but you get much more for your money out here. (It was Simon's turn to do a bit of told-you-so to Daddy this time!) And because we now had more bedrooms, I took this as a sign that we could now have more children. We never really discussed it, of course, but why else would he have bought us a bigger house? And so I stopped taking my Pill completely, and it took me a while but I did indeed fall pregnant again.

I told Scarlett first, she was so excited – she was 5 then and thought the baby would be like a little dolly that she could push round in her pram. But Simon – well, he didn't try to persuade me to have an abortion this time, but I could tell he wasn't exactly ecstatic about it. Fortunately he was filming away from home as usual and so I didn't have to cope with his mood swings, and anyway I was all wrapped up in the cotton wool of pregnancy.

I don't really want to go into the miscarriages again. It's still all too painful, even now, and we've covered all that many times before, haven't we? But I still wonder what happened to my lost babies, where they went, how they would have been if they'd managed to stay with me. In my mind, I kiss them every night before I go to sleep. The only comfort I can get from this is that perhaps God had not made them perfectly, that they would have had an unhappy life on this earth. And yet I would have loved them, I know I could – oh it's just too awful, I'm going to stop for a minute. Cup of tea, I think.

Sorry, sweetheart, just had a quick weep over the kettle. It's funny, when you're used to crying a lot you seem to be able to do practical things at the same time, don't you? It's probably because you know it'll pass. I remember when Daddy died I thought I'd never stop, I was so scared of the pain. And it made it worse that he'd been so good with me about the babies, held me so tight, just let me ramble on until it stopped. I mean – don't get me wrong – Simon was fantastic when Dad went, but somehow it just wasn't the same. I hope I've been as helpful to him about his mother, but it's odd, he doesn't seem to want to talk about it very much. He was almost clinical about going up to Glasgow this week to sort out the house and everything, quite emotionally detached – it's like he can't face the grief yet. I suppose I'll have to wait until he feels ready to deal with it all. Or Della dumps him. Oh dear, let's just not go there, I'll deal with all that later. Where were we?

Oh yes – it was different when I found out I was pregnant again so soon after Dad died. I didn't dare be happy. Week 6 was the worst, I hardly moved for fear of dislodging anything. It was an almost impossible time, I was still so upset about Daddy but knew that this could harm the pregnancy and so just tried to distract myself with daytime tv, watching videos, reading books, doing jigsaws, anything that wasn't too strenuous really. I could hardly believe it when we reached 12 weeks, further than I had ever got before. Three whole months, a third of the way there.

Scarlett came with me for my 18-week scan (Simon had to rehearse that day) and we positively bounced along the hospital corridor, so excited that we were going to get a look at the little baby. And then that awful silence. The lady scanner went and got the professor, and he did a vaginal scan, and yes, there was a lump on the brain and a hole in your heart. I can remember them saying that one of these things on its own usually mended itself, but when there were two 'soft signs' together it was sometimes an indication of something being wrong. Scarlett kept asking what was the matter, but I couldn't even speak, I could only stare at that man's face as he studied the screen.

They called Simon, tracked him down somehow, and they explained our options to us, though I didn't really hear any of them. As it was Queen Charlotte's (which is a teaching hospital) they had done lots of research on foetal testing, and I seem to remember them saying that McDonalds had just donated a brand-new machine which did a better test than amniocentesis, more efficient. So Simon said yes, and I was whisked into a gown and taken to a room full of people (I suppose they must have been students) and I had to lie down, just lie there while they took a needle and punctured it through my tummy and into my womb, and then chased you round until they speared your liver and took two whole syringes of blood from a baby who was only a few inches long, still tiny. It felt like rape then and it still feels like that now. Oh god, I'm welling up again. Well I'm not going to stop this time, I don't have to — it's only us, isn't it.

I know we've been through all this before, but it helps me to talk about it, you don't mind do you? I still feel so bad about letting them do that to you. I wish I had said no. I'm haunted by the image of you being assaulted by something so terrifying, so huge and painful, with nowhere to run, no escape, you were trapped inside me. I just didn't have time to think it through, it all happened so fast. I kept looking at Simon cuddling Scarlett on a chair on the other side of the room, making sure she didn't see anything; I suppose I just wanted what was best for my family. I couldn't think, I didn't know, I was paralysed, literally: they told me

I couldn't move as this was such a tricky procedure, any sudden jerks could harm the baby.

And then we had to wait 24 long hours for the result. Scarlett went to stay with Mother because I thought it best that she was away from all this, I didn't want her to see me so upset. Simon dealt with it by not dealing with it at all, saying stupid things like 'don't worry', making me cups of tea which I forgot to drink. We went to the cinema in the end, still can't remember what the film was. I just kept hoping the test hadn't killed you, that I hadn't let them kill you. But I knew that couldn't be true, as you were still moving around in my tummy. I kept my hand on you all night, stroking you, it was the closest I could get.

I rang the hospital in the afternoon, even though they said to wait until they called me. I did it when Simon was out picking up Scarlett because for some reason I wanted to be by myself when I found out. They said they didn't have the results yet, wait until Monday. I tried to explain that I couldn't go through the weekend not knowing, they must know something by now, they'd promised us the results within 24 hours, today, Friday. I was very upset. Eventually Simon got on the phone and threatened to contact the newspapers, and so they tracked the professor down and he rang us back.

'Your baby's got an extra chromosome,' he said, 'but we can't say which one it is.' Just like that. He said that it could be Down's Syndrome, but that was unlikely; it might be something more serious which could mean severe retardation and the baby would die during the first few days of life. Or it could be brain damaged, but we wouldn't know how badly until the child was older. But they didn't know exactly what it was yet, so much can go wrong with chromosomes. In any case, if the result was not very good, he would quite understand if I wanted to terminate, but they'd have the full diagnosis on Tuesday. Sorry not to be more clear. He did try to be nice.

The worst weekend of my life. Not knowing. Knowing there was something wrong. Certain that they had made a mistake. Simon trying to keep everything going for Scarlett. She could have gone back to Mother's, but we wanted her with us now. We found ourselves in Oxford Street, bought her a hideous bright blue fun-fur coat, put up that curtain rail in the kitchen at last. Couldn't talk. Kept hiding in your room, hugging you. So sad.

'Good news,' he said on Tuesday. 'It's only XYY Syndrome. You can still have a termination if you want, though.' Went to see the geneticist, she explained, and I know this stuff off by heart now. We all have 46 chromosomes, arranged in 23 pairs. The Xs are female, the Ys male. When genetic research began in the 1950s they took compulsory blood samples from inmates of prisons and mental institutions and discovered an inordinately high proportion of male prisoners had an extra Y chromosome. As a result, lots of couples choose to end their pregnancies when they find out that's what they're having.

I think this is when Simon stopped listening, when he thought you'd be a criminal. I heard the rest, though, and I studied all the information she'd photocopied for us, and I found out that although these boys are more susceptible to learning, speech and behavioural problems and grow to be extra tall, nurture could triumph over nature and most went on to lead normal lives. I read nothing that made me want to send you away, in fact I thought that God had probably specially chosen me to look after you as he knew I would be able to make your life a happy one.

But Simon didn't agree. He thought it was unfair to bring someone into this cut-throat world who was already at a disadvantage, that it would be too much pressure on us, that it just wasn't right. I tried to gather together as much information as I could to convince him otherwise, but to be honest there wasn't that much out there. (I now know that this is probably because one in a thousand men are born with XYY, and most don't even know it, so, as it's not that much of a problem, it's not been worth investigating.) But he kept saying that you would be a retard, a hooligan, a murderer, perhaps even a rapist and that we just couldn't do this. You'd be teased by the other kids at school, you'd be a really aggressive teenager, you'd never be prime minister.

I really fought for you, my darling, I really did. Harder than I had for Scarlett, you needed me even more. I argued that you'd be special, that we had enough love to cope with any problems you might have, that it wouldn't be as hard as he thought. I tried everything I could, I promised to take full responsibility, I wanted my Dad.

I've never told you this before, but I think you'd understand now. He said that if I insisted on having this baby, he would leave me.

What a terrible thing for you to know. That I chose him over you. But I think you know your mum well enough by now to understand that it wasn't an easy decision. I couldn't have managed on my own, Sebastian, I wasn't strong enough then. I don't know if this makes any sense at all, but I did it for you. I couldn't have given you the life you deserve, my darling. I didn't feel I could be a proper mummy to you on my own. I hung on for as long as I could, but I finally said goodbye to you on Friday, 24 October – physically, that is. You're still alive here in my heart; not a day passes without me thinking of you, saying a little hello to your soul, wherever it is. I give you my love, guidance and protection every day. He can't stop me thinking my thoughts.

You'd be 3 now, a naughty little boy, a 'cheeky wee monkey' as Dad would say. You'd be calling me Mummy. Doesn't bear thinking about. I wish I could say that I made the right decision but, as you know, the more I've gone on to find out about your condition, the more I see that it wouldn't have been a problem for us after all. There's more and more research being done, and it turns out that the 'criminal' element was only a result of being easily led, not being quite as bright as your peers. As that lady at the Unique conference said, you'd be the one sent over the wall into the orchard to get the apples and be caught when the others had scarpered! And, of course, there are no records of XYY men being murderers or rapists, quite the reverse – every parent I speak to assures me you're all lovely boys, very charming, a little too sensitive if anything. I know I can never justify what I did to you, Sebastian, but at least I saved you from being born into unhappiness.

And anyway, I have you all to myself now. I can talk to

you whenever I want, I carry you round with me all day, we're great friends, aren't we? I love you, Sebastian, and I know you have it in your heart to forgive me, even if I can't forgive myself. Bless you, my darling, to me you will always be my lost boy.

But I'm going to get you back, aren't I? Now I came up with this plan the other day, see what you think. (I'll have to be quick, because I've got to pick Scarlett up from school soon.) OK. As you know, I've not been pregnant again since I said goodbye to you. I just can't face the pain of it all going wrong again, and Simon very rarely comes near me now anyway. But, Sebastian, I'm ready to try again. I'm ready for you now, I want you here with me. Desperately. I know we've tried all sorts of different things before, but I've come up with a new plan, a really good one.

The thing is, I'm beginning to think that it's not by accident Simon and me keep having babies that don't want to be here, and that perhaps his sperm and my eggs aren't very well matched or something. I know they said you were an accident at conception, just one of those things, but I'm not so sure. The hospital can't find anything wrong with either of us – I got a letter from them this morning and apparently we've both got rare blood groups which we knew about already, but that's all. His sperm count is fine (that was funny, scraping the sperm off the toothbrushes, wasn't it?!) and I've got lots of perfectly healthy eggs just waiting to be turned into babies.

So I thought, what about going to a sperm bank? I've just been going into it on the internet and it seems it's not as complicated as you might think. In fact, it's really easy!

First of all, I did a search on the world wide web and I could hardly believe my eyes when it came up with 62 matches! Some of the places were about whales, and there were some very disappointing sites that turned out to have poor jokes on them about holding up a spermbank and making the nurse drink the samples, but most of them seemed genuine enough – there was even a site called hellobaby.com! It seems this method is very popular with lesbians in America and all the clinics sound most helpful. And it's not too expensive either, there was even one man willing to give his donor sperm away for free, isn't that nice?

Anyway, I thought it might be a bit tricky to find an excuse to go by myself to America, so then I did another search on the UK and I got 46 matches! There's even one right here in London, which was most informative – did you know that a sperm donor is not allowed to father more than 10 pregnancies? It's to make sure that it would be almost impossible for a genetic brother and sister to meet and marry and have children of their own. But he can father as many as you want if you've already got one baby by him – so I could have two more babies, or even three! One of the websites even gets you to tick the boxes for preferred hair colour, etc. You can order up whatever you want, it's fantastic. (Sainsbury's will be doing them next!) Anyway, I've printed them off and I'm going to hide the pages in your chest of drawers, I thought under the teddy lining paper would be a good place, and I'll go through them tomorrow and see what I can discover.

You see I think that if I get an anonymous donor who

has the same colouring and physical features as Simon, and they screen them thoroughly for defects by the way, then I stand a better chance of getting a perfect baby, don't I? And Simon need never know, it'll be our secret. I'll just make him succumb to me during one of my fertile times – tonight is one of those nights by the way, and don't you worry, I've made sure he won't be able to resist me! And even if that doesn't work, I can always literally force myself upon him one night when he's asleep, he always used to find that a bit of a turn-on. And if I do that once I know I'm already pregnant, then we can just say the baby came a bit early.

Now I know what you're thinking, that he'll be all furious again when I announce the pregnancy. Well things are different now, aren't they? I can manage a lot better these days. Even if he threatens to leave me again, I think I'm strong enough to cope with it all. But I really don't think I'll have to, he'll love you when he sees you, I know he will. We've both changed since then. You'll probably bring us closer again too. I don't think even Della is ruthless enough to carry on an affair with a man whose wife is expecting their baby, do you?

So that's my new project. Brilliant, isn't it?! I'm going to get cracking on it tomorrow and find out more – I'll keep you posted on all developments!

Better get going now. I'm going to save this onto your special disk and hide it under your cot mattress as usual. Oh I can't wait to meet you, my darling, it really does seem possible now. And as we know, when I decide to get something . . .

Until we speak again, my darling baby boy, be safe in the knowledge that Mummy loves you. xxxxxxxxxxxxxxxxx

*

Friday, 21 May
Home, 10.15 a.m.

My darling Sebastian,

Just a quickie as I've got to get on with the new project, but I just had to tell you this.

Last night, at my birthday supper, Simon announced to me and Scarlett that when he was going through his mother's desk drawer, he found a brown envelope addressed to him in her handwriting. Inside was a letter informing him that he was adopted! She said she couldn't give him any more details as she had been sworn to secrecy, but she couldn't bear for him not to know.

Can you imagine?! I think he's still in shock about it, it's completely disorientated him. Scarlett and I said that he simply must find out more – she said we could all be related to the Queen for all we know! Poor man, he's really in a pickle about it.

Anyway, got to go and find that sperm – mission accomplished last night (just about) but better to be safe than sorry . . .

Lots of love as ever,
Mum xxxxxxxxxxxxxxxxxxxxxxxxxxxxxxxxxxxxxxxxxxxx

PS He gave me one of those Psion Organizer thingies for my birthday; I'd rather have had something a little more personal, like jewellery or something, but I don't think he's thinking straight at the moment. xxx

JESSICA ROSE
40 on Saturday

JESSICA ROSE

CELEBRATES HER BIRTHDAY
WITH SHOWBIZ PALS

Talented top TV presenter and popular personality Jessica Rose celebrated her 35th birthday in style last week at one of London's hottest nitespots. Jessica, stunning as ever in Gucci (above right, fending off George Clooney) said 'it's so great to be amongst my closest friends. I'm thrilled that dear Brad and Jennifer (above left) took time out of their busy schedules to fly in for my little party, and my new boyfriend Prince William (right) said it was the highlight of his year.' Sadly there wasn't room for all Jessica's friends however; many big stars (left, Liz Hurley in tears) had to be turned away ...

19 June

Millicent let herself into the flat and was not quite as horrified as she had been the first time. She was getting used to being greeted by this kind of devastation now. Even though most of her employers weren't as tidy and clean as she'd like them to be, the men were better than the women; but this girl was most definitely one of the worst. How could anybody live like this? They should warn you when they stick their advertisements in the newsagent's window: 'I live like a pig' the card should say.

Still, she was getting used to the different ways of this country now, she'd been here nearly four months – few things surprised her any more. She took off her hat and coat and hung them on the back of the door – the hooks were always empty, this girl didn't seem to know what they were for – and picking her way through the miscellaneous detritus on the floor walked straight past the bathroom and into the kitchen, trying not to look to the right where she knew the worst of the mess would be, all over the sitting room. What was the point of having such a beautiful place if you weren't going to keep it nice? Still, it was none of her business – after all, it was her job to keep it nice, that's what she was paid for. Millicent shuddered – who'd have thought she'd end up a cleaner?

Not sure whether Jessica was still in bed or just out, she

decided to make herself a nice cup of tea before tackling the kitchen. No water in the kettle as usual, not a mug in the cupboard, just one tea bag left in the hastily opened box of PG Tips and – yes, as she thought, no milk in the fridge. Botheration, thought Millicent; she was really looking forward to that cup of tea. (She was tired this morning, Della and her so-called boyfriend had kept her awake most of the night, doing their thing in the bedroom, thinking she didn't know he was there, as usual.)

I'll go and get some bits and bobs for her, that would be a nice thing to do. And if she doesn't give me the money, I'll take it all back home with me. I need some Mr Sheen anyway, I'm certain she won't have got it for me yet. She bent down to pick up her handbag which was slightly stuck to the kitchen floor, the result of what looked like some spilt orange juice which hadn't been mopped up. Ugh, thought Millicent with the smugness of those who always cleaned up after themselves, and she left the flat not quite as concerned about slamming the door as she could have been.

A dull thud registered itself in Jessica's brain. She stirred. Pretended she hadn't heard it, tried to go back to sleep; but there was an unidentified horrible smell creeping up her nose, so she decided to turn over to face the other way. Without success, she didn't seem able to move. Still paralysed, not enough sleep yet, go away.

But a nagging internal voice told her she wasn't supposed to be asleep any more, there was a feeling of anticipation in her stomach, but she couldn't remember what it was about. She managed a half turn onto her back and lay still with her eyes shut and waited for it to hit her. Was she supposed to get up for work? Unlikely. Man trouble of some sort? No, men were always trouble but she couldn't think of anything specific to be concerned about today. What was it, what's happening?

Wham! Party! Of course, it was on Saturday and today was Wednesday or Thursday or something and there was still loads to do. Shit! What's the time?

Opening one eye with difficulty (due to last night's mascara clumping her eyelashes together) she managed a peep at the Fifties retro alarm clock on the bedside table. Its minty green face said ten past ten – no it didn't, it said ten to two. What?! How come? And how come she could see it so clearly? Oh no, that meant she'd gone to sleep still wearing her contact lenses, which meant only one thing . . .

She tried to swivel her head to have a look at the other side of the bed but it was too heavy and too far. So she slowly eased her reluctant body to turn back to where she'd started. That revolting smell hit again. She opened her eyes.

Facing her on the other pillow was somebody's head, or rather an open mouth framed by lots of dark greasy curly hair. Who the fuck was this? Jessica uncomfortably swivelled over to face the window, to try and remember what happened last night.

But before she could get the heavy machinery that was her brain to heave into action and work it out, a hand had landed on her shoulder. 'Mornin',' it said.

'Yes, hello,' said Jessica, a bit too quickly. Now what? I can't say 'Who are you?' or it'll think I don't remember. Which I don't. Oh god, where are my faculties?

'Got a fag?'

How disgusting. At this time of the morn–afternoon? 'No, sorry.' This is ridiculous, she thought, and cupping her hand over her nose she turned over to get a proper look.

Aagh! It was that twat from the video shop, grinning like the simpleton he was.

'Good night, huh?' He adopted a lascivious look which rang a few bells from last night. 'I always wanted to shag you, even when I was a kid. You were my favourite on *Krazy Kids*, you know. I've always gone for the more weird-looking birds, don't know why. Have you had a nose job since then?'

Right. 'Well I'm so glad to have been able to help you fulfil your ambition, but if you don't mind I've got to get up, I've got a lot to do today.' Hangover aside, she somehow managed to leap right out of the bed.

He lay back on her previously white, crisp Conran pillow which was now probably covered in some ghastly chainstore hair oil, and spread his arms behind his head. 'You carry on, darlin', I'll just watch if that's OK.' The grin was back. He was so – well, common-looking – she could see why she'd done it.

'No, it's not OK. You're going to have to go. I've got to organize' – don't tell him about the party, he'll only want to come – 'something very big and I have to do it on my own, d'you see?' Jessica grabbed the nearest item of something-or-other to protect her modesty.

'All right, all right, I'm going.' He eased his young and frankly fit body over the side of the bed, and as he was pulling on some surprisingly Paul Smith boxer shorts said, 'What about my money?'

Oh god, she hadn't paid him, had she? Had she really stooped that low? 'What money?'

'For the coke – you said you'd go halves.' Ah, all was explained.

'Well I haven't got it here, have I? I'll drop it in at the shop later.' Phew.

'What shop?'

'What?'

'You don't remember, do you? I don't believe this –' He clambered into his trousers at great speed and began buttoning up a blue shirt. 'You haven't got a clue, have you? What's my name, then?'

Blimey, she thought, he's really insulted. 'Look,' Jessica was thrashing about here, willing her normally sharp tongue to get off the roof of her mouth and do something more useful, 'there's no need to be like this, I –'

'There's every fucking need – you bitch.' She was alarmed to see him sling a tie round his neck. 'I don't believe you, all that bunny you gave me last night, I thought we were onto something good.' He rubbed his face in both hands. 'So let me get this straight – you're not interested in me at all, you just wanted what I had in my pocket – and my trousers, come to that. Well you're no great shakes yourself, darlin', you're a lousy shag if you want to know. I've had more fun on my own.' He looked quite angry now. 'Well you just made a mistake, Jessica Rose, a big mistake. You're going to really regret this, you stupid COW.' And grabbing his suit jacket from the top of the pile on the chair, he stormed out of the room.

Quite a long speech really, Jessica thought – you had to admire him, little sensitive soul. She heard him try to make an exit through the broom cupboard – 'Fuck!' – and shut it again. 'It's the next door along,' she called out, 'the one with the locks on it!' He may not be the twat from the video shop but he was still a twat.

She came out of the bedroom and watched him from behind as he fumbled with the latch, eventually flinging it open to reveal a startled Millicent standing on the doormat with a key poised in her hand. 'Good afternoon,' she said, the whites of her eyes whiter than ever. 'Oh fuck off!' he spat and flew past her down the stairwell.

'Everything all right, Jessica?' Millicent asked as she closed the door behind her. 'Can you remember where you put your dressing gown?'

'Oh god, sorry, Millicent.' Quickly identifying the item as a tiny singlet that was hiding nothing, she pulled it on over her head while dashing back into the bedroom for the favourite Gap trackie bottoms. 'Listen, I'm sorry about the mess,' she shouted out, 'don't worry if you can't do it all today!'

Millicent was rolling up her sleeves, preparing herself for the kitchen sink. 'I can always do more hours if you like . . .' she volunteered.

Jessica made a beeline for the kettle. 'Er no, that's OK, just do what you can. Tell you what Millicent, you couldn't make me a cup of tea could you? Only I seem to have overslept and I've just got to get on.'

'I'll bring it in to you.'

Jessica winced at the state of the sitting room. Minimal décor, maximum mess. The polished wooden floor was covered in everything she must have been wearing last night; the glass coffee table was sporting wine bottles and the emergency bottle of Stolichnaya from the freezer, all empty of course; there were some half-full glasses there with the sticky rings to match and it looked like someone had mistaken her big crackle-glazed ceramic bowl full of curved rainforest shavings from Peru for an ashtray. The candles had melted all over the fireplace making it look like a sorry attempt at set-dressing for a Gothic horror movie, and the entire room had been liberally sprinkled with sparkling cds. Every available surface was covered in over-flowing ashtrays and there was a smell to match. Both lamps were still burning a faded yellow, the LEDs on the stereo system were still twinkling away and the answer machine was flashing and nagging. Evidently this *Marie Celeste* had had a bit of a party.

Jessica slumped onto the sofa, noticing as she did that there was still a Simply Red cd cover on the coffee table with a give-away rolled-up twenty-pound note and a credit card. She automatically licked her finger and rubbed it over the tiny granules of white powder still there and put it to her gums. Bitter sweet but good. She flattened out the note, left it on the table until she'd tracked down her purse and looked at the card more closely.

It wasn't a credit card, and it wasn't hers. It was a Selfridges store card, and the name on it was P Hartley. That's quite a funny name actually, put it together and you get phartley. He must have got the piss taken out of him relentlessly at school. Expires end 06/04. Signature on the back, quite easy to forge. No, thought Jessica, I mustn't. Or must I? The phone rang. From somewhere.

'Jess? It's Simon. Listen, I've got to see you today.'

'Do I have a choice?'

'Well no, sorry, I've got a very important favour to ask you.'

'What sort of favour?'

'I'll tell you when I see you. Where and when?'

Irritated but intrigued, Jessica tried to think of somewhere expensive. 'Well I'm very busy today trying to get the party together . . . by the way, how're you doing with the cast of *EastEnders*?'

'Look, I'm doing my best – my director friend says he's told them all about it, but he can't promise any of them will turn up. I've managed to get Steve Venables to say he'll come, though.'

'What, that old has-been? You're going to have to do a bit better than that – *Hello!* say I have to guarantee current household names if they're going to cover it. They're not going to take very kindly to some crappy actor from an old BBC series from the Eighties based in a bloody post office, are they?'

'Shall I not bother to turn up in that case?'

'Oh for god's sake, Simon, I didn't mean you – don't be so over-sensitive. Thanks, you're a darling.' Millicent placed the mug of tea on the coffee table, but not before wiping the bottom of it with a cloth first.

'What?'

'I wasn't talking to you. OK, look, let's meet at The Pharmacy at about three thirty – they're open all day, I think. In the meantime you can compile a list of everybody you know who's at least from the Nineties – the Naughties would be even better – and we'll go through it then. OK?'

'Well all right, then. I knew I wouldn't get away with just asking for a straightforward favour, I'd have to do something in return. You are awful, Jess.'

'Yeah, but you like me. And you're not exactly up for a sainthood yourself. I'll see you later.' Now click off.

Jessica launched into her routine for mornings like these. She got up, opened the curtains and pushed up the sash windows behind the muslin drapes. A cold rush of air greeted her nipples, which stood out like stalks under the little vest already straining over the perfectly rounded orbs placed there by Dr Koi a few years ago. He was a genius, that man. And hopefully *Hello!* were going to be funding the next stage of keep young and beautiful – a facelift with a spot of liposuction for good measure. And fat lips please.

She turned off the lamps and turned to the answer machine next. Only eight calls? She was losing her touch. Not a pen or paper in sight, as usual, just a stub of eye pencil sitting on the mantelpiece under the mirror, covered in wax. She picked it out with a fibreglass fingernail and spotted an empty fag packet – Embassy, yuk. Pressing the play button, she settled down in the armchair and ripped open the cardboard carton to write on.

'Jessica? Are you there?' boomed out her agent's voice. 'It's me, Sandy, pick up the phone, darling. Hello? Counting down – five, four, three, two, one – no, not there? Well, OK, I'll try your mobile but if that's off can you call me as soon as you get this message? I've had a request come in for you which you might be interested in. Speak to you later then. Bye.' Beep. Good, get on to that in a minute.

'Hi, Auntie Jess, it's me, Scarlett. I'm just ringing to tell you the good news. Mummy says I can come to your party after all! Isn't that great! She says I can come for the first couple of hours and then she'll take me home because she doesn't really want a late night because she's a bit tired at the moment, so isn't that good! I don't know what I'm going to wear, you'll have to come round and help me decide, and please will you do my hair for me? Anyway, I'm really excited! So – bye, then!' Good, that means soppy Sophie won't be hanging around all night being shocked at everything as usual. Beep.

'Hi, darling, it's me.' Kerry, new best friend. They'd known each other for years, but had recently become better friends, in a who's-still-left kind of way. They were still dancing the dance of impress-me which was a bit tedious, but she seemed to know a lot of the filthy rich; could be useful. 'Listen, last night's blind date turned out to be the most fabulous man ever – and what's more he knows lots more fabulous men. So I thought I'd ask him to bring a couple of them along on Saturday, if that's all right.' No, it bloody well isn't, this is going to cost me a fortune. 'In the meantime, can you look up Scorpio man Pisces woman in Linda Goodman for me? I don't think I've done this combination before – well if I have, I can't remember it!

Call me as soon as you can for the full low-down – wow, what a night! Byeeee!' Later, later. Beep.

'Oh hello, this is the Cobden Club. Just calling to say we still haven't received your deposit for Saturday night, it didn't arrive this morning as promised. Perhaps you could call in today with a cheque, or we could always take a credit card number over the phone? Could you please get back to me as soon as possible? Thank you.' Beep. Arsey cow.

'Hi, Jessica, it's Mark McAndrew here. Thank you so much for the invitation to your birthday party, it was a bit of a blast from the past but I'd love to come. Is it OK if I bring my girlfriend? You might know her, actually, she's in the same business as us – Suki Samprah? Presents *Hip 'n' Happnin?* You might have seen us in the papers a bit recently, really boring, they seem to follow us everywhere – but I'm sure a woman of your class and distinction doesn't bother with rags like that. Anyway, looking forward to it, see you Saturday – it'll be good to see you after all these years. Bye.' Silly fucker, did he think she'd invited him because she wanted to be friends again? After she'd dumped him when *Krazy Kids* was cancelled, and then, contrary to all expectations, he'd gone on to have a fulfilling career? Arrogant shit. No, it was his Plus One she needed, jumped-up little tart, but only to keep *Hello!* happy. Beep.

'This is Dr Longworth's surgery, just calling to say that we do have your repeat prescriptions here still waiting to be picked up. Thank you.' Beep. Prozac and Mogadon, a match made in heaven.

'Hi darling, just calling in to say hi.' Nigel! 'Listen, about

Sat – ni – it OK – bring – kkkssshhh – ssscccooossshhhzzz
– sk – bg – tttx – mind, do you? Bye now.' Fucking mobiles.

'Jessica, where the hell are you? Call me.' Sandy again,
sounding quite peeved. Maybe it was a big job after all,
better call him back. After a bath.

But Millicent was faffing about in there. 'I'm not sure
what to do about this . . .' she was saying, pointing to the
loo. 'There's something in there.'

'Oh just flush it again,' said an unashamed Jessica. 'That's
the trouble with being a vegetarian, your poos float.'

'Well, you might want to take this out.'

What? For god's sake, she'd tried every cleaning lady
from every different ethnic minority there was, and each
one seemed to have a fixation about something. The
last one, an illegal immigrant from Croatia, used to unplug
everything from the sockets and not put them back in
again. Now it turns out that this big black woman from
Africa or wherever wanted Jessica to pick up her own turds.

'Millicent, I really don't think –' Jessica peered into the
loo. Lurking at the bottom of the bowl was a mobile phone.
'Oh. Well I don't know how that got there – it certainly
wasn't via the usual route. If it was I'd be in the circus!' She
laughed at Millicent, who wasn't amused. 'I'll fish it out,
shall I?'

The berubbergloved Millicent did the deed, and handed
it to Jessica, rather defeating the hygiene objective. As she
turned it over she was relieved to see it wasn't hers, even
though it was the same Nokia model – but hers had a shiny
silver cover, not a rubberized black one. Must belong to
the boy Phartley. She had a vague memory of snatching it

out of his hand last night because it kept ringing and he was rude enough to keep answering.

'Right then, is there anything else in the bath – a map of Australia, a pair of roller skates perhaps?'

She couldn't believe that Millicent actually bothered to look.

'I can't believe you've been hounding me all day for something as crap as this.' Jessica was pacing round the flat as she always did when she was on the phone, treading a well-worn path from one room to the other, gesticulating wildly with her free hand. 'Let me repeat this back to you, Sandy, and then maybe you'll see how stupid it sounds – a cable tv company has come up with the remarkably original idea of sending round a chef to knock on celebrities' doors and cook them a meal from whatever they've got in their fridge. And because they want so-called real tv, you're not allowed to know when they're coming? Well that's ridiculous – as you should be aware, I've worked very hard on my girl-next-door image and quite frankly I don't fancy some grinning asshole in a whacky hat wielding a wooden spoon on my doorstep first thing in the morning with a film crew, expecting to make a meal out of some nasturtium jelly my stupid sister made for me, and a novelty hangover kit. Oh, and I've got an old plum pudding from Fortnums in the cupboard, would that be helpful? I mean honestly, be serious, Sandy – do the public need to know that I'm not really living on a healthy diet of pasta, vegetables and pulses? That the only protein I get is carried in men's sperm?' She turned into the sitting room to see if there were any long enough dog-ends left in the ashtrays, but they'd all been cleared away. Straight into the kitchen then, have a quick rummage through the bin while Millicent was wrestling with the bedroom.

'Yes yes I know we need the exposure Sandy, you don't have to remind me. But for god's sake, do we have to do shit like this?' Aha, there's one on top which looks quite long. Light it off the gas – damn, she just caught the edge of her nail, which melted in one corner. Fucking hell.

'Well how much? Two hundred and fifty quid? I suppose that's better than usual, normally these things are about seventy-five . . . look, tell you what, I'll think about it, OK? But it might be worth getting back to them and asking if a researcher could just come and stock up the fridge in advance or something; yes I know what the whole point is, Sandy, but nobody really believes these things aren't set up in advance, do they? Well if that's the way tv's going nowadays, then I want out.' She had her second drag and stubbed it out in what turned out to be the sugar bowl. Bollocks. 'Look, just tell them I'll act shocked and delighted – well remind them I've been in a couple of pantomimes then, I don't know . . . yeah, OK, bye.' Fuckwit.

As usual, there was nowhere to park. As usual, Jessica was late. And as usual, she decided this was an emergency and parked in a residents' bay, slapping her fake permit (£100 from a guy at the Town Hall, worth every penny) onto the windscreen. Quick check in the rear-view mirror – why did BMW not acknowledge that women drove cars too and only kit out the passenger side with its own visor mirror?

– and yes, everything looked in place despite her head banging to a very loud beat. Quick application of lipstick just before making the entrance, otherwise it bleeds before you've even got there, a ruffle of the hair for that just-got-out-of-bed look (if only they knew) and unplug the mobile phone car charger, hoping it's done something to revive the dead battery during the ten-minute drive.

'Yes?' said an immaculately groomed young woman with a certain air of I'm-only-doing-this-until-I-start-at-Cambridge-to-study-law. 'Can I help you?'

'I'm meeting somebody here,' said Jessica, looking over Little Miss Tasteful's shoulder.

'Name?'

Pause. Blink. 'Jessica Rose.'

'Have you booked?'

'What, for a drink in the middle of the afternoon? Hardly, I – Ah, there he is.' Simon was waving, but seemed to be sitting at a table with another man. Jessica sashayed on through, hoping the other diners were noticing her.

'Jess, hi, nice to see you.' Simon stood up and gave her a bear-hug, as this is what actors did when somebody made an entrance. Jessica disentangled herself immediately. 'D'you know –'

His companion had stood up and turned round, proffering a hand to shake. His smile went from genuine to fake in a split second. 'Er, hi, Jessica, how are you?'

'Fine thank you, Ivan – and you?'

'Great, yeah, great, you know, fine, really good.' He's going to say 'mustn't grumble' in a minute, thought Jessica.

'And how's your wife?' He paled. 'Still married?' She

smiled at him full frontal, brazenly, in a really, really scary way. 'How's your daughter? Rebecca, wasn't it?'

'Er Becca, yes. She's fine, bit of a tearaway teen now, but –' He smiled back. 'We've had another one since then, a little boy, Anton –'

'How lovely look Simon, I don't want to be rude but can we get on with it? Only I've got lots to do, and can't really waste too much time on idle chit-chat.'

'Yes, sure – look, Ivan, let's catch up soon, OK? You and er, well you, must come over to dinner one night, I'll get Soph onto it.' Jessica took him by the arm and manhandled him to an empty table just far enough away for Ivan not to hear their conversation, but just near enough for her to be able to see who he was waiting for. 'Bye then,' Simon called, but Ivan was busy fiddling with his mobile phone. Probably sending a text message to his latest mistress, Jessica thought with a flash of envy. Happy days. Bastard.

'So – you're a dark horse, Jess, how do you know Ivan? He directed those furniture-warehouse commercials I did, but I don't remember you being in any ads.'

'Let's just say we're old friends.' Simon raised his eyebrows and smiled at her. 'Yes yes, all right, if you must know he was the love of my life during my most attractive years. He kept making promises to me, but in the end he didn't have the nerve – or the cash as it turned out – to leave his wife and so I had to break it off. Oh don't look so shocked, Simon, there's no such thing as a family man any more. All men fuck around on their wives as you well know . . .' Jessica always knew exactly when to play the don't-go-there card on him, and this was a perfect time.

'Well he's not married now,' said Simon. 'Lucky sod.'

What? 'What?! How d'you know?' She glanced over, couldn't see his wedding-ring finger from here.

'He just told me, we were doing a bit of male bonding.'

'Oh.' Well why hadn't he called? 'What happened?'

'Well he just sort of opened up to me, people do that all the –'

'No, who left whom?' As Shakespeare probably really meant to say, all the world's a twat.

'Oh, I don't know. We didn't really discuss it.'

'I thought you said you were doing some male bonding?'

'Well yes, but we didn't talk about the finer details. Men don't talk about that sort of thing you know.' No, most of them can't really talk about any sort of thing. They can only do Top Five lists if Nick Hornby is to be believed. 'I could put in a word for you if you like . . .' Simon grinned.

'Look,' he was irritating her now, 'why don't you just shut up and cut to the chase – what d'you want?'

'A bottle of Becks, please,' said Simon to the waiter who'd magically appeared at their table.

Jessica sighed and ordered a Bloody Mary, the bigger and bloodier the better. 'So why are we here?'

He sighed. 'Well, you know I found out when my mother died that I was adopted?'

'No, I didn't actually, but carry on.' She hooked a long tress of dark hair behind her ear. She did know actually, Sophie had told Mother who'd told Jess – but this way was more fun.

'What – nobody told you?' He was genuinely surprised.

'No, why should they? I haven't spoken to Sophie at any length for ages and I've been extremely busy organizing my party – funnily enough your personal life hasn't really been uppermost in my mind lately.'

'Oh. Well anyway, you know now.' He eased back in his chair, sweeping the hair off his forehead in the self-conscious manner of a man who knew perfectly well it would flop back down again straightaway. 'It came as a bit of a shock, as you can imagine. I mean I had no idea, not even an inkling. I never questioned the fact that they were my real parents, I loved my mother. And my father too, of course, but – well, you know what they say about boys and their mums.'

'No, what?' said Jessica as she scrabbled about in her bag, not quite interested enough because she was experiencing a delayed discombobulation from seeing Ivan.

'Oh you know, stuff about Oedipus and things. I mean, not that I didn't love my father, you see, I did, of course I did, only he was a little distant. But my mother worshipped him; as a child I used to be quite jealous of their relationship. Is that a bad thing to say?'

'No, not at all – it's certainly something to say,' replied Jessica, knowing that he didn't really need an answer and sure enough, he carried on. She looked at him as he spoke, watching his mouth move but not bothering to take any of it in. He really was one of the most feeble, weedy, self-obsessed men she'd ever met, and that was saying something. What on earth did Sophie see in him? Seldom had a man been adored so much for so little. It was quite extraordinary, he was completely unremarkable.

'. . . you see, I think he was always emotionally unavailable to me, it was quite sad really.' Simon gazed out into space, wrapped up in his boyhood memories. Jessica took this opportunity to check out Ivan – nobody there yet. 'Though he did make a supreme effort when we went to Largs every year for our holiday – he used to bury me in the freezing cold sand, laughing his head off while my mother looked on from her deckchair and smiled, and I used to think, can't she see that I don't like this? But I somehow knew not to make a fuss, I was always very perceptive, even as a child . . . Jess? You OK?'

'D'you think they bring you fags here, or have they got a machine?'

'No idea. Anyway. I'm sorry, I don't want to keep banging on about this' – he continued – 'but I think I'm still in shock about it all, even though I've known for a couple of months now. It's funny, when Dad died I wasn't really that upset – sad, obviously, but not, you know, devastated. I was more concerned for Mum, she took it really badly at first – once I'd moved to London she'd made him the centre of her world and suddenly she had no one to look after any more.' Ivan's phone rang. 'But she coped, of course, she was a very strong woman – always out on her little magical mystery tours with the other widows on the coach, knitting for other people's grandchildren, happy to come and stay with us every Christmas.' He let it ring one more time and then he answered it. 'Though she'd never fly, said she wouldn't until someone could explain to her how they managed to keep the plane up in the air. Sweet, really.' Ivan was clearly very fond of whoever was on the other end. 'She was a good woman, Jess, never complained, took everything in her stride – not like the have-it-all lot of today, never happy, want everything yesterday. Look, just get up and ask the waiter!'

'Sorry, Simon, I am listening, really I am – I just can't quite see where I fit into all this.' She waved at the waiter. Ivan waved back. They both smoothed their hair.

'Well since I found out that the woman I have loved as a mother all my life wasn't really my mother at all, I've been through every emotion in the book. At first I was shocked, of course, but then I experienced a great deal of anger about this – I mean Mum and Dad had been living a lie for thirty-seven years, how could they not tell me? And then I felt foolish, for not having suspected a thing – you hear about people in this kind of situation always having a feeling that they never really fitted in but I didn't think anything of the sort; and of course I kept wondering who else knew.' You should have been wondering who else cared, thought Jessica. 'The shame attached to this kind of thing is immense, you see, suddenly you just don't know who you are any more, it's a terrible thing to have to live with. And then I was totally overwhelmed with an enormous feeling of –'

But Jessica had left the table in search of twenty Marlboro Lights, just happening to pick the waiter nearest Ivan's table, leaving Simon to wallow in his own self-indulgence for a while. She came back a little flushed.

'So, Simon, what d'you want me to do about all this?' She knew she sounded impatient, but couldn't face another speech on Simon's favourite subject. Me.

'Well the fact is that I've decided to try and trace my real mother – birth mother, I think they call it.'

'Why? I'd leave it alone if I were you – she might be dead, or not want to know you. After all, she gave you away. She clearly doesn't care about you or she'd have tried to find you herself.'

Stinging words. 'Look, Jessica, I don't want your opinion on what I should or shouldn't do –'

'And anyway, what if you were the result of a brutal rape? Or your mother is some scuzzy alcoholic living in a council flat with damp running down the walls? Ooh no, I'd rather not know if it was me.'

Simon was losing his patience. 'Well it's not you, it's me, and I do want to know and that's all there is to it! Have you any idea what it's like? Walking around, looking at every old woman thinking is that her? Wondering what made her give me away? Maybe, just maybe, she thinks about me every day and has been in mourning for her baby boy ever since she let me go. Who knows? And apart from anything else,' he knew this would grab Jessica's attention, 'I might even be the love child of somebody famous.'

The waiter arrived with Jessica's cigarettes. 'Doubt it, they'd have used it to promote their flagging career by now. "My Shameful Secret" by – actually, that's quite exciting, who would it be? Um . . .' She pounced on the packet like the true addict she was and, as she was scrabbling about with the cellophane and silvery paper, tried to come up with a few suggestions. 'Joan Collins? Nah.' She fiddled with the bookmatches. 'Sophia Loren? No, you'd be much more handsome if that was the case. Too glamorous. Oh no,' she drew deeply as she lit the cigarette, 'what if your real mother is Edwina Currie?'

'Jessica!' Simon slammed his hand down on the table, causing Ivan to look over. 'This is no laughing matter. This is my life we're talking about, not some stupid parlour game! For god's sake, show some respect and compassion, will you?' Good heavens, he was really angry. He should do that more often, it was quite exciting.

'OK, OK. So, Simon, I ask you yet again, exactly what part do you want me to play in this?'

'Well didn't you work on that tv programme that helps people trace their lost relations?'

'What, *Family Matters*? Yes, but I was only the roving reporter; they gave the main presenter's job to a vet, if you remember.' She blew the smoke out in disdain.

'But you must have some contacts in that world.'

'Hardly. I was driven to the location, handed some questions to ask, made the right upset noises for the tragedy and joyful ones for the reunion and then fucked off home again. It's not as if I was slaving over a hot phone line to the Salvation Army all day long.'

'Yes, but you must have some idea of how I start trying to trace her.' Simon used his best little boy face and meant it this time. 'Please?' It was obviously important to him, too important maybe.

'Well – I suppose I could make a few calls. Try to track down one of the researchers or something.' She resisted the temptation to make a joke here about tracing people to trace people. 'That's really the best I can do though.'

'Thanks, Jess, I'd really appreciate it.' Simon reached into the back pocket of his jeans. 'And before you ask, here's the list I made for you of my showbiz pals. I've put their phone numbers on there too – you can use my name if you want.'

Jessica's handbag started to ring to the tune of 'Super Trooperper'. She didn't recognize the caller ID and so gathered up all her belongings and quickly walked to the door, safe in the knowledge that Simon would be left with the bill.

Bloody hell, it was the bank, better take this outside. Was she aware that she had exceeded her overdraft limit of £5,000? From now on, they would be grateful if she didn't issue any more cheques until she had rectified the situation. Only this morning they had been forced to return two items, marked them 'refer to drawer'. And they didn't buy her best I'm-so-shocked reaction at all; had she not received any of their correspondence?

'Well yes, but I send all that sort of thing on to my accountant – I never open your letters. It's not what I'm for.'

Not falling for the ditsy thing either, the woman with a voice from Surbiton said that perhaps she would like to meet with the manager who could explain everything more clearly to her, if she was having trouble working it all out for herself.

'Is the manager male or female?' She scrummaged in her bag for the car keys. 'Well then it would be a complete waste of time. Look, I'll pay some money in later on today, I've got loads of cheques in a pile on my desk at home, I just haven't got round to them yet. Goodbye.'

Simon came out of the restaurant, tucking his wallet into

the breast pocket of his denim jacket as he did so. 'Right then, I'm off. Let me know if you get any joy.' He gave her a huge bear-hug, as this is what actors did when somebody made an exit. Walking backwards into a bus queue, he said, 'I've paid for the drinks, but not your cancer sticks – since I gave up I can't be associated with them, bad karma. Cheers!' He straightened the little pensioner up again and put her back in pole position at the front of the line.

Jessica left anyway – what was a packet of fags to a big restaurant like that? As she squeezed her car out of its space, she saw new-best-friend Kerry in her rear-view mirror. Rushing into The Pharmacy. Looks as if she's late to meet someone there. Oh no.

Later that afternoon, Sandy on the mobile: 'Where are you?'

'Why do you always ask that?'

'Because I'm fascinated by your lifestyle, Jessica, you never seem to be anywhere for very long.'

'Well if you must know, I'm in a shop buying something to wear on Saturday night.'

'Designer?'

'Of course.' Aware that the middle-aged assistant was getting a bit peeved at having to wait for her to get off the phone, Jess performed a big look skywards for her benefit and said, 'What d'you want, anyway?'

'I've had a catalogue company on the phone.'

'I beg your pardon?'

'You know, one of those ones that has lots of new inventions in it.'

'What?'

'They've decided to go upmarket, get a bit of celebrity endorsement going, and so they're asking for people to lend their names to a product.'

'I can hardly contain my excitement. This is hilarious! And which piece of fabulous moulded plastic did they have in mind for me to do?'

'Well there's a few you can choose from, I've got a list here.'

'Hit me with it.'

'An automatic loo-paper dispenser? At the press of a button, it gives you three sheets at a time.'

'No, you're not serious!'

'Or, still on a bathroom theme, there's a musical towel rail up for grabs.'

'Does it play "I'm Forever Blowing Bubbles"?'

'How did you know?'

'What else?'

'A cat car seat.'

'What?!'

'"Give your pet a better view during those boring journeys to the vet, or maybe you'd like to take your feline friend for a relaxing drive in the country on Sunday afternoons."'

'I have never heard anything so absurd in my life, though it does present a very amusing picture, a cat sitting up strapped into a car seat like a baby, smiling at other drivers at the traffic lights. But no, Sandy – are you ready for this – I'm afraid I'm going to have to send you off with a flea in your ear on this one!'

'Oh ha ha, very funny. Big money, though.'

'How much?'

'Ten grand.'

'Fuck.' The shop woman winced. 'Really? Oh god, it's so unfair – why do crappy jobs like this pay so much and yet you're expected to work for the BBC for next to nothing?'

'Because, as I keep telling you, shit is popular and prestige isn't. You're going to have to start lowering your standards, my darling. The more work I turn down for you, the less you get offered. That's how it works, you see –'

'Yeah yeah OK Sandy, spare me the speech. Look, my battery's about to go – I'll think about it, OK? Bye.' As Jessica replaced the phone in her handbag, she smiled at the disapproving saleswoman. 'Sorry about that, *Tatler* pestering me yet again. I mean really, like I want to be paid a lot of money to model Versace's latest collection alongside a gaggle of giggling It Girls. Frankly, I've got better things to do with my time.' The woman looked unconvinced. Well too bad. 'Now then, why don't you have a look through this bag and see what you like, while I rifle through your rails and we'll see what kind of deal we can come up with. OK?'

'Can I have a receipt?' Jessica asked the minicab driver as they stopped abruptly outside the house.

'What d'you mean?' He sounded confused.

'I mean, can I have a receipt?'

'What for?'

'For the money I have just given you to perform an

emergency stop at every available opportunity, thus making me feel utterly sick.'

'Oh, right.' He looked a bit blank.

'It's customary to write it down on a business card – you know, those things you shove through our letter boxes? The ones that say you offer a twenty-four-hour service, meaning that's how long it takes you to come and pick us up?'

'OK, OK.' He found one in the hollow under the radio. 'Have you got a pen?'

'What?!'

'A pen – you know, those things you use to write with?'

'No, I haven't.' Cheeky fucker. 'Just give me the card, I'll fill it in myself later.' Making it more expensive for the benefit of the Inland Revenue.

He handed it to her over his shoulder. 'Don't forget to add on the tip you didn't give me.'

'Yeah, well,' said Jessica as she tried to work out how to open the door, 'don't forget to get a life.'

As she tried to slam the minicab door shut, but couldn't because it was too stiff, Jessica resolved to go back to taking proper taxis. This economy-drive thing really wasn't working, but her mother wouldn't let her drink if she'd brought the car and they were still working their way through Archie's considerable wine cellar.

Walking up the steps to Constance's Holland Park mansion, the usual irritation passed through her mind. Why on earth didn't Mother sell the old family home and get something smaller? It wasn't as if she had to keep all the bedrooms free for hordes of visiting grandchildren – there was only Scarlett and she always slept with her grandmother anyway. And there certainly weren't going to be any more grandchildren at this rate – Jessica couldn't think of anything she'd less like to have, and Sophie couldn't even hold on to a pregnancy for very long. But whenever she raised the subject with Constance her mother got very sniffy indeed, told her it was her house to do what she liked with. But wasn't there some tax thing about death duties being really hefty and so it was better to give your descendants the money when you were still alive? That would sort out all her problems, Jess thought as she lifted the huge brass door knocker and did her usual knock three times.

It took a while, but Jessica knew not to bother to knock again. As she waited on the doorstep, Jessica wondered what sort of mood her mother would be in tonight. She wouldn't be down, that was for sure – Constance was always up-tempo. But sometimes she was a little too bright, a little too energetic – to be honest, Jessica found her quite exhausting most of the time. She always had some project on the go – once she'd adopted a poor man serving behind the counter in the local deli and decided to take it upon herself to teach him how to speak English fluently in a month. Jessica felt sorry for him – if his English had been better he would have been able to tell her to bog off. If she had finished writing one of her plays (the main part was always a glamorous older woman who had experienced terrible adversity but somehow fought it and won), Jessica would have to read it right then and there in front of her and offer an opinion on it; finding the right words to say was becoming increasingly difficult, the wrong ones were usually more appropriate. Fortunately her dramatic efforts had yet to make it into the West End, despite the fact that all the impresarios and their accompanying anecdotes were frequently invited to dinner. But she didn't seem to mind, she just kept churning them out. The woman's energy was boundless – last week they'd been moving furniture around until one o'clock in the morning, the week before that she'd marched Jessica off to Madame JoJo's, a club in Soho that featured some admittedly talented drag acts, but they didn't get home till three. There had been talk of going on one of those Jack The Ripper guided walking tours of London one night – that would be too much, Jessica would have to put her foot down. She didn't have the shoes for that kind of walking.

At last the big wide front door opened slowly in front of her, but there was nobody there. Jess marched in and without bothering to look behind the door said, 'Evening, Mrs Mac, everything all right?' as she took off her leather Top-Shop-copy-of-Gucci jacket and slung it over the highly polished wooden stairpost. 'Mother in the drawing room?'

But the little old woman who resembled a beer barrel on spindly legs was still absorbed in the whole business of shutting the door and so Jessica tottered briskly across the tiled hallway, the clack-clacking of her heels echoing as she did so. She'd been having dinner with her mother every Thursday evening for years now, and knew the routine. Flinging the double doors open with all the drama of a 1930s starlet expecting to see another, she was taken aback not to see Constance assuming the usual position; normally she would be found standing with her back to the door at the fireplace, holding a glass of sherry in her hand and looking up at the oil painting of Dad that hung above the mantelpiece, only to be supposedly surprised by Jessica's entrance.

Instead, she could see an elegant pair of legs sticking out from the pale-blue wing-back armchair, stilettoed feet resting on an embroidered footstool. And she seemed to be watching tv, if you please. Jessica realized that she hadn't even known there was a television in this room, she'd always thought that piece of furniture was an eighteenth-century tallboy, but now its doors were opened to reveal a whole armoury of twenty-first-century gadgetry.

'Hello Mother,' she said, somewhat thrown by all this.

'Ssshh!' hissed Constance, and motioned for her to sit down. 'It's my new toy!'

As Jessica parked her semi-toned bottom in the chair that had always been her father's, she saw that her mother wasn't watching a tv programme after all, unless Mrs Mac had been given her own show. Which wouldn't quite frankly surprise Jessica, it seemed that anyone could be a television star these days – except her.

'Watch, watch this bit!' exclaimed Constance, clearly delighted and amused by what was to come.

The camera-work was slightly shaky, and the picture was very dark, but Jessica could ascertain from the soundtrack of heavy snoring that we were in Mrs Mac's cluttered bedroom downstairs. The camera showed us that she was lying on her back, face covered in cold cream (surely too late for all that, thought Jessica) with just the one roller perched in the front of her hair. A hand reached out from behind the camera and picked up the alarm clock beside the bed. The screen went fuzzy, and then back on to a new viewpoint from the bedroom doorway. Constance's voice, slightly distorted from being too close to the built-in microphone, said quietly, 'It's four thirty in the morning' and then the alarm shrilled out its piercing call. (Jessica wasn't surprised at this unkind practical joke as she'd grown up with her mother's predilection for laughing at other people's expense.)

Mrs Mac sat bolt upright in bed, rubbed her eyes like a cartoon character and switched off the alarm. She then turned on the bedside lamp, which lit up the fact that she wasn't wearing a nightie – yes, Mrs Mac slept in the nude.

'Yuk!' exclaimed Jessica, turning away. 'How revolting!' She'd never managed to see old people's nudity as a thing of wonder, no matter how many exhibitions there were on the subject in the smartest Mayfair art galleries. She shuddered.

Constance freeze-framed the video with the remote control. 'Silly girl, you didn't see it, did you?'

'I've seen enough, thank you very much,' said Jessica, feeling decidedly queasy.

'Look again,' commanded Constance, pressing rewind.

The video wound too far back and we saw Mrs Mac on wobbly tippy toes trying to hang out the washing (Constance had probably raised the height of the line) and then it cut to the bedroom scene again. Only this time Jessica forced herself to watch further.

Mrs Mac sat up again, rubbed her eyes again, switched

off the clock again and switched on the lamp. As Jessica was looking more closely now (feeling like a rubbernecker at a car crash) she could see that the old woman's barrel chest was flatter than she'd thought it would be; added to which there seemed to be a sort of shadow across it. Then, as Mrs Mac slowly pushed back the covers with her feet and swung her mini-stick legs over the side of the bed to stand up, Constance shrieked, 'There it is!' and freeze-framed the video again.

She'd obviously done this before as the tape had stopped at just the right moment. Mrs Mac was suspended in animation walking towards the bedroom door.

'Can you see it now?'

Oh yes. There, dangling between Mrs Mac's legs, was a willy.

'How long have you known?' They were in the dining room now, having just been served the soup by you-know-who. Jessica was floundering between disbelief and hysterics, somehow managing to avoid Constance's beady eye throughout the laborious shaky ladling. She'd kept her head down, holding her napkin over her lap – she didn't want anything to happen to her favourite black pants from Joseph.

'For as long as I've known her. She was my dresser when I was in *An Ideal Husband* at the King's Theatre in Glasgow ooh, nearly forty years ago now.' Constance grimaced as she tasted the soup. 'Oh dear, this really is disgusting, isn't it? Probably tinned. You don't have to eat it if you don't want to.'

'What and upset the chef? I'd probably get beaten up. Has she got any tattoos?'

'Oh don't be so narrow-minded, Jessica. You're really shocked, aren't you?' Constance was loving this.

'Well wouldn't you be? This is the woman – man – person who brought me up while you were away perfecting your craft in glamorous locations around the world. I used to see her as a second mother, and now you're telling me she was really Mrs Bloody Doubtfire! Did Dad know?'

'Of course not, he would have had a fit – or wasted money on a sex change for her. Nobody knows, except you now.'

'And why've you told me? There are some things I'd rather not know, and this has to be one of them.'

'Jessica, as you know, I'm sixty soon and I just thought that if by chance I die before her . . .' Constance looked from under her eyelashes for a reaction from her daughter but didn't get one '. . . then someone's got to deal with the undertaker, haven't they? She's got no family, poor love, well not to speak to – they disowned her, apparently. And don't tell Sophie, she'll probably go and jump off a cliff.' She got up and poured her soup into the elegant Chinese vase holding a huge dried-flower arrangement in the fireplace. 'How's the party coming along?'

'Don't change the subject, Mother, I'm still trying to take all this in. So why did you employ her – him – whatever to come and look after us? What was wrong with having a normal nanny? Honestly, this is so typical, you just have to be different, don't you – did it never occur to you that we could have been seriously psychologically damaged if we'd found out when we were little – god, no wonder she would never come swimming with me. Lying old bat always said she was afraid of water. I always thought that if that was the case, how come she managed to do the washing-up?' Jessica drained her wine glass and poured herself another one.

'Now Jessica, I won't have you being disrespectful about Mrs Mac. She's been part of this family for years and if I'd thought you were going to react in this negative fashion I would never have let you find out. And whatever you do, don't let her know that you know – it would break her heart. This subject is now closed.' And that was that. Not for the first time, Jessica marvelled at her mother's ability to control everything around her, including not only what came out of her mouth but yours as well. Constance slid her hand under the table and pressed the button to summon the next course. 'So how are your birthday arrangements coming along? Are you looking forward to it?' Her bright blue eyes flashed with excitement, Constance had always loved a party.

'Well to be honest, I've hit a bit of a major stumbling block. It's not anything I can't handle of course, but –'

'Money?' interjected Constance, frowning.

'Well, yes . . .' Jessica looked down, knowing what was coming next.

'I thought you had arranged for one of those dreadful magazines to pay for it.' Constance's painted left eyebrow arched above her powdered face.

'Yes, but they don't give you the fee until after the party just in case nobody of interest turns up and they can't print

it. And the club is really hounding me for the deposit.'
Jessica hated admitting that she was in trouble, especially
to Constance. But her mother had a way of looking right
through you, there was no hiding from her. She'd always
get it out of you in the end.

'And what about your father's money? Surely you've got
some of that left?' The painted right eyebrow joined its
partner.

Jessica shook her head.

'Well where on earth has it all gone? I just don't under-
stand it. It's not as if you've got anything to show for it,
Jessica; you live in that grubby little shoebox in Wormwood
Scrubs – and don't even try to tell me it's North Notting
Hill because that just doesn't wash with me, you drive a
BMW that is practically pre-war and you come round here
looking a complete tramp covered head-to-toe in dog hairs.
At least Sophie's used Daddy's money sensibly, giving
Scarlett a proper education. Though I dare say most of it's
gone on supporting that wastrel husband of hers –'

'I thought you liked Simon?' said Jessica, grateful for
the opportunity to interrupt Constance's flow.

'Oh he's all right, bit spineless though, not like the actors
of my day . . .' Oh god, we'll be here all night.

'But the thing is, Mum, I'm owed lots of money at the
moment and only today my agent called me with two very
lucrative offers. It's just a cash-flow crisis really.' Constance's
jaw was setting. Go for her weak spot. 'I just hope the club
doesn't tell the papers that Jessica Rose hasn't got any
money, that's all . . .'

Pause. The older woman sighed. 'I'm not stupid, Jessica.

I can see what you're up to. How much d'you need to keep them off your back?'

Yes! 'A thousand should do it. No, actually, maybe two – just to tide me over until I get the fee from that Belgian yoghurt commercial.' The two women eyeballed each other and there was a tense silence, apart from the sound of Mrs Mac fumbling with the door handle. Jessica held her breath until she saw Constance's face soften around the edges.

'Well, all right.' Phew. 'But this time you're going to have to pay me back. I'm getting a bit tired of this, Jessica. I can only bail you out so many times, you know. You're getting a bit old to be relying on your mummy to look after you now.' She glared at Jessica and shook her expensive coiffure from side to side. 'And it's not as if I'm a rich woman any more, I'm struggling to make ends meet myself. I don't know what I would do without the kindness of Luigi – at least I don't have to fork out for my own supper every night of the week. Why on earth can't you just find yourself a rich man?'

But Jessica didn't have to answer that one as Mrs Mac had managed to flip the soup plate and its contents onto her lap.

On Friday morning she began to panic. Less than forty-eight hours to go until the party and there was absolute chaos.

The phone hadn't stopped ringing, and while she was on that line the mobile kept going off with people trying to get through to her because her landline was engaged, and there was a constant procession of beauty professionals throughout the morning: the nail technician, the hairdresser, the masseuse who complained that Jessica was wasting her time by being on the phone throughout what was after all supposed to be a relaxing process.

Having fielded calls from everyone ranging from the unpaid printers of the invitations to soon-to-be-ex-best-friend Kerry wanting to wax lyrical about Ivan, who it turned out was indeed now officially separated and leading the life of bloody riley, she was just closing her front door on the way to a midday appointment at the salon for a sunbed and a St Tropez to cover up the redness, when a bland-looking middle-aged man popped out of a nearby bush and screamed, 'Hi!'

Alarmed, she peered over her sunglasses (vital when leaving the house with no make-up and loose clothing) and said, 'Do I know you?'

'It's all right, I'm not going to tell anyone.'

'Tell anyone what?'

'Where you live.' He grinned, reminding Jessica to book an appointment at the dental hygienist as soon as she had some money. 'It'll be our secret.'

'Are you stalking me?' She hoped so, it'd be a good diary piece for one of the nationals.

'No, Liz, no. Just come to say hello.' He winked.

'Liz?'

'Oh sorry, do you prefer Elizabeth? I do apologize. Is it lonely without Hugh for you now?' Why do these people never wash their hair?

'Look, why don't you just go away and spot some trains – share your bloater-paste sandwiches with your mates and leave me alone. Goodbye!' And she walked round him towards her car – or she would have done if she could remember where she'd left it.

'You're not going now, are you?' He also had bad breath.

'Looks like it to me.' Where the hell was the bloody car? She started to walk up the street.

'But you can't!' he shrieked, running after her now. 'I want your autograph!'

She grabbed his tatty book and scribbled in it. Ah, there was the car, at the other end of the street. Being given a parking ticket by that bloody Indian traffic warden who seemed to spend his life tracking her car around West London. She shoved the autograph book into the pestiferous little man's face, crying, 'No no no, I'm here, don't do that! Stop!' and ran past him.

Later that evening, the pestiferous little man and his elderly bedridden mother were trying to work out what she'd written. It looked like 'I am a lesbian. Now fuck off. Liz Hurley x' but they didn't think that could be right – could it?

'Have you put on weight recently, Jess?' Sophie asked through a mouthful of pins.

'No!' replied Jessica sharply, looking down at Sophie from her lofty position on the pine kitchen table. 'Why?'

'Well I'm sure I copied this dress exactly from the one you gave me, but it doesn't seem to fit. Have you still got the old one so's I can check?' Those baby-blue eyes peeped up at her sister in a puppy-dog way.

'No, I had to return it to the shop the next day. What d'you mean, it doesn't fit?'

'Well it's too small. Maybe you're a 10 after all, and not an 8.'

'Oh Sophieeeee,' wailed Jessica in time-honoured fashion, 'what have you done?'

'Nothing, honest Jess. I don't know what's happened.' She slumped into a chair.

Jessica got down from the table and looked at her reflection in the glass of the back door. There was no way the two sides were going to meet over her bottom, or round her waist for that matter, there simply wasn't enough material. Ohmigod. 'You bloody idiot, Soph, what am I supposed to do now? I haven't got time to go shopping for something else, I was relying on you. I don't believe this. Oh god!'

Sophie sat up in her chair. 'I know, I could always put a panel in the back!' she said brightly.

'Oh don't be so bloody silly, then everyone'll know it's not genuine Gucci. I take it you've still got the label?'

'Yes, somewhere.' And then Sophie burst into tears. Brilliant, thought Jessica. Typical. 'I'm so sorry, Jess, I really wanted to make you a dress you would treasure for your birthday present, and now I've messed everything up. I'm such a fool, I just can't seem to get anything right these days . . .' She boo-hooed like a baby.

Jessica knew it would be mean to get angry with Sophie; after all, her sister had done her best, it was a loving gesture, she hadn't meant to get it wrong. But for fuck's sake, there was a limit. 'You ARSE! What am I supposed to do now? You absolute fuckwit, you can't do anything right, everything you touch turns to SHIT! I don't fucking believe this, you've ruined EVERYTHING, as usual. The party is tomorrow night, I haven't got time to go shopping, I was relying on YOU. What the fuck is the matter with you? I keep giving you another chance and you keep blowing it – I'm beginning to think you do it on purpose. AND STOP – BLOODY – CRYING!' As she said this, Jessica walked over to where Sophie was sitting and slapped her in the face. Really hard.

Silence. Both girls a bit shocked. Very shocked. Sophie with her hand on her cheek, looking up at her elder sister towering over her. Jessica looking down at her pitiful younger sister, feeling nothing but a distant flash of the green-eyed monster child, too old to be sweet herself, sitting in the corner watching them fuss over the new baby. Packed off to boarding school so they could spend more time with the baby. Never loved properly after that. Still angry about it now blah blah blah – she'd had more therapy than Woody Allen, hadn't done any good of course, just made her feel worse.

'Sorry,' said Sophie, not Jessica.

'Yeah.' But she didn't mean it. In fact, she'd got a certain amount of satisfaction out of hitting that stupid fat face.

'I'm such a twit.'

'It's twat now.'

'Oh. Can't even get that right.'

Funny. They exchanged cautious smiles. 'Look, Soph, I know I shouldn't have done that, but –'

'I know, I know – it's fine. I know my always crying is

really annoying, but I'm even more emotional than usual at the moment – you know.'

Yes, she did. 'Got your period again?'

'Um, well no, not yet. But I'm trying to get it all out and then I can move on.'

'Right. Well speaking of moving on, I've got to go.' Jessica stepped out of Sophie's latest fuck-up and began to put her clothes back on.

'Oh dear, surely you've got time for a cup of tea?' Sophie got up and walked over to the kettle, dabbing her nose with her hankie as she went.

'Not really,' replied her sister, fumbling in her handbag and picking out her phone, which Sophie clearly hadn't even known was ringing because she didn't have mobile-friendly hearing. 'Hello? Yes, I did but it's not really a good time for me right now. I'm just about to leave a meeting – I'll call you back from the car. And for god's sake answer my call, Darren, I know what you're like. Bye.'

'Darren?' Sophie turned round. 'Not Della's Darren?'

'No no no, totally different Darren, work Darren. Trying to track down someone from *Family Matters*, see if they can help Simon trace his real mother. Which reminds me, Soph, why didn't you tell me about all that?'

'Oh didn't I say?' Jessica was never sure if it was genuine vagueness with her or actual stupidity. 'Sorry, I've had a lot on my mind recently. Yes, isn't it strange? Who'd have thought – he's terribly upset about it all, they were quite close. But give him his due, he's absolutely determined to find his real mother, it's all he ever talks about these days. He's like a man possessed.'

And obsessed, thought Jessica, who'd had a barrage of calls from him already to remind her of her promise to help. Very tiresome, but he had mentioned that he might know the second assistant on Madonna's new video, who was going to have a word with her about the party. 'How is Della, anyway? You still letting her loose on your hair? She's a crap hairdresser you know Soph, you should really go somewhere else. She was OK when she was working in that salon, but she got sloppy when she went freelance. But my old friend Kerry still swears by her – mind you, you should see her hair, that's enough to make anybody swear. There's quite a good place near me just opened up – It's A Snip, I think it's called; looks quite cheap, you should try it, let me know if it's any good.'

'Oh I don't know, it doesn't really matter what my hair's like, nobody ever really sees it except Simon and the school mothers. And anyway, I like Della – she's um, very entertaining. Ooh – speaking of entertainers, have you seen Mother lately?'

'Yes, I saw her the other day, why?' Jessica and Constance kept their Thursday night rendezvous a secret from Sophie, for fear of her wanting to join in.

'Well has she said any more about her sixtieth birthday?'

'No, not a word, she's probably forgotten all about it. I think she only ever used to say it to wind Dad up, and don't let on that you remember or she'll do the same thing to you. And we've always known that she'd never have the nerve to actually go through with it. And anyway, look on the bright side – you could end up with the painting of Dad sooner than you think! You haven't been wasting time worrying about it, have you?' Was there anything Sophie didn't worry about?

'Well no, not really,' said Sophie, a patent lie. 'But it is only a few months away. She hasn't mentioned it at all, then?'

'Nope. Nothing. Probably too busy shagging Luigi to remember. Now –'

'Oh Jess, I do wish you wouldn't say things like that, it's horrible,' said a visibly shocked Sophie.

'For god's sake lighten up Sophie, you're going to have to accept it sooner or later. Now listen, I've got to fly – I'll see you tomorrow night with your newly illegitimate husband and Scarlett then, yes? And make sure she gets that bag of old make-up I've given you for her. It's her first grown-up party and she'll want to look cool. No ringlets and smocked frocks, please.' She picked up her car keys from the table. 'And Soph, cheer up, will you? I'll see myself out. Bye!'

She'd known this would happen, and Sophie's fuck-up didn't really bother her at all. Rather than risk something home-made she'd taken the precaution of securing a slinky little number by Jasper Conran from the second-hand shop.

Jessica couldn't remember the last time she'd spent a Friday night at home, but tonight was dedicated to preparing herself for the party. Normally, of course, she'd be meeting a not-quite-as-attractive girlfriend in the new hottest bar in town, getting pissed up and coked up, pouncing on a couple of suits, then taking them on to a club and fucking 'em all night. And not always in a standard boy–girl combination either, though these days it was hard to know who you could trust not to spill the beans to the tabloids. She'd had a couple of near-misses, but she was good at this game and knew to leave no trail behind her – no photos, no phone numbers, no proof.

There had been a rather close shave (which reminded her, did she have any new razors in the house?) when she'd shagged Nigel in the hot tub at his friends' party, and their bloody neighbour had done a David Bailey, but he'd sorted that out for her quite neatly in the end. Though Jessica suspected it was more to do with not wanting to get into trouble himself than protecting her reputation – a solicitor could presumably get struck off for this sort of behaviour.

Ah, Nigel. The one that kept getting away. Who would have guessed that she, Jessica Rose, emotional hardnut, girl-about-town, fuck 'n' go girl would actually feel the urge to settle down, get married and have babies with someone? But anyone who knew her emotional history would indeed have guessed that she had picked a someone who would run a mile if he knew how she loved him, who had an on-off off-on girlfriend, and whose mission in life seemed to be to sleep with as many women as possible. But he had something she wanted and she didn't know what that was. He was a little on the chubby side these days, not quite as handsome as he had once been, and yet for some reason he just did it for her. But he was completely unreliable, utterly selfish, fickle, rich, quite funny, unpredictable and unattainable – everything a challenge should be.

She'd tried every trick in the book to ensnare him and

he would be happily led up her garden path, only to turn round at the door and run back down it without even shutting the gate behind him. This had been their pattern for the last couple of years, almost since they met really. But they were so well matched mentally, they really sparked off each other in an it-takes-one-to-know-one way. He once said they were both evil, she'd said wicked and they'd argued about the difference for the rest of dinner – they stimulated each other, fired each other up, couldn't he see what fun they would have together? But old Kerry had thought he was a bit of a wanker, reckoned that he was so committo-phobic he'd never even give it a go. And Jessica didn't trust her own judgement any more, so she had to pay attention to what the old bag said. An emotional retard, she'd called him.

Well bollocks to him, thought Jessica, as she turned on the telly. Let him just see her in her element tomorrow night, with everyone adoring her, the centre of attention. Cameras flashing, celebrity chums, party queen. Then at last he'd realize how great she was – is – well, could be sometimes. Hmm, better have a quick flick through *Force Him To Fall For You* before going to sleep tonight for a few handy hints.

Nothing of any interest on terrestrial tv till *Friends* and *Frasier*, quick flick through cable channels . . . what's this? Bloody Mark McAndrew's landed himself yet another job in what looks like an updated version of *Candid Camera*, but with celebrities. Only it was really obvious that even this sportsman (the easiest targets in the Gotcha business) knew what was going on and was just playing along with it for the exposure. And the so-called celebrities were of a very poor standard, all has-beens from the Eighties.

During the commercial break Jessica went into the kitchen and looked into the fridge. No food at all, of course – where was that silly Greek boy with her pizza, she'd ordered it ages ago – and no white wine either, it was going to have to be Sophie's home-made elderflower wine which tasted like liquid perfume but packed a punch all the same.

As she hunted round for the corkscrew (damn that Millicent, always inventing new places for things) she smiled at the memory of the very naughty thing she'd done today, after leaving Sophie's. Bold as you like (but disguised by hat and glasses, civilians were so easily fooled), she'd marched straight into the designer room at Selfridge's, picked herself a nicely expensive Dolce e Gabbana evening dress with shoes to match, and forged Phartley's signature so well that nobody suspected a thing. And then, just as she was leaving the store, she dropped it on the floor in Small Leathers to avoid detection. Well she had to wear something tomorrow night, didn't she? And anyway, it served him right for drinking all her wine. Which was always Chablis. She was strictly ABC – Anything But Chardonnay.

As she walked back into the sitting room, she heard the nauseating Mark McAndrew's voice booming out in its accustomed smugness, 'Welcome back! Now as you know, one of our favourite things to do here on *Catch Them If We Can* is to surprise celebrities in their home surroundings, so here's our roving reporter Jimbo Reynolds – in full disguise, as ever – with this week's Star Stalker!'

Jessica had a horrible feeling as she suddenly remembered

the autograph hunter outside her house. They wouldn't, would they? Surely not. Oh no – she was going to be all over the papers now for abusing a fan . . . but no. They'd only filmed a major Hollywood star taking something back to a shop because it was too small for her. Phew.

'And that, ladies and gentlemen, was filmed only last night – as you know, we always catch them before the lawyers can catch us!' Huge applause all round.

The phone rang. Don't answer it, never let anyone know you're in on a Friday night.

'Jessica!' Sandy's voice blared out from the answer machine. 'Pick up the phone, I know you're there, you told me you were in tonight.' No way. 'Look, I've just had a brilliant idea. Why don't we set you up on Mark McAndrew's new show? Everyone's doing it now, you just have to act surprised when you're caught. We'll have to think of something good though, the standard's quite high. What about sex with an Alsatian? I dunno, let me know what you think. And by the way, this afternoon I've had various members of the press on the phone about your party – is the deal with *Hello!* exclusive? Let me know, babe, bye.' End of message.

Newspapers interested, eh? That'll be good. Yes, the *Hello!* deal was supposed to be exclusive but fuck it. The whole point of this party was to get herself back in the public eye – only the family knew it was her fortieth.

Mark McAndrew was now apparently pissing himself about somebody's toupee and so Jessica flicked over to MTV to see what the young people were watching, her form of research, keep in touch. She pumped up the volume and went into the bathroom, to gather together all the products necessary for tonight's beautification process. The old grumpster in the flat downstairs was thumping on his ceiling with a broom handle again, as was his wont – he could at least do it in time with the beat, thought Jessica, ignoring it, as was her wont.

Half an hour later she was standing up, naked, in front of the telly watching *Friends*. Not able to laugh or even smile because of the mud face pack. Her hair was wrapped in clingfilm, with strips of cotton wool carefully arranged around the crown of her head to stop the henna (cheaper than the hairdresser's version) running down her face and neck to form a dribbly tattoo. She'd applied the leftovers of the mud face pack to her nipples which evoked a surprisingly pleasant tingling sensation, even though they had turned a fetching shade of olive green. Her pussy was entirely covered in hair-removing cream apart from a little strip in the middle (a Brazilian mohican, porn-style) and so were her legs from the knee down. Her wet red toenails were held apart from each other with blue foam separators and she was swinging her arms to and fro to make her fingernails hurry up and dry. Every now and then she winced as the Slendertone machine strapped around her waist sent huge electric currents down the dangling wires to the pads which were obediently scrunching her stomach, bottom and thighs.

A knock on the door. Fuck! Who could this be? Oh no, it's OK, it must be that stupid boy from Hippos who'd rung the wrong bell as usual and so the grumpster had let him in. Well about bloody time too, thought Jessica as she hobbled towards the door on her heels, I'm starving.

Gingerly turning the latch to avoid smudging the nails, she stuck her head round the door, only to be nearly blinded by an extremely bright light shining right in her face.

'Jessica Rose?' said a male voice as it walked in through the door, followed by the camera light which swivelled round to catch her in her full blinking glory. 'We're from *Fantasy Fridge*, and I've come to cook you supper! Oh sorry, is this a bad time?'

At last, the day of the party. This was the first time Jessica had seen this side of Saturday morning for ages and she resolved to do it again, it felt good. The early summer sun was diffusing its way into her sitting room through the muslin drapes as they waved in the breeze of the crisp morning air; Alanis Morissette was crooning softly through the stereo system, filling the room with sweet songs of ill-fated affairs with artistic lovers; the delicate fragrance of ylang ylang emanated from a joss stick burning on the mantelpiece, its thin grey twist of smoke curling up into the beyond – christ, thought Jessica, all I need now is some freshly squeezed orange juice and a white linen shirt and I could be in a building-society commercial.

She was sitting on the sofa, feet perched on the coffee table, making a list entitled 'Still To Do' on the back of an envelope which had held a birthday card from her gynaecologist reminding her that now she was forty she had to have smear tests more frequently. But there was nothing actually on the list yet as she'd got caught up in the old copy of *Vogue* (marked 'Reception Do Not Remove') that she was going to use to lean on.

The phone rang. First call of the day. Someone cancelling tonight with the lame excuse that their mother had fallen downstairs and broken her hip. Immediately followed by another call with an equally feeble reason for not coming – couldn't get a babysitter. She'd actually managed to send out the invitations six weeks in advance, how much notice did these people need? The third call was more cheering, though – Adam Crompton, a red-faced, chubbyboy researcher she'd taken the precaution of befriending last year on a daytime panel game show; he'd risen rapidly through the ranks, as only those who work in tv can, to become executive producer on a new programme for Channel 5 about shopping. And she'd heard they needed a presenter, so she'd put in a call and sent him an invite. She'd taken him out for lunch last week as well – he didn't get back to the office until gone five o'clock, but she had managed to ascertain that he was probably gay.

'You're not cancelling are you, Adam?' Damn, don't sound desperate.

'No no, darling, quite the opposite. I'm ringing to tell you I'm going to be bringing a couple of people from Network Centre along with me to your party, only I had a meeting with them yesterday and we got chatting about you, told them I'd be seeing you tonight and they expressed an interest . . .'

Wow, he was bringing the head honchos with him, the

job was probably hers already. 'Brilliant – I'll put you plus two on the guest list, shall I?'

'Plus five or six actually, a few people from the office want to come too.'

'Great, great, the more the merrier!' Why was it that when she was speaking to important people she began to trot out phrases her mother would use?

'And it's still OK to get us sorted, you know, on arrival?'

'Er sure, sure, no problem.'

'OK then darling, see you later.' What, not even a *ciao*? From a man who'd just asked her to provide six more people with a gram of cocaine each? She'd promised Adam (and various other important work contacts) that she'd have some there for him, as an added incentive to get them to come, but this was a bit of a tall order. Still, she really wanted that job – could re-launch her back into the hearts of the nation, especially after last night's débâcle. Didn't want to piss them off at this crucial stage.

Better warn her dealer. Jessica dialled his number, which was one of the few she knew off by heart. Damn. She didn't normally like to leave a message, and he was even more paranoid about the police bugging his phone than she was, but this was an emergency. 'Hi, it's Jessica here, just ringing about tonight. Um, could you bring a few more bottles of champagne with you, about seven in fact, and I'll square it up with you then. Thanks, sorry about this, thanks.' Shit.

Just as well she had the Fun Fund stashed away under her mattress. Jessica got up and went into the bedroom, which was already messy again since Millicent's visit. Slight panic, better check how much is there – what if it's not enough, the cashpoint wasn't paying out any more – where would she get the money from on a Saturday morning?

She heaved up the mattress. Nothing there! Oh yes there was – the brown envelope had moved a bit, that's all. If I was in a film, I would kiss this envelope, she thought.

But she could tell without even opening it that there was no money inside. Nothing. But that's ridiculous, thought Jessica, I put a fifty-pound note in there only last week, it was part of my fee from that charity gig. Nobody else had been in here since then. Except Phartley, and he wouldn't have known about it. Whirr, click. Millicent!

By the time she'd tracked down Millicent's phone number (which was no mean feat, it wasn't under M in the address section of her Filofax but under W instead for some reason, an indication of her upside-down life probably) Jessica was in a complete frenzy. As she punched the number into her phone, a fingernail snapped off and plopped into her coffee cup.

'Hello?'

'Millicent?'

'No, she's out. Who's that?'

'My name is Jessica, Millicent's my cleaner. D'you –'

'Jessica Rose?'

'Yes.' Oh god, a fan. Not now. 'Look –'

'Oh hello Jessica, it's Della.'

'Della who?'

'Della, hairdresser Della, you know, I used to do your hair. Until you decided I wasn't good enough.'

Bloody hell, she'd forgotten how upfront Della was. 'Oh yes, that's right.' Always best to be honest with these feisty young girls.

'I still do your sister's hair actually, and Scarlett's, and I do Simon.' She sounded irritatingly cheerful.

'So how come you're answering Millicent's phone? Are you friends with her?' Maybe it was a black thing that she didn't understand.

'This is my home phone. Millicent's my mother. She's staying with me.'

'Really? I didn't know that. Well look, small world innit and everything but listen, Della, I've got to speak to her, it's really urgent.'

'She's gone out. Can I help?' She was clearly loving this.

'I doubt it. Unless you've got a few hundred pounds lying about the place.'

'Some hope. You lost some money then?'

'Well to put it bluntly, yes.'

'And you think my mother's stolen it, do you?' Oh bloody hell, here we go.

'Well no, of course not, I just –'

'Listen – we may not be as posh as you lot, but we're not thiefs either, so you can just f–'

'Della, listen, I'm sure it's just a misunderstanding. D'you know where she is, I really need to talk to her.' Jessica seldom used this word: 'Please.'

'Well she's either at church or at my Auntie Ellen's.'

'Number? Please?' There it was again.

'I'm not sure God's on the phone, but my Auntie Ellen is.' Oh well done, very funny. As Jessica was writing it down, Della said, 'I'm going to be seeing you tonight, in fact.'

Of course. 'You coming with Darren?'

'Course. Who else would he bring?'

Jessica wasn't sure if Della knew exactly why Darren was invited. 'I don't suppose he's there with you now, is he?'

'Nah, you know what he's like. Could be anywhere.' Della had obviously used up her quota of helpfulness for the day now.

'OK, well never mind. I'll see you tonight then.' Just get off the bloody phone.

She was driving like a madwoman. Millicent, once she had calmed Jessica down, had thought that she was being accused of dishonesty and handed in her notice on the spot. Once Jessica had calmed Millicent down, the truth had (very slowly) emerged.

On Thursday, after the gentleman caller had left, Millicent had noticed that the bedsheets needed changing. Pregnant pause. So she'd stripped the bed, and decided to turn the mattress over as that was the way to stop it getting lumpy – you should do that every six weeks, you know.

So that's what she had done, and when she had lifted it up, she had noticed the brown envelope and could see through the little window that there was money inside. Well now everybody knows that the first place a burglar looks for cash is under the mattress, and so just to be safe she'd taken the money out of the envelope and placed it in the pocket of a dress hanging up in the wardrobe. If Jessica had turned the envelope over and looked on the other side, she would have seen that Millicent had written on it 'See me – M'.

What a pity she hadn't done that, all this confusion could have been avoided. But Jessica had gone out before she'd managed to tell her about it, and of course she hadn't liked to leave a note saying what she'd done as the burglar might read it and then know where the money was hidden.

During this lengthy explanation, Jessica had been frantically rummaging through all the pockets of all the clothes still in the cupboard, and a few on the floor as well, but hadn't found anything except some phone numbers with no names and a stick of Juicy Fruit.

'Which dress was it, Millicent?' she asked, trying not to sound impatient enough to fluster the woman.

'Oh that's easy,' replied Millicent, 'it was the red one, halter neck, sequin trim. Very well cut. My mother used to be a seamstress you know, I remember dresses like that.'

Yes so do I, thought Jessica. I remember taking it to the second-hand shop two days ago to be sold.

Having left the car with its hazard lights flashing on a double-yellow line right outside, Jessica burst in through the shop door and almost flattened the portly saleswoman who was hovering near the window.

'Oh thank god,' wheezed Jessica, 'it's you! I thought you might not be here on a Saturday.'

'Unfortunately, yes,' said the other woman, straightening her beads. 'Some of us have to work hard for our daily bread. And I'm pleased to see you too. I've been trying to ring you all day, but your phone has been constantly engaged. That cheque you gave me on Thursday had the wrong year on it.'

'Yes yes, never mind, I'll write you another one. Where's my red dress?' Jessica shut her eyes and promised to be good from now on if it was still here.

'Which red dress? We get so many clothes brought in here, it's almost impossible to remember each one individually.'

'Oh you'd remember this one – it's red –'

'Ye-es,' said the shop woman in a tone normally reserved for small children.

'Low-cut halter neck, sequins round the edges, just above the knee . . .' But even with her miming the dress as she spoke, the stupid woman was not even attempting to look for it. 'With pockets, yes, a patch pocket either side with a sequin trim. Come on, you must remember it, it's a pretty spectacular frock. The sort of thing Samantha would wear.' The woman looked blank. 'The blonde one from *Sex and The City.*'

'Oh that red dress! Ah yes, I remember it now. Original label cut out, Armani label sewn in?' Two ladies who had been flicking through the circular rail of coloured jackets looked at each other.

'Yes! That's it! I need it back.'

Mrs Portly adopted an apologetic expression. 'I'm afraid that's not possible.' She smiled. 'I sold it yesterday.'

'No! You didn't?! Who to?'

'I'm sorry, I can't tell you that.'

'What, is there some bloody secrecy clause in the second-hand trade now or something?' The two ladies raised their eyebrows at each other.

'No, I can't tell you because I don't know who she was.'

'Well why not, isn't her name on the cheque?'

'It was a cash sale.'

'Didn't she bring in stuff to sell, leave a phone number or anything?' The two ladies thought that was a good question.

'No,' Mrs Portly replied, moving towards the door, 'she didn't look that desperate for money.' She opened the door. 'Are you aware that you're being given a parking ticket?'

Jessica ran out of the shop uttering a series of expletives the like of which the two ladies had rarely heard before. But the Indian traffic warden didn't even flinch – he'd heard it all before.

The rest of the day had been a complete write-off – the Bureau de Change had refused to cash in the thousands of lire she'd had left over from a dirty weekend with Ivan in Milan years ago, claiming Italian bank notes had been re-designed since then and so they were worthless; the pawnbroker had turned down her Tiffany heart necklace saying they were two-a-penny these days; and the loose change from the bottom of all her handbags amounted to only £9.36.

But fuck it, right at this moment she felt goooooood. The party was in full swing and she'd just had her third line of coke. Darren had said that as she was such a good customer she could pay him on Monday, he'd call round for it. She knew what that meant, but didn't care right now, she was having a good time.

Mother and Luigi had been the first to arrive, taking eight o'clock to literally mean eight o'clock; they'd then left an hour later, Constance complaining that the music was too loud, Luigi shrugging his shoulders with a lap-dog smile as he left the present in the huge Whistles carrier bag specially left for this purpose on the table by the door.

Simon and Sophie had come early too with Scarlett, who looked like the Tin Man from the *Wizard of Oz*, all decked out in a silver disco-dolly outfit which apparently she'd borrowed from her friend Jade. She'd done her best with the make-up but gone a bit overboard with the glitter gel, which made her look like she had a dirty face. She'd managed to persuade one of Jessica's single girlfriends to dance with her – probably trying to show some man what a good mother she'd be – what did they think this was, a wedding?

Still, Scarlett had made more of an effort with her appearance tonight than Sophie, who was wearing a long, supposed-to-be-baggy, navy-blue velvet dress that could easily be mistaken for a Betty Jackson but Jessica knew was really M&S. She'd made a beeline for Della, who was looking very sexy in a pair of skimpy black leather shorts and matching bikini top with very high knee boots, little cow – and Della was chatting away to her in a very animated fashion; Sophie's probably mistaking this for friendship, thought Jessica, who could tell it was drug-induced.

Simon was sitting on a stool at the bar, boring Sandy stiff by the look of it; every now and then he'd glance over in Sophie's direction, a look of concern on his face. Surely he wasn't worried she'd get off with another bloke, smirked Jessica inwardly. She would never understand how their marriage had lasted so long – soppy Sophie and simple Simon – perhaps they were well matched after all.

Looking round the rest of the room as she waited impatiently for a handsome young runner from his influential father's production company to buy her another glass of champagne – the so-called free bar had run out much quicker than she thought it would – Jessica felt pretty damn proud of herself.

Everybody was here. Just everybody who was anybody. Her party was in the middle of being a Roaring Success. The *Hello!* photographer's camera was flashing away and the social coordinator from the magazine with him seemed very pleased with the turnout, despite being followed around the room by Steve Venables, desperate to be in every shot. Every soap was well represented by various fat girls in ill-fitting frocks, there were even a couple of Australians here from *Home and Away* or *Neighbours*. This was truly a star-studded celebrity bash.

And all the top television industry personnel had turned up (except Adam Crompton and his cronies, and they'd better come soon or she'd have done all their cocaine, which was still sitting in her handbag) and even the forty-something spinster producers were being chatted up by young fruity researchers. Jessica didn't actually know everyone, of course, but the networkers were networking and all probably talking about her. After all, everyone kept saying to her what a great party it was, how beautiful she looked, how nice it was to see her again. Jessica was on top of her world.

'Mum says we've got to go,' wailed Scarlett, 'tell her Auntie Jess, tell her.'

Sophie was standing behind her, hands protectively resting on her daughter's shoulders. 'Sorry, Jess, but it is midnight and I've got to get her home. The Brownies are visiting the elderly tomorrow morning.' Scarlett did a like-I-care look. 'And I've got a splitting headache. Simon's going to stay for a bit longer though, he'll get a cab home – he's a bit drunk actually, you will look after him, won't you?'

'Yeah yeah, off you go.' Jessica spotted Mark McAndrew pushing his way through the crowd towards her. 'Come on, Scarlett, I'll see you out.'

As she made her way to the exit, waving and smiling to everyone as she went like Fergie on royal walkabout, she overheard a woman's voice saying, 'Thank you – I bought it yesterday, it's Armani.'

Jessica stopped dead in her tracks and looked round. Ex-best-friend Kerry, resplendent in the red dress, surrounded by men including a slavering Ivan. She couldn't believe it and wanted to say something but couldn't decide what.

As she carried on carving out a path towards the door, her champagne/cocaine-coated brain worked out that she couldn't say anything as then Kerry would know that she sold her clothes, thus letting down the I'm-so-successful drawbridge to her castle of poverty. And, of course, Kerry would never say anything about finding the money either, as then Jessica would know that she'd bought second-hand.

'Wow, Auntie Jess, look how many presents you've got!' said Scarlett in amazement. 'Can we open them now?' The bag was now full, and there were many more glittering packages and bottles of champagne with cards stuck precariously onto their beautiful phallic gold necks, all jostling for prime position on the heaving table.

Jessica cheered up instantly. 'No, I'll take them home with me tonight and then I'll come round and open them with you tomorrow afternoon,' promised Jessica. 'Night night.' She kissed them both goodbye and waved as they disappeared down the staircase. Good – now she could really let her hair down.

Nigel passed them on his way up. Her heart flipped inside her skinny rib cage. 'Sorry we're a bit late, darling,' he said, 'Baboushka couldn't decide what to wear.'

Jessica couldn't believe he'd had the nerve to bring the On-off-off-on to her birthday party, especially as they'd never met. And here she was, right behind him. Towering over him, long blonde hair, face like a fucking horse with lipstick on. Looking bored already.

'Got anything on you?' he murmured as he kissed her on the cheek. 'We've had all ours,' he said into the other ear.

'Yes, but only for you,' muttered Jessica, ignoring longlegs as she knew her English wasn't very good. 'Follow me.'

As they squeezed themselves into the doorway, Jessica saw to her horror that Mark McAndrew had been lying in wait.

'Jessicaaa!' He grabbed her round the wrists and held

her at arm's length, pretending to drink in her beauty. 'I've been trying to talk to you all night. You look gorgeous!'

'Scuse me,' said Nigel as he took the Russian round the waist and steered her away towards the bar. Damn, lost him.

'Better than ever,' the slimeball continued, 'which is amazing since you must be, ooh, let's see now – forty-one, forty-two?'

'Oh fuck off,' said Jessica, and tried to shake his firm grip away from her arms.

'No, look listen, I've just heard about *Fantasy Fridge*!' he laughed. 'Sounds hilarious, what are you like? You're not cross about that, are you? Best career move you could make, that show gets quite high ratings for non-terrestrial tv and they've already sent it to Denis Norden apparently – big honour, Jess. It's just brilliant, I'm so pleased for you!'

'Why is that brilliant? It hardly fits in with my girl-next-door image, does it?' He was quite clearly drunk on her champagne and his own success.

'But that's so *passé* now, they all want a bit of edge – you're going to get a lot of exposure out of this, you know. Literally!' He was actually guffawing.

'Yes, but the wrong kind. I'd rather be famous than infamous, thank you very much.' Though she was beginning to understand why Suki Samprah had let it be known she was bisexual.

'Well suit yourself. Only trying to give you a bit of advice.'

'Yes well thank you very much but the last thing I need is –'

A huge shout rang out above the loud music and over Mark's shoulder Jessica could detect bodily movement of the wrong kind right in the heart of the party. Oh no.

She made her way through to the edge of the circle that had instantly formed around the cause of the disturbance. Everyone had stopped talking, but the music was still declaring itself horny, horny, horny.

It seemed that Darren had punched Simon's lights out. He was lying sparko on the floor, and the big black man was stepping over him, making for the door, hand-in-hand with Della who was not quite as shocked as she might have been, in fact in this light she looked as if she was smiling.

'What's going on?' asked Nigel, appearing as if by magic at Jessica's side.

'Fuck knows,' replied Jessica. 'Looks like my drunken brother-in-law's made a pass at his wife's hairdresser.' As Nigel tried to work that out, she looked around the room. Fortunately the *Hello!* photographer had already left, and two burly bouncers were making their way towards Simon in order to pick him up and pour him into a cab. At least she hoped that's what they were going to do – she simply couldn't be associated with this, not in front of all these people. The crowd began to talk to each other again, and the volume went from 0 to 60 in ten seconds. And she'd got Nigel to herself.

'Come on, follow me,' she said to him. 'I'll give you what you want.' A quick check over at the bar revealed that his stupid foreign girlfriend was being chatted up by Adam Crompton and his crowd, who must've just arrived. She'd give them their drugs in a minute. 'Ladies or Gents?' Jessica asked as she led him into the corridor outside. Her fanny already felt like it was on fire.

'Ladies, turns me on.'

As they marched past the girls primping and preening themselves along the line of basins, but not actually washing their hands, one turned to the other and said 'Who's that?' but Jessica pretended not to hear as she and Nigel had already queue-jumped their way into the end cubicle, the disabled one. Enough room for two.

'Lock the door,' said Jessica as she fiddled with the tiny packet and her video rental card on top of the cistern.

'No, it's more dangerous not to, means we could be caught,' he said as he scratched his hands down her back. 'Good party, Jess.'

'Thanks,' said Jessica as she rolled up a five-pound note. 'Good of you to come.'

'Oh OK then, now you're asking,' he said as he lifted her skirt with one hand and undid his belt with the other. She heard his trousers fall round his ankles with a satisfying flumpf.

Jessica bent down to take one of the fat lines she'd chopped out. As she did so, he barged his way into her, sending a delicious shiver up her spine. God, she loved this!

The cubicle door banged open and there was a flash. And another, and as she turned round another.

By the time they'd straightened themselves up, the man with the photographer was holding out his business card. 'Hello, Jessica. You may remember me from the other night. Phil Hartley, *Daily Mirror.* And this –' another man poked his head round the cubicle door '– is Detective Inspector Anstee, Drugs Squad. And the man behind him is my friend Bill – he's from the Fraud Squad. We all want a little chat with you.'

MILLICENT O'HARA
50 tomorrow

Higher Power,
Grant me the serenity to accept the things I cannot change,
The courage to change the things I can,
And the wisdom to know the difference.
Grant me patience with the changes that take time,
Appreciation of all that I have,
Tolerance of those with different struggles,
And the strength to get up and try again,
One day at a time.

12 September

'My name's Millicent and I'm an alcoholic.'

'Hi Millicent,' said the rest of the group.

'I'm a bit nervous this evening. I'm not sure what I'm going to say.' Millicent looked around at the expectant faces. Some of them politely looked down at the floor, knowing that it was easier to share if you didn't think anybody was looking.

'It's strange. I used to be very good at public speaking, but since I came here I have lost a lot of confidence. Not to the meeting, of course. I mean since I came to this country.' This wasn't going very well at all. Jim, who was quite new to the group and still had a lot of anger, got up and left the room. Not worth hanging around for her chair? Right, she'd show him.

'It's my birthday tomorrow, I'm fifty. But my real age is twenty-two.' Always start a speech with a dramatic line. She could sense that she had their full attention now. 'I haven't touched alcohol for twenty-two years. But I've never felt more like having a slip than I do today. Perhaps I should say a sip, but I don't think it would be just one drink, would it?' The rest of the group smiled, knowing this to be true.

'I was a secret drinker. I was never what you might call a roaring drunk; I made sure I never let go enough to let people see how out of control I was. That was probably because it made me feel as if I was in charge of the situation. And anyway, on the small Caribbean island I come from, we never acknowledged problems of this nature. My uncle was what we all know as an alcoholic, although he would never have admitted it, and I'd seen enough of his bad behaviour when I was a child to make sure that I would never be like him. Oh no. In fact, when he first made me taste alcohol, when I was eleven years old, I hated it – I thought it tasted disgusting.' A few people nodded in recognition.

'So when I tried it again a few years later, at his funeral in fact, and found I liked it after all, I was horrified. But I loved the feeling it gave me, everything got further away. I was the oldest child and had a lot of responsibility in the family. When I was sober, it felt like a burden. When I was drinking, it was easier to cope.

'After my uncle died, my mother carried on with her job as a seamstress but it wasn't enough to keep the family going, so she decided that I had to get a good job. My brother and sister were still halfway through school at the time. They both wanted to leave, but she wouldn't let them – her brother, who was the head of our household, had always been very keen on us passing our examinations. He didn't want us letting the side down, he had been one of the solicitor's clerks and had great plans for us. As I was nearly at the end of my education, she decided I must become a teacher.

'I didn't want to, of course. Even though I was only sixteen, I was popular enough. I had many friends, I was good fun, especially if I could manage to get a drink inside me. Why would I want to work in a boring school? I was very angry with her, but she wouldn't listen. So I took a correspondence course for my teacher training, which I did under her watchful eye in the evenings, and by day I was a civil servant – I worked at the post office. But I also got an extra job for the weekends, just to make a little bit more money for the family you understand. In one of the hotel bars, naturally.' Some of the group smiled – many of them had always managed to make sure they worked around alcohol too. 'I was very popular as a barmaid; we used the American measures, pour the bottle for a count of five – but I always did six. And it was only polite to accept a drink for myself when it was offered.

'It was not my intention to teach for ever, just until the twins were old enough to do their bit for the family, share the responsibility. But I was always a bit of a perfectionist, Diligent Millicent my sister used to call me, and so I became a very good teacher. In fact I found I quite enjoyed it in the end. The best way to teach children is to make the lessons fun, make them want to learn, you know.

'But I didn't let my career get in the way of my drinking. I had to be very careful, of course. It was fine in the school holidays, I could disappear; sometimes I would go up to the waterfall with my ready-mixed Mount Gay and coke in a thermos flask. When I came home, I would tell them I was tired. It was a very long walk up there, everybody knew that. And then I would pass out on my bed and pretend in the morning that my headache was from too much sun.

'In term-time, though, it was a different matter. I could manage to go quite a long time without a drink, weeks sometimes. I think the correct term for what I was is a "dry drunk". But if there was a jump-up at the weekend I found it difficult to stop. Everybody else would be drunk then of course, so it was easier for me to get away with it. And even though the island was very small, there were plenty of places to hide.

'But one Monday morning I got caught out. The headmistress had had her suspicions, and followed me silently to my locker in the staff room where I kept a small bottle of vodka for emergencies such as these. I pleaded with her to let me keep my job; she gave me a second chance as I was one of her best members of staff, and I promised not to drink again at school. But I didn't stick to it, of course, how could I? My addiction was beginning to take a hold of me by now. I was just more careful.

'Then we had a family tragedy.' Millicent paused and took a deep breath. 'My little brother was killed in a car accident. We all took it very badly. His twin, my sister, began to hate everybody and everything, she was very angry. My mother was never the same again, he had been her favourite, we all knew that. And me? Well, I used it as an excuse to drink even more, drown my sorrows I told myself. The irony of the situation didn't even occur to me – actually he had been killed by a drunk driver.

'Fortunately, everyone was too wrapped up in their own grief to notice my erratic behaviour. The headmistress put it down to Edric's death and nobody in the island's bars was surprised to see me there, they were all very sympathetic towards me and knew that what I really needed was another drink. But I always managed to leave before I got out of control. I'd buy a bottle of rum, saying it was for my mother, for medicinal purposes; and I'd go off to drink it quietly somewhere in the dark.

'I was twenty-five years old when my brother died. Even though I still kept up a respectable front, my life quickly became unmanageable. I was finding it more and more difficult to hide my problem; some people were beginning to talk. That's the trouble with living on a small island, everybody knows your business. I began to take days off from school, I'd get my sister to send a message that I was sick, which she would do willingly. Anything to avoid the rest of the island knowing the truth.

'It was not a lie, I was sick. I was spending all my wages on drink, we were getting into financial difficulties. My mother and sister wouldn't seek help for me because then everybody would know I was an alcoholic and it would bring shame upon the family. They did everything to try and make me stop: they banned all alcohol from the house, they only gave me enough money for my bus fare to and from the school every day. They would lock me in the house when they went shopping. I was only allowed out to go to church.

'But I was too clever for them. I'd slip away during the service. I knew all the rum shacks – places they'd never go to – and I had friends there who were just as addicted as me and so they would help me out. Alcoholics are kind to each other, as you know. I took to drinking plastic, a vicious concoction brewed illegally on the island. And I would smuggle some back into the house in an old nail-polish-remover bottle, just to see me through.

'I still can't quite believe I managed to hold on to my job, I don't know how I did it. I think the headmistress must have decided to turn a blind eye – after all, there was no one on the island to replace me. I can't even remember my twenty-sixth birthday, or my twenty-seventh, or much about the year in between come to that.' She laughed to herself as she remembered how much she'd forgotten. 'Birthdays have always been important to me, you see. I used to like them because it was a good reason to celebrate, the one time of the year (apart from Christmas) when I could get away with having "one too many". But towards the end, I realized that I could find a reason to pick up a drink any time I liked – it was nearly the weekend, it was the weekend, it was a little something to get me through the week, it was a Wednesday, it was nearly the weekend again, and so on.' More nods of identification from the other people now safely in recovery.

'But by the time my twenty-eighth birthday came around, I was sober. You see, I'd done a very bad thing.'

The room was completely pin-drop silent, Millicent noticed. She thought about it. No.

'I can't talk about it yet. Soon.' She could almost hear their disappointment. 'But it was my rock bottom. Enough to make me realize that unless I changed my behaviour, more terrible things would happen and people would get very badly hurt.

'So I turned to God for help and guidance.' Jim came back into the room, noisily scraped back his chair and sighed loudly as he sat down. Millicent waited until he had settled himself and then continued.

'I had always gone to church of course, we all did, but I had never really embraced the Lord properly. But from the day I asked Him for His help, for Him to take care of me as I was a lost soul, from that day on I have never had another drink. I gave myself to Him, I let Him choose what happened to me next. There was nothing else I could do, I had no choice but to trust Him. And in return for my faith, He looked after me. You see before you one of God's miracles.' Jim snorted into his folded arms.

'Just before my thirtieth birthday, I was promoted – to headmistress. And I have managed to remain strong for the last twenty-two years. But now my life has changed so much since I left home, I don't know who I am any more or what I am to do next. I need my Higher Power even more than ever. All I can do is ask Him for His guidance and clarity.' Jim offered a look skywards to whoever his Higher Power might be.

But Millicent was determined to finish her piece in peace, and so she did. 'However. One blessing I have received from the Lord bringing me over here is discovering this programme. There were meetings over there, I knew that, but I never went to one. I didn't trust other people enough to realize that no one would have said anything about the headmistress being there, which I regret now. But as soon as I arrived over here, six months ago, I found out about it all, and I am slowly working my way through the steps with the help of my sponsor. With her help, I have just completed Step Four. It was difficult, and pain-ful, but I can see that it will be rewarding. Even though it's hard to work on myself sometimes, I can see that it's having an effect. I am so very grateful to be here. Thank you.'

'Thanks, Millicent,' replied the group in unison.

'Right then,' said the secretary, 'the rest of the meeting's open for general sharing.'

'My name's Jim and I'm really f***** off with all this god c***.'

'Hi, Jim,' chorused the group, with as much enthusiasm as they could muster.

Sitting on the top deck of the number 52 bus on the way back to Della's, looking down through the black-beaded raindrops on the window at all the Londoners scurrying about like wet beetles with nowhere to go, Millicent's thoughts turned to home, as they always did in her idle moments. And this was going to be a long journey. Until she'd come over here, she always thought the red double-deckers she'd seen in the films just raced to and fro across London's bridges. She didn't realize that they were slow, lumbering, dirty things that took a very long time to pass through the busy capital.

Montserrat was a beautiful, beautiful place – a paradise. She realized that now. Correction. Had been a beautiful place. How ungrateful they had been for their heaven on earth, they had just taken it for granted. They had been living in God's Garden of Eden, and they hadn't known it. Of course, everybody knew that Chances Peak was a real volcano but they never dreamed that it would actually erupt. As she herself had said many a time, 'the last time was more than three hundred and fifty years ago'. Millicent had taken her pupils up there on school outings many times. They always complained that it smelt of rotten eggs, so she would explain that it was the sulphur in the air, which also accounted for the cars rusting so quickly. And the sand on the beaches was black due to the volcano too. Many a project had been done on the Soufrière Hills, under the heading of Geography. She'd always told them they were very lucky to be so close to a natural phenomenon, and then made them spell it. Any smart alec who had written i-t would be given an immediate detention.

But their luck had run out. Everything had changed and all they had now were their memories of the way it used to be. In History she'd told them all about Christopher Columbus discovering their tiny island in 1493, calling it Montserrat after a place in Spain which had a similar landscape of jagged peaks. Their ancestors were Carib Indians who lived here quite happily (outing to the Montserrat Museum to see bows and arrows from those days, which always made the boys over-excited and the girls bored); until the English and Irish settlers came in 1632 to grow tobacco and indigo, then cotton and sugar (another outing, Art this time, to draw the old sugar mills still standing like proud windmills without arms all over the island); then an attacking party from France arrived and tried to take over (which was why you must pay special attention in French so that you can tell them to go away if they try to do it again) but eventually things settled down and the black people became slaves to the white landowners.

Millicent always found this part a bit tricky, as she didn't want to stir up any uncomfortable feelings on an island where black and white people lived happily alongside each other. And there was often a white child or two in the class whose parents had opened a business here, though they seldom stayed on the island for very long. (Most of the white people were retired Brits or Canadians, and there was the occasional pop star who'd fallen in love with the island enough to buy a holiday home here.) So she used to diffuse the issue by telling them that slavery was abolished in 1834 and the land was divided up and given to the black people who took on the surnames of their masters. And if we go round the class, I will be able to tell you if your ancestors belonged to an English family or an Irish family. Now, my surname is O'Hara, so I'm what?

Then they would understand why Montserrat was known as the Emerald Isle and why their flag had not only a Union Jack on it, but also a woman holding a harp and clasping a Christian cross. She'd go on to ask them what their families did now, to show what had happened over the centuries. There was a lot of poverty on the island of course, but most of her pupils' parents were gainfully employed. Some were still farmers, mostly of cotton now and not limes any more; many were connected with the building trade, or they were shopkeepers, or worked for the British Government, had office jobs – which was something to be proud of in their community, some of the more strident young men grew their nails long to show they didn't have to work on the land any more – and many were involved in one way or another with tourism. Which means what? Yes? That's right. We have a beautiful island and we must take care of it, and not become litterbugs. This will make sure the visitors keep coming and we will have enough food on our tables. Speaking of tables, what are six eights?

And so it would go on. She liked to keep them on their toes. Her pupils enjoyed her lessons but never became rowdy; they liked her but they were a little bit afraid of her at the same time. This was exactly as she wanted it. Miss O'Hara commanded a great deal of respect and produced very good results. So much so that when the headmistress retired, Millicent was promoted to the position. And thus, over the years, the fiery young girl with the secret drinking problem had become a respected pillar of the community who'd always chosen a Ting and ice over a rum and coke.

Two young lads, probably football hooligans thrown out of Hyde Park for kicking mud in children's faces or something similar, stomped up the stairs to the top deck of the bus and raced to the back, shouting at the top of their voices about getting away with paying half fares again and swearing at the bad weather.

It's only a spot of rain, she wanted to say. That's what they all used to say when the heavens opened up without warning back home. But even the rain was different here. It was a spitting affair, made everything grey and dull, put everybody in a bad mood. There, the raindrops were big and splashy, made everything green and shiny, a bit of welcome relief from the stifling heat. The soil was already fertile from the volcano, the rain just made everything grow more quickly. Millicent smiled to herself as she remembered her first sighting of a lovingly nurtured rubber plant over here, in an expensive-looking pot in Jessica's flat. The ones back home just grew like huge weeds overnight, nobody would actually bother to cultivate one! She'd tried to explain to the silly girl that it would be more useful to grow an aloe plant; then if you were unfortunate enough to cut yourself at home you could just slice a leaf open and rub it on the wound, that would speed up the healing process. But Jessica hadn't listened of course. That was the problem, nobody listened to Millicent any more.

She was putting a brave face on it, she had to. But nobody knew how much she was hurting inside, because she had nobody to tell. Della was avoiding her most of the time, she didn't seem to understand that her mother only wanted to get to know her daughter again after all these years apart. Admittedly, she had played it all wrong when she first got here and tried too hard to make up for all that lost time, but Millicent put that down to her own disorientation. Then she'd tried to interest Della in Caribbean life, but that hadn't worked either. Now her sponsor had suggested that she leave it to God to show her when the time was right to say something, and so that's what she was trying really hard to do. But it wasn't easy, Millicent was really having to bite her tongue – not something she was used to doing.

And Ellen wasn't interested in anything her sister had to say either. She made herself too busy to listen, and dismissed any attempts to reminisce about home with Millicent as being too long ago for her to remember. Desmond was quite simply never there, and if he was he was glued to the television. They'd managed a conversation about cricket, but that was it.

Barbara had listened respectfully at first, but eventually

had had the cheek to tell her aunt that she should try to adapt to the change in her circumstances, say goodbye to her old life and embrace her future.

But it wasn't as easy as that. How could she forget the last fifty years? Was she supposed to just write it off, pretend nothing had happened, start again with a blank sheet of paper? She had a story to tell, and she wanted someone to hear it.

Millicent had an idea. It suddenly came to her. (Later, she would tell the group that this was a Higher Power Moment.) Write it all down! Of course. Then her memories would be real, would exist in this new world she was being so brave in. Now that was good, Millicent thought to herself, a literary reference. Her extensive knowledge of Montserrat could be passed down, through future generations. Though it would probably be lost on Della, whose education was almost invisible. Her handwriting was very messy, and she seemed to rely purely on colloquialisms in her speech. Her enunciation was appalling too, except when she swore, which she did far too often – a good indication of a badly limited vocabulary, as Millicent had always told her pupils.

She smiled to herself as she remembered the time she had marked an exercise book with 'Please try harder' and the child had written back in pencil 'I am you nit' and obviously forgotten to rub it out when he handed in his book the next time. So the next Nature class had been all about headlice, and the lesson had been learnt.

Yes, writing it all down would be a good exercise. Maybe she could turn this into a book. After all, Montserrat was a British colony, people would be interested in life on the island. Sadly, it was now just a part of their social history. But not only would she enjoy the process (after all English Language had been her favourite subject), it might help to exorcize the demons from her mind that were coming back to haunt her now that she was around Della again. She had had another dream about it only last night. In some ways, this was encouraging. If she could remember something that happened all those years ago so clearly, then the rest of her memoirs would be easy to recollect.

But she couldn't write about that. It was a story full of shame and scandal, wrongdoing and regret, people wouldn't be interested. Who wanted to read about that sort of thing? No, this was going to be an important book, an accurate record of island life. She could have called it 'Paradise Lost' only that had been done already.

To while the long journey away, Millicent started planning it right now. She would start with the history of the island, of course. People would find that absolutely fascinating. And then maybe go into volcanic eruptions past and present and describe the hurricanes as well. What had they said about Hugo, in '89? That it was the work of the devil, yes that was it, because all the churches had been flattened in its wake, but the flimsy rum shacks had been left standing. No, better not mention that, people might get the wrong impression.

And then – well, then she would write about the flora and fauna which would be very interesting. She would describe the luscious vegetation in great detail. Of course she'd have to go to the library for confirmation of some of the Latin names of plants that she wasn't completely sure about, though she did know most of them.

And she could tell her readers all about eating from the land. Yams, breadfruit, christophene, a bit of callaloo – which they should be told was much more tasty than the spinach they have here. And all the fruit, which we just picked off the trees and bushes; she'd never even seen tamarind over here and mango was a terrible price, free in Montserrat. The difference between a banana and a plantain would make a good section.

Fauna. Where to begin? There were several species of goat to be covered, though only one kind of dog. When she was a child she had thought it was always the same one barking at her wherever she went, Millicent remembered with amusement. And the cows and egrets who lived together, the bird picking the flies and bugs off the bits the cow couldn't reach. She'd skim over the donkeys, they weren't very exciting. Though she hadn't seen or heard of many over here. But iguanas were of great interest, and agoutis would be too – even though they were just glorified rats – and she could describe the mountain chicken very well, having caught many herself as a young girl by shining a torch into their eyes and slipping a sack over their stunned heads. Even Della might enjoy eating the giant frog, it was very tender. Millicent resolved to try and find some over here, cook it up for Della as a special treat, not tell her what it really was until after she'd eaten it, as a surprise! In fact she must include some traditional recipes. Goat water was very popular back home, they might like it over here. Yes, she'd call that section A Taste of Montserrat.

What about the fish? They would have to have their own chapter, there were so many of them. Maybe she'd call it Flying Fish No Chips, for a light-hearted touch. This was very exciting indeed, Millicent was enjoying herself.

She would have to go into the economy of the island, so that people could familiarize themselves with the EC dollar and how it worked. Administration and Social Conditions would both be very lengthy chapters, as would The Effect of the British Government on Island Life, From 1871 to the Present Day. Yes, this was really a very good idea, she must start on it right away. It might even be a best-seller. Perhaps a blockbuster!

The bus stopped yet again, this time outside a big department store, to let on the shoppers who had been taking advantage of the late-night opening hours. That was part of the trouble with this country, thought Millicent: it places too much importance on the consumer. It was buy, buy, buy all the time. The BBC World Service had painted an entirely different picture. Yes, they had been warned of the rising crime rate and vandalism and violence, but they'd not explained things like how everything had to have a beep or a code number, or, if it was really important, a beep and a code number. This country seemed to be entirely run by computer now, it was ww this and com dot that all the time.

She'd been saddened to discover that people didn't actually speak to each other except on the mobile phone, there was no proper sense of community here. Nobody stopped to exchange pleasantries with you, they were all too busy having to make more and more money. It seemed you had to be a millionaire to survive over here, everything was so expensive. Her limited funds were being eaten away extremely quickly, though Jessica still owed her quite a few pounds. She'd have to get that somehow, but how?

As Millicent looked down at the shopaholics jumping anxiously from one store into the next, she decided that it was the little things that showed the biggest differences. Everybody looked so scruffy all the time, few people looked like they'd taken any care with their appearance. The Royal Family were totally disrespected by their own press, which was a shocking state of affairs. The newspapers themselves had very little actual news in them, they seemed to be more preoccupied with the personal lives of scantily clad film stars and badly behaved musicians, who were not setting a good example to the young people at all. And many of those seemed to be content to sleep in doorways with their flea-ridden dogs, only being moved on in the daytime by the people who wanted to smoke cigarettes there.

She'd heard quite a lot of people openly swearing on the streets too – in Montserrat you could be threatened with imprisonment for that, the Government there just wouldn't put up with it. (Though this rarely happened, the prison was still a Victorian place, the prisoners really did get only bread and water. Even though the warden used to turn a blind eye when the inmates jumped over the wall for national holidays and suchlike, as long as they were back in their cells by the morning.)

She had been shocked to discover that a German car was a sign of prestige over here, if you please, after all they had done to this country. Millicent realized that she hadn't driven herself for weeks. The little white car (Japanese, but it was all they could get) that she had spent so many years saving up for had been her pride and joy, she had been very important driving it around the island. Which didn't take long, as it was only five miles wide and nine miles long. They used to laugh about only needing cars with three gears, the fourth was never used on their winding roads. But Mother had enjoyed a drive on a Sunday afternoon and it had been invaluable for visiting parents whose children had been misbehaving.

But if they could see me now, Millicent thought, they'd be as horrified as I am. Sitting on a dirty bus, reduced to cleaning up after people who live like ungrateful pigs. If she had the energy, she'd be angry. But the outrage of her situation just wore her out, she found acceptance easier to live with. However, she refused to get used to this, she'd get back on her feet again, she knew she would. In the meantime, it was just a case of handing it all over to God and waiting patiently for Him to show her His plan for her, Thy will be done. But right now she was waiting impatiently for yet more people to get on the bus with yet more foolish purchases. When did these people stop? Why were they always in such a hurry to get nowhere? What did they do to relax? Did they –

'Could you move your bag?' said a woman with red hair impatiently. Millicent had been so busy comparing and contrasting that she hadn't noticed the bus had filled right up and this was now the only spare seat.

'Oh, yes, I'm sorry,' replied Millicent, who couldn't believe she had just left her handbag sitting beside her, anyone could have taken it. She really must be more care-ful in this wicked city. She smiled up at the young lady apologetically.

'Miss O'Hara!' The woman sat down as well as she could manage with all her expensive-looking carrier bags. 'I don't believe it!'

'Have we met?' asked Millicent, scrutinizing the freckled face with brown button eyes in front of her.

'It's Liz! Liz Wilson-Gough. God, this is incredible, it's mad! Surely you remember me – I came to Montserrat as a student teacher ooh, about ten years ago!' She was screeching with excitement.

'Oh yes,' said Millicent slowly as it dawned on her, 'I remember you now. Elizabeth. Miss Wilson-Gough.' Each year the school had been assigned a British student, for work experience. Or at least that's what they said. The fact that there was no salary or living expenses involved meant that Millicent had had to suffer the consequences of sons and daughters of rich parents with no real application for teaching thinking they could get away with anything. She'd done her best with each of them, of course, but it was a thankless task as they left the island after a year and she'd had to start all over again with the next one. And this girl had been one of the worst, she'd thought she was on holiday instead of being there to work. Insisted on trying to get a suntan too, pointlessly and painfully. Silly. It was only polite to show an interest, though. 'How are you?'

'Oh I'm fine. I'm not teaching any more, you'll be glad to know. I wasn't very good at it, was I?' She nudged Millicent and laughed.

'You could have been,' replied Millicent, 'if you'd put as much effort into your work as you did into your social life.' She went on, 'You certainly had the focus necessary for being a good teacher, only you were looking in the wrong direction.'

'Yes, well I hated it anyway, not really my style saying things like "don't answer back". I remember one girl asking me what that meant, and I realized that it actually meant that she wasn't entitled to her own opinion, which didn't seem very fair to me! No, I wasn't really cut out to be a teacher, so it was just as well I gave up. Never even took my finals.' Millicent despaired out of the window to the Royal Albert Hall. 'Got married instead. To a Frenchman, actually. I live in Paris now.'

'Do you?' Millicent knew how to sound interested even if she wasn't. 'Why are you here then?'

'Well you know, Paris is OK but the shopping's better here. For a start, there isn't a Harrods over there! And besides, I love to pop over to London every now and then on the train.' On the train? She must be delusional. Even her youngest Geography students knew France was across the English Channel. Unfortunately as the foolish girl chattered on, Millicent *did* remember hearing about something called a chunnel on the World Service, but never mind about that now. 'And it's great to catch up with everyone back in dear old Blighty and all that! There's no place like home, you know.' Millicent knew.

'Anyway,' she continued, 'what are you doing here? I just can't believe that we've met on a bus! Classic! I heard about the earthquake of course, it must have been awful. I bet you got out of there as soon as you could!'

'I didn't, actually. I stayed for as long as possible. But in the end –' Millicent shut her eyes and resented the girl for making her think about it. 'Well for one reason and another it became impossible to stay.'

'Yes, god, I can imagine!' I don't think you can, thought Millicent. 'Actually I went to a couple of benefits for the hurricanes at the Brixton Academy a few years ago, you know, to do my bit. It was a good night, in fact, got completely pissed on Malibu and coke. Didn't do anything for the volcano, though; there wasn't much fuss made about it in France.'

'I don't think there was much made about it over here either,' said Millicent with a certain amount of bitterness. She would have gone into the whole débâcle of the appalling lack of support from the British Government, how they had been left to fend for themselves, but knew it would be wasted on this girl. 'In fact, I've decided to write a book on the subject.'

'Gosh, what a brilliant idea!' gushed Elizabeth. 'I've been dining out on stories of Montserrat for years. I always say it was like living on an island stuck in a sort of two-zone time warp, part Victorian, part 1950s.'

'I seem to remember you enjoying the benefits of a very modern nightlife,' said Millicent, sourly.

'Oh god, that was hilarious! Only one disco in town – La Cave, wasn't it? – and it played the same old records every Friday and Saturday night, only in a different order!

Mind you, we were always too pissed to notice by then, the booze was so cheap over there. Andy's was the best bar in town, only it wasn't in town was it, where was it again?'

'Salem,' replied Millicent, whose jaw was hardening.

'That's right. God, it was brilliant. We'd start there on a Friday night, with one of us VSOs driving – didn't matter if you got rat-arsed, nobody would stop you – and we'd have some of his delicious fried chicken which was out of this world – d'you remember those posters he had on the walls, drawings in luminous paint of suggested sexual positions for all the star signs?'

'No I don't,' said Millicent through somewhat gritted teeth.

'Oh they were hilarious, really kitsch! Mind you, wasn't as bad as Nepcoden, was it? Looked like a normal house from the outside, but in the basement it was a very lively bar, all done up to look like you were under the sea, with flashing fairy lights inside crab shells and lots of cotton wool stuck on the ceiling to make you think you were under the waves. Quite disgusting and unhygienic really as all the flies got stuck in it and died there, quite put you off your roti.'

This girl was using her knowledge of the Caribbean to great effect, thought Millicent. She must be a very popular dinner-party guest indeed. There was a momentary silence as they both looked down onto Kensington High Street.

'And the shops! God! I don't know how they managed to keep going. I mean there's only so many novelties you can buy, aren't there? And the food was so expensive – still, that's what comes of only having one supermarket, I suppose.'

It was pricey because people like you shopped there and the food was flown in from America, thought Millicent. We would only use it for the essentials that you couldn't get anywhere else. And the owner refused to employ local people on his staff, he flew them in from India instead. And mistreated them, thus exploiting their poverty and expanding ours.

'I've still got my t-shirts, though; the Sea Island Cotton shop kept me in cheap clean clothes for ages!' chirruped Elizabeth. 'I always thought it was so funny when you'd see an old lady sitting on the side of the road selling her fruit wearing a Dire Straits t-shirt, which had obviously been given to her by someone who worked at Air Studios. Rather incongruous, don't you think?'

'Yes,' said Millicent quietly, knowing full well that this was most likely all she'd had to wear and that the poor woman would have had to get up at dawn to pick the mangoes off the road before the cars squashed them.

'The whole island was a bit like that, actually. I mean when I first arrived at the airport on that scary little plane, I thought I was coming to a very efficient place that was all bound up in doing things properly. You know, the way they make you stand behind the yellow line in the customs shed and really cross-examine you about why you're here and go through every single piece of your luggage. And then they'd take ages to decide if they were going to stamp a shamrock in your passport, when you knew perfectly well they were going to in the end, wasn't that funny?'

Millicent didn't know if it was funny or not, she'd never arrived at Blackburne Airport, only seen people off. Years ago now, but she could still feel the wrench. Still feel the pain, still feel the tears. She pressed her head against the cool glass of the window. Good, they were coming up to Notting Hill Gate. Millicent had been in London long enough to realize that this idiotic girl would most likely be getting off there.

Liz's flow flowed. 'But then if you put a Montserratian in a uniform, he'll turn into a little Hitler!' She laughed at her own flawed imagery. 'What about that bloke whose job it was to stand outside the library all day in his smart white uniform and gloves in that terrible heat, just to make sure nobody nicked the Governor's parking space?'

What about him, thought Millicent. He was one of her most compliant students and had been given a good job accordingly.

'It was a funny old place,' she chattered on merrily, completely oblivious to Millicent's mounting disapproval, 'nothing was what it was supposed to be. I mean if you wanted an ice cream, you'd have to go to the hardware store. An electric fan from the stationery shop. And you could only get Brie from the cinema, of all places – did you know the owners flew it back with them from Guadeloupe when they went to collect those dreadful Kung Fu films?'

Actually Millicent hadn't known that. She hadn't much use for French things. But the cinema hadn't always shown those movies, she'd spent many a pleasurable evening there when she was younger, watching epics like *Gone With The Wind* under the romantic starlit sky. You couldn't have an open-air cinema here, she thought with a shudder, it was too cold. But why the people of Notting Hill Gate needed two indoor ones almost next door to each other was a complete mystery.

'I remember once,' said the stupid girl, launching into another amusing anecdote, which would no doubt be at their expense, 'taking my car into the garage for a service and the mechanic told me that it needed a spare part but they didn't have it in stock. So when I went home for Christmas, I tracked it down with great difficulty from Hyundai and took it into the garage when I got back. The man asked where I'd got it from as it wasn't in the usual box, and when I told him he just laughed and asked why I hadn't gone to the travel agents for it! "Oh yes, of course," I said, "silly me!" I mean really, how was I supposed to know?'

You didn't need to know. We all knew how to find anything we needed. It was us who lived there, you were just visiting. 'Was there anything you liked about Montserrat?' enquired Millicent with as much patience as she could manage. She was beginning to think they had been living on two separate islands.

'Oh don't get me wrong, I loved it!' answered Elizabeth. 'It was an idyllic place to live. Lots of sunshine, lovely people, peaceful way of life. What more could you want?'

What more indeed.

When she finally got off the bus, Millicent went into the newsagent's and bought herself a large exercise book. It had a silly picture of a fluffy puppy on it, but that didn't matter too much, this was only going to be the first draft. That was one good thing about London she thought, as she tried to cross the road without being run over, the shops were open late. Never shut, in fact. She still couldn't get used to the twenty-four-hourness of Ladbroke Grove. When she first got here, she'd thought there was about to be a riot, everyone seemed so restless. They were all out in the street most of the night. Now she knew that it was like this all the time. Sleeping had been a problem at first, but she had purchased some earplugs from the chemist which had helped a little. Not that they had managed to drown out the noise of Della and her boyfriend.

Ah Della, sighed Millicent as she let herself into the flat. What are we going to do with you? So beautiful and smooth on the outside, so ugly and prickly within. When she had first seen her daughter at the airport, she had been taken aback at her beauty. She was taller and slimmer than she'd expected, with the face of an angel, under all that make-up. She'd found it difficult to look at Della completely and honestly for a while, it was almost too much to take in, it was like staring into a bright light. Her cheeky little girl had turned into a beautiful brown woman with fine, sloping features and a naturally graceful way about her; if she wore proper clothes she would look so – well, elegant, poised. It seemed incredible that she (and he) had created something so perfect, and yet of course it wasn't.

She'd discovered pretty soon that Ellen had not done as good a job as Millicent had hoped, and Della was one of these modern girls who could not communicate properly. She was impolite and ill-mannered, completely self-centred.

This had to change. Millicent was determined about that. She was here now, she would make sure it happened.

'I'm home!' Millicent called out as she stepped through the door. (She'd learnt to give Della some warning.) She was out, of course. Probably gadding about with that man of hers. Millicent took off her coat and folded it up neatly, placing it on the back of the sofa. She put the kettle on and opened the fridge door to get the milk out. All those bottles of champagne were still there, queuing up for something to celebrate. Their twinkling chilled green glass made them seem very tempting especially as she'd never tasted proper French champagne before, but Millicent knew she wasn't going to have a drink today, maybe tomorrow. She hoped Della hadn't inherited the alcoholic gene, it was probably still too early to tell. But I expect she'll drink them all in one go once I've found somewhere else to live, thought Millicent. Well bad luck, Missy, you've got a long wait ahead of you. I'm not leaving until we've got you back on the straight and narrow.

Fancy her daughter being a thief. She'd tried to confront her about it, of course, but Della had just laughed it off and said Jessica had it coming to her. It had been quite a surprise to discover that the two girls knew each other in the first place, but a real shock to find out that Della had stolen all the birthday presents from her party.

'Serves her b***** right for calling you a thief, Mum,' Della had said as she unwrapped each package the next morning, throwing the cards and paper away but keeping the contents. She'd even offered Millicent a very nice silk scarf, but of course she couldn't accept it.

Millicent had tried to explain that the misunderstanding had been sorted out in the end, but Della wouldn't listen. She just didn't seem to understand. She had even quoted the Old Testament, 'an eye for an eye and all that', and Millicent had naturally pointed out that the New Testament told them to turn the other cheek. She would have fetched the confirmation bible from Della's bedroom to prove it, but realized this would let her daughter know that she knew its true contents. She'd been horrified at that discovery, recognized the marijuana immediately – you had to know all about this kind of thing if you were running a school, keep one step ahead. But she was trying to follow her sponsor's advice, and years of experience in dealing with naughty children told her to wait, wait, wait. Collect your information and use it at the right time. Which was going to be very soon. In the meantime, she had allowed Della to get away with some very disrespectful behaviour.

As she had always explained to her pupils when one had been bullying another, people were only unkind to others when they were hurting inside themselves. Which meant that Della was very unhappy indeed.

She'd gathered bits and pieces, of course, after Della came back home on the evening of her birthday in a very distressed state. Millicent had known to keep quiet, just watch the drama unfold. She'd sat there, pretending to watch a blasphemous comedy about a woman vicar on the television. The telephone had rung and rung and rung, with her friend Nancy's voice coming out of the tape recorder, asking – no begging – Della to speak to her. But

Della had shut herself in her bedroom and wasn't coming out.

Then she'd heard her speaking to somebody, and so Millicent had carefully tiptoed down the corridor, avoiding the squeaky bits (she'd worked out where they were one day when Della was out) to listen at the door. She was arranging to meet someone at the chemist, of all places. And then they were going to check into an hotel. What a terrible waste of money, she had a perfectly good bed here. Though maybe she wouldn't mind if her mother slept there instead, just one night in a proper bed would be nice.

As Della said goodbye to her friend, Millicent had ducked into the bathroom to use the lavatory and locked the door. This had caused Della to become extremely agitated, as she wanted yet another bath before she went out. She had lost her temper, called her own mother a b******. Which was technically true, her parents hadn't been married when she was born, but this was the Caribbean way. Millicent had realized that she was perfectly entitled to call Della the same name back, but chose not to.

Since then, relations between them had really deteriorated. Ignoring her mother's suggestion of replacing Nancy with Barbara, Della avoided her as much as possible. She kept just the right side of civil when they did meet, but only just. Millicent was going to have to make her move soon as it had been a few months now, but she'd decided at the time to let her daughter get over this latest upset, patch it up with the boyfriend, feel a little better inside before she confronted her. That's what she'd told Nancy, when she'd come round to the flat the next day looking for her friend. 'Just leave it for a while, my dear, let things blow over,' she'd advised. The poor girl hadn't told her what had happened of course, but she didn't need to. It was written all over her guilty face. And besides, having sexual relations with the wrong man was something Millicent knew all about.

The next day, she decided to make a start on her masterpiece after *This Morning* had finished. She'd grown to like this programme, it was nice to see a happily married couple on the television for a change. They were pleasant people with a good moral code. Also, it provided her with quite a clear picture of exactly what was going on in this country. She'd managed to find a very good station called Radio 4 on Della's transistor radio which was most informative and entertaining too – it had some of her favourite panel games from the World Service on occasionally; but she had to remember to re-tune it when she'd finished listening as Della liked to keep her wireless permanently tuned to Capital 95.8FM.

Not that she was one to sit in front of the television all morning of course, that would be a terrible waste of God's precious hours. No, she'd have it on while she was tidying the place up, get it nice for Della when she came home. Millicent decided to gut the kitchenette this morning, just in case there was a cockroach infestation there after all. She hadn't seen any yet. They were much better at hiding over here, probably didn't like the cold.

'Coming up,' said Judy, who was looking very nice today in a smart navy-blue suit teamed with a pale-pink blouse, 'we've got an update on our slimmers, actor Simon Matthews is popping in for a chat, and there's a chance to win a trip to Paris on the Eurostar.'

'That's after the break!' said Richard, smiling his cheeky grin. Millicent hummed along to the tune they used before the adverts came on as she started to open the cupboards. She realized that she hadn't heard herself sing for ages, apart from when she was at church of course. Good, she'd hummed all the time as she pottered about the house back home, she must be feeling a bit better.

Trying to ignore the commercials, as she didn't intend to be bamboozled into buying items she neither wanted nor needed, she began to empty out the contents of what was now the larder cupboard onto the worktop, checking for anything past its expiry date – as advised by Richard and Judy's cook on the Hygiene In The Home report last week. This was a good thing, she thought, mentally awarding Britain a tick, the date-stamping idea; it would keep those weevils at bay.

She checked the flour for the tiny insects. No, there wouldn't be any here yet as she'd bought it herself quite recently, on Della's birthday in actual fact. She'd decided to make Della a twenty-first birthday cake, which she'd taken great trouble with. She'd even taken the bus for a special trip to the library that day to borrow a cake cookbook. She'd found a marvellous one by a lady called Jane Asher, and this had inspired Millicent to make Della's in the shape of a lovely blue hairdryer. But she hadn't had the chance to surprise her with it, as planned. Della had brought another one home with her which she'd insisted on taking to Ellen's and so Millicent's had remained in the fridge. (She wasn't even sure Della had seen hers, she hadn't said anything about it if she had.) Then Ellen had insisted on them taking the other one home again as she didn't want cake in the house, they'd only eat it. It had really been very tasty. Which was just as well. Not wishing to see good food go to waste, Millicent had had to eat both cakes very quickly before the cream went off. Slim chance of someone baking a cake for her today, unless Della was going to buy one on her way home. Not very likely. She probably didn't even know it was her mother's birthday. Ellen certainly wouldn't have told her, Millicent thought with some dismay. How the mighty have fallen – if things had been as they were supposed to be at home, the headmistress's fiftieth birthday would have been declared a school holiday and there would have been at least a concert to celebrate.

'Welcome back,' said Richard, as he replaced his coffee cup on the table and smiled at Judy sitting proudly beside him. He turned to face the man on the sofa. 'Now he hasn't been on our screens for a while, but actor Simon Matthews is here with us today. Hi, Simon!'

'Hi Richard, how are you?' Millicent was appalled to see that the Pickle from Branston had expired two months ago.

'Fine thanks, fine,' replied Richard. 'Now we haven't seen you on the box for ages, where've you been?'

'Well after I left *Knock*, I did lots of important theatre work –' Simon began.

'Actually,' interrupted Judy, 'we should explain to our younger viewers what you mean by *Knock*, shouldn't we?'

Millicent could imagine Judy shooting one of her Looks to her husband, even though she wasn't watching.

'Yes, Simon, d'you want to tell us?' said Richard, deflecting the issue with his customary charm.

'Well,' said the actor, '*Postman's Knock* was a very popular drama series that was first made by the BBC about twelve years ago –'

'Gosh,' interjected Judy, 'was it that long ago? I didn't realize!'

'Yes, it's been a while now,' said the actor. 'Makes you feel quite old, doesn't it?'

'Huh, you speak for yourself!' said Richard. 'I can barely remember it.'

'Oh don't be so silly,' said Judy, 'honestly!'

'Anyway,' continued Simon, a bit tetchily Millicent thought, 'it was set in a post office – this was in the days before Royal Mail, of course – and I played Robbie, the heart-throb postman.'

'That's right,' said Judy, 'you were always having affairs with the housewives on your rounds, weren't you? I seem to remember one very sexy scene, quite daring for the time, we saw your bare bottom bobbing up and down –'

'Now now!' said Richard. Quite right, thought Millicent, it's only eleven o'clock in the morning. She'd have to wipe the lid of the tomato ketchup, it was revolting. May be better to soak it.

'That wasn't all I did, of course,' said the actor. 'It was a very demanding part in many ways. There was one episode, for example, where my mother had died – which is why I'm –'

'Oh yes, I remember that one,' said Richard. 'Hadn't she been burnt to death in a yachting accident or something?'

This rang a bell with Millicent. She had a distant memory of something like this being the talk of the island at one point. She'd never been one to bother with the television much (even though Mother had liked it on all the time) as the man who had the satellite dish they were all linked up to had the irritating habit of switching channels when he got bored, so you seldom got to see the end of anything. They'd all been up in arms because they never found out who started the fire. She turned round to have a look.

'. . . totally improbable, of course,' the actor was saying. Millicent realized with horror that this was the man who had been making improper suggestions to Della on her birthday. He had been standing right here, in this very room. No wonder she'd thought he looked familiar at the time. And now here he was on Richard and Judy! She came out from behind the breakfast bar to get a better look.

'Tell us about Jessica Rose,' said Judy, 'she's your sister-in-law, isn't she?'

What? This was like something from *The Young and The Restless*. Millicent decided she'd better sit down.

'Um, well yes,' replied Simon who looked nearly as shocked as Millicent felt. 'How did you know that?'

'Oh you can't keep much from us!' said Richard, tapping the side of his nose. 'How's she doing?' he asked, looking concerned.

'Well I don't really know, we haven't heard from her — she sort of disappeared after that night.' Yes, she did, thought Millicent, who also hadn't seen her since. And just as well – the newspapers had been full of all sorts of terrible stories, which Millicent hoped weren't true. And she'd been asked some very personal questions by reporters waiting outside Jessica's flat when she'd gone there a few days later. But she hadn't told them anything of course, it wasn't any of her business or indeed theirs – she despised all gossip.

'Were you at that party?' asked Judy.

'Well yes, but I'd left before it happened. Anyway –'

'So did she appear to be on drugs?'

'Um, I don't know, I didn't really talk to her, there were so many people there. Can I –'

'Yes, we were invited actually,' said Richard, 'glad we didn't go now.'

'Yes, well we didn't really know her, did we?' said Judy with a shudder. 'But when you do see her, Simon, please pass on our best wishes, won't you?'

'Yes,' said Richard, looking into the camera, 'get well soon, Jessica, if you're watching.'

Millicent was amazed – fancy this nice couple being actually invited to that sort of a party, a Bacchanalian orgy like that. And everybody seemed to know each other. She was beginning to think that London was just one big village after all.

The actor looked uncomfortable. 'Can I talk about my mother now?' he asked. Millicent hoped she didn't know her as well, that would be just too much.

'Yes, of course,' said Judy, 'that's why you're here, isn't it?'

'Yes' – Richard now – 'I gather you have an interesting tale to tell?'

'Well it's a bit of a mystery, actually.' He settled down, relishing the limelight, Millicent thought to herself. Obviously this man was a bit of a show-off.

'My father died some years ago –'

'We're sorry to hear that,' interjected Richard.

'Thanks – yes, it was a terrible wrench,' said the actor, looking sad. 'But my mother passed away quite recently –'

'Oh dear,' said Judy.

'Yes, makes me an orphan now.' He put on a little boy face. Millicent decided she didn't like him. 'But when I was going through her papers, I discovered a letter she'd written to me to be read after her death. I have it here, in fact. I can read it to you if you like?'

'No, I think we can do better than that,' said Richard. 'Can we roll VT?' he said to nobody in particular.

Some swirly music came on, and the letter came up on the screen. It had been written in ballpoint pen on lined paper, Millicent noticed with disapproval, and was lying on a background of pale-blue satin, held down at the corners by a pair of knitted baby bootees, a dummy and a rattle.

'Dear Simon,' said a thin, reedy woman's voice in what Millicent now recognized to be a Scotch accent – there seemed to be so many of them in London there can't be many left in Scotland, she thought. 'I feel it is my duty as your mother to let you know that you are not my son. Your father and I were not able [unable, Millicent couldn't help herself] to have children of our own and so I asked God to help me.' [Forgiven.]

The music swirled on. 'My prayers were answered when one day an angel brought you to me. You were a miracle boy, and we loved you as if you were our own. I hope you feel we gave you a happy childhood. Even though we were never rich, we gave your our hearts which is more than money can buy. We did our best, son.'

New paragraph, the violins soared higher. 'I felt you should know about this, even if your father didn't want you to. I have lived with this secret for many years and now it is yours. I am not able [hmm] to give you any information on your real parents, as the angel would not tell me, he had been sworn to secretcy. [Secretcy? Oh dear.] I am sorry about this, but please know in your heart that you were a special boy, one of God's chosen children.'

The music rose higher and higher, now at its peak, surely. 'If you are reading this, it means I have passed on. Your father and I will be waiting for you in heaven. We always loved you. That is true. Until we meet again, be a good boy and love your family with all your heart. Mum'

Back to the studio. 'That's just so moving,' said Judy, as she wiped away a tear. Millicent thought it badly constructed, but the sentiment was there all the same.

'So how can we help you, Simon?' asked Richard.

'Well,' he replied, 'once I'd got over the shock of it all, I decided that I would like to trace my birth parents. Not that they could ever take the place of my real ones, you understand.'

'No, quite,' said Judy, as she regained her composure.

'So how far have you got?' asked Richard.

'Nowhere very fast,' replied Simon. 'I've tried everything I can think of, I've tried all the usual channels plus a few strange ones via the internet, I've even set my alarm to call

Australia in the middle of the night, see if they've got anything about me over there. I'm determined to find out who I really am, you see, where I came from. But the trouble is, my birth certificate has my normal parents' names on it, which I've since found out means that it must have been an illegal adoption, not done through the usual channels. So all the various professional agencies I've been in contact with haven't been able to help me, as they've got absolutely nothing to go on.'

'So it would have been done within the family, perhaps?' asked Richard, he was so intelligent.

'Well maybe, I don't know.'

'Have you tried asking your other relations?' said Judy.

'That's the trouble, there don't seem to be any still alive. We were a very insular family. And none of her friends know anything about this, I've asked everyone who knew her and they always presumed I was their son, as did I. I do have a vague memory of my mother talking about a brother who'd moved from Glasgow down to London' – told you so, said Millicent to herself, they all do – 'but I think they must have fallen out or lost touch as she didn't seem to have any contact with him. Or maybe he died, I don't know. Her friends couldn't throw any light on that either.'

'The plot thickens,' said Richard. 'So let's get all the facts together, and perhaps we can jog the memory of one of our many viewers into helping you piece this puzzle together.' He turned to the camera. 'So if you were living in – Glasgow, wasn't it?' Simon nodded. 'About what, forty years ago?'

'Thirty-seven,' said Simon firmly.

'And you knew the Matthews family –'

'Actually that's my stage name,' said Simon. 'My father's name was Ferguson and my mother's maiden name was McArthur.' He cleared his throat. 'And my Christian name was Sean, middle name Donald.'

'As in where's your troosers?' asked Judy brightly. Millicent didn't understand why, but they all laughed.

'Yes, OK then,' continued Richard, 'now if any of that means anything to you and you remember the family, or are able to help Simon in his search in any way – perhaps you know the angel who brought him as a baby to his parents –'

'You never know, his real mother might be watching,' said Judy.

'Yes, or even that, stranger things have happened on this show!' said Richard. 'So please, if you can help do call our switchboard and we'll pass any information you have on to Simon.'

'And you will come back to tell us how you get on, won't you?' asked Judy.

'Of course,' said Simon, 'I'd be glad to.'

'Moving on, fascinating story there, cheers, Simon,' said the urbane Richard as he got up, 'now – let's go over to the weigh-in and see how much our guinea pigs have lost this week.'

Really, thought Millicent, this country is so weight-obsessed they're even putting their pets on diets. She got up and went back into the kitchen to tackle the dirty-mug situation with a bottle of trusty bleach.

Della came home later on, and Millicent told her about Simon's appearance, calling him her 'client' – she didn't want to give anything away just yet.

Della had pretended not to be interested. Millicent told her of his search for his real mother, who had given him away when he was just a baby.

'For f****'s sake, not that again,' said Della. 'He goes on about it all the time. I wouldn't want to know if I was him. I mean, what kind of woman would do a thing like that?'

As it was a Thursday afternoon, Millicent went over to Jessica's flat as usual. Even though she hadn't seen the girl for some time, not since that shocking photograph had been splashed all over the papers, she still went there each week. Just to keep an eye on things really; even though Millicent disapproved of her behaviour, she felt some kind of loyalty towards this wayward girl. She knew how it felt to be the subject of people's talk through your own wrongdoing, fairly or unfairly. Jessica would be very grateful for her support and advice when she did eventually resurface, Millicent was sure of that.

She let herself in through the front door and sorted through the mail, which had been left scattered around the doormat as usual. The ground-floor flat door opened and a scruffy old man in a very dirty vest said, 'Where's she gone, then?'

'I don't know,' replied Millicent. 'She'll be back soon, I'm sure.'

'Better 'ad be,' he said, 'they keep on coming round 'ere, all hours of the day and night. I'm sick of it.'

'Still? You'd think they'd be tired of it all by now, wouldn't you?'

'That's what I said. I've told 'em everything I know, but they still want more.'

'Oh well,' Millicent sighed, moving towards the stairs, 'today's news, tomorrow's fish and chip paper.'

'They've not been allowed to do that for years now,' said the old man after her. 'EEC, innit. Where've you been, living in a cave?' Feels like that sometimes, thought Millicent as he slammed his door.

As soon as she got into Jessica's flat, she saw that it was exactly as she had left it the week before. She had to admit, she was a bit disappointed. Like the rest of the country, she wanted to know where Jessica had been all this time.

She hung up her coat and hat on the hooks on the back of the door, and placed the letters and business cards left by members of the press on the coffee table, along with the others.

The flat had taken on a completely different personality without its owner, Millicent thought to herself. She had taken Jessica's absence as a good opportunity to give it a very thorough spring clean. She'd tidied and folded all the clothes in the bedroom, sorting out what belonged in the drawers and what should live in the cupboard. As there was not enough furniture to accommodate all the clothing, she had cast her beady eye over each item and made three separate piles on the bed of what needed dry cleaning, what needed mending, and what was only in a fit state to be given to the poor. There had been some pretty peculiar stuff in that bedroom, which clearly didn't belong in there

– she'd placed the electrical items back in the drawer with the other kitchen gadgets. And under the bed there had been some things she didn't want to think about even now, they had been disposed of accordingly.

The bathroom was sparkling and so was the kitchen, but Millicent still poured most of a bottle of bleach down the drains in order to keep the germs at bay. She watered the plants in the sitting room, and indulged in a little chat with the rubber plant, which was looking rather forlorn. Prince Charles had said it was a good idea to talk to them, and so Millicent began to tell it the sad news from home.

There was a loud buzz from somewhere. Millicent stood upright with alarm, even though she knew no one could see what she'd been doing. There it was again, it seemed to be coming from the telephone on the wall by the door into the flat. She picked it up and said hello, but it just buzzed again, very loudly, right into her ear. She said hello again, louder this time – nothing. She decided to ignore it, it wouldn't be for her anyway, and replaced the receiver.

Then she heard the old man downstairs swearing loudly as he came out of his flat and shuffled along the hallway. Millicent opened Jessica's door an inch, so that she could hear what was going on.

'Is there nobody up there?' she heard a lady's voice say.

'I've told you people before,' the man said, 'she's not 'ere. Now b***** off.'

'I am well aware of that, it's not her I've come to see.' This lady sounded very authoritative.

'Well the darkie's up there, if that's what you mean.'

'That's really not a term you should be using in this day

and age,' said the woman as she must have pushed past him. Millicent realized to her horror that she was coming up the stairs and quickly shut Jessica's door.

'Hello? Are you in there?' Now she was knocking sharply on the door.

Taking a deep breath, Millicent opened it and said, 'I can't help you with your enquiries. I'm sorry. Good day.'

But the elegant woman who looked just like Joan Collins from *Dynasty* put her hand on the door as Millicent tried to close it and said, 'Ah, you must be Millicent. I'm Constance Rose. Jessica's mother.'

'. . . wonders with the place!' Constance was saying as she did a tour of the flat while Millicent waited for the kettle to boil. 'I never realized this carpet was such good quality. Typical Jessica, living above her means.'

'Do you mind taking it black?' asked Millicent from the kitchen. 'There is no milk.'

'That'll be fine,' replied Constance, 'I'll drink anything. No sugar for me, though – constant battle with the bulge, I'm afraid.' She sat down on one end of the sofa. 'It even smells better in here now. I do hate smoking, don't you?'

'Oh yes,' replied Millicent as she brought in the mugs, 'it's a disgusting habit. And so bad for your health, as well.' The two women shook their heads and tutted at the same time, which made them smile at each other. As Millicent sat herself down on the other end of the sofa, she said to Constance, 'I'm always telling my daughter to give up, but she won't listen. Della. Do you know her?'

'I don't think I do, no. Should I?'

'Well she lives here in London.'

'Good lord, Millicent!' Constance laughed. 'London's a big city, we don't know everyone who lives here!' She fixed her piercing blue eyes on the big black woman. 'You don't come from London yourself, I take it?'

'No, I'm from the Caribbean, a small island called Montserrat. It's near Antigua, just –'

'Yes, yes I know where it is, we went on holiday to Antigua many years ago, before it became spoilt by tourism of course . . . wasn't there a volcano there? I remember my husband saying all the beaches were black.' She looked as if she liked her beaches white.

'Yes, that's why I had to leave, because of –'

'The volcano?' finished Constance. 'That's right, of course, I remember reading about it, watching the news reports. Dreadful business. It must have been awful for you. I can't even begin to imagine how it must feel to have your home destroyed in that way.'

'No. It was a terrible thing,' said Millicent. And it all came pouring out, she couldn't stop it, just like the lava, rocks and ash that had covered two-thirds of the island during those last few years.

She told Constance how she and her mother had been forced to abandon their home in the south of the island and go to the north, sleeping on the floor of her own office in the very school she had been in charge of, now a shelter for others rendered homeless by the choking, scorching path of the angry Soufrière.

How everyone had tried so hard to keep their spirits up

at first, but it had become harder as the volcano reclaimed more and more of the island. She'd done her best to keep the school going, for the children's sake, but as the situation worsened more and more of the families evacuated, leaving only a small minority behind to make the best of a terrible situation. Many of those had wanted to leave, but didn't have the means, they had lost everything. The buildings that had been made of concrete were still standing, just about, but anything of value inside had been burnt. She told Constance that the remaining Montserratians were brave people. Many had decided to see it as a privilege to have experienced this, none of their ancestors had seen anything like it. And most of the men had elected to stay on the streets, they were too proud to live in the makeshift shelters with the women and children. Even the Tourist Board, in an attempt to entice visitors back to the island, had tried to turn the live volcano into an attraction by describing the 'wonderful glow at night'. Everyone had tried to make the best of their bad situation, despite their personal losses.

'Did many people die?' asked Constance, who Millicent could see was very interested in what she had to say.

'Nineteen poor souls perished in the biggest explosion,' Millicent explained. 'The scientists told those who wanted to hear that they hadn't stood a chance. It came at them at 100 miles per hour, at a temperature of 800 degrees centigrade. Their clothes would have caught fire straight-away, and they would only be able to take two breaths before the blood in their lungs suffocated them. They were burnt alive in seconds.'

'What a ghastly way to go.' Constance shuddered at the thought. 'Did you ever get back to your house?' She seemed to be fascinated.

'Well, we weren't supposed to go back to that side of the island – it was declared unsafe, and if the police caught you that meant you had to pay a fine, or get a two-year custodial sentence. That wasn't as much of a threat as it once was, however; the prison had been reduced to rubble.'

'So you did go back, then?'

Millicent was grateful for this opportunity, she realized she hadn't talked about it properly since she arrived here. 'Yes, just before I left the island. I hitched a ride on a speedboat that was taking a journalist there. I felt I had nothing more to lose. If there had been another pyroclastic flow while I was in the area, then the good Lord would take me within four minutes, and I was finally ready to go. Besides, I was a property owner. It wasn't a big house, of course, just a modest bungalow but I was still paying the mortgage. The bank kept up their demands, but the insurance company cancelled our policies. The building society quickly declared itself bankrupt.'

'How appallingly typical,' said Constance, who was not as shocked at this as Millicent had been. 'So what did you find when you got there?'

'Well, we lived just beyond Government House, near St Patrick's, so I had to go through Plymouth, the capital, to get there. I had to walk very quickly, because the ash stays hot for a long time after each eruption and I could feel it burning through the big hiking boots I had borrowed for the purpose.'

Constance smiled. She is a very sympathetic woman, thought Millicent. And a good listener – she liked that.

'It was like a ghost town that had been covered in a thick grey carpet, over a foot high in some places. There were twisted telegraph poles lying in the streets, a few foolish dogs and donkeys roaming around, sniffing the carcasses of other animals that had already died. There was an eerie silence everywhere, so different from the usual hubbub. The shops were all smashed up, melted, useless now even though the signs were still up on the walls, advertising their wares. The door to the red telephone box in the centre of town had been jammed shut with ash, and the clocks on the war memorial had stopped. I didn't notice much more than that because I wanted to get up the hill to my home.'

'And did you?'

'No.' Millicent paused, trying to swallow away the lump in her throat. 'It was too hot, I was choking in the dust and the sulphur. My feet were burning. I had to turn back.'

'So you never saw your home again?'

'No.' The frustration and disappointment was too much now as it had been then, and much to Millicent's alarm she began to cry. 'I'm sorry, I –'

'You carry on.' Constance rummaged in her big handbag and produced a Kleenex. 'Do you good, get it all out.'

'I just wanted –' Millicent couldn't hold back now. 'I just wanted to see my home for the last time. I had worked so hard for it, I couldn't believe I had lost everything. And I wanted to take something from our house with me, anything I could find that had belonged to my mother.'

'Had she been burnt to death?'

'No, no,' Millicent dabbed her eyes, 'she hung on until the bitter end. It was the insanitation of the living conditions that killed her in the end, though some might say it was old age. It was ironic in many ways, before the eruption we were just about to open our brand-new hospital, which had cost the British Government thirty million pounds to build. But it was in Plymouth, so it never got used.' She blew her nose. 'That was why I finally decided to leave. I had buried my mother and it was time to say goodbye to the island. I hadn't seen my daughter for many years and I had just enough money left for a one-way air ticket here. If I'd stayed any longer I would never have been able to afford to leave. So – here I am.' She tried to smile.

'Your daughter didn't live with you?' She looked surprised.

'No – she has been living over here with my sister since she was a little girl.' Constance looked even more surprised, she had better justify that. 'It's quite normal for parents to do that in the Caribbean, it happens all the time.'

'So you were reunited with your daughter, at least. So there is a happy ending after all?' asked Constance.

Millicent hoped she wasn't going to cry again. 'I'm hoping there will be soon. Della has not turned out to be the way I would have liked.'

'Yes, well, I know how that feels,' said Constance.

'Oh my goodness, I am so sorry,' said Millicent, pulling herself back into the present day. 'Here am I carrying on about my troubles, when we haven't even mentioned your Jessica.'

'Doesn't matter at all,' soothed Constance, 'other

people's problems are so much more interesting than your own, aren't they?'

'Is she all right?' ventured Millicent.

'Oh yes, she's surviving. Always has, always will – as long as it's at someone else's expense. She's hidden away in The Priory at the moment, which is costing a fortune, and she's expecting me to pay for it, if you please!'

Millicent was shocked. 'You have to pay over here, for someone to join a religious order?'

Constance laughed and looked at Millicent with a twinkle in her eye. 'Well anyway, she told me you might be here today, so I've come to get the keys and settle up with you. I presume she owes you money?' Millicent nodded.

Looking around the room, Constance declared, 'I must say, I do think you've done a marvellous job. It can't have been easy, my daughter has the living habits of a slattern. It's probably my fault for paying people to pick up after her when she was a child. You've managed to get it looking far better than it ever did while she was here. Well done!' She beamed at Millicent, who was pleased to have someone notice her hard work at last.

'In fact . . .' Constance continued, looking closely at Millicent, 'what are your present circumstances? Are you looking for a proper job?'

'I would like to use my qualifications and time in a more useful way, certainly.'

'Well I can't promise you it would be an educational position, though perhaps we could learn a thing or two from each other,' Constance smiled. 'You see, my beloved housekeeper has just died on me. She was an old family friend; it was a great shock, totally devastating in many ways.' Constance paused, obviously still feeling the pain of losing a loved one. 'But my point is this – I'm looking for someone to fill the position. I've been trying to find a replacement for some time now, but I won't just hire any old body and I seem to have interviewed all the old bodies in London. I desperately need someone who would be capable of doing the job properly – I take it you cook?'

'Of course, if I can find the right ingredients.' Millicent wasn't too enthusiastic, she'd wanted to move on to some kind of teaching position next; but not being one to look a gift-horse in the mouth, she decided to hear the lady out.

'And it's quite clear that you clean to an excellent standard.'

'I try to do everything as well as I possibly can.'

'Yes,' continued Constance, 'I could tell that straightaway, soon as I saw you.' Millicent blossomed at this praise. At last, someone as discerning as herself.

'You see, I think we would be good company for each other. You're obviously a well-educated person – not at all as Jessica described you to me – and to be quite honest I get a little lonely sometimes, rattling about in my house all on my own. It would suit both of us perfectly: I would be providing you with board and lodging and a good wage – I always say that if you pay peanuts, you get monk – anyway, in return you would be my housekeeper and companion.' She flashed Millicent a winning smile. 'What d'you think?'

'Well . . .' Millicent wasn't sure.

'You're not sure, are you? Well perhaps you should give

it a go, just for the meantime. And if you don't like it, then we could always find you something else.'

It was the 'we' that did it. Suddenly Millicent felt as if she wasn't going to be so alone in this world any more. This woman was offering her a home and a job and extending the hand of friendship all at the same time. She had visions of them reading the same books, going on outings to places of historical interest, discussing world events by the fire when they were snowed-in, looking after each other through the long winter nights she'd heard so much about, and had been dreading.

'I would be happy to accept your kind offer, thank you.' As soon as she said it, Millicent could feel God lift an enormous weight from her shoulders.

'Excellent!' Constance leapt to her feet and clapped her hands in delight. 'You can move in tonight. I think we're going to get on like a house on – er, famously – don't you?'

Instead of going straight home, Millicent had decided to pay Ellen a visit. Tell her the good news. Maybe they would get to talk properly for once, they hadn't really had a good old chat since Millicent got here. This would give her something to smile about. She was really a very grumpy woman these days, not at all how she used to be – well, before Edric died. She was a lively girl then, with a great big laugh to match her great big personality – and now she seemed worn out, dull, lethargic, far older than her forty-one years.

But if I was surprised when I saw her again, I wonder what she thought of me? Was I as she imagined? Millicent thanked the good Lord once again for her sobriety. She was pleased with the progress she had made over the years; she'd learnt from the twelve-step programme to let go, let God. And today, her patience was being rewarded. He did indeed move in mysterious ways – who would have thought that cleaning up after that naughty girl would lead to this new development?

As she walked past the houses in Ellen and Desmond's road, she could hear the usual loud thumpings coming out onto the street, each house moving to a different beat. All Saints Road indeed, Millicent said to herself. Whoever had decided to call it that obviously had no idea that its inhabitants would lead such ungodly lives. It was like this day and night. She didn't know how Ellen could stand it.

But today it didn't bother Millicent so much. Strange, she thought, something good happens to you and it changes your whole view of the world in a split second. She noticed for the first time that September day that the sun was out. Her feet didn't feel as heavy as usual, she was walking with a little spring in her step. She breathed in the crisp, cold air and thanked the Lord that now she would be able to afford some warmer underwear.

She even managed to bid good afternoon to a couple of grumpy teenagers lurking on a wall, who didn't look up from staring intently into the little machines they were holding in their hands, which were beeping of course. They didn't even bother to acknowledge her greeting. Well that's their problem, she thought, if they choose to miss out on their education for the sake of going blind. Heavens above, she was in a good mood! She hummed 'Abide With

Me' the rest of the way, to feel closer to God and further away from the madness of this street.

Having tried to close the wrought-iron gate behind her, but not managing to as it obviously hadn't been oiled yet this year, she walked up the leaf-strewn path and rang the doorbell. She decided to have a big smile on her face for whoever opened the door.

Nothing happened. She rang the bell once more. She knew they were in, Felix's record player was on full blast, as ever, inflicting his taste in so-called music onto the whole street from the attic window. And the television was on in the front room, she could see the cartoons flickering through the net curtains. Michael was probably in his usual catatonic trance in the armchair in the bay window. As she looked up to Ellen and Desmond's bedroom above, she thought she saw the curtains flicker. They were closed, or had just been closed. Third time lucky? Still no answer.

If they had the sense to have a door knocker I would use it, Millicent thought as she bent down as far as her well-covered knees would let her and peered through the letter box.

She could see right past the stairs down into the kitchen where Barbara was studying like the good student she was at the kitchen table, with her back to the door.

'Michael!' she called out to her brother, without looking up. No reply. Barbara tried again, louder. 'Mi-chael!' she shouted at the ceiling. Nothing. He's in the front room, Millicent wanted to tell her, but she didn't have to as the young girl slammed her pen down and shut her book in frustration. She got up, and so Millicent let the letter box go and stood up smiling, ready for the door to open now.

But it still didn't do that. She heard Barbara in the front room now, shouting at her younger brother. 'Are you deaf or what?' Millicent moved slightly nearer the window, headmistress's ears on full bionic alert.

'Well answer the door, then.'

'No.'

'Why not? You're nearer to it than I am.'

'Because Mum said not to.'

'When?'

'Last week.'

'What, so we never answer the door again?'

'Not when it's Aunt Millicent.'

Aunt Millicent felt as if he had stabbed her. 'Oh for god's sake,' said Barbara, 'this is stupid. I'm going to let her in.'

Millicent sprang back onto the doormat. She wasn't going to let an eleven-year-old ill-mannered boy spoil her day, and so she put on a very happy face.

The door opened. 'Hi, Aunt Millicent, what a nice surprise!' said Barbara, also with a very happy face. 'How are you?'

'I'm just fine, thank you, Barbara. And you?'

'Oh you know, studying all the time, as usual.'

'It'll be well worth it in the end, you'll see,' Millicent reassured her.

'Hope so.'

'Is it all right to come in?'

'Oh, yes, sorry, of course,' said Barbara, as she turned and walked back down into the kitchen, kicking the front-room door really hard with her right leg as she passed. Millicent closed the front door behind her, and pushed the snib down on the lock, just in case. She followed Barbara into the kitchen.

'Is your mother here?' asked Millicent as she removed her hat and unbuttoned her coat.

'Yes, she's upstairs,' replied the young girl, packing her books away into a dirty green rucksack.

'She's asleep,' said Michael, who had come to lurk in the doorway.

'No she's not,' said Barbara, glaring at the young boy who appeared to be wearing clothes that must belong to his older brother, they were far too big for him. 'She's only just gone up. Go upstairs and get her, Michael.'

'But –'

'Now!' said Barbara, with an authority Millicent admired.

He actually went. 'You'll make a good teacher, Barbara,' said Millicent. If only Della was more like her cousin.

'That's if I ever pass my exams. Honestly, it's impossible to study round here,' she said as she did up her bag. 'There's so much noise, they don't understand how important this is to me. I wish Mum was more like you.' She lugged it onto her shoulders. 'I sometimes think Della and me must have been swopped at birth!'

Della and I. A sizeable part of Millicent often wished they had been. Then Ellen and Della could go around being spiky together and leave her and Barbara to follow their path of learning in peace.

Barbara smiled. 'Hope you don't mind if I don't stay, but I'm going off to the library.'

'Not at all,' replied Millicent, 'I think that's a very good idea.' And, as an afterthought, she called to Barbara as she fiddled with the front-door snib, 'Don't forget, if you need any help, I'm always here!'

'Yes, right, thanks,' Barbara called back as she got it open. 'Bye!' Slam.

While she was waiting for Ellen, Millicent carefully folded up her coat, lining on the outside to protect the fabric, and put it on the back of a chair. She looked around the kitchen and sighed.

They had been burgled twice, as far as Millicent knew. If you were a burglar, she thought, you would never know that this family had come over here from the Caribbean. There were no signs of their heritage at all, this just looked like the kitchen of people who had never even been outside London. She had never once seen them use the Map of Montserrat tea towel she'd sent them one Christmas; or the round oven glove fashioned after the face of a local woman in a spotted headscarf, with coca-cola ring pulls for earrings, made by the old people in the Red Cross home. Even the yellowing toaster had a brown scene of rolling fields and haystacks on it, not a palm tree in sight. The burglar wouldn't even have known they were black.

'Ladies and gentlemen,' said Michael from the doorway, announcing his mother's arrival with arms outstretched, 'Mrs Ellen Dublin!'

'Oh shut up Michael and go and watch the telly,' snapped Ellen as she pushed past him towards the kettle. 'Hello Millicent,' she said, without looking at her sister, as she tightened her dressing gown around her girth, slippers swishing along the lino floor.

'Good afternoon, Ellen,' said Millicent.

'And before you start, I'm working double shifts at the moment. NHS cutbacks, if you know what that means.'

'Of course I do,' said Millicent, who wasn't sure that she did. 'I wasn't going to say anything about you being in your dressing gown at this time of day, Ellen.' She sat down at the table.

'You're staying, then,' said Ellen as she filled up the kettle. 'Tea?'

'No thank you,' said Millicent, who could still remember the inside of her mug from last time, 'I'll have a glass of water instead.'

'What, tap water?'

'Yes please.'

'Have you tasted the London water yet? It's not like the Montserrat stuff –'

'Ah, so you do remember something good about home after all!' Millicent was pleased with herself.

'Oh for God's sake, Millicent, just drop it, will you? I am getting so sick of this. Can you talk of nothing else?' She could obviously tell that her words were hurtful, because she sat down at the other side of the table and looked at her sister with one of her best sympathetic faces. I raised you, I know you too well, thought Millicent.

'Look,' Ellen said, calmly. She'd obviously decided to Say Something Next Time. 'You've just got to let the whole "Back Home" thing go. Start living in the present, leave the past behind. You're a forty-whatever-year-old woman, you've got years ahead of you. You behave like an old person who keeps going on about the good old days.' Fifty today, in actual fact. Half a century. You've forgotten. 'The Montserrat you knew has gone, for ever. Face it, Millicent, it was a tiny island in the middle of nowhere that nobody knew about and nobody cared about.'

'I cared,' said Millicent quietly. 'The people who lived there cared.'

'Yes, I know you did.' Ellen rubbed her face in her hands. 'But what was it famous for? Nothing. No one over here has ever even heard of it! Montserrat's only claim to fame was the recording studios, because Sting and Elton John and people like that went there. And even that wasn't Montserratian music – unless you count Arrow feeling hot hot hot. Come on, Millicent, what is there to be so d***** proud of?'

'Everything.' She was taken aback by the force of what she knew was just her sister's opinion, but it seemed more like a personal attack. Ellen's disloyalty to their home felt like a betrayal. For the second time that day, Millicent thought she was going to cry. 'It was a beautiful place, it had magic.'

'It was a shit-hole! It had too many rats, too many cockroaches, too many termites eating away at our houses. The standard of living was bad, many people had no electricity, there wasn't enough money to go round and so nothing happened there; the people were too lazy to make anything happen, too drunk to care about their surround–'

Sore point. 'It wasn't like that! It changed after you left.'

'No, it didn't, Millicent. You changed. You had to. And don't get me wrong, we're all very glad you did. But you must leave all your memories behind, where they belong.' She looked at the door and lowered her voice. 'Let's face it, some of them are bad ones.'

'No they're not!' How dare Ellen speak to her like this? 'I loved Montserrat, it was perfect!'

'No, Millicent, it wasn't. You just think it was. It's like people are when someone dies, I see it all the time at the hospital. You start to remember them as better than they actually were.'

'And how do you remember Mother, Ellen?'

'What's that got to do with it?'

'Just answer the question.'

'All right, but you're not going to like it.' Ellen took a deep breath. 'I don't like to speak ill of the dead, but she was an old battleaxe who always got her own way. As you well know. She saw us as her slaves. She certainly had you under her thumb.'

'Well she wasn't like that at the end. She was a confused old woman who had no idea of where she was, who she was, what was going on around her. She was incontinent. She couldn't speak. She was almost blind. She relied on me for everything. She would wake up in the night, screaming, not able to tell me what was the matter. You have no idea what it's like having to look after someone like that –'

'Yes I do, it's my job!' Ellen despaired up at her peeling ceiling.

Millicent paused momentarily. 'Well, anyway, the point is that I didn't want to spoil your memory of her. I also decided not to tell you because I didn't want to worry you or make you feel guilty for leaving. Her condition worsened after you left us, you see –'

Ellen stood up and frowned at her sister. 'I hope you're not trying to pin Mother going gaga on me!' Millicent was astounded at her sister's lack of compassion for their mother's demise. 'Look, I'm sorry that you had to deal with it alone, Millicent, I really am, but you know perfectly well that she started to go downhill after Edric died, it had nothing to do with me leaving the island. And of course your little scandal had nothing to do with her decline, I suppose?' She went over to the worktop and flicked the kettle on to boil again. 'Well I'm sorry, I just did what I thought was best at the time.'

'What, leaving me to deal with Mother? Not coming back to see us, as you'd promised? Not even sending any money?'

Ellen spun round, angry. 'We needed every penny we had to bring up your daughter!'

'I sent you money for that.'

'Well it wasn't enough.'

Millicent decided to say this now. 'Is that why you didn't do a very good job?'

Ellen's mouth dropped open and her hands went to her hips. 'And what's that supposed to mean?'

'Well . . .' She'd rehearsed this moment over and over again and now it was here. Lord, please help me. 'She's not a very nice girl, is she? She has no morals, she carries herself badly most of the time and she doesn't seem to know the difference between right and wrong. She's selfish, self-centred and self-obsessed. And she behaves like a common prostitute.'

Ellen raised an eyebrow. 'Like mother, like daughter.'

Millicent's turn now. 'And what exactly is that supposed to mean?'

'I don't think I need to spell it out, do I? Surely you haven't forgotten how she was conceived? Letting a man take advantage of you like that, for a bottle of rum?'

Silence.

Ellen continued. 'I don't believe this! You should be thanking me for what I did for Della — I worked very hard to raise her, we all did; and now you have the nerve to sit here, in my kitchen, and tell me it wasn't good enough! You are unbelievable, Millicent, you really are.' She shook her head in angry disbelief. 'Well while we're telling each other how it really was, you might as well know that we had a very tough time of it over here too. We've had to work very hard for all of this.' She indicated her grubby kitchen. 'As you are now beginning to realize, things are very expensive here. We'd arrived with very little money, if you remember. I had to complete my training, and Desmond didn't earn very much as a postman then, still doesn't in fact. We could hardly support ourselves, let alone three children. We were all living in one room at that time, Millicent, it was tough. We were hardly surviving, there was barely enough to go round.'

Millicent was surprised to hear this, Ellen's letters had been full of how wonderful everything was in London. She had been pleased, smug even, to know she had made the right choice for Della.

'What did you think, that the streets were paved with gold? Well so did we, but we soon found out that wasn't the case. It was hard, really hard. We didn't tell you or anybody back home because we didn't want to worry you.' Ellen laughed without smiling. 'But the point is, Millicent, that Della had exactly the same treatment as Felix and Barbara and then Michael. And Barbara seems to have turned out quite well, don't you think?'

Millicent knew she had to agree. 'So what went wrong with Della?' She couldn't let it go. 'Did you give her enough attention?'

Ellen wasn't going to let it go either. 'Well more than she got from her mother.'

Millicent stood up now. 'What more could I have done, from over there?'

'Looked after your own child, that's what. But no, you were too wrapped up in yourself, your life at the school. Too busy looking after other people's children to bother with your own.'

'That's not true!' This was so unfair. 'I worked very hard to send you that money, I sent every spare cent I had. I wanted her to have everything she needed.'

'Or was it that you thought you might start drinking again, and you wanted her out of the way?'

'How dare you say such a thing!' Millicent grabbed her sister's arm. 'You know perfectly well I had to stay in Montserrat, to look after Mother.'

'Well I wouldn't count on Della looking after you in your old age!' retorted Ellen, shaking herself free from Millicent's grip. 'You get out of people what you put into them, you know.' Ellen snorted. 'That's the sort of thing you used to put in your letters to her, isn't it?' She laughed and shook her head as she rinsed out a dirty cup from the sink.

Then it dawned on Millicent. 'You didn't give them to her, did you?'

Ellen moved past her to open the fridge door. 'No,' she said into it.

Millicent was flabbergasted. Why not? 'Why not?' she demanded.

'Because,' said her stupid, idiotic, supposedly well-meaning younger sister, 'I didn't know if she would ever see you again. I assumed you'd die of cirrhosis of the liver sooner or later. And anyway, you didn't exactly race over here to find out how we were, did you?'

'I couldn't, I –'

'Don't tell me, you had to look after Mother blah blah blah. Well I thought it best for Della to adapt to her new life over here, feel a part of our family, which you had decided was now her family. She couldn't remember much about you anyway. We never talked about you, we didn't want to. You had done enough damage to the family and, for all I knew, could be about to do some more. And besides, she needed food and clothes and trainers, not rambling letters about God. I did give her the confirmation bible though.'

'Yes, I know,' said Millicent, who was outraged at the injustice of her sister's behaviour. This explained so much. 'So you just threw my letters away?' How could Ellen do this? She had spent hours of her precious time composing them, putting all the love she had in her bursting heart for her missing little girl into them, writing them out so carefully, starting again and again if she'd made even one mistake. She'd save up all her news and snippets from the local paper for the first Sunday of every month, then she'd sit down in the evening once Mother was asleep and write until her hand ached.

'No, as a matter of fact I didn't throw them away,' said Ellen carelessly, 'they're in an old shoebox at the back of the cupboard under the stairs. I thought I'd give them back to you if you ever did turn up, let you see for yourself how Della would have just laughed at them. You were so high and mighty! I'd forgotten they were there in fact. You can have them back if you want, they're only cluttering up the place.' Ellen yawned and looked insolently at her sister. 'Now if you don't mind, I'm going to bed.' And off she went with her cup of tea, leaving Millicent just standing there in the kitchen. Dazed.

Eventually, she went into the front room to ask Michael to go into the cupboard and get the box out for her. He wouldn't, he just said, 'What am I, your slave?' So she had to do it herself. She got a certain amount of satisfaction when she noticed the cupboard was also occupied by several cockroaches, and there were plenty of rat droppings there too.

'That's great!' exclaimed Della, once she'd had her tea and Millicent had told her of Mrs Rose's kind offer. 'Fantastic news! Brilliant! B***** h***, I'm really pleased!'

'I thought you might be,' said Millicent.

'There really is a god!' said Della.

286

'Yes, there always has been.'

'So when d'you start?'

'Mrs Rose said I could move in this evening.'

'Right then!' said Della as she turned *Pet Rescue* to mute and sprang up from the sofa. 'We'd better get you all packed up.' She looked at her mother behind the breakfast bar and said brightly, 'I'll help you if you like. Be quicker.'

'Thank you, Della,' replied Millicent, wiping her hands on her apron, 'that's very kind of you.' And she just stopped herself from saying well done. 'But I'm not going to take anything with me.'

'You what?' That pretty little face went into a frown.

'It's a new start. A fresh beginning. She offered me the job as I am, I'm going to take it as I am. Ellen and Barbara were right. It's time to leave those memories behind. I don't need physical reminders anyway, it's all here.' She patted her well-upholstered heart.

'Oh. OK then, fair enough.' She sat down again and turned the volume back up with the remote control. Millicent came out from behind the breakfast bar and walked over to the television which she turned off. 'Oi! I was watching that.'

'No you weren't. You were trying to avoid me, as usual. That donkey is a beast of burden, a working animal. The last thing it needs is to be treated like a member of the family. There are plenty of starving people still in the world.' She steeled herself. 'I want to talk to you, Della, before I go.'

'I knew there'd be a catch,' muttered Della, getting up again. 'Well I've got to go out now, so –'

'SIT DOWN!' roared Millicent.

She did.

'You'll be pleased to know that after you've heard what I have to say, you won't have to talk to me again if you don't wish to. But first, before you finally get rid of me, you have to hear me out.'

Della folded her arms and did that face that children do when they're about to get a lecture.

Used to this, Millicent sat down in the armchair opposite her daughter and launched into the first part of her speech. She said that she knew about everything – Darren, Simon, the sins in the bible, Nancy and Darren, all of it. But it didn't seem to matter to the girl what her mother knew, she wasn't even slightly ashamed of herself; Millicent could see she was having no effect on her daughter whatsoever, there wasn't the slightest trace of remorse on that doe-like face.

So she moved on to the next part, the bit she'd thought long and hard about on the bus back from Ellen's. The bit she understood now.

Della soon stopped huffing and puffing and just stared at her mother, listening.

'. . . You must have thought I'd just left you. Given you away. Forgotten about you. Abandoned you. You must have felt that nobody really cared about you, what happened to you, nobody loved you enough. You probably thought they didn't want to give you the love you craved so badly. The love you needed. That you deserved. Because you weren't really theirs.'

Della looked up at the ceiling and bit her lip.

'But when you were naughty, then they looked at you, didn't they? Then you got some attention, even if it was of the wrong kind. Even if they were shouting at you, at least they noticed you. I bet you even said to Ellen many times, "You're not my mother, you can't tell me what to do!" Yes?'

Della sort of nodded, and looked down at her lap.

Millicent continued, softly and slowly. 'They're not bad people, Ellen and Desmond. They were just too busy trying to keep you warm and clothed and fed. They must have been too tired to give you love as well. That's a much harder thing to give than money. But you know, don't you, Della, that it doesn't matter how much food you've got in your stomach, if your heart isn't full you still feel empty, don't you? It doesn't matter how hard you try to fill that big hole with sex and drugs, how much "fun" you try to have, it's never enough, is it? Well, not for very long.'

Della began to cry. Little tears at first. Millicent got up and tore off a piece of kitchen roll from where it stood on the counter and handed it to Della. She sat down on the sofa with her daughter and put her hand on Della's tiny knee.

But Della pushed it away. 'If you knew how it felt,' she cried, 'then where the f*** were you? All those years,' she sobbed, 'not knowing anything. I know nothing about who I am, I don't even know my father's name! I used to aks them about both of you, but she always changed the subject. I learnt not to in the end, it was like I'd ruin their day or something. All I had was that old photograph of you, and when I was little I'd stare into it and just wish and wish that it would come to life and you'd be standing there in front of me like magic. Or I'd think that if I looked at it hard enough I'd see something I hadn't seen before, some sign in your eyes, a secret message to just me, nobody else.' She scorned into the coarse tissue. 'So pathetic!'

'Didn't you remember me at all?' Millicent asked quietly.

'Don't be stupid, I was three years old! All I knew was that we came over here on a plane and that I had to be grateful to Ellen and Desmond for giving me a home, I was an extra mouth to feed. I mean it wasn't awful or anything like that but I always had to fight for anything I wanted, nothing came easy. I used to dream that you would come and get me one day, that we'd go and live in a little house together, just us. I used to look for you at the school gates, even though I couldn't really remember you . . .' She glared at her mother. 'I wanted you to be my mum, not her!'

'I'm so sorry,' said Millicent, 'I thought –'

'Sorry?' spat Della. 'Sorry! Sorry just doesn't cover it! Oh god, god . . .' She buried her wet face in her hands and Millicent let her cry some more. When she raised her head again, she looked her mother straight in the eye and said, 'And then when you did turn up – well, you're not what I wanted. Not what I thought you'd be like. I thought you'd be fun, like me, that that's where I get it from –'

'Oh I used to be fun all right. It's hard to believe, I know.' Millicent breathed in, and then out. 'There's something else I want to tell you.' Nearly done now.

'No, I don't want to hear any more. You've got to stop now, I can't deal with any more, can't take it –'

'Yes you can. You're a strong young woman, have a bit of faith in yourself, girl.' Millicent smiled. This seemed to work. Della sat back and blew her nose.

Millicent suddenly realized she didn't know how much Ellen had told Della. 'What do you know about your father?'

'Nothing. Oh god.'

'You've thought about him, though?'

'Of course.'

'How did you imagine him to be?'

'Just tell me.'

'What do you want to know?'

'Oh for f***'s sake, just –'

'All right, all right.' Now that she was here, now that this was the moment, Millicent realized she didn't want to talk about it. Couldn't. 'I can't. I just can't.'

'Yes you can,' said Della. 'You're a strong woman, where's your faith?'

This made them both smile. Tension released, pressure still on.

'I don't know where to start.'

'All right then, um – what's his name?'

It was Millicent's turn to look down at her lap. 'I don't know.'

'What?! What d'you mean, you don't know?'

Millicent looked up. 'I was drunk.'

'Drunk?!' Della repeated the word with the force it deserved. 'You?! You're joking.'

'I wish I was,' said Millicent sadly. And she told Della everything she'd told them at the meeting the evening before, arriving at the same point, at that shameful sin, unable to go any further.

She had only spoken of that night once, years ago, soon after it had happened, to Ellen. Her sister had caught her stealing the money from under their mother's mattress and so she'd had to confess. (Ellen had told Mother, of course, who'd added it to her catalogue of family disasters. The young Millicent was well and truly in her power from that moment on.) And then when she found out her sister was going to use the money to have an abortion in Antigua, Ellen had made it her business to tell every Tom, Dick and Harry on the island. She, along with the rest of them, saw a child as a gift from God, to be loved and cherished – not thrown away.

And so Millicent had given birth in the old hospital, since destroyed as it was deemed a danger to public health. They'd said it was killing more people than it cured. She'd had no painkillers, no help from the nurses and there wasn't even anybody there to hold her hand. Just her, alone with her pain. She couldn't even cry out, you just didn't, it was seen as a sign of weakness amongst the other women.

But Della didn't need to know about all that.

'Come on, Mum – please? Tell me about it, about him. I can take it – honest. Come on.' Della took her mother's hand. Millicent closed her eyes and prayed to Him to love her, help her and guide her through this.

She took a deep breath, a very deep breath. 'I was sitting in one of my favourite hiding places, on the beach under the stilts of the Yacht Club. It was a Friday night. The calypso band was playing inside, people were enjoying the party, rubbing up, flirting with each other and the visitors to the island, getting drunk on their wages from a hard week's work.

'But I wasn't enjoying myself. My drinking had got to the stage where it was no longer fun, but necessary. I couldn't function without alcohol. I couldn't function with it either, but I had no choice in the matter, I was powerless.

'I was so drunk I couldn't move. I wanted to, the sandflies were biting me, I knew they were even though I couldn't feel it. I knew I couldn't leave until I had finished my bottle, wouldn't leave until I had to. It was strange, even though I was a drunk, I always somehow managed to get myself home. I didn't want to pass out anywhere, the shame of being discovered the next day was too awful to contemplate.' Millicent smiled to herself. 'Even in my darkest times, I've always had a strong sense of self-preservation, some little voice telling me to keep going. It was probably the good Lord trying to get through to me. That's probably why I'm not dead now – I should be.'

'Go on,' said Della.

Encouraged by the tender tone in her daughter's voice, Millicent continued. 'It was getting quite late, the courting couples were coming down from the party onto the beach. I remember looking at them, wondering what it felt like to be in love. To have a boyfriend, someone to hold hands with, to kiss, to be intim–'

'How old were you then?'

'Let me see, I was twenty-seven, nearly twenty-eight.'

'And you didn't have a boyfriend?' Della was amazed.

'No. And I told myself I didn't want one either. I didn't

think I needed a man, my life was complicated enough already. I had the alcohol for company. And anyway, Ellen was the pretty one of the family.'

'Pretty? Auntie Ellen?!'

'Oh yes, she had many boyfriends. George, Felix's father, was her first love –'

'Are you telling me Desmond isn't Felix's father?'

'I thought I'd explained the system back home to you –'

'Well yeah, but – b*****h***. Auntie Ellen, what a goer! She kept that quiet.'

She kept a lot quiet, thought Millicent bitterly. And who was she to correct Della's impression of her aunt, even if her behaviour had been the norm on Montserrat. It was Millicent who had been the abnormal one. But now here she was, bursting the bubble of her sister's silence. And now that she had started to tell all, Millicent didn't want to stop.

'So there I was, watching the couples walking along the beach hand in hand, laughing, whispering, sharing the warm night together and I began to cry. I felt sorry for myself, I suppose. I wanted someone to come along and rescue me, save me from this living hell. But who would want me? I was a wreck. I wanted to die that night. I wanted to be able to stop drinking, Della, I really did but I didn't think I could. Little did I know that God was there for me all the time, that He was just waiting for me with an outstretched hand, ready to love –'

Della squeezed her mother's hand. 'So you were crying on the beach.'

'Oh, yes, and I couldn't stop. Whether it was the alcohol,

or my self-pity, I don't know, but it must have been quite a show as a man appeared as if from nowhere beside me and asked if I was all right.

'I think I told him to go away, to leave me alone but he wouldn't. He sat down beside me, just sat there in silence until I stopped. And then I started talking, I told him all about the mess I had made of my life and he just listened.

'He had such a kind face, Della, such blue eyes. I'll never forget that face. He was a handsome man, white, you know –'

'Yes, I worked that much out,' said Della, indicating their hands which were still clasped together. 'Did he live on Montserrat?'

'No, he was just visiting, a business trip he said. I'd never seen him before, I'd have remembered that face. I don't know much more about him than that, I'm sorry.'

'That's OK,' said Della. 'It really is. Loads of people at school didn't know who their fathers were. I see Desmond as my dad anyway. It's OK, honest.' Millicent noticed an understanding, a warmth in her daughter she had never seen before. 'So how did you get on to shag– er, you know – doing it?'

'I don't know, it just sort of happened.'

Della looked at her mother with a raised eyebrow. Millicent realized she knew enough about the birds and the bees to know that this was a ridiculous thing to say.

'All right. Yes, I know. I haven't convinced myself over the years that that was the case either. The truth is that, well, that I started kissing him.' The shame, oh the shame of it. But Della's face didn't seem to be judging her, so she carried on. For the first time in her life, Millicent told God, herself and another human being the exact nature of her wrongs. This was the real version, not the one she'd told Ellen.

He gently moved himself away from her. 'I'm sorry, I really am but – well, I'm married.' What with his accent and her drunkenness, she hadn't understood everything he'd been saying, but the m-word was unmistakable.

'Oh.' She thought about that as the waves gently came lap, lap, lapping onto the dark sparkling sand. It was almost as hot now as it had been during the day. But she didn't need to be thirsty to drink. Millicent tried to screw the lid off the bottle of rum, but couldn't.

He laughed gently. 'It's already off,' he said.

'What is?' What?

'Come on, I think you've probably had enough, don't you?' He smiled, she could see a warm gentle smile as he picked up the little gold shiny cap from the sand, and wiped it clean with the corner of his crisp white shirt.

'I've never had enough,' she tried to retort but it came out as a slur. She lifted the rim of the bottle to her lips and let the liquid burn its way down to the hell that was raging inside her.

'Where d'you live?' he asked, still smiling. He was either simple or kind.

'Why?' She looked at him through narrowed eyes.

'I thought I might walk you home, if you'll let me.' Kind.

'Why?' Or had she said that already?

'Because it's a beautiful night, and you're a beautiful

woman. It would be an honour.' No one had ever called her beautiful before. He probably didn't mean it.

'No.'

'Why not?'

'Want to stay here.' Want to cry some more. Go away, stop spoiling it for me.

'Then I'll stay too.' He sat back and played with the bottle top in his fingers. She watched him and took him in. He was a big man, broad and burly-built; the moon was lighting his silvering hair and shining on his shoulders as his heavy hands made delicate patterns on the sand in front of him. She'd caught his smell when she'd kissed him, it was different, the smell of a creature she hadn't come across before, sickly and sweet and musky. Nice. Better than she'd expected. She wanted to smell him again. She wanted to be near to him, she wanted to feel his cheek on her cheek, his lips on hers. He looked up from his play and smiled as he caught her looking at him.

'Just go away, go back to your wife.' She tried to turn her back, but couldn't really move.

He laughed softly. 'She's not here. We left them in Antigua. Just as well, she wouldn't like it.'

'Why not?'

'Too rough and ready for her.' He threw a little pebble out towards the sea. 'Too unsophisticated.'

'Oh.' A couple further down the beach lay down on the sand. 'D'you have sex with her?'

'Of course, she's my wife.'

'D'you want to have sex with me?' She didn't mean to say that, it just popped out.

'Come on, let's get you home.' He said it in such a way that it suddenly seemed like a good idea. So she let him help her to her feet, savouring his strength and the comfort of his steadying arm. 'Which way are you going?'

'The same way you are,' she drawled.

'Well where's Government House from here?'

'You staying there? So'm I then.' She was a bit unsteady on her feet, but it was probably the sand.

He laughed. 'I don't think you are! My daughter wouldn't be very impressed if I came back to the room with you now, would she? Not to mention the Governor – whoops –' He caught her in his big hands, she leant on him, she felt she could.

'Thank you, that's nice.' She closed her eyes and held on tight, willing herself to remember this moment so that she could call it up again. Nobody put their arms round Millicent any more, hadn't since she was a child. 'I do live near Government House in actual fact, come on, I'll show you.'

'You are a funny thing,' he said as they slowly left the beach and climbed onto the road. 'Why are you so sad?' He stroked her upper arm with his hand, which was softer inside than she'd expected.

'I told you, didn't I? Nobody likes me. I don't even like myself.' The crickets and the tree frogs were really loud tonight. Tsing tsing they went in her head, tsing tsing.

'I like you.' He had such a kind voice.

'You don't even know me. Nobody does. I'm a lonely person. A loner.'

'Surely you've got a boyfriend?' He squeezed her round the waist.

'No.'

'Ever had one?'

Might as well tell him the truth, nothing more to lose now. 'No.'

He didn't speak as they slowly made their way up the winding hill, past the driveway to the Coconut Grove Hotel. She didn't say anything either, she didn't want to spoil it. She was happy just to feel protected. Even though she hardly knew him, she felt as if she was being cared for and cherished by an old friend. She felt safe.

The old man was out on the hotel verandah smoking in his rocking chair as usual, she hoped he hadn't seen them.

'Actually,' Millicent took a deep breath, 'I'm a virgin.' He didn't say anything. 'I'm twenty-seven years old, and I'm a virgin. Probably the only one on the island.' This hill was steeper than ever.

'So you're saving yourself for the right man, then?' He caught her just before she stumbled into the deep gutter.

'No – there isn't one. I told you – I'm the respectable schoolteacher. I can't have some boy bragging about his conquest to the whole island. And if he found out about my – y'know, drinking habits, I'd be finished. But it doesn't matter now.' She couldn't let go of him, didn't want to loosen her grip.

'What d'you mean, it doesn't matter? Of course it matters, we all deserve to be loved.' He looked at her, she caught his warmth.

'I don't.' Her chin was quivering like a child's. 'I'm going to die soon.'

'Don't be sill–'

'I am!' She stopped walking and turned to face him. She didn't feel drunk at all any more. 'I want to die! I can't live here, like this. I'm messing everything up for everybody, they hate me!' The tears ran fast down her shiny cheeks. 'And you know what upsets me most? It's not that I'm hurting my family, it's not that I could damage my pupils, it's not even that I'm killing myself. The thing that really – really –' she could hardly speak for the sobs that were hurting her chest '– I can't bear it – I have never known any passion – that thing they call love, what all the songs are about, the love I hear about and read about and see all around me but never feel myself! I've never felt it, I've never gone to bed with a warm heart, I'll never know what it is to feel a man inside me, it's too late for –'

A car's headlights were flashing down the hill towards them. Millicent grabbed him by the sleeve and pulled him inside the gates of Rose Hill, an old-style gingerbread house. The lights weren't on, nobody was home. They waited silently behind the cold stone pillars until the car had hurtled past, the loud thumping of its sexy bass music pulsating through the song of the night.

But they didn't move when they could, when it was all right to carry on their journey home. They were looking at each other, reading each other's eyes. Millicent was still crying, but silently. He brushed her cheek lightly with his fingers, as if he wanted to clear the pain away for her.

Without saying a word, she took him by the hand and

led him down through the long damp garden to the edge of the cliff. They stood together for a while, just looking down at the sea, drinking in the heady perfume of the hibiscus wafting its way around them.

He took off his shirt and laid it on the grass for her. They lay down together in one close movement, and he kissed her tears away. For the first time in her life Millicent gave herself up, she trusted herself to trust him and his flow, let him be in charge of them both now.

His big hands were kindly healing hands, he covered her in a warm glow of love and care and tenderness. His skin was silky smooth, and soon hers was too. He was gentle and silent, and so was she, they were one with another and it was a blissful peace.

They lay together for some time, hands and hearts entwined, star-bathing. The tiny twinkly lights became brighter the longer they looked, and the moon gave a soft light to illuminate their faces as they smiled and warmed with each other.

'Thank you,' Millicent whispered as it was her turn to trace his face with her finger this time. He kissed her sweetly in return, tenderly soothing.

They talked on and he spoke of his life and his love, his truth and his passion and they listened and learnt from each other under the moonlight until dawn, when reality crept back to claim its focus.

As they made their way back up the garden to the road, Millicent wanted to say something to him, but couldn't. This feeling had no words, it was a beauty of calm purity, a smoothing feeling of soft.

Just before they went through the gates, he stopped and held her to him. She knew it was for the last time.

'Promise me one thing.'

'Yes?' Anything.

'That the next time you make love, it's with a man who loves you, adores you, worships you – as you do him. Don't accept anything less for yourself. Promise?'

'Yes.'

'And did you? Did they?'

'No.'

'Why not?'

'I never did it again.' For the third time that day, Millicent wanted to cry. Why would she want sex, when she had been freely given a love like that? She'd never have that love again, but she didn't need to. She didn't want anybody else, she could still remember him.

Della was stunned. 'Let me get this straight – you've only had sex once in your whole life?' Millicent nodded. 'And that was when you got pregnant with me?' Millicent nodded again. 'B***** h***, that's incredible!'

'But I'm proud of that, Della. Because as soon as I found I was having a baby, I stopped drinking. With God's help, I managed to turn a bad situation into a good one. And of course,' she put her hand on Della's shoulder, 'I have to thank you for the part you played too.'

Della looked a little bit embarrassed. 'Did you ever see him again?'

'No, he was leaving the next day.'

'And you never found out who he was?'

'I didn't ask him his name. It wasn't mine to know.'

'So he never knew about me?' Her little face wanted him to, despite her brave talk of not caring.

'No, but he would have loved you, I'm sure of that. You were a beautiful, beautiful baby.' Millicent smiled at her lovely daughter. 'As soon as I saw you, I fell into your big brown eyes. You were a very pretty child, with a sweet nature. We all loved you, once you were born.'

'So why,' this was obviously difficult for Della, 'why did you send me away?'

'I really did think I was doing the best I could for you. Ellen and Desmond were emigrating over here with Felix and Barbara. You were the same age as her, you were the best of friends, like sisters in fact. Many, many young families came over here; we'd always been told that Great Britain was the land of opportunity, and I thought you would be lonely at home with just Mother and myself for company. And now that Ellen was going, I had to stay to support Mother which meant I would have to remain headmistress at the school, so I couldn't have been with you as much as I would have wanted anyway. Normally your grandmother would have looked after you, but she was already showing signs of frailty by then.' Millicent sighed and looked into her baby's beautiful face. 'I know this must be hard for you to believe, but I thought I was putting your needs above my own. It was very hard for me, very difficult – very painful.'

'Why didn't you come to see me?'

'Many reasons, and not all the right ones – I can see that now. Money, Mother, the school. I always intended to come here eventually. It's a terrible thing to say, but it just never seemed to be the right time. And Ellen's letters were full of how well you were doing at first, she used to send me your school photo. But she stopped writing eventually – though we did get a Christmas card every year, which just said that you were happy and settled. I didn't feel it was my place to disturb your new life, even though I was desperate to know all about it.'

'But you didn't even write to me, or –'

'I did. Once a month, every month.'

'Well I never got them.'

'I know. But you can have them now. They're over there, sitting on top of my Pile of – ahem – Pile of Shit, as you call it.' She smiled as she got up and walked over to her suitcase.

This time, Della had the grace to be a bit ashamed. 'You really do know everything, don't you?' she said.

'Not everything, no,' said Millicent. 'But enough.'

'I'm a bad girl, aren't I?'

'No,' said Millicent, as she picked up the tatty shoebox, 'I don't think you are as a matter of fact.' She handed it to Della. 'You can read those later if you wish, when I've gone. Or you can throw them away.'

'Why would I want to do that?'

'Because,' replied Millicent as she picked up her coat and started to put it on, 'you have a choice. You can keep on running, Della, running away from the one thing you really want. Or you can let me stop you, turn you round and hold you. I'm here now, I've come here to love you and if we try really hard to be gentle with each other, then I think we can make up for those lost years. One day at a time.'

Della was completely silent, listening, neither agreeing nor disagreeing. But Millicent noticed that she was clasping the old shoebox tightly in her arms, as if she wasn't going to let it go. With hope in her heart Millicent put on her hat, picked up her handbag and walked towards the doorway, into the hall. 'I've left my new telephone number and address by the telephone,' she called out, 'so you know where I am – if you need me.'

Just one more look. She couldn't resist it. Turning back into the doorway, gazing through her tears at her beautiful daughter for one last time, Millicent said, 'I love you, Della. I always have, you know, and I always will. You live in my heart, and I hope one day I will have a place in yours. Goodbye.'

And off she went.

'Are you sure this is it?' Millicent asked the driver. This house was huge, enormous, very wide and very tall.

'Yes, I'm sure,' he replied, wearily. 'That's seven quid, please.'

'How much?'

'Seven quid. Seven pounds.'

'But I haven't got that much.'

'Then why the feck did you get a cab, then?'

'Because I didn't know where it was, I told you.'

'Well it's here. And it's seven pounds.'

'I've only got five.'

'What?! That wouldn't even get you to Hammersmith from Ladbroke Grove these days.'

'Now look here,' said Millicent in her best headmistress voice, 'I used to have a Datsun Cherry just like this – only it was clean – and I know very well that it doesn't cost you nearly that much to bring me here. It was only a short drive and I won't be' – what was that phrase? oh yes – 'ripped off by you. I'll give you five pounds, take it or leave it, yes or no?'

She obviously wasn't losing her touch – the driver slumped onto the steering wheel. 'I give up!' he cried. 'I can't do this any more!'

Taking that to be a yes, Millicent leaned forward and dropped her last five-pound note onto the passenger seat. 'You're a very bad man,' she said as she got out, shut the car door, went up the steps to Mrs Rose's house and knocked on the door, making a mental note as she did that the knocker needed a good polish.

I like the new me, Millicent thought to herself as she waited for the door to open, it's about time I took control of the situation. Good.

'Millicent!' Constance threw open the door. 'You're here at last! Come to save me from my infernal struggle with all things domestic – come on in!'

She'd only seen pictures of houses like this. It was like a stately home inside, a lot of marble and polished wood. It was like a palace.

'I'll show you to your quarters straightaway,' Constance

was saying, 'so that you can unpack your – oh. Haven't you got any luggage?'

'No,' Millicent said as she followed the lady down some dark stairs into the basement, 'I've just brought myself.'

'Fair enough,' said Constance, as she opened a door, 'I'd planned to get your uniform sorted out in the morning anyway.'

Uniform? Millicent didn't like the sound of that. But she didn't say anything, as she was a bit taken aback by her surroundings. 'I'll leave you to settle in,' said Constance. 'I'll be in the drawing room. Come up when you're ready and I'll go through your duties with you then.'

She left Millicent to look round the apartment. There was a sitting room, with its own television, and a small kitchen off to one side. The bathroom was a very pretty peach colour with not one but two lavatories and the bedroom – well. Millicent knew she was going to be happy here. She took off her coat and hat, and her shoes and lay down on the bed. It was soft, it was clean, it was de luxe. Her sofa days were over. She was exhausted, it had been a long and very emotional day. As she closed her eyes she said a prayer of gratitude to the good Lord, who had clearly performed one of His miracles.

Somewhere, a telephone was ringing. And ringing.

Millicent woke up with a start – she hadn't even realized there was one in the room. But there was, and it was ringing, beside the bed.

'Hello?'

'Millicent! It's almost nine o'clock – I normally eat at eight thirty.'

'Oh. Yes. I'm sorry, I must have fallen asleep.' She turned the bedside light on.

'Come upstairs straightaway. I'm in the drawing room. Still.'

Millicent wasn't sure she liked her attitude. She hadn't even said goodbye. As she sat up and swung her legs onto the floor, she noticed that she was just about to put her foot in a dog mess that was just sitting there, on the carpet. How peculiar, she thought, I'm sure it wasn't there before. And she hadn't seen any sign of a dog.

Carefully stepping over it, she went into the bathroom for some toilet tissue to clean it up. When she tried to do that, she discovered it was made of plastic. Hmm.

She eventually found the drawing room. It had to be through these doors, she'd tried all the others. She opened them, and as she entered the large room, she saw that Mrs Rose was standing with her back to the door at the fireplace, holding a glass of sherry in her hand and looking up at an oil painting hanging above the mantelpiece.

She recognized the face in the picture immediately. It was a man with clear blue, twinkling eyes. It was Della's father.

CONSTANCE ROSE
<u>60</u>

CHASUBLE: What do you think this means, Lady
   Bracknell?
LADY BRACKNELL: I dare not even suspect,
   Dr Chasuble. I need hardly tell you that in
   families of high position strange coincidences
   are not supposed to occur. They are hardly
   considered the thing.

(from *The Importance of Being Earnest*
by Oscar Wilde)

23 November

It was bloody freezing at Heathrow Airport. OK, so it's November, but why is it, thought Jessica, that no matter what time of year it is when you land, it is always cold here? And why is it that no matter what time it is when you land, the taxi queue is always at least twenty people long? She shuddered, and tried to pull her little jacket tight around her so that the two sides would at least meet.

'I'm going to North Notting Hill,' she eventually said to her designated cabbie as his window wound down.

'Where?' He frowned.

'Barlby Road,' Jessica said as she opened the door, 'W10.'

The cab driver guffawed like someone in an Ealing comedy. 'That's not North Notting Hill, luv,' he laughed as he set the meter, 'that's Wormwood Scrubs!'

'Oh whatever,' said Jessica, as she flumped herself into the back seat, glad to be taking the weight off her slingbacks, 'it is W10 though.'

'Yeah, and Notting Hill's W11,' he said as he swung the cab out. 'But officially speaking, W10's the arse end of Ladbroke Grove and beyond. D'you know how they went about numbering the London postal districts?'

No, but I think I'm about to find out, thought Jessica.

'Now it's best demonstrated using West London as an example. I mean W1 and W2 were easy enough of course because they're central, but then it goes W3 – Acton, W4 – Chiswick, W5 Ealing, W6 Hammersmith and so on, dunnit?'

'If you say so,' said Jessica, who'd never really bothered to think about it before and didn't really want to do so now.

'Well that's the point, it's not me that says so, is it? They wouldn't think to consult the humble cab drivers on such an important matter, would they? Oh no, they like to make life as difficult for us as possible, and so you've got your numbered postal districts all over the place, intcha, making no sense at all geographically speaking.'

'Right,' said Jessica, thinking she could have said 'your mother's a whore' and it wouldn't have stopped his flow.

'So what did they do? They numbered 'em in alphabetical order, that's what. Now it don't take a genius to work out that numbers and letters don't mix – you've got your Greek and your Arabic there with a little bit of Roman thrown in for good measure, and as we all know you can't mix that lot up without expecting a war . . .'

And he went on and on and on, like Fred fucking Housego, all the way to the Hogarth fucking Roundabout. 'I'll turn off here, if you don't mind, it gets chocka this time of day with small women in big cars ferrying their little darlin's home from posh school, we're better off nipping round the back of the Bush.'

'Whatever you say, you seem to be the expert.' Jessica was too cold, too tired and too bored witless to care.

'You're not back off your holidays, then?' How he managed to look at her with one eye and keep the other on the road was a complete mystery.

'How d'you know that?'

'Handbaggage.' He tapped the side of his nose. 'You can't keep much from us cabbies! Mind you, I'm not complaining, I just dropped off some old bat who looked like she was emigrating she had that many suitcases, nearly killed me humping that lot out of the cab. I told her she'd have to pay excess baggage, but she didn't seem to care. Honestly, some people just have money to burn. Now if I was that rich, I'd . . .'

Fuck off and leave us all alone, I hope. Jessica managed to lean forward and push the taxi heater button on, hoping its whoosh would drown him out. It didn't.

' . . . live abroad, then?'

'Yes, the Caribbean, actually.' That should shut him up.

'Oh yeah, whereabouts?'

'Antigua.'

'Oh I've been there, my brother got married over there last Christmas. I thought it was a bit of a shit-hole actually. They did it at one of those special wedding hotels, y'know.'

'No, I don't.' Avoid them like the plague, in fact – too full of nosy British tourists.

'Now if you want a really good holiday, you want to go to Mauritius . . .'

Blah blah blah, thought Jessica, as they passed that quirky little vegetarian restaurant with the same name in the Goldhawk Road. Funny, thought Jessica, I thought everything would have completely changed in the few months I've been away, but no – the cabbies are still boring, my old haunts are still here and London town is still as grey as ever. Though that probably wasn't helped by having to wear sunglasses in November. Over there she'd dreamed of magazines, Marmite and men. Now that she was here they'd lost their appeal.

Having run out of idyllic holiday spots for Jessica to remember to never ever visit for fear of running into people like him, the driver changed tack – doubtless looking for a feed line to launch his next speech. 'So – you here for work, then?'

'No.' Soon though, soon – Sandy had been emailing her with various job offers that had come in since The Exposé. She just had to wait a bit longer and then she'd be free to take up the better ones. He didn't know where she was, of course, nobody did – except Mother. Who took great delight in posting her the clippings from various publications she'd sold her 'My Drugs Hell' stories to via the internet – well how else was she to finance her extended absence? Constance had written all over the cuttings in red pen, remarks like 'this can't be true' and 'sue immediately'. Little did she know Jessica had made a lot of it up – each fat cheque required a different angle, and a little bit more juice than the one before.

Good, nearly home. She was looking forward to being in her old flat again, it would provide a bit of protection from the prying eyes of the outside world.

'Family?'

'No thanks.'

'What?'

Jessica sighed. 'It was a joke.'

'Oh, right.' He paused. 'What I meant was, are you here to see your family?'

'Yes. Now please stop talking to me or I'll have to kill you.'

She'd been surprised at how excited she was when Constance had sent over an air ticket, even if she was supposed to go back into exile the next day. But maybe once Mother saw her she'd relent, extend the visit to a week, give her the chance to do some proper shopping. The retail therapy in Antigua was not what she'd been used to, but Jessica had found the perfect birthday present there – a really grotesque kitsch little ornament fish thing made out of coconut shells, Constance was going to scream with delight when she saw it.

Jessica had found herself strangely over-excited at the thought of seeing her mother again, and was even nearly looking forward to seeing Sophie tonight. These feelings had come as a bit of a shock, as had all the other emotions she'd experienced since being clean and sober. Well, almost. Constance had spread a rumour that she was in The Priory, but thankfully Jessica had managed to persuade her mother that she wasn't an addict at all and that to merely disappear for a while would be more beneficial. (Lots of her friends had checked into treatment centres when they'd overdone it, and had come out with horror stories of having to tell alcoholics and druggies your innermost secrets and, even worse, hug them.) Once Jessica had pointed out that this was also the cheaper option, Constance had packed her off to the hotel in Antigua they'd stayed at years ago, but it was full of tourists and so Jessica had rented out a tiny villa instead. And there she'd languished ever since, for the last four months or so.

It had been OK at first. She'd thought the Caribbean would be quite a glamorous hideaway location with lots of sun, sea, sand and sex, but it hadn't been like that at all. As Constance had said that if anyone discovered her whereabouts she'd withdraw all funds, Jessica had had to live in virtual solitary confinement, disguising herself with enormous hats and local dresses when she had to go out. When she did, she got to watch from afar as other people had holidays of a lifetime, Jolly Rogering themselves stupid. It was hell in heaven.

So she'd had a lot of time on her hands. Too much time. She'd started to keep a diary ('My Isolation Hell') with the intention of selling it to a magazine later on, when this was all over; but it had evolved into a journal far too intimate to share with the rest of the world. She had slowly come to tell her dear lap-top diary everything, all about the pain and the fame and the difficulty and the horror of being Jessica Rose. How everything was fine until Sophie came along and she had to share. How her father had given all his time and energy and spare moments to his empire when Jessica was growing up, and then decided to give all his time and energy and spare moments to Sophie instead. How she had managed to keep her mother's attention only by doing everything she was told. How it felt to be packed off to boarding school because her father thought she was going off the rails, when it was quite obvious that he just wanted Sophie to himself. Mother should have stuck up for her more. How she wanted so badly to be famous, because it meant that they were definitely looking at you and not your fat baby sister.

She could see now that it had all started to get out of control when she'd left home to lead her own life, away from Mother. It had been hard to rebel against a mother who was more exciting and dangerous than you, but Jess had somehow managed. She hadn't known how to behave, there was no one there to tell her now. She didn't even know how to look after herself, school and Mrs/Mr Mac had always organized the parts of her life Mother hadn't. So she'd made it up as she went along, and some of the time she'd got it right. She'd done well with her career, anyone who worked with her always wanted to again, she was both professional and talented. Even Jessica herself believed that.

But it was the people bit she wasn't very good at. Until recently she'd assumed she was popular. She'd always wanted to be part of a gang, in a crowd, have the sort of friends who'd known each other for years, through weddings and kids and serious illnesses. The kind of people who had photos of each other on holiday in Crete ten years ago neatly stuck into maroon plastic albums on their bookshelves. But it hadn't quite worked out that way, she could see now that she'd quickly move from one group to the next. And nobody had tried to track her down since she'd left. Very disappointing.

And as for the men – well. At first she'd made a game of it, listing all the ones she could remember, and dealt with them like the figures of fun she thought they were, giving them marks out of ten for various qualities they did or didn't have. There was something wrong with each of them of course, which was why they had been dumped.

But one day she realized with a shock that there was one thing they all had in common. Her. Ah.

For lack of anything better to do, Jessica took a good long look at herself. It was a painful process, in fact it really hurt at times. But as she slowly peeled back the layers of artifice and designer and status and money and cool, she eventually discovered a woman whom she realized, with horror, she didn't know at all. Herself.

All her life she'd done what everyone else was doing. She'd copied the cool people. She'd lived a 'glamorous' life because that's what everyone wanted for themselves, wasn't it? She'd worn the clothes the magazines had told her she must, regardless of whether they suited her or not; she'd eaten some of the most revolting food the planet had to offer because it was in a restaurant one simply had to be seen in; and her flat was supposed to be like a glossy double-page spread from *Elle Décor*. In fact she'd only really taken drugs because everyone else was and that was what had got her here in the first place. How feeble to be so easily led.

Jessica despised herself more than ever, especially now that she had discovered that the real Jessica Rose was such a dullard. But she realized that now she had a choice, that this was her chance to change, to make amends, to re-invent herself as a person with depth and interest, warmth and love.

But fuck it, why do that? That sounded like very hard work indeed, no thanks. And anyway, who wants to be Mother Teresa? Apart from Sophie? No, being bad was what she was really good at. And Mother could go fuck herself actually, it was time to lead her own life now, shake off Constance's control. No need to have her approval now, it was too late for all that. She'd start an empire of her own. The sense of freedom from this decision had been awesome, she'd gone out that night to celebrate and come home with a nice big black man called Augustus.

'This is it, East Wormwood Scrubs – what number?' Thank christ for that.

'Anywhere here will do fine.' As she got out of the cab and paid him his ludicrous fare (they should give you a discount for auditory abuse) she noticed a For Sale sign outside next door's house. No, she saw as she walked towards the house that the sign was strapped to her gate-post. Well, their gatepost – thank fuck for that, she thought, the old grumpster downstairs had finally died. Hurrah.

Ah good, the spare key was still under the terraplastica flowerpot. She could hardly get the door open for all the mail that was behind it. Charming, she thought, you'd think someone would have taken it upstairs. But who, actually – Millicent was working for Mother now and the old bastard and his cooking-cabbage smells were dead, though still lingering. It would probably take years for the smell to go away – right now it was making her feel nauseous. Deal with all this junk mail later, don't need it now. And anyway, how many pizza emporiums did you need to ring at one time?

As she trudged up the stairs, Jessica glanced at her watch. Good, just enough time to have a nice hot bath to get the chill out of her bones, and a lie-down in her dear old bed, a mosquito-free zone. She was absolutely exhausted, it had been a long plane journey full of stupid Caribbean men and women all dressed up in their church-going suits and hats, with screaming sticky children head-to-toe in nylon clothing running riot up and down the gangway, pushing the air hostess's manicured patience to its limit. And the woman next door to her had declined their kind offer of putting her bouquet of flowers in the overhead locker, insisting instead on clasping them to her bony chest throughout the entire flight; which meant that every time Jess had tried to sleep the loud creaking and tickling of the cellophane had woken her up again. Well never mind, she'd have a nap now to refresh herself before the evening's festivities. Wonder if she could get away with a glass of wine or two?

When she let herself into her flat, Jessica was absolutely horrified at the devastation that greeted her. It was such a shock. There was just – well, stuff everywhere. And someone else's stuff at that. Many, many pairs of trainers, a bicycle missing the front wheel, a pair of filthy roller-blades, a crash helmet, empty fag packets, old copies of the *Sun*, the *Mirror* and *Racing Post* all over the place – what the fuck was going on? She was alarmed to feel tears pricking at her eyes, but some pig had trampled all over her home, how could they do this?

Picking her way through the miscellaneous detritus on the floor, she walked straight past the bathroom (which she didn't need to look at, the smell told her all she needed to know) and into the kitchen. Disgusting. You couldn't even see the worktops for all the dirty plates, cups, glasses, knives, forks, bowls – she noted with horror that they'd even left some half-finished muesli in her favourite vase. And as she tried to turn round, her shoes seemed to be stuck to the floor – looked like someone had decided to paint it orange with juice.

Jessica cupped her hand over her mouth at the state of the sitting room. The once-polished wooden floor was covered with the cardboard boxes of a million dead pizzas; the glass coffee table was sporting every cup, glass and mug that wasn't in the kitchen, all full of mould of course; there were a million sticky rings around her big crackle-glazed ceramic bowl which was still full of curved wood shavings from Peru but now had a top layer of dirty socks. The mantelpiece was sporting what looked like a sorry attempt at modern art, which could be entitled Lager Can Designs of the Twenty-First Century, and the entire room had been liberally sprinkled with sparkling tin-foil takeaway cartons. Indian or Chinese with your fag ends? Every available surface was now unavailable, being mostly covered with porn mags and videos and *Loaded*s, with the odd *What Car?* chucked in for good measure. The stereo system was missing, just not there any more, as was the answer machine. And horror of horrors, it looked like one of the arms of her beautiful sofa from Heals' sale was broken, from some fat twat sitting on it no doubt. She also noticed (how could she not) that one of her muslin drapes was lying in a crumpled heap on the floor. Evidently this *Marie Celeste* had had a bloke living in it.

This can't be happening to me, thought Jessica, as she contemplated not looking in the bedroom, for fear of passing out at what might be lurking in there. Who is he, and how can he live like this? Must be a squatter, nobody else would treat such a beautiful place with this amount of disrespect.

She'd half-hoped to find some slob snoring in her bed, so that she could leap on him, flatten him and punch his bloody lights out, but no such luck. Just more of the same, only her beautiful clothes weren't hanging in the cupboard – nothing was, just a few mangled wire hangers – and the chest of drawers held no trace of her either, just some neatly folded nasty nylon football shirts. The rest of the clothes were just strewn around the room, she couldn't even see the carpet, typical male. There were signs of female company though – he'd just chucked his used condoms on the floor, disgusting animal.

Bastard! I thought squatters normally changed the locks, thought Jessica. And the only person who has keys is Millicent – this was certainly not the work of any friend of hers. What to do? Phone. At least that still worked, even though it was covered in what looked like congealed lumps of tomato ketchup.

But who to ring? She'd try some other people before Mother, but who? Sandy mustn't know she's in town – Sophie was not a good person to call in a crisis. Turned out she wasn't in anyway. Kerry hadn't answered any of her emails, but it might be worth a shot: 'Hi, Kerry and Ivan aren't in right now –' Bloody hell! She clicked off the phone in disgust. Maybe she should – No, he would still be furious, he must surely hate her, he hadn't replied to her either – there again, he was a lawyer, he'd know what to do . . .

'Moakes, Cowell and Bilton, how may I help you?'

'Nigel Moore, please.'

'Who?'

'Nigel Moore?'

'I'm sorry, we don't have anyone of that name working here.'

'What?'

'I said I'm sorry, we –'

'Well where's he gone?'

'I'm afraid I don't know who you're talking about.'

'But you must know Nigel, he used to work there, he –'

'Exactly. Good day to you.' And the cheeky cow put the phone down. Fuck, the fall-out from the newspapers must have been worse than she thought. Well – oh, she'd sort it out later. She'd asked Mother to track him down, perhaps she'd know what had happened to him.

As Jessica made her way slowly down the stairs again, she thought she heard somebody moving about in the flat below.

Sure enough, as she went to open the door out onto the street, the dead man's door opened and his unmistakably Steptoe voice said, 'You're back then?'

'And who are you, Jacob fucking Marley?' She didn't bother to turn round, just walked out, slamming the door behind her.

Constance had told her to come to the house immediately. But Jessica had been hoping to put this latest revelation off for a little longer, she wasn't sure how Mother was going to take it. As she climbed into her second black cab of the day, she realized that she was experiencing one emotion she hadn't felt for a long time – fear.

*

At that precise moment, Millicent was on her preferred method of transport, a double-decker bus. Mrs Rose had tried to make her use the London Underground as she'd said it was quicker, but Millicent hadn't liked it at all. She'd felt like a rat, scurrying about in confusing tunnels, mixing with the dregs of humanity – the other passengers were either drunk or asleep, never both, it had been a very depressing experience. And there were far too many tourists, getting lost, taking up too much room with their enormous rucksacks. Nobody smiled, ever. No, the bus was a far better way of getting around London – she prided herself on knowing the routes in and out of Holland Park off by heart now. And if you sat on the top deck you saw a lot more than if you were at street level. You could admire the architecture, see into people's windows in the early evening, just before they drew their curtains. And she knew a lot of the drivers and conductors too, though not by name, of course. Just to smile to.

It had been a long day. But all her days were long days, she liked it that way. It wasn't just Mrs Rose's fault, though she was quite a demanding, highly strung woman. It had been very difficult working with her at first. Neither woman would completely relinquish her power to the other, and it had been a bit of a battle. Constance had kept trying to catch Millicent out, but the younger yet wiser woman was always one step ahead. She'd tried every practical joke in the book, and a few more that Millicent had indeed fallen for (there had been a most embarrassing evening when Millicent had thought the Queen herself was coming to dinner, and had gone to much trouble accordingly; the guest turned out to be an effeminate man who couldn't stop tittering), but she had made it clear that she would stand for no nonsense, and the two women had now settled into a better working relationship. Compromise had always been one of Millicent's favourite words, and at last Constance was beginning to understand its meaning.

The first tussle had been over the uniform. Millicent had agreed to wear the apron, but not the rest of it and that included the silly little hat her boss tried to get her to wear for dinner parties. In return, she had consented to be available for work twenty-four hours a day, seven days a week, carrying a pager with her whenever she left the house. (Naturally it had a very loud beep, which Millicent had become used to now. Though if the request was a silly time-wasting one, she would tell her employer that it hadn't worked, or she'd find a way out of it. Buy a bottle of still mineral water indeed. What a waste of money – Millicent just topped up the empty bottles from the tap. She still hadn't noticed.) Mrs Rose had been pleased to think that she had someone permanently on call for her; Millicent had realized very quickly that there wasn't much to be done if you only had one able-bodied person and an almost empty house to look after.

And the telephone had been the source of much amusement when she'd first arrived. For all her love of gadgetry, Constance wouldn't use a machine to take messages – which suited Millicent as she wasn't sure she'd ever master such a thing. It had clicks as well as beeps. So it was her job to answer the phone, to say 'Rose Residence' when she picked it up. But Millicent had managed to persuade her employer to take messages for her too when she was out of the house, as this was only fair. Which Constance had duly done, causing her unsuspecting housekeeper to make several crank calls to companies such as Durex, asking to speak to a Mr R Johnny.

So when she'd got the message to call a Mrs Bleat at a primary school in Shepherd's Bush, she'd ignored it. But the woman had rung again, and Millicent had answered this time. Barbara had been doing some work experience there, and had recommended her aunt to the headmistress. She was looking for someone to work part-time with the children who had fallen behind, but purely on a voluntary basis as the school couldn't afford another salary. In her prayers that night, Millicent had thanked the good Lord over and over again for leading His lost lamb back to her flock.

The headmistress (real name Mrs Pleat) had been an ineffectual woman, far too young for such a responsible position. And what she'd seen at the interview had been a real eye-opener. No wonder her own daughter was almost illiterate – if this school was anything to go by, the standard of education in this country was truly appalling. There had been scant evidence of the 3 Rs, even amongst those children considered to be doing well. She'd accepted the job on the spot, thus immersing herself in the world of Janet and John, geometry and joined-up writing once more.

Mrs Rose had kicked up a terrible fuss of course. Began weeping and wailing all over the house and sulking, just like a child. Threw a temper tantrum, selfishly wanted to keep Millicent all to herself, wouldn't share her. There had been a huge row, during which Constance sacked Millicent who'd already handed in her notice anyway. But then both women knew that they needed each other and so they had negotiated a way forward, and from then on they'd slowly become friends. Each respected the other for her tenacity, high standards and honour with nobility, and neither felt she was waging a one-woman war against the wicked world any more. And each had been surprised to discover that actually the other was much nicer than she'd originally thought.

They took to having a late-night cup of something hot (Horlicks for Millicent, green tea for Constance) together at the kitchen table, and then they added a snack to that (Penguin for Millicent, Ginger Thin for Constance) and eventually that turned into supper if they were both in for the evening. It was an unlikely combination but it worked – both women were sufficiently interested in the other's very different life to keep the relationship well balanced. Though each one thought she had the last word. Of course.

And they had much in common. They were both creative people, for a start. Millicent had read much of her employer's writing – Constance was most prolific, short stories, film scripts, theatre plays, radio monologues, and now she was hard at work on a novel, and there was talk of an autobiography too. Millicent thought the storylines rather melodramatic and unlikely – there was far too much emphasis on the plot and not enough on the emotional resolves – and she'd been brave enough to say so too, though she did cushion her criticisms with compliments on the spelling and layout. Her style was more Victorian novella than modern-day commentator, which is how she described herself. Constance should really pay more attention to the old adage of writing about what you know, Millicent had said. Meanwhile she was still waiting for feedback on the first three chapters of her book, Montserrat – Memories and Memoirs. She was certainly taking her time with it, clearly savouring the information contained within the 385-odd handwritten pages of what was going to be hailed by historians as a most important work.

And both women had nursed a sick parent, although Constance was much younger than Millicent had been when her mother died, she was still in her twenties. She was an only child, from a more humble background than Millicent had imagined – her father had worked as a station master but her mother had also been a dressmaker. Both had early memories of strange women standing on their kitchen tables having their hems pinned. Both had mothers who had wanted more for their daughters, both had obligingly gone out and got it.

And, of course, they'd both slept with the same man. Had children by him too.

Millicent had decided not to say anything. She had been tempted, naturally, especially now that they were good friends. Constance often spoke of him, how she had allowed him to sweep her off her feet when she was only twenty and he was thirty-two, how if she was honest it was the money that she found more alluring at first, how he was far too boring and too in love with her ever to have had an affair.

Every day Millicent dusted that mantelpiece. Every day

she looked at his picture. Every day she wondered if it really was him, or was she just imagining it. After all, it was over twenty years ago and it had been dark. There again, it was as if it was only yesterday in her memory, and they had stayed together until dawn. She would know that blue twinkle anywhere. Or would she?

Once, soon after Millicent had started working there, she'd waited for Constance to go out and straight after she'd heard the front door shut she'd fetched the stepladder from the cellar and climbed up it in order to get a really, really good look at his face. Of course Constance had come back in for her scarf and seen Millicent wobbling about precariously perched at the top, eyeballing Archie. 'Honestly, Millicent,' she'd laughed, 'a quick whizz with the feather duster will do, there's no need to lick it clean!'

And how lifelike was the painting anyway? She'd looked round the house for photographs of him, of course, but there weren't any – not even in the main bedroom. She'd managed to work it into the conversation one night – Constance had said she'd put them away, out of respect to Luigi.

And so the painting was all Millicent had to go on. But she still wasn't absolutely sure it was him, and it began to torture her. She would feel such a fool if it wasn't, gazing lovingly every day into the painted eyes of a man she'd never met. But how would she ever know? And so she decided for her own peace of mind that yes, this was the man she'd loved for one night only, and who she believed loved her too for that special night, this was Della's father. And she took great comfort from that. She even enjoyed hearing Constance talk about him, which she did all the time. It made her heart warm, like she was getting to know him a bit better. Sometimes she even found herself sticking up for him, if Constance was being unkind. And when she was on her own in the house, she'd chat to him. She knew he could hear, she could feel him there all the time. His presence was very healing, and every time she thought of him nowadays it wasn't a stab that shot through her heart, but a glow that wrapped itself around her soul.

As she got off the bus and started to walk home with a few last-minute bits and bobs for tonight's dinner rustling in their carrier bags around her knees, Millicent realized that for the first time in ages, certainly this year, she was actually happy. It was a nice feeling.

Jessica poured her mother a stiff sherry and handed it to her. Constance took the glass and motioned to her daughter to sit down in the armchair opposite. You are the only person I know who can boss people around using just one hand and no words, thought Jessica as she obeyed the order.

'Why on earth didn't you tell me?' Constance eventually said.

'I didn't realize until recently.'

'You didn't realize?' she spluttered. 'Weren't there a few tell-tale signs?'

'Well yes, but I thought it was because I was eating more out there. And one day just turned into the next, I wasn't keeping track.'

'Oh really, Jessica!' Constance took another sip. 'I have

to say I am absolutely flabbergasted, I don't know where to start.' She had another sip. 'At the beginning, I suppose. It's a very good place to start, if Julie Andrews is to be believed. Who's the father?'

Pause. Jessica looked down at her tanned hands with the little white bits in between the fingers. 'I don't know.'

'What?!'

'You heard.'

'Jessica!' Constance sat up in her chair, her pale face pulsating with a mixture of anger and shock. 'There is absolutely no need for that attitude, especially in this time of crisis.' Another sip. 'I didn't even know you had a boyfriend.'

'I haven't.'

'Oh my god!' Constance was appalled. 'Well when did you get pregnant?'

'Oh I don't know, sometime around my birthday.'

Constance's thin painted lips withered into a smile. 'Well then, Jessica, it shouldn't be too hard for you to work out, should it? I think the whole country knows who you were having sex with that night.'

'Look, it might not have been then, there were various dogs sniffing around my lamp-post at that time – by the way, did you ever find out what happened to Nigel?' She didn't really want to know but had to.

'I tried, but all old Geller knows for sure is that he certainly won't be working in London as a solicitor again. However he did say that legal rumour has it he's turned into some sort of art dealer, importing hideous paintings from Russia or something. It's not Nigel's, is it? That wouldn't be too bad – he's from a very good family – or was, anyway . . .'

'I've told you, I don't know. And I don't want to know either.' Of course Jessica had tried to work out who'd fathered it for herself, but it was a bit like looking for a needle in a haystack. So to speak. And some of the possibilities just didn't bear thinking about. 'Anyway do calm down, Mother, it's not the end of the world. Look on the bright side, you're going to be a grandmother again.'

'Stop it, Jessica! This is really the last straw.' She drained her glass and held it out for another. 'So how far gone does that make you?'

'They think I'm about five months.'

'Too late to get rid of it, then?'

'Yup.' Jessica took the glass and walked over to the drinks cabinet.

'Well, then, what are we going to do?'

'What d'you mean, "we"?'

'What d'you mean, what do I mean "we"?'

The door opened and Millicent poked her head round. 'I'm back.'

'Oh yes, Millicent, so you are. I can see that now for myself, very clearly. Thank you so much.' Constance shot a look skywards. So did Millicent as she shut the door again.

'I don't need your help,' said Jessica as she crossed the elegant Chinese rug to hand Mother the next sherry, 'I do have a plan, you know.'

'Oh really?' said Constance with a raised eyebrow. 'And what does that involve, may I ask? Shoes!'

'Well first of all I'm going to get rid of the squatters in

my flat –' said Jessica as she released her swollen feet from their inappropriately strappy sandals, and then – aaah, that's better – I'm going to sell it.' She swung her legs back up onto the cool lemon damask and began to rearrange the cushions around the armrest in order to prop up her head, which was feeling heavier by the minute.

Great minds think alike, thought Constance. 'And then?'

'Well I was going to travel round the world.'

'Really? How interesting. Doing what?'

Being bad. 'Sightseeing.'

'And aren't you forgetting about somebody?'

'Who?'

Constance closed her eyes, exasperated. She flashed them open again. 'The baby! You'll never be able to single-parent your way around the world, Jessica, you're not the type.'

Jessica sighed and leaned back onto the cushions. 'I wasn't going to take the baby with me.'

'Oh?'

Silence.

'Why not?'

'Because I'm not going to keep it.'

'But I thought –'

'I'm going to give it up for adoption or something.'

Silence.

'No.'

'Yes.' Here we go.

'No, Jessica!' Constance was getting angry. 'I can't let you do that!'

'Well tough shit, Mummy dear!' Jessica spat with the last

of her energy as she sat up again. 'You can't stop me! It's my life, and the life inside me is my life too, and I'll decide what's going to happen to it, not you! I'm sick of your interfering ways, I've had enough of you telling me what I can and can't do, what I should and shouldn't, I just want to be able to – oh I don't know, I – well anyway.' She just had to lie down now.

Constance put her glass down on the mother-of-pearl coaster sitting on the side table beside her. 'Quite a speech, Jessica, well done.'

'Thank you.'

'Tailed off towards the end though.'

'Whatever.'

Silence.

'You'll regret it.'

'Really.' Jessica shut her eyes.

'Yes.'

Silence.

'I did.'

'You did what?'

'Regretted it.'

Oh for god's sake. 'Regretted what?'

'Giving my baby away.'

Jessica forced her eyes open once more. 'What?'

'I gave my baby away.'

'What baby?'

Constance tried to sound casual. 'The one I had after you.'

'Before Sophie?'

'That's right.'

Bloody typical. Just when you think you've dropped a bombshell, she drops a bigger one. Only it usually turned out to be a wind-up. 'Oh for god's sake, Mother. I'm sorry, but I don't believe you. This is one of your sick jokes, isn't it? Well can you tell me all about it later, I've just got to go to sleep.'

Having given birth once before, Cecily knew what to do. But this was different. It was horrible. It was more prolonged, it was more painful. Even though dear Donnie was there to hold her hand, she felt very alone. I'm sorry to say she wasn't very brave, she screamed like a wild animal from start to finish.

Cecily never saw her baby. That was what they'd agreed when they'd struck the deal. He would take it away for her and she would give Donnie a new life. She didn't even know if she'd had a boy or a girl. She thought it was for the best – how wrong she was.

Much to the astonishment of her assembled family, Cecily began to cry. (She had always been terrifically strong in front of them, you see, they had no idea of the pain she had lived with for all these years.) 'I never even held my baby. I didn't even touch the little life that had been borne out of love, born into a cold world. Donnie just wrapped the tiny thing up in a warm blanket and took it away, leaving me completely alone in that cold place with just my torture for company. My baby's milk had flowed into my breasts, I yearned for my suckling infant, I wanted Donnie to bring my baby back, but of course he didn't. I just had to wait and watch and suffer while my motherhood subsided. I cried for my sins, I cried for my lost little soul, I've never forgiven myself. Ever.' Cecily's trim frame heaved with racking sobs and her daughter noticed how beautiful she looked, even when in great distress.

'You see, my darling, there are some things you never get over, you just learn to live with them instead. Once I'd come home I poured all the extra love I had into you, and I know it's hard to believe, but I never had an affair again. But scarcely a day passed without me thinking about that baby, wondering what happened to it.'

Scarlett peered at the screen, to see if she'd made any mistakes. Becca's emails were always full of wrong spellings and shit punctuation, so she tried to do the same, sometimes putting them in on purpose. Though this had gone a bit wrong one time, when Becca'd said she couldn't make any sense of what Scarlett had written, but what could you expect from someone (in fact she'd typed 'sum1', which had taken Scarlett ages to work out) who went to a privit school? (At least they teach us to spell, Scarlett had thought privately.)

She thought this would make Becca laugh though. (She still seemed to be a bit fed up, especially after her dad had left, which was odd as Scarlett knew he was a bastard.) It was a joke that Jade had emailed her yesterday and Scarlett had changed it so that Becca would like it more: why did the fucking chewing gum cross the road? Because it was stuck to the chicken's buggering foot, you wanker.

Sophie stuck her head with dripping wet hair round the study door. 'Hurry up, darling, we're leaving in half an hour. Oh Scarlett, you're not even dressed.'

'I'm wearing this,' said Scarlett, not looking up from the screen.

'You most certainly are not!' said her mother. 'What on

earth would your grandmother say if you turned up in jeans and a vest?'

'It's not a vest, it's a singlet. And if Constance loves me, which she does, she'll just be happy that I'm there – whatever I'm wearing.' She looked up at her mum. 'You shouldn't be so worried about what other people think, it means you're very not deep.'

Sophie was puzzled, but carried on anyway. 'Well all right, then, *I* would like you to look nice this evening, will you at least do that for me?'

Scarlett slumped back in her chair with an enormous sigh. She's getting more Kevinish every day, thought Sophie. 'Oh Mum,' Scarlett wailed, 'do I have to?'

'Yes.' Sophie was being really quite firm on this one, she didn't want to give her mother the chance to criticize. 'I've picked out a nice dress for you and laid it out on your bed.'

'A nice dress?!' Scarlett folded her arms. 'No. I'm not wearing a dress. Anyway, I don't have any nice dresses.'

'Yes you do – I've put out that lovely yellow one we got for your party, you know, the one with the little daisies on it.'

'Oh Mu-um!' whined Scarlett in that tone of voice that brought Sophie out in a rash. 'Don't make me do this, please?'

'Don't make you do what?' Simon crowded into the tiny room.

'She's making me wear that really gross dress that I was going to wear for the birthday party that I never had because you never got round to organizing another one because nobody cares about me these days.'

'Scarlett, that's just not true –' spluttered Sophie.

'What dress?' said Simon.

'That horrible babyish one.'

'It's very pretty,' Sophie appealed to Simon. 'And it cost an absolute fortune.'

'I don't remember it,' said Simon, who was always amazed at women's instant recall of articles of clothing from years back.

'That's because I've never worn it,' said Scarlett, 'and I'm not going to – ever.' She looked at her parents' faces and put on her best little girl face. 'Please don't make me, please – Dad?'

'Well . . .' Simon thought about it.

'Simon?!'

'Look, just put something on that is at least clean, and brush your hair or something.'

Sophie pushed past him and left the room.

'Thanks Dad,' said Scarlett, and Simon looked down at her and smiled the old way, their smile.

'No make-up, mind,' he said.

'Course not,' said Scarlett, who was surprised that he couldn't see she already had some on – Becca said it made you feel better around yourself.

'But hurry up, we're leaving in about fifteen minutes,' he said, tapping his watch as he left the room.

That's not what Mum had said, but who cares. Scarlett got online to send her emails and receive new ones. Blimey – no, bloody hell, she'd got loads! Mostly from people at school, though. Mum was always going on about how she'd see them all the next day and so why did they phone and email each other as soon as they got in the door, she just didn't get it. Scarlett always said it was about homework, but of course it wasn't. They were mostly quizzes on your personality, and letters that if you didn't pass them on you'd die straightaway.

Ooh goodie, one from Becca:

'Hi Fuckface thougt this would make you wet your pantsits v. funny B:)'

Go to attachment. Open.

A photograph began to come up on the screen. It turned itself out to be a picture of a dead cat that had been run over, its blood and guts spread out all over the road.

Sophie was sitting at her dressing table, struggling a bit with the new chrome supersonic salon-standard hairdryer Della had recommended she bought – it was quite heavy and unwieldy. 'Why did you do that?' she asked Simon's reflection in the mirror as he came in.

'Don't shout!' he said.

'What?'

'I said don't shout!' he shouted.

'Oh right, sorry!' she shouted back as she tried to find the switch to turn it off. The ruddy thing blew into her open tub of loose face powder, spraying the glass top and the mirror and everything else on the dressing table with a shower of flesh-coloured dots. 'Damn! Oh no, look at my dress, it's covered!' She brushed the navy-blue velvet with her hand, which only turned the dots into dashes. 'Oh dear . . .'

'Don't cry,' said Simon as he opened his cupboard, the

one on the right-hand side of the fireplace. 'Just don't bloody cry.'

'Oh I wouldn't,' said Sophie as she stood up, 'I've got far more to cry about than a little bit of spilt powder.'

'And don't even think about coming over here,' he said as he held his affluent barrister/confident businessman/ sexy older man audition suit protectively against himself, 'I don't want you anywhere near me.'

'Yes, I know,' she said, as she struggled with the zip at the back of her dress, 'that's the trouble.'

Simon decided not to say anything because he knew she wanted him to.

'Perish the thought,' said Sophie as she pulled the dress up over her head. But it got stuck on her big bosoms. Perhaps this wasn't great timing, but *carpe diem*, as Robin Williams would say. 'You don't fancy me any more, do you?' she asked quietly.

Simon looked at her, standing there with her arms out like a penguin, skirt pulled up over her belly, pink-and-white-mottled sloppy flesh spilling over the sides of her comfy pants, pop sox already working their way down to her ankles. Yuk.

'Don't be silly,' he lied as he stepped out of his chinos, 'of course I do.'

'Fuck me then.'

'I beg your pardon?'

'You heard.' This Talking Dirty thing had better work. It's what they said to each other on his favourite website. As she'd discovered when she'd clicked Favourites by mistake.

'Um, well – haven't we got to go soon?'

'We've got time for a quickie.' She shut the bedroom door.

Simon began to feel trapped. Normally a quickie would appeal to him, he wouldn't have to bother with the overture before getting on with the show, but not now and not with her. He shuddered.

Sophie took a deep breath. 'You can do it up the Gary if you want.'

Now he didn't say anything because he didn't know what to say.

'You know, it's rhyming slang – Gary Glitter, sh –'

'Yes all right, thanks, I know what it means. I haven't turned gay, if that's what you're hinting at.' What the devil had got into her? Better talk her down. 'Look, Soph, it's not that bad – we did it only the other day . . .'

'The other day?' She tried another escape route from her velvet prison. 'It wasn't the other day, Simon, it was nearly six months ago.'

'Six months? Are you sure?' He hastily put on his suit trousers, before she could come over and manhandle him.

'Positive. It was the night of my birthday, if you remember.' There was an expensive ripping sound in her left ear.

Oh yes, he remembered all right. That had been the night she'd performed her own peculiar version of the dance of the seven veils – but it had been more Salami than Salome. 'Look, I'm sorry, Soph, it's just that – well, I've had a lot on my mind lately –'

'It's not your mind I want.' She finally struggled free and put the dress over the back of the chair. Now Simon could see she wasn't wearing a bra. They really were enormous, but he was used to little brown ones now. 'I want my lover back.' He didn't react. She sat down on the bed and continued. 'Anyway, I don't know why you think you've got a lot on your mind. Everything's fine – work's OK now, we'll get some money in –'

'OK? It's bloody brilliant – at last the bastards have realized what's been sitting right under their noses all these years. Simon Matthews rides again! I always thought I'd make a good gynaecologist – and now it turns out, so does the BBC!' The power surged through his loins at the thought of being back on top. He looked at Sophie, who was smiling at him strangely, showing him her tongue. His loins had a power cut. 'Though it does mean I'll be away a lot.' Thank god.

'Oh I think we'll cope. We managed perfectly well while you were away in Edinburgh this summer, didn't we?'

'Well if you don't count the bath overflowing through the kitchen ceiling, managing to lose Baldrick –'

'Poor Jill.'

'Baldrick, and allowing my car to be towed away as an abandoned vehicle because you hadn't paid the tax disc – then yes, everything was fine, Sophie.' He went to select a tie.

Sophie lay back on the big brass bed and put her hand down her pants. 'So you have nothing to worry about, then,' she said, 'so why don't you come over here and –' she breathed heavily '– relax . . .'

When Della did that, it really turned him on. When Sophie did it, she looked like she was scratching an itch.

'Look, Soph, we really haven't got time for this.' He nearly strangled himself with his own tie.

'Oh yes, I think we have . . .' she said, panting like a thirsty Old English Sheepdog, 'come on, baby, come to mama . . .'

Bing! 'Well that's just it, Soph, I think that's why I don't feel very sexy at the moment, what with not knowing about my real parents and everything –'

'Oh really Simon!' snapped Sophie. 'You've just got to let that go, it's got all out of proportion now, you're like a man obsessed.'

'Possessed.' Simon began to pace round the room. 'It's not as easy as that! I can't just write it off, pretend nothing happened. It's all right for you, you know where you came from. I just can't stop thinking about it, it's driving me mad.'

And me, thought Sophie, who stopped mucking about down there as it quite clearly wasn't having the desired effect. It had been very hard living with his obsession, his mind was elsewhere all the time and yet he wouldn't share whatever was going on inside it. She'd left him to it in the end – fortunately she'd had a project of her own to concentrate on.

He looked genuinely upset actually, poor lamb. Sophie sat up again. 'Didn't that tv thing help at all? I thought you got a big response from your appeal.' This was encouraging, it looked like he was willing to talk about it at last.

'No, not really.' He slumped down on his side of the bed, with his back to her. 'It was mostly little old ladies ringing in to offer their mothering skills, to adopt me, completely missing the point.' And plenty of ladies offering other womanly skills, which had been nice but even he had his standards. He'd kept some of the letters, though, from the better-looking ones who'd attached photographs. Hidden them in the baby's room under the chest of drawers. 'And I followed up a few calls from people in similar circumstances, which just depressed me more – they hadn't got anywhere either.' He buried his face in his hands.

'This isn't really about that though, is it?'

'What isn't?'

'Well, you not wanting to make love to me any more.'

'Oh come on Soph, we've had sex-free zones before.' He got up and walked over to the dressing table. Keeping his back to her, he crouched down to check his hair in the mirror. 'You've not wanted to before, for weeks sometimes. And what about when I've been on location for months on end?'

'Well you haven't exactly been a sex-free zone then, have you?'

His hands paused momentarily as they ran through his hair. 'I don't know what you're talking about – if you mean filming sex scenes then I thought we'd been through all this before –'

'No, I mean what goes on off-camera.'

Simon spun round with a big frown on his face. 'What are you talking about?'

'Oh stop it Simon, I know. I worked in the theatre myself, remember? I am more than familiar with the sordid ways of actors and actresses. I know about the "if it's on location it doesn't count" rule and I can see that it works for some of you, the ones too feeble to go a few weeks without sex. But this one's different.'

'This one?' Simon still wasn't sure, decided to tough it out, look at her as if she was mad.

'Della.'

Shit. 'Oh.'

'It's gone on too long, Simon, it's got to stop.' Strange, she wasn't even shaking.

He sat down on the dressing-table stool.

She looked at him through the bars of their big brass bed. Taking a deep breath, Sophie asked, 'Do you love her?'

'Um . . .'

The whole world stopped while she waited.

'. . . I don't know.'

'Well when will you know?' Good, she was getting angry now, that would help her through. The silly boy just shook his head and stared at the floor. 'Simon?'

The trouble was, he really didn't know. He fancied her, of course, and they still had great sex – when she let him. He'd thought that once that boyfriend of hers had finally been put away, she'd want to see him more. But no matter how much attention he'd been willing to give her, she'd still been very cool towards him. Simon wanted to take it further, but he was pretty sure Della didn't. He was relieved now that Sophie had brought it to a head, he wanted to get it sorted out too. It was one thing to shag the continuity girl in your Winnebago, quite another to fall in love with a girl who's young enough to be your daughter.

'Are you giving me an ultimatum, Soph?'

'Is that what you want?' she asked, softly.

She knew him so well. 'Well, I – oh god, I don't know what I want, I don't know what I'm doing, I –' He placed his face in his hands in despair.

The bedroom door flew open. 'Mu-um . . .'

'What?' snapped Sophie.

Scarlett was a bit taken aback at her mother's tone, but kept her position by the door with her arms folded. 'I was just coming to say that I'm not going to wear that dress. I refuse.'

'Fine. You can wear a bin bag for all I care. Now please go away, we'll be out in a minute.'

'But –'

'Just go!' said Simon, too loudly.

She went.

They looked at each other.

'Is Della worth leaving us for?'

Silence.

'Because you either stop it right now, Simon, or you go.' Yes, good girl.

'Will you have the baby anyway?'

'Um – sorry?' She couldn't believe her ears. Surely, he –

'If you manage to get pregnant. Will you still have it if I go?'

'How on earth –'

'Sophie.' He looked up at the ceiling. 'Computers aren't nearly as complicated as you think. It's very easy to trace what sites other people have visited, if you know what you're doing. I know about the sperm banks, I've been following your correspondence very closely.' He stood up. 'I think your new-found nymphomania is more to do with getting me to think I've fathered a child than wanting to keep our marriage intact, don't you?'

Her turn to keep quiet now.

'Sophie?'

The trouble was she really didn't know. Ideally she'd like Simon and Scarlett and her and Sebastian to live happily ever after. But he'd been more than clear about his views on having another child the last time. Could she really manage on her own now, was she strong enough to cope without him?

'Are you giving me an ultimatum?'

Nobody said anything, nobody moved. They looked across the room at each other and stopped.

Sophie was the first to speak. 'What are we doing?' she asked, quietly. 'Is this what we want?'

'I don't know,' he said, simply.

'Come here.' She held her hand out to him.

He sat on the bed beside her and looked at her soft moon face. 'I'm sorry, Soph.'

'So'm I.'

'I don't know what I'm doing any more. It's like I'm having an out-of-body experience – I watch myself and I don't recognize me any more. It's as if when my mother died she took me away with her. I didn't mean for any of this to happen, I'm so sorry –'

Simon sobbed like a little boy. Sophie took him in her arms and listened as he hated the woman who'd just left him, given him away. Forgotten about him. Abandoned him.

Didn't care about him, what happened to him, didn't love him enough.

Sophie had to help him. She swung into caretaker mode, the part she knew best and the part she did best. She put herself into him and it came. 'I've got an idea,' she said softly into his ear.

Simon looked up. 'What?'

'Why don't we go up there, together?'

He turned round. 'What, to Glasgow?'

'Yes. Together. I mean, why not? We could ask a few questions around Cambuslang, see if anyone remembers anything.'

'But they won't.'

'How d'you know? Not everyone will have seen Richard and Judy, and even though we haven't been there for years, I do remember it being like a sort of village. I'm sure someone will remember the magical arrival of a new baby, especially if it was completely out of the blue. And even if they can't help us, we can have a look in the library at the old newspapers, or go to see Births, Marriages and Deaths.' She was warming to her theme. 'Your mum must have had to register you somewhere, somehow – I did with Scarlett.'

He warmed to her theme too. 'Actually, it would be quite nice to go up there after all these years – we could go for a long weekend, the three of us – I could show you my old school, and where I passed my driving test, the bakery – maybe we'll bump into some of my old friends, I bet they're all still there . . .'

'Exactly! And even if we don't discover anything about

your real parents, you'll still feel like you exist – it'll remind you where you came from. Who you are.'

'God, Soph, that's a brilliant idea!' He hugged her tight.

Sophie was really pleased with herself, and really pleased for him.

He looked at her, into her warm baby-blue eyes rounded with love. 'You are such a good friend to me, Sophie – I don't deserve you.'

'Yes you do. And anyway, I'm sure you'd do the same for me. We love each other so much, don't we?'

He really hoped so. He covered up his reply with a kiss, and then another and another. He could feel himself beginning to come back to her, wanting to come home. Reassured by her unconditional love for him, and her soft squashy motherly warmth, he found that he had the desire for her after all. Kicking off his trousers, he despised himself for having to turn her onto her stomach; but he did so gently, with tenderness, so she wouldn't know it was because he felt so guilty looking at her happy moon-like face, a picture of perfect bliss. It'll just take time, that's all.

And she obligingly went up on all fours, big white tits slapping about, just like the old days when she knew it was a special treat, his favourite position. Just he was about to shoot into her fleshy folds, the bedroom door opened.

'I was just coming to say I'm ready,' said a white-faced Scarlett.

'Is that you, Della?'

'Hi, Mum.'

'Are you still all right for Sunday?'

'Well actually . . .'

'Della –'

'I know, I know – it's just that I'm waiting to hear about a work thing, that's all.'

A roaring silence from the other end.

Oh fucking hell. 'Look, it's important, Mum. Honest. Come on, you know I'd rather see you, but this could make me lots of money.'

Baby steps. One day at a time. 'All right then, but you be sure to call me when you know, OK?'

'OK.'

'And I'll be thinking of you tonight.'

'Thanks.'

'Just be big-hearted.'

'OK, thanks.'

'And try not to be judgemental.'

'Right. Bye –'

'Or opinionated. Let her say her piece. And don't keep telling her what to do.'

'Okthanksmumcallyalaterbye.'

Millicent smiled to herself as she put down the phone and picked up a kitchen knife. It had been slow, and painstaking, but bit by bit she was getting to know her daughter once more. She'd realized eventually that if she gave Della enough space, she'd come to her in the end. It had been a hard lesson to learn, but a very worthwhile one. So she'd given it all up to the good Lord who seemed to be taking very good care of them; and now it sounded like Della was receiving some benefits from Him too.

It was *Just A Minute* on Radio 4 now – she'd listen to it as she prepared the supper. She'd promised Constance a traditional Caribbean spread, and had gone to some lengths to track down various delicacies. She just hoped frozen mountain chicken tasted as good as it did fresh.

The atmosphere in the car over to Constance's house in Holland Park was a little strained to say the least. Nobody said much: Simon was irritated because the minicab hadn't turned up so he'd had to drive, which meant he couldn't drink; Sophie knew she'd be cross-examined as to why she wasn't wearing The Dress so she was busy feeling the fear and doing it anyway; and Scarlett was cross because the new puppy Kenny (the parents hadn't caught on to the *South Park* thing yet) had chewed Auntie Jess's red stilettos that she'd promised to lend to Jade for her Austin Powers party. Or at least that's what they all told each other.

After Sophie had gone back to the car to get the presents, they walked up the steps to Constance's imposing front door in silence, and Simon banged the gleaming door knocker three times.

Almost before he had finished, the huge door opened and Millicent was standing there, a little too close for comfort. 'Good evening, Mr and Mrs Matthews, Miss Scarlett,' she said.

They all took a step back.

'Hi Miss O'Hara!' said Scarlett, who knew this lady's bark was worse than her bite, having had many a giggly session round the kitchen table as they'd all three played gin rummy for real money well into the night. 'We're here!'

'Yes,' said the big black woman, bulging eyes taking in Scarlett's casual dress, 'I can see that.'

'Well shall we come in?' said Sophie, who wanted to get this evening over and done with. She supposed Constance would sit her next to Luigi as usual.

But Millicent was staring at Sophie. So like him, she was thinking.

Sophie looked at Simon. They'd not met this woman before but they'd heard all about her from Constance and Scarlett, who both adored her. To be quite honest Sophie was a bit suspicious of her, she'd read in the *Daily Mail* time and time again about housekeepers drugging their elderly bosses and getting them to change their wills at the last minute.

Millicent snapped out of it. 'Excuse me, yes of course.' She smiled as she opened the door, reminding Scarlett yet again of that horrible nurse. Forgetting that she was supposed to be cool and not be keen about anything now, she ran on ahead and threw open the drawing-room doors. 'Happy birthday, Constance!'

Her grandmother was at her usual place by the fireplace, under the picture of Grandad, wearing a dress Scarlett hadn't seen before but it was beautiful and long and sparkly and like a film star at a party. 'Wow! You look dead-drop gorgeous!' Now why on earth didn't her mum wear stuff like that?

'Hi, Scarlett!'

'Auntie Jess!' She ran over to her aunt who'd stood up from the sofa to throw her arms around her, but Jess moved away just in time and she caught her by the arms instead.

'Let's have a look at you. Hmm, you've changed a bit since I last saw you.' She scrutinized the excited little face in front of her. 'You sure you're still a virgin?'

'Jessica!' Sophie was in the doorway. 'You're back!'

'Glad to see your powers of observation are still intact,' said her sister.

'Hi, Jess!' Simon made his way across the room and gave her a bear-hug. But he soon realized something was different and stood back.

Jessica was irritated to see that everyone was looking at Sophie, who appeared to be frozen to the spot. 'You're pregnant,' she said quietly.

'Two out of two Soph, well done.'

She couldn't take her eyes off the bump. 'How come?'

'Well, I just lay down and opened my legs and –'

'Yes all right Jessica, thank you,' interbutted Constance. 'Come on in, Sophie, won't you have a glass of champagne? It seems we have more to celebrate than we thought!'

At that precise moment, just down the road in Ladbroke Grove, Della was cutting Nancy's hair.

'I like your new couch, Della,' said Nancy as Della snipped away to the tinny beat of Capital blaring out from her little radio sitting in front of them on the kitchen table.

'It's not new, you silly cow,' retorted Della. 'I've just chucked a throw on it, that's all.'

'Oh. Sorry.' Nancy tried again. 'Where d'you get it, then? It's really nice.'

'From Selfridges. Cost a fucking bomb.' She hadn't got it there, actually – it was from the market, really cheap, but she wasn't going to tell Nance that or she'd only get one for herself.

The two girls fell silent. Nancy had thought it would go a bit better than this, she'd been really excited when Della had agreed to do her hair. But her friend was still being very cool with her. Nancy just wanted them to get back to how it was in the old days. She'd really missed Della, it had been awful not seeing her and not talking to her every day. So she'd come up with a plan all by her own, well sort of, she'd tried to talk about it to Boring Barbara who had helped her a bit – she just decided to keep reminding Della that they'd agreed they were always going to be best mates for ever, no man was ever going to split them up. So she'd left a message on Della's machine every day, she'd written letters and sent cards, left a bunch of flowers on her doorstep every Sunday morning; she'd even drawn her a really good picture of the two of them together when they were kids. And framed it in one of those clip things. And then left it with Maggie in the launderette next door, for the next time she came in. She'd also secretly given all the clients from her new work (Scissor Happy) who weren't satisfied with their hairdo (which was basically anyone under seventy) Della's phone number, on the condition that they say who give it them. And she'd sent her just one Rolo in an envelope.

Then Della had answered the phone one day, took Nance a bit by surprise actually, she was about to give up. So they'd started talking again, not about you-know-what though, and bit by bit things had got better. Nancy had managed to get Della to meet up this evening (the first time since Then) by begging her to do her hair, as she was just the best in the world. Della had agreed, but Nance had to bring the Bacardi Breezers. So she'd got four of every kind, which cost her a bloody fortune, but it was going to be worth it. She hoped so, anyway.

And Della had her own plan, of course. She knew it was bad, but she wanted Nancy to suffer. Well, a bit anyway. She had, after all, betrayed her and even her mum would say that was a bad thing to do. But Millicent had said to give Nancy another chance, let bygones be bygones. And in fact, if Della was being truthful (she was doing her best to try that out now, at least to herself) she missed her old mate. She'd done another thing Millicent had suggested and given Barbara a go but she'd had one of the most boring nights of her whole life at some bloody theatre, watching some stupid play about Lady Somebody's Fan. Lady Somebody's Fanny would have been better.

So she was pleased at Nancy's trying to get back in with her. But she wasn't going to let her get too close, not yet – even though she was dying to tell someone all about her new plan.

'So, er,' Nancy said, 'what've you been up to?'

'Oh y'know, this and that,' said Della, not wanting to give too much away.

'You got rid of the nun, then?'

'Who?'

'Your mum.'

'Oh, yeah. How d'you know that?' Had she been spying on her?

'Pile of Shit's gone.'

'Oh yeah.' It hadn't gone in actual fact, it was all packed away in Millicent's shabby old suitcase on top of the wardrobe in the bedroom. And the letters were still in their shoebox, under the bed. She hadn't read them again since that night or anything soppy like that, but she knew they were there. 'We're getting along all right now, in actual fact.'

'Really?'

'Yeah, she's all right really, just a bit old-fashioned. She's getting better, though.'

'What, d'you like her now then?'

'She's all right. I meet up with her once a week, it's quite sweet really. Except that she always drags me along to the bloody zoo when it's her turn to choose.'

'What?' Things really had changed round here. 'Why?'

'Penguin mad.'

'No!'

'Yeah. Loves 'em. Can't get enough of them.' Della laughed at Millicent's laughing. 'Mad.'

'Where's she live now, then?'

'She found herself a fucking great mansion in Holland Park.'

'No!' Nancy was shocked, nearly dropped the bottle. 'How come?'

'She's living with an older woman.'

Nancy stopped mid-swig. 'What, lezzies?'

Della laughed, she knew Nance would think that, she was so stupid. 'Nah, idiot, she's working for Jessica Rose's mum.'

'What, that girl off the telly?'

'Yeah, her mother.'

'Fuck me, how'd she get that?'

'Oh I don't know – look, Nance, stop moving about, or I'll cut your ear off. By accident.' But that would be a nice idea.

She could almost hear Nancy's brain clanking round. 'Didn't you used to know her? Wasn't she the one who –'

'Yes.'

'Had that party –'

'Yes.'

'Where she –'

'Yes.'

'You were there, weren't you? Didn't you go with – um, did you see anything?'

'No, we – I – left before it happened.' Leave it.

'Bloody hell. Who'd have thought, your mum, ending up being in the same house with the mother of someone like that.'

'Oh don't be so bloody saintish Nancy, it's not as if we didn't do our bit in that department. I seem to remember you being off your face all the bloody time on just half an E! Going round begging people to snog you, I do believe.'

'Yeah well,' said Nancy, trying to take a drink without moving her head but she couldn't so she decided to have another fag instead, 'I don't do any of that any more, not since, well, you know . . .' She trailed off, not wanting to be the first one to mention it, so she decided to concentrate on lighting her cigarette.

'What, nothing? Not even weed?' said Della, as she pushed Nancy's fat head forwards a bit roughly, to do the little bits at the back.

There was a weird crackling sound, followed almost immediately by a burning smell.

'Ohmigod, Nance!' Della moved round to the front and couldn't quite believe what she could see. The front of her head looked like a burnt stubbly cornfield, like the one she'd seen on a daytrip to the countryside with Darr– Well anyway, that's what it looked like.

'It's OK, really,' said Nancy, trying not to sound too pissed off, brushing away the remaining bits of burnt hair that hadn't gone up in smoke. 'I didn't really want a fringe anyway, honest – doesn't really suit me I don't think, does it?'

'Um, no,' said Della as she went back to where she'd been, grateful that Nancy couldn't see her smiling. She couldn't have planned it better herself.

'So anyway, where were we?' Nancy took an enormous drag on her fag, to steady her nerves.

Della knew perfectly well what they were both trying to avoid talking about, but she didn't want to go there either – and so she changed the subject. 'Seen any good films lately?'

But Nancy wasn't going to be palmed off with standard hairdresser talk. 'You still shagging T.o.m.?'

'Who?'

'That actor.'

'Oh. Yeah.'

'Really? Even though you don't have to now that –' It was no use, all roads led to *him*.

'Yeah. He's OK, buys me loads of presents. Works out quite well in actual fact. Less I do it with him, more he buys.'

'Oh. That's nice, then.'

'Yeah.'

But Nancy wanted to get back to when they told each other everything, and she wasn't going to give up. 'You seeing somebody else now?'

She knows then, Della thought. 'No. I'm busy concentrating on work, trying to make as much money as I can.'

'Oh that's really good, Della, good on ya.' This was really not going very well at all, they were like people who hardly knew each other. They just had to get it out of the way. Sod it. Nancy decided to come out with it now. 'Look, Della, I –'

'All done!' said Della, even though she hadn't quite finished but who cares. 'D'you want to have a look?' She went into the kitchenette and got a mirror out of the work drawer.

'Fucking hell, that's beautiful!' said Nancy, gazing at the mirror.

Della was a bit taken aback, she'd deliberately given Nancy the worst haircut in the world, she'd planned a Worzel Gummidge. 'Oh, d'you like it?'

'It's gorgeous, the silver frame's really old – where'd it come from?'

'Oh that – um, it was a present from Jessica Rose.' To Jessica Rose more like.

'Was it, you know, to make up for – well, you know?'

So Nancy knew everything then.

'I heard, Della, through the grapevine, you know how people love a gossip – she shopped him, didn't she? He goes to prison, she gets to go free. That's not fair if you ask me, I think –'

'Look, Nancy, I don't really want to talk about all that right now.' I'll decide when, thank you. 'What d'you think of your hair?'

Nancy put the mirror down on the table and looked back up at Della. 'It's horrible. I knew it would be.'

'And what exactly d'you mean by that, may I ask?' Della put her hands on her hips.

Nancy stood up, big chunks of mousy hair falling to the floor, and looked at her old friend fair and square. 'Della, I know you very well. Too well. I had to be punished for what I done, didn't I?'

'I don't know what you're talking about.' Bloody hell, she'd been rumbled.

'Oh hello – Nancy calling Della? Look, you silly arse, it's me – the one you used to plot how to get people back with, remember? I thought you'd do this and d'you know what – I don't even care that I look really crap, I just want to be friends again, that's all. I thought the burning my head off part was a bit over the top though.'

Della couldn't help herself. She began to laugh – Nancy looked terrible, like she had cancer or something. And when she laughed, Nancy laughed, and then they both laughed together. And laughed and laughed, especially when Della told her the next part of her plan was to dress Nance up in a horrible rank dress she'd been given by one of her clients, which she knew would look really shit and then take her out for a drink – she was going to pass it off as a kind of make-over, a nice thing to do, to help her get a boyfriend.

'No need,' said Nancy, opening the other bottle of watermelon for Della and taking two fags out of her packet, just like the old days. 'I already have a little man in my life, thank you very much.'

Della went cold. 'You didn't fall pregnant, did you?'

'Don't be so fucking stupid, course not.' I don't think you can that way, can you? 'Nah, I'm going out with someone now.'

Thank fuck for that. 'Who?'

'You're not going to believe this.' Nancy was bursting with it.

'Do I know him then?'

'Oh yes.'

'Well come on, Nance, fucking spit it out!' This was incredible, who on earth did they know who would go out with her?

'Guess.'

'No.'

'Go on.'

'I can't. Oh hurry up Nancy, I want to go for a piss but I can't till you tell me.'

'Kevin Khan.'

'No!'

'Yes!'

'You're joking!'

'No.'

'But he – you – Kevin Khan, brother of Raj the traffic warden? The one we were at school with, that Kevin Khan? Kevin Khan the King Kunt?'

Nancy nodded.

'But he's really nice now.' She looked a bit embarrassed.

'Is it lurve?'

'I think so, yes.'

'Really?!'

'Yes. Definitely.' Nancy smiled shyly. 'He's gorgeous . . .'

'I'm sorry, Nance, I can't hold it any longer. C'mon.'

Funny how you just swing back into things with some people, Della thought as Nancy followed her down the squeaky corridor into the bathroom. Only minutes ago she'd wanted to see Nancy squeal and squirm like a stuck pig, now she was coming with her to the toilet. Mad. 'What's he doing now, then?' she asked as she sat down.

'Oh I don't know, something to do with computers. He's loaded.'

'Rich? Kevin Khan?!'

'Yeah, it's great! Takes me all over the place.'

'What's the sex like?' Not that Nancy would know – as far as Della was aware she'd only had sex with – well, with one other person.

'Great, yeah, good – he's still got that scar on his little bum!'

'No!'

'Yes – still doesn't know who did it, still angry about it now in fact!'

'You never told him then?'

'No, I wouldn't do a thing like that, you know that.'

'Wouldn't you, Nancy?' She looked her old mate straight in the eye. 'You a woman of standards now, then?'

'Look, Della, we've got to talk about this –'

Della stood up and flushed the toilet. She looked down at Nancy squatting uncomfortably on the floor. 'He still a midget?'

Nancy got up. 'Well he's quite short, yeah.'

'How short?'

'Five foot three, why?'

'Just wondering what we'd look like together. Scuse me.' She squeezed past Nancy and went back up the passageway.

Nancy followed, as ever. 'You wouldn't.'

'I could,' said Della as she picked up her bottle from the kitchen table. 'I'd only be six inches taller than him, and what's six inches between friends, eh Nancy?'

'Della, please, let's just keep calm about this –'

'Calm?! Calm, you fucking whore! I'm afraid it's not something I feel calm about, you sleeping with my bloody boyfriend! Why did you do it, Nancy, why? I tried to patch it up with him, but it was never the same after that, you spoilt everything. And then – oh god, I miss him so much, he won't even let me visit him . . .' She clapped her hand over her mouth and went all quiet, but her eyes were filling up.

The phone rang. Phew, saved by the bell, thought Nancy with relief as she picked up her fags and lighter and went over to sit on the sofa. She'd kind of practised this moment over and over again and now it was here.

Della pounced on it before the machine could kick in. Maybe this was the call she'd been waiting for. 'Hello?' Yes, it was him!

'Yes, that's right, yes . . . Well Sunday would be good for me . . . Can you park round there? . . . Do I need to bring anything with me?' Laugh. 'OK then, I'll see you Sunday, at eleven. Yeah, cheers, bye.' Della put the phone down and punched the air. 'Yes!'

'What's that, then?' said Nancy, who hadn't been able to guess.

'None of your fucking business, that's what that is — same as it wasn't any of your business to go shagging my boyfriend! Come on then, Nance, let's have it!' She sat down in the armchair opposite her old best friend and took a swig of Breezer. 'Come on! I'm all ears,' she said, trying to be big-hearted, whatever that was.

'OK, then,' said Nancy, who'd rehearsed this speech many times. She cleared her throat. 'I'd invited Darren over to my place as a surprise for you. The plan was that you'd get all pissed off that he'd forgotten and then be really shocked to see him round at mine —'

'You certainly got that bit right.' Fuck, mustn't interrupt.

Nancy continued anyway. 'And then we'd go on to have a mad night and have a real laugh and so on. But he arrived early, and he had just pocketfuls of gear, Della, and so — well he wanted to start early. You know what he's like, Dell — it's really hard to say no to him, innit?'

Della didn't say anything.

'Now you know I've got no head for drugs but, well, I'd been looking forward to it for so long – I just got carried away.'

Della frowned at her friend. Was she supposed to believe this shit?

'And there's no need to look at me like that neither, you've done it and all. Many's the time I've looked after you when you've taken more than you can handle. D'you remember that time when I had to talk you down over the phone at four o'clock in the morning, and I made you mop the kitchen floor so's you had something else to think about? That was really funny, you –'

'Go on.'

'Well anyway, by about eight thirty he'd given me loads of coke, some really strong weed which was like an oil he put in a fag and two Es. I was off my tits, Della, really off it. I didn't know what I was doing.'

'Oh fuck off Nance, you seemed to be perfectly awake to me. I think you were even smiling.' That horrible picture came up in Della's mind's eye again. So was he.

'Look Della, I've asked myself all the questions you want to ask me over and over and yes, I would be lying if I said it wasn't in the back of my mind to get one over on you. I was getting pissed off with you it's true, you were spending more time with him and less time with me. I was jealous. And I was fucked off with still being a virgin. So it could have been for all those reasons, I don't know. What I do know is that it was the lowest thing I ever did, and I ain't never going to go that low again.'

Nancy went all quiet, and Della couldn't really think of

anything to say except, 'I'm over him now, anyway.' She wasn't, but she'd been hoping that if she said it enough times it would start to be true.

'Well that's the other thing I wanted to say, and I think it's really important. What kind of bloke is it that does that to his girlfriend's best mate? Plies her with drugs when he knows full well she gets really off it really easy, and then shags her up the arse? I could have done him for rape, Della.'

Now she'd never thought of that. Della had been so busy blaming Nancy that she hadn't seen it from Darren's point of view before. Bastard. Fucking bastard. Well it just so happens that prison's just the right place for him after all. She'd heard about what they get up to in there. She looked at Nancy, who was waiting for her to say something.

'Fucking hurts, doesn't it? I couldn't face doing a shit for at least a week after that!'

Nancy squealed long and loud with all the joy of a pig who'd just become unstuck and the rest of the evening was spent reminiscing and catching up on the missing months, getting pissed and smoking too much. The two girls parted at two o'clock in the morning, having got most of their friendship back; it was a bit like the good old bad old days, but different. And Mickey didn't take Nancy home. He'd sold his minicab and was now a van driver for Royal Mail. So Nance had a fucking scary ride home, with a grinning Spiros at the wheel.

'Can I go and watch tv?'

'Scarlett!' cried both parents at once.

'You haven't eaten nearly enough –' said Simon '– and it's your grandmother's birthday,' added Sophie.

'But it's horrible!' protested Scarlett.

'Scarlett!' cried both parents again.

'She's quite right,' Constance declared. 'D'you want to . . .' She indicated the fireplace to Scarlett.

'Oh yes, thanks.' Scarlett got up and took her plate over to the elegant Chinese vase standing there, took out the dried-flower arrangement, scraped the contents of her plate into it and replaced the flowers. She then put her plate back, being very careful to place the knife and fork together, and waved smugly to her parents as she left the dining room.

Everyone looked at Constance. 'Well how d'you think I keep my figure? I only employ bad cooks, they make much better cleaners. Which is why Luigi and I eat out most of the time, isn't it?' She raised her glass and smiled at him, sitting quietly at the other end of the table behind a barrage of silver and candelabra and glinting crystal.

Sitting in Dad's place, thought Sophie, who had drunk more than usual in her despair and was feeling quite tipsy now.

'In fact, darling, would you like to come with me for a moment?' She scraped her antique carver back as she stood up. 'Do excuse us, everyone.' Smiling, she took Luigi's proffered arm and they too left the room.

'Oh god, they're not going to put on a show, are they?' Jessica shuddered at the memory of supposedly impromptu concerts at the end of Big Events, which had been quite excruciating. Dad had pretended to play the piano (which they all knew was one of those that did it all for you, from

Harrods), Constance had pretended to be able to sing, and they'd all pretended to enjoy it.

'Isn't that your speciality?' Sophie said into her glass.

'I'm sorry?' Jessica had no time for this.

'Soph –' Simon reached over and put his hand on her knee.

'Putting on a show? Making a display? Embarrassing us all? What the hell' – she could feel she was going red but she didn't care – 'did you think you were doing? You've never even said sorry! You just disappeared into thin air – where've you been?'

Jessica really didn't see why she should explain anything to anybody. Hadn't Mother sorted this out for her?

Grateful for this opportunity to Say Something while Mother wasn't here to defend her favourite daughter, Sophie carried on. 'You have no idea, have you? Well, it was hell for us – we had journalists crawling all over the place, camping out outside our house, asking Scarlett questions as she was dropped off from school even. Poor Simon's reputation was publicly tarnished because of his association with you, which was my fault not his. You could at least have rung to explain yourself, but no, you left us to deal with it all while you, you – you were busy getting Pregnant!'

'Oh fuck off Sophie, what d'you know about getting pregnant? You're so bloody useless, you can't even get that right!'

She knew it was a blow below the belt and Sophie was indeed winded.

'How dare you.'

Simon!

'How dare you speak to Sophie like that! How could you say such a thing?' He glared across the table at his sulky sister-in-law. 'Why would you want to wound your own sister, your own flesh and blood, probably the only person you know who is loyal, kind, compassionate, all-forgiving – my wife, my beautiful wife, has a simplicity and a purity that you will never know, let alone understand.' He got up and stood behind Sophie's chair, placing his hands protectively on her shoulders. 'This is a woman who has experienced more pain and suffering than you can ever imagine, but who has the strength to get up and try again and again and again. You, on the other hand, seem to think it's OK to run off at the first sign of difficulty, you –'

'Oh shut up and sit down Simon, nobody's filming this.' Who did he think he was, a barrister in a mini-series?

'What's going on?' Constance breezed back in and took her place at the head of the table. 'Sit down, Simon, I have a speech to deliver.'

Sophie squeezed his hand before he left her and as he sat down they exchanged a sideways look of love and unity that she hadn't experienced for some time. She was moved by his words and held them close.

Oh no, wise words from Mother. 'Where's Luigi?' asked Jessica, hoping to put the moment off for a bit longer.

'He's left.' Constance sought Dutch courage in her French claret. 'Well, in fact, I've left him. Either way, he's not here.' She rang the bell for Millicent.

The door opened immediately.

'Is he – um, are you – um, have er –'

'Yes, Sophie, you will be glad to hear that we are no longer a couple.' She cleared her throat to make her grand announcement. 'I am cutting all ties.'

Everyone had the same thought. What does that mean?

'I'm sure you're all wondering what that means. Well, let me explain.'

Throughout her life Cecily had been bound up with responsibility. Tied down with it, held down with it, never allowed her freedom except once when she had made a terrible mess of things.

She was an only child, born to elderly parents. Her father, who worked for a national transport network, was a domineering man who died when Cecily was merely thirteen years of age. Her weak and delicate mother did her best to bring up Cecily alone and, being a talented seamstress, quickly became a much-valued and cherished member of Richmond Theatre's costume department.

Young Cecily often sat in the wings and admired the actors and actresses as they entertained the enthralled audience, and she resolved one day to join the ranks of those responsible for bringing so much joy to others' lives.

Being an exceptionally bright and beautiful child, she studied hard and used her talents well, resulting in great acclaim from critics and colleagues alike. ('An absolute triumph' – Richmond and Twickenham Times.)

But tragedy was never far away, and when Cecily was just at the beginning of her adult life, her poor struggling mother was struck down by a terrible illness. At the same time, a kindly Scottish man came calling at the Stage Door and, to cut a long story short, they married and Cecily's poor mother came to live with them. Tragically, she passed away when their daughter was a mere babe in arms.

*

'So just when Jessica was getting old enough to look after herself, Sophie was born. Another rope to tie me down.'

Thanks a lot, thought Sophie.

'Really, Mother, this is nothing we don't know already, can we just cut to the chase?'

'Patience, Jessica, patience.' Everyone took a drink. 'Once Sophie had left home, I begged your father to retire and come away with me but he wouldn't. It was quite ridiculous, we had more than enough money, but it seems he was worried about Sophie and felt he should "be there" as they say nowadays, to help her with her troubles.' Sophie looked down at her lap, a tiny bit smug that her father had put her before everything else.

'Added to which he was, of course, a complete work-aholic, and the thought of leaving the blasted office brought him out in a cold sweat. No wonder he had a heart attack, he was under so much strain, poor darling. Constantly looking after those who couldn't, or wouldn't, look after themselves.' Sophie didn't look up.

'And then, once he'd died, once I'd got over the shock of finding him dead in the bed beside me that awful morning, I couldn't – oh really, Sophie, this has got to stop, it's almost Pavlovian – well, I didn't feel ready to go. I still had Mrs Mac to look after, of course, and I'd promised her a home for life. And I had to keep an eye on Jessica, who had already purchased her one-way ticket to hell by then.' She took a deep breath and laid a hand on her chest. 'Archie's death affected me far more than any of you will ever know. I was never in love with Luigi – and I never let him think otherwise. He always knew I was going to do this.'

'Do what?' Sophie was getting worried.

'Ah, you still remember that, do you?' Constance smiled. 'I only said it because I didn't want to be a burden on my family, as my mother had been to me. It is one thing to say you're going to kill yourself at sixty, and quite another to do it.' She smoothed over her hair. 'It's really not that bad once you get here.'

Jessica had always suspected she'd threatened suicide because she didn't want to start looking old.

'And so I'm going to do the next best thing.'

The old bat is so over-dramatic, thought Simon, who'd never seen Constance's work but suspected her to be crap.

'Which is what?' Jessica was tiring of this now. And she was tired, sleepy-tired too, it was probably something like five o'clock in the morning to her.

'I'm going to stage my own disappearance.' She smiled triumphantly as she watched their faces work it out. Nobody asked but she explained. 'I'm going to go. Leave. Cut the ropes. Fly away. Travel the world.'

'Sightseeing?' asked Jessica.

'No,' replied Constance, 'being bad.'

'I think that's a great idea,' said Simon.

'Yes, good for you,' said Sophie, who was only copying Simon. She made a mental note to process all this later.

'I can't believe you'd be that selfish,' said Jessica. 'When are you coming back?'

'I'm not.'

'What, never?' asked Sophie, who on second thoughts realized she'd better start processing it now.

'No.'

'Oh don't be ridiculous!' Jessica folded her arms into the space between her bosoms and her bump. This was the tedious part of Constance's pranks, the catch-me-out-if-you-can part. 'Where are you going to go?'

'I don't know yet. I'm just going to turn up at the airport tomorrow morning, with just handbaggage and my passport, and pick a destination. It's going to be such an adventure, I've always wanted to do something like this, I can't wait!' Constance looked like a little girl, almost bouncing in her chair with the excitement of it all.

Jessica thought of another one. 'Who are you going to go with?' She knew her mother liked to be surrounded by people whenever possible, she'd always been a party girl.

'Nobody. I'm going on my own.'

'Really?' asked Sophie, who thought this rather brave.

'Yes, really. It's out with the old and in with the new – tomorrow will be the first day of the rest of my life. Isn't it thrilling?!' She looked at them all in one move, the way an actress takes in the whole of an audience at once.

'It is – I have to say I'm very jealous,' Simon said, and he really meant it. 'You are lucky.'

'Luck has nothing to do with it, Simon,' pronounced Constance. 'We make our own luck. We're all given the same tools in life, it's how we use them that counts –'

'How are you going to pay for all this?' Aha, thought Jess, that's got her!

'Your father was a very shrewd businessman,' replied

Constance. 'All sorts of pensions and other clever invest-
ments of his have come to fruition now that I'm sixty –
and of course I inherited all his properties on his death.
I've sold a few of them already, and the rent from those
remaining is just about enough to keep little old me going
for quite some time. No overheads, you see!'

She really has worked this out quite well, thought Jessica,
no wonder she looks so bloody pleased with herself. Oh no.
'You haven't sold this house though, have you?'

'No no no, of course not.'

Phew.

'I've given it away.'

'What?!' Both sisters were astonished.

'Yes, to a marvellous new charitable foundation for
wayward children. They're going to turn it into a school, I
believe.'

'No! You can't . . .' Jessica began to panic as she felt her
financial security blanket being snatched away.

'I'm afraid I can! I can do what I like now.' A beaming
Constance rang the bell for Millicent to clear the plates,
too busy enjoying herself to notice that she was doing so
already.

'Oh, and I'm also selling your flat, Jessica.'

'What?!' She'd forgotten all about that, it seemed like
ages ago now. 'But you can't!' The baby kicked. 'It's got
squatters in it, and anyway, it's mine. I won't let you.'

'That's no squatter, that's the young man I've let it out
to in the meantime. Rather a nice chap, works round the
corner from you, in the video rental shop.'

'What, that twat! You've let him live in my flat?!'

'I had to, he was the only person who answered my ad in the newsagent's window. And it's not your flat, it's still in your father's name.'

Simon was enjoying this little show, she'd planned it very well. Quite a performance. And it was very gratifying to see Jessica lost for words, probably for the first time in her life.

'There's no point protesting, Jess, there's nothing you can do. I'll tell you why I've done this, to save you the bother of asking.' Constance was clearly loving this. Her two daughters were clearly hating it.

'Since you committed your worst crime to date and finally managed to drag the family name down into the gutter with you, I've had time to think. It was an enormous shock to me to realize that you're not a very nice person, Jessica.'

Sophie exchanged a look with Simon. They quickly looked away again, knowing they'd get a chance to giggle about this later. Or at least go 'hell-o!' like they do on *Rikki*.

'I couldn't understand what had possessed you, why you would imagine your behaviour to be acceptable to anyone, let alone yourself. It distresses me to think that you had so little regard for your own life that you would treat your own body and soul so badly.'

Sophie thought this made a lot of sense actually. Low self-esteem, you see, it's a killer.

'To me, you are very precious. Too precious. And that's the problem. I've never let you take responsibility for your own life, because I've been too busy doing that for you. I thought I was being kind, but no – I've been nothing but unhelpful to you. I'd do anything for you, Jessica, you know that, and this is breaking my heart, but now I have to let you stand on your own two feet and learn to look after yourself. We're too close, we're too similar, it's time to break our bond and get our relationship onto a healthier footing. I was very pleased to hear this afternoon that you have arrived at the same conclusion – it means I've made the right decision.'

'Yes, but you don't have to go selling my flat –'

'Ah but I do. You've never experienced a moment's difficulty in life, and I think this would be an excellent time to start. You need something horrible to happen to you, something life-changing, to make you stop and think.'

'But I've had a horrible time recently, it's been really awful . . .'

'What, living in the Caribbean for months on end at my expense?' Sophie and Simon looked at each other again, this time with an 'ohmigod!' expression each.

'That newspaper business didn't mean anything to you, Jessica, you just ran away and left me to clear up your mess as usual. Well it's not going to happen any more.' Constance took a sip of water and sighed. 'It upsets me that you seem to have no real friendships, no man to speak of and you're not even nice to your own sister. Family is everything, I thought you knew that. We used to get on, we were very close, but nowadays I think you just see me as some sort of money dispenser, a cashpoint if you like. Put simply, you've forgotten how to be nice, Jessica. A bit of humility and hardship will do you a power of good.'

'You're just punishing me for making people stare at you in the hairdresser's.'

Constance ignored this remark, although it was true. The juniors had been instructed by André to cut out all mention of Jessica from the salon's magazines, resulting in a certain amount of resentment towards Constance from the rest of the clientèle. Only *Good Housekeeping* had remained intact.

'I'm sorry, Jessica, but you're on your own now. You've still got your return ticket to Antigua, so you'd better go back there and think about how you're going to start looking after yourself.'

'But I'm having a baby –'

'Ah, but you're not, are you?' The two women glared at each other.

'Mango and ice cream!' Millicent announced as she burst through the door.

'Oh whoopee,' said Jessica, who'd eaten very little else over the last few months.

'I'm sorry – I don't understand –' said Sophie.

'I'm going to give it away!' spat Jessica. 'I was going to have it adopted, but now it looks like I'd be better off selling it on the internet!'

'No!' cried Sophie and Constance. And Millicent.

An alarm bell went off in Simon's head. 'Look, Constance, I'm sorry to rush you but it is getting late and we should really be getting Scarlett home –'

'Yes yes, of course. Just one more thing. It concerns you, Sophie.'

Oh help, thought Sophie, what can she do to me? She

looked to Simon for support, but he was too busy praying that his real mother wouldn't turn out to be as monstrous as Sophie's.

'You mustn't do this!' hissed Millicent into Jessica's ear as she put the dessert down in front of her. 'You'll regret it!'

'Poor Sophie, I realize I haven't been a very good mother to you. It's not your fault, you've done nothing wrong. The truth is, I didn't really want you.'

Sophie was going to say 'That's OK' but thought better of it.

Millicent winced as she served Simon. Really, Constance had to learn to cushion her feelings more sympathetically, she could come across as so tactless sometimes. She caught her boss's eye and glared.

'Well,' said Constance, lifting her spoon and fork, 'that sounds a bit brutal probably, and of course once you were here I wouldn't have given you back for love nor money, even if I could –' Millicent nodded her approval as she tended to the drinks '– but when I discovered I was pregnant again I was absolutely devastated, it was the end of the world.'

'You're going to have it!' said Alistair to a distraught Cecily. 'I absolutely insist upon it.'

'But why?' she wept as she beat against his manly chest with her tiny fists. He could be so cold sometimes, so non-understanding. Cecily had explained to him over and over again that she had no desire for another child, and neither did their daughter Jessamy who was now

*over ten years old. Dear Cecily herself was just beginning to think
about returning to work.*

*But Alistair was having none of it. 'I missed out on Jessamy's
childhood because I was too busy earning money to support us all and
so I am grateful for this second chance,' he said, very forcefully.*

*Cecily did her best to stand up to him. 'Well then I shall go ahead
and get rid of it and leave you both, so that I might fulfil my true
vocation and live out the rest of my days in the theatre!' She spoke
bravely with great spirit and prettily flushed cheeks.*

*'You will have this baby!' he roared. Any woman would have
been absolutely terrified, but a strange part of Cecily rather liked it,
he was very masterful when he was like this.*

*Cecily tried one more time. 'But I might die in childbirth,' she
pitifully ventured.*

*'Unlikely in this day and age,' he said, with no compassion
whatsoever, 'it's the nineteenseventies.'*

'We made a sort of pact, that he would be more hands-on
with you and I would try to contain Jessica, who was already
showing signs of becoming a bit of a wildcat.'

The wildcat ignored her, she was busy trying to work
out how she could get Mother to give her the money from
the sale of her flat.

Constance sighed. 'And so I embarked on yet more years
of child-rearing. Who knows what would have happened
if I had been allowed to pursue my dream of bringing the
theatre to the masses?'

Who cares, thought Simon.

'But I have to confess, and there's no nice way of putting

this –' Constance glared back at Millicent who was on her way out to the kitchen '– I just didn't feel as much for you as I should have. Whether it was resentment at your getting in the way of my career, or that we just didn't click – I don't know.' She looked straight into Sophie's rounded blue eyes. 'I'm sorry, Sophie.'

Sophie hated being looked at by Constance, and so she did say 'That's OK' after all.

'No, it's not!' insisted Constance. 'It's an appalling state of affairs. I tried, I really did – but actually I had difficulty getting in there, your father seemed to want you all to himself.'

Sophie understood how that felt, but couldn't really say so right now.

'So there it is – the truth. I'm sure all this comes as no surprise to you, Sophie dear, but – well, one can't roll back the years and start again. Pity.' She looked almost wistful, quite fragile in the candlelight. Sophie did feel a little bit sorry for her.

'So.' Constance stood up. 'I find myself at sixty years old with two daughters who were born into similar circumstances but who have turned out completely differently. One is a scary monster who's been given too much by me, and the other is scared by monsters because she's not had enough from me.'

She's quite pleased with that one, thought Simon to himself as he watched her walk over to the sideboard. No doubt she'll create a character around that line in her next shitty screenplay.

'Now I have thought and I've thought about how I can

make this up to you, Sophie.' She opened the top drawer and took something out, they couldn't see what. Keeping her back to the audience, Constance said, 'I just hope you will take this in the spirit in which it is given.'

As she returned to her seat, she added, 'I see it as a kind of compensation. Of course, I understand that money can't buy love . . .'

Who wants love when you can have shoes, thought Jessica bitterly.

'. . . but I hope this will go some way to helping you along a bit once I've gone.' Constance handed a cheque to Simon to pass to Sophie. He couldn't help but look at the amount. Wow!

'May I suggest that you put it to good use, start a business with it perhaps? I've always thought you'd make a very good caterer, business lunches, that kind of thing. Whatever you do with it, don't waste it on everyday things.' She looked at Sophie. 'Keep it safely, you never know when you may need it.' There was a Message in there somewhere, but it went straight over Sophie's head as she was just staring at the cheque. 'Well, what d'you think?'

'I – think –' spluttered Sophie '– I think – I think you're a wicked, wicked woman!' She was laughing and crying at the same time, she was veering out of control. 'I just don't believe this – you – what are you – how dare you?! You can't give me money! It's not your money I want, there's nothing you can do for me that I want – I just – I don't believe this, of course I know you've never really loved me, the only person who did was Dad and you didn't love him either!'

Oh yes I did, thought Constance, you've got that completely wrong.

'You might as well have this baby,' Alistair continued, 'because you'll never return to the theatre.'

'I'll do what I jolly well like,' retorted Cecily audaciously and attractively. 'You can't stop me.'

'If you leave, I won't let you back. You see, I know what happened seven years ago, when you went on tour.' He went on to say that he had known about the affair, and the baby — the other actor had spinelessly confessed to his wife, who'd contacted Alistair and spilt the beans.

'You — knew — all these years?' she asked her husband.

'Yes, and it nearly broke my heart. However, I shall never mention it again and neither will you.'

And so their second child was born.

And do you know, from that moment on Cecily had a respect for Alistair which eventually turned into a very deep love. For here was a man stronger than herself, a man who had fought his own emotions and won.

That's not to say he wasn't a little dull at times, but theirs was a good life and Cecily had had enough excitement for one lifetime. Or so she thought.

'I don't want your money!' Sophie pushed the cheque away. 'And I don't want you either!' She was raspberry-puce in the face with rage and emotion, but this was the first time in Sophie's life that she had felt powerful. 'I'm glad you're going away, good riddance to bad rubbish, that's what I say! You can't buy me — I don't deal in money, I deal in people and love and nice things like that!' She stood up so quickly that her chair fell back onto the floor. 'This is just too much, Mother, you've gone too far this time. Come on Simon, we're going!' Simon got up and followed her out of the room. Tucking the cheque into his inside breast pocket as he did so.

Jessica got up too. 'Wait, I'm coming with you!' She looked at her mother with what might have been a little tear in her eye. 'You really mean this, don't you?'

'It's for the best, you'll see.' Constance stood.

Her little chin was quivering. Constance wanted to say 'Come with me!' and whisk her away, but she knew she mustn't.

'Bye.' And though she was clearly hurting, tough-nut Jessica managed to kiss her mother farewell. Constance wanted to cling on to her, but knew she mustn't. Time to let go.

'Is Auntie Jess coming with us?' asked Scarlett as they stood at the top of the steps of the big house in Holland Park and wondered what to do now.

'Um, yes, if she wants to,' was all Sophie could say. She was having trouble taking everything in.

'Might as well.' Jessica looked almost vulnerable. 'I haven't got anywhere else to go now' she realized with a shudder.

'I'll go and get the car,' said Simon, who reckoned that's what men do at times like this. 'You come with me, Scarlett.'

Scarlett suddenly remembered she was supposed to be difficult now. And she'd been cross at not being able to see the end of that rude film on Channel 5. 'Oh do I have to?'

As Simon led her away, Jessica turned to Sophie and said, 'Well – that's that, then.'

'Yes.'

They thought for a moment.

'It's funny, isn't it,' said Sophie, 'you've got what I want and I've got what you want. Paying me off indeed! Doesn't seem right, does it?'

'No,' said Jessica.

The two girls gazed out in silence from the top of the steps at the wide, leafy avenue in front of them. Then they slowly turned to look at each other.

When Simon and Scarlett drove up, they were smiling, with shiny bright eyes. He'd never seen it before, but they actually looked like sisters now.

'One thing,' said Sophie brightly, as she got into the car. 'Now we know why the dress I made you didn't fit, don't we?'

'No,' replied Jess as she eased herself in beside Scarlett, 'I wasn't pregnant then. Or if I was, it would only have been days. That was a genuine fuck-up.'

'Oh.' Damn.

'It all went according to plan, then?' asked Millicent as she cuddled her cup of Horlicks in her hands.

'Oh I think they'll work it out,' said Constance. 'And anyway, it's not as if they've heard the last of me. Neither of them thought to ask, but my mobile will work anywhere, apparently. And of course, there's always email. They'll want to speak to me again soon, you mark my words.'

'Of course they will. It won't take long for them to realize that you've helped them along after all.'

Constance looked at her friend for reassurance. 'It was a good plan we came up with in the end, wasn't it, Millicent? I did do the right thing, didn't I?'

'Of course you did.' Millicent reached across the kitchen table and squeezed Constance's hand. 'You have the freedom you've always wanted, and now they are free to make their own choices as well.'

'You don't think I should phone, just to –'

'No.' Millicent smiled at her friend, the first person to have shown her any kindness in this big city. 'Let them be. Now come on, you should go to bed. We don't want you making bad decisions at the airport, you'll end up in Timbuctoo!'

Both women had slightly watery eyes. They smiled at each other and looked into their hot drinks. Constance felt decidedly wobbly. 'You know – now that the time has come, I'm not sure I'm brave enough to go through with it. Can't I stay here and help you?'

Millicent laughed her big wide rumbling laugh that Constance had grown to love so much. 'No! You are the last person I need helping me run the school – I don't know who would be more trouble, you or the children!'

'You're absolutely right, of course.' Constance stood up, weary now. 'Oh Millicent, thank you so much. Thank you for listening, and understanding and helping and – well, it sounds silly, but thank you for liking me.' She smiled a crumply smile and Millicent came round and gave her a big old-fashioned hug.

'You don't scare me, you old bossy boots,' said Millicent as they parted.

'You're fired!' laughed Constance as she bent down to pick up her shoes. Millicent watched her pad across the kitchen in her stockinged feet. 'Oh one thing –' Constance turned in the doorway '– I nearly forgot.'

'Yes?' said Millicent as she picked up the dirty cups from the table.

'I thought that as it's going to be called the Archibald Rose School, it might be a nice idea to keep that painting of him hanging above the fireplace. I know you're very fond of it and I think it would be fitting for him to stay there, watching over you – don't you?' Constance had a twinkle in her eye. She smiled. 'Goodnight, Millicent.'

'Goodnight.' She nearly added 'I'll miss you', but she didn't want to make things worse.

As she peered into the Chinese vase in the dining-room fireplace, which did indeed need emptying, Millicent smiled to herself.

It's a small world, she thought. We all lead similar lives, and similar events happen to us all; but how you cope with what life throws at you depends very much on who you are.

She made a mental note to try and squeeze that into her book somehow as she turned the dining-room lights out and went to check the locks on all the doors and all the windows, just one more time.

SCARLETT MATTHEWS
11 today

What I want for my Birthday:-

Belly button pierced
Eminem hoodie
Lots of hairdye, any colours exept brown
Any videos that are a 15
Miss Selfridge or vouchers from Top Shop
New York on concord for weekend with Jade
   or if that's too much Thorpe Park with no
   parents
CDs but I'll choose
My own phone in my room which is just mine
Sony Play Station 2
NOTHING with cats on it, I mean it.

25 February

'Never again.' Simon shut the bedroom door behind him. 'Next year she can have her party somewhere else. I'm knackered!'

'All asleep now?' Sophie didn't look up.

'You're joking! They're all wide awake, giggling about Felix.' He sat down on the end of the bed.

'Who's Felix?' asked Sophie, still reading.

'The DJ. I had to pay him in cash, by the way, he wouldn't take a cheque. Kindly offered to give that girl Becca a lift home, though. Are you sure she's the same age as Scarlett?' Simon had been somewhat disconcerted by her physical attributes.

'Um, I don't know.'

'What are you reading?'

'Mmm?'

'I said, what are you reading?'

'Oh, sorry.' She put the sheaf of papers face-down on the duvet and shifted in the bed. 'It's that thing Mother sent me to read. Her new novel. It's absolutely dreadful, really hard going. I don't know what I'm going to say to her when she asks what I think.'

Simon laughed. 'What's it about?'

Sophie smiled. 'Well surprise surprise, a beautiful and

talented young actress marries a Scottish man and they have two daughters.'

'Not much imagination plot-wise, then.'

'Well no, except that she then crowbars in this really far-fetched sub-plot about going on tour and having a baby by another actor – and then it gets really silly.' Sophie began to giggle. 'She's got this mad bit where her dresser from the theatre takes the baby away and then turns into a woman if you please –'

'No!'

'Yes, and then comes to live with Cecily's family as their housekeeper! Poor old Mrs Mac must be spinning in her grave!'

'Where is she anyway?'

'Mortlake Cemetery, I think.'

'No, Soph, your mother.'

'Oh, sorry.' Sophie yawned. 'She keeps being all mysterious, saying she can't reveal her whereabouts. Jess and I decided that we'd never ask but the parcel with the book in it was postmarked Paris.'

'How long's she been gone now?' said Simon as he stood up.

'Three months.'

'That long?' He stretched. 'You sure?'

'Positive.' Three months and two missed periods, to be precise.

'Right, well I'm going to quickly check my email, see if that adoption agency in Australia's managed to come up with anything.' He walked over to the door.

'OK,' said Sophie, picking up Constance's manuscript

once more, only a few more pages to wade through now. 'And can you read the riot act to the girls on your way to bed?'

'What, if-you-lot-don't-shut-up-I'll-have-to-split-you-up, that one?'

'That's the one,' said Sophie, wondering if tonight would be a good night to tell him.

'OK, won't be long.' Simon closed the door behind him, eager to log on to Della's website. Well if he couldn't have her in the flesh any more, this was the next best thing.

When it came to sorting out her dearly departed housekeeper's belongings, Cecily couldn't help but notice amongst the boxes, bags and envelopes – the woman had been a frightful hoarder – an old shoebox.

Now as you know, dear reader, Cecily wasn't a nosy person by any means, but for some reason she decided to take the lid off and have a look inside.

Imagine her surprise when she discovered that Mrs Jock had had a sister! Cecily had known none of this, her dearly departed housekeeper had seldom mentioned his/her family, except to say that they had been understandably ashamed of her leanings toward transvestitism.

(Now as I mentioned before but I'll remind you again, the baby had been whisked away at birth and taken Cecily knew not where. Cecily's part of the bargain had been to keep mum about Mrs Jock's real identity and to provide her with a home for life. Both had agreed to keep the other's secret and the matter was never raised again.)

But it turned out that Mrs Jock had been in constant touch with Cecily's baby's adoptive mother – who turned out to be his/her own sister! She and her husband had been unable to have children of their own and so Mrs Jock had obligingly turned up on their doorstep one day with Cecily's little bundle, like an angel bearing a gift from heaven. There it was, all in this box, hundreds of letters and photographs, conveniently arranged into chronological order for Cecily. It was as if Mrs Jock had known she would stumble across them one day.

The letters were frankly rather tedious, detailing years of suburban life for an ordinary Scots family. (Cecily knew not to say Scotch, for her husband had corrected her many times about this.) However, it was the photographs that caught her attention. Let me take you through a few, if I may:

A black-and-white snapshot showed the baby sitting on a car blanket, covered in jam. As a toddler he had been put in unattractive yellow shorts, with a matching bow tie. Then followed one of those terrible school photographs with a blue cloudy background – he'd lost his front teeth by then – and another, as a teenager.

Cecily's hair was just about standing on end by this time, it couldn't be – could it? She gingerly unfolded a page that looked like it had been torn out of a magazine, the Radio Times *in fact. Mrs Jock's sister had written in her spidery handwriting along the margin 'our wee boy's first professional engagement!' It was a photograph of a young man, horrifyingly familiar to Cecily, and he was dressed as a postman.*

Cecily's blood ran cold as the truth raced through her veins to freeze her heart. Oh the horror of it! To discover that her long-lost son was married to her own daughter! Poor Cecily recoil–

'You've got an email from Jess, asking you to come out and help when the baby's born next – Soph, are you all right?' Simon shut the bedroom door behind him. 'What's the matter?'

She didn't answer.

He sat down on the bed, and took her hand. 'Sophie?'

She looked at him. A strange look, a kind of frightened frown, a look he'd never seen on her soft moon-face before. 'Stop it, Soph. What's happened?'

She was about to say something, but then she changed her mind. 'Nothing,' she said, looking at him. She sort of smiled at her husband. 'Doesn't matter.'

A big thank you to:

Jonny Geller for changing my life, literally and literarily

Top Bird Louise Moore and all the other lovely penguins for making this such an enjoyable journey

Minh Phuong Ti Nguyen and Deyna McFarland for loving my children

Dr Tania Abdulezer (www.mindyourlanguage.com) for keeping me mentally fit

Liz Anstee for support and belief

Kerry Clark, Howell James, Jill Sinclair, Kim Wilson-Gough and all my other lovely friends for being so patient with me

Unique, the rare chromosome disorder support group (www.rarechromo.org)

Dr Joan Patterson, Consultant Clinical Geneticist at the Kennedy Galton Centre

The Salvation Army Family Tracing Service (020 7367 4747)

Dymphna Flynn at Radio 4

Rosalind Rathouse at Montserrat Aid Committee 89, 13 Hyde Park Gardens, London N21 2PN

Janice Panton, the Montserrat Government UK Representative

Codependents Anonymous – 020 7376 8191